W9-ANG-211

Praise for Karen Schaler's

CHRISTMAS CAMP

"With its perfectly evoked New England winter wonderland setting and cast of charming characters, Schaler's delightful debut will warm the heart of even the most hardened Scrooge." —*Booklist*

"A charming movie-to-book crossover that would be right at home on the Hallmark Channel and a winner for fans looking for a touching holiday read."
 —*Library Journal*

"Schaler knows just what audiences hunger for at Christmas and sprinkles it generously throughout this title."
 —*Entertainment Weekly*

By Karen Schaler

Fiction
CHRISTMAS CAMP
CHRISTMAS CAMP WEDDING (novella)
FINDING CHRISTMAS

Nonfiction
TRAVEL THERAPY: WHERE DO YOU NEED TO GO?

ATTENTION: ORGANIZATIONS AND CORPORATIONS
HarperCollins books may be purchased for educational, business, or sales promotional use. For information, please e-mail the Special Markets Department at SPsales@harpercollins.com.

CHRISTMAS CAMP

A Novel

KAREN SCHALER

AVONBOOKS

An Imprint of HarperCollins*Publishers*

This is a work of fiction. Names, characters, places, and incidents are products of the author's imagination or are used fictitiously and are not to be construed as real. Any resemblance to actual events, locales, organizations, or persons, living or dead, is entirely coincidental.

"Christmas Camp Wedding" copyright © 2019 by Karen Schaler.

"Christmas Camp Wedding" was originally published as an e-book novella January 2019 by William Morrow, an Imprint of Harper-Collins Publishers.

CHRISTMAS CAMP. Copyright © 2018 by Karen Schaler. All rights reserved. Printed in the United States of America. No part of this book may be used or reproduced in any manner whatsoever without written permission except in the case of brief quotations embodied in critical articles and reviews. For information, address HarperCollins Publishers, 195 Broadway, New York, NY 10007.

First Avon Books mass market printing: October 2019
First William Morrow paperback printing: October 2018
First William Morrow hardcover printing: October 2018

Print Edition ISBN: 978-0-06-295023-9
Digital Edition ISBN: 978-0-06-288368-1

Cover design by Danielle Christopher
Cover photographs © dszc/Getty Images (front porch);
© Hannamariah/Shutterstock (wreath); © Luc Brousseau/
Shutterstock (dog); © Alhovik/Shutterstock (snow)
Chapter opener art © Danny Smythe/Shutterstock, Inc.

Avon, Avon & logo, and Avon Books & logo are registered trademarks of HarperCollins Publishers in the United States of America and other countries.

HarperCollins is a registered trademark of HarperCollins Publishers in the United States of America and other countries.

19 20 21 22 23   DIX/QGM   10 9 8 7 6 5 4 3 2 1

If you purchased this book without a cover, you should be aware that this book is stolen property. It was reported as "unsold and destroyed" to the publisher, and neither the author nor the publisher has received any payment for this "stripped book."

This book is dedicated to everyone
who holds Christmas in their heart,
and everyone who needs to let Christmas into their heart.
Find a pinecone. Make a wish. Believe.

CHRISTMAS CAMP

CHAPTER 1

Haley Hanson was having a staring contest—with a bunch of dolls. And they were winning. Lined up on her desk, the adorable dolls were dressed in beautiful, classic red velvet and emerald-green Christmas dresses. Each dress was meticulously trimmed with delicate white lace and had tiny pearl-like buttons up the front. But it was their perfectly painted smiles that made Haley's frown deepen. They weren't fooling her for a minute. She knew they might look innocent enough, but the truth was that these Christmas dolls were about to decide her entire future. They were everything.

"So, here's what we need to do," she said to the dolls as she leaned in closer to them. "We need to work together if I'm going to get this promotion, understand?" Haley gave them a stern look, waited a beat, and then laughed. People always said she had an active imagination. It was a useful trait to have in her advertising job as a brand strategist. But not even her imagination could make those dolls talk back.

She decided to let the dolls win this round. But she

wasn't giving up. She had too much to lose. To remind herself exactly what was at stake, she walked over to the biggest piece of furniture in her office, a chic glass bookcase filled with all the awards she had won working at Bergman Advertising. It was an impressive collection.

She had started working for the agency right out of college eight years ago. She had chosen advertising and working specifically with building brands because it was a way to combine her creative skills with her storytelling ability, and she loved being able to help people and companies connect in an authentic way with their customers.

She picked up one of her awards. It vaguely resembled a Hollywood Oscar, and she was always surprised by how heavy it was. It was called an Addie. It was silver instead of gold, and smaller than an Oscar, but if you worked in advertising, it was about the equivalent. It was the most prestigious award you could get.

She'd won it right after she had started at the agency, working on a campaign for one of her first clients, the Massachusetts Board of Education. They had wanted a big television ad campaign to promote literacy, but their budget was tiny. She had found a way to get some top celebrities to donate their time and sponsor the ads. The campaign was such a huge success, it was used as a model for other school districts, helping children across the country. When Haley was put in charge of the national campaign, it had jump-started her career, and she never looked back. She quickly went from representing small mom-and-pop businesses to some of the top brands and companies in Boston.

Sure, she had given up some things along the way to become one of the youngest vice presidents the company had ever had—like a personal life, vacations, and weekends—but she had never regretted it, and now she was finally getting everything she had worked so hard for: a promotion to partner.

Her boss, the owner of the agency, Larry, had promised to make her partner if she could land a multimillion-dollar account before the end of the year. That's where the Christmas dolls came in. Haley glanced back at them. They weren't just any ordinary dolls. They were dolls from Tyler Toys, one of the largest toy companies in the country, which was about to go international. It was exactly the kind of account Haley needed to land if she wanted to make partner.

She'd come to the point where she didn't want to just work for a company—she wanted a stake in the business, a business she had helped build into one of the top ad agencies on the East Coast. She had worked hard, and she knew she deserved it.

As an only child, she had grown up in a family where money had always been tight, but she had been lucky. While her parents couldn't give her a lot of material things, like fancy clothes and vacations, and she'd had to miss out on dance and gymnastics lessons, she always knew she was loved. Her parents encouraged her to believe anything was possible, so she decided early on that when she grew up, she never wanted to have to worry about money like her parents always did. And neither would her parents. She'd take care of them.

Haley walked back over to the dolls. An account like Tyler Toys didn't come along very often. This was her chance.

There was just one small thing standing in her way, or more like one very important person—her boss. To Haley, Larry had always been much more than just a boss. He was her mentor. He had taken a chance on her, hiring her right out of school. He had been tough but always fair, always pushing her to exceed expectations. He had taught her how to always think outside the box, to never take no for an answer, and to always stay one step ahead of the competition.

So, when Haley got an insider tip that Tyler Toys was thinking about hiring a new ad agency, she immediately worked her contacts and found out that Tyler Toys' president was attending a baseball game in Boston. She pulled some strings and made sure to get tickets for that game in the same box. By the third inning, she had him agreeing to come in for a pitch meeting. The meeting was in two weeks, right before Christmas. It was perfect, right up until Larry decided that another VP at the agency, Tom, should do the pitch.

Haley shuddered just thinking about it. There was no way she could let that happen. Tom was also vying for a chance to make partner, and they had been competing against each other for the last two years. Haley had nothing against Tom, personally. He was about ten years older than her, married, with two kids under ten. He was a nice enough guy. He just wasn't the guy she was ever going to let steal her promotion. It wasn't personal. It was business.

Haley sat back down at her desk. Her eyes filled with determination as she stared down the dolls. Her little one-on-one with them was suddenly interrupted when Larry walked into her office. Immediately she sat up straighter and smoothed an imaginary wrinkle out of her impeccable black dress.

"Good morning," she said.

"Good morning." He smiled back at her and then did a double take when he saw all of the dolls lined up on her desk. "Haley, what are you doing with the Tyler Toys dolls? Those were supposed to be sent over to Tom."

When Haley quickly stood up, she accidentally bumped her desk, sending the dolls toppling over like dominoes. She ignored the mess. She was on a mission, feet apart, hands on her hips, chest lifted, and head held high. She was assuming the position—the Wonder Woman position. She had perfected the power pose over the years after learning how it was supposed to give you an instant shot of confidence. It had always worked for her before, and she was counting on it to work this time.

She smiled her most winning smile. "Larry, I want to pitch the Tyler Toys account. I'm the one who brought us the lead. Exactly what you asked me to do, to bring in a big account. I should be running this pitch, not Tom." She locked eyes with Larry. She wanted to make sure he knew just how serious she was. When she saw the look of surprise in his eyes, she just kept smiling—and posing. Wonder Woman would have been proud. The only way you ever would know she was nervous was that her hands on her hips were pressing into her skin, hard.

She watched and waited as Larry walked up to her desk and picked up one of the Tyler Toys Christmas dolls. The doll's hair was messy from her tumble, but somehow this made her look even more endearing.

Larry smiled at the doll. "You know a Tyler Toys doll was the first doll I ever bought my daughter Shannon." He shook his head. "We gave it to her for Christmas when she was about six. It was the only thing she wanted. She was so excited about it, she didn't even open any of her other presents." He shook his head as he remembered. "She named her Grace and insisted the doll had its own plate at Christmas dinner. Grace instantly became part of our family. Shannon took that doll with her everywhere. Even on a vacation to Hawaii where there was an unfortunate swimming pool incident. But it never mattered how soggy or worn and torn Grace got, my daughter loved her. It's hard to believe Shannon's already a sophomore in college, but you know what, she still has that doll, and every year she gets Grace out for Christmas. That's what makes Tyler Toys so special. Every doll comes with a Christmas memory—"

Haley jumped in. "I know all about Tyler Toys and the Christmas dolls." She hated interrupting, but she needed to show Larry just how hard she had worked researching the company. "I know the company is family owned and has been making these dolls for decades, and every year at Christmas, they introduce a new doll, like this one." She went to grab one of the dolls but accidentally ended up knocking the pile of dolls off her desk.

Larry arched one eyebrow.

Haley laughed as she scrambled to pick up the dolls, but when she noticed Larry wasn't laughing, she quickly put her game face back on. "Tyler Toys' president told me they're looking for something truly special for next year's Christmas doll. It's their seventieth anniversary, and I already have some great ideas. I want this pitch, Larry. I know I can get us this account."

But Larry didn't look so sure. He walked over to her bookcase and pointed at all her awards. "Haley, I know how talented you are. You've proven that over and over again. You're always my go-to person when I need to pitch a client something fresh and unique, something out of the box, but Tyler Toys . . . they need to stay in the box. That's who they are. They're all about Christmas and tradition."

"I can do Christmas and tradition."

Larry folded his arms and stared back at her. "Really?"

Haley, excited, nodded.

Larry took her arm and led her out of the office. When they got into the hallway, he pointed to an intern who was struggling to put up a fake Christmas tree. Tree branches were all over the place, and there were unopened boxes of Christmas decorations stacked up everywhere. When the intern tried to cram the latest branch into the sad-looking tree, the whole tree toppled over.

"So then explain to me what's going on here?" Larry asked.

Haley cringed, then recovered quickly. "I can explain."

"This year I put you in charge of scheduling the decorators," he said. "I wanted all the Christmas decorations up by November first. It's two weeks until Christmas, and all we have is our intern wrestling with a tree. And it's fake. We're supposed to have a real tree."

Haley took a deep breath. She knew she needed to turn this conversation around fast. "I'm sorry. I just got so busy finishing up the Time Right Beauty TV ads and getting the Perfect Perfume billboards up in Times Square . . . by the time I got around to calling the decorators, they were all booked up, and I couldn't find anyone else."

"So you thought it was a good idea to have our intern do it? He doesn't even celebrate Christmas. He's Jewish!"

Haley opened her mouth to say something—but had nothing.

Larry pointed across the hall. "And have you seen Tom's office? He found time to decorate. He loves Christmas."

Haley reluctantly followed Larry's stare. She knew what Tom's office looked like. It was impossible to miss. He was the self-proclaimed Christmas king and had more decorations than a Hallmark Christmas movie. She forced a smile. "Larry, just because Tom can decorate doesn't mean he's the best person for the pitch."

Larry wasn't smiling, and when he looked her straight in the eye, she squirmed inside. She knew that look. That was Larry's "I've made up my mind so don't mess with me" look. She had to do something. She assumed the position—the power pose. Only this time her chest wasn't puffed out quite so much and her head wasn't held quite so high. She fought to keep calm. She couldn't lose this promotion. She wasn't the kind of person to lose anything.

When Larry spoke, he didn't pull any punches. "I'm putting Tom on the Tyler Toys account because he embraces the Christmas spirit, just like Tyler Toys does. He's our best chance at winning the account." He gave her a curt nod, discussion over, and started to walk back to his office.

But Haley wasn't giving up. Her adrenaline kicked in, and she cut in front of him, talking a mile a minute.

"I can embrace Christmas! I can decorate my office! I can put up the tree!"

"Haley, I appreciate your enthusiasm, but I just don't believe you're the right person for this pitch. You run off to the Caribbean every year at Christmas and completely ignore the holiday when you're there."

Haley stood her ground. "You know that's because I make it a work trip and always see our Caribbean client when I'm there. I take my parents. It's our winter vacation. I work, they get to relax, it's a win-win."

"But that's the point, you're working, you're not celebrating Christmas." Larry continued walking.

Haley cut him off again. Her desperation was starting to show, and it wasn't pretty. "Larry, look, please, you know how hard I've worked for you, for this agency. You said this was my year to finally make partner—"

Larry interrupted her. "But part of being partner means knowing what's best for our company—"

"I know, and that's why I'm telling you I'm the best person to pitch this account. I know I can do this. You have to give me a chance. Just tell me what I need to do to convince you, and I'll do it."

Larry took a deep breath. Haley held hers.

He glanced at Tom's office, then at the intern who was still struggling with the pathetic tree, then back at Haley. He looked like he was about to regret what he was going to do next, but he did it anyway.

"My office, in ten minutes. Be there." Larry turned and walked away.

CHAPTER 2

This time when Larry walked away, Haley didn't follow him. She was too busy doing a victory dance. She looked like a football player who had just made a touchdown and was dancing around with her arms up in the air. Kathy, the agency's top graphic designer and Haley's bohemian, fabulous best friend, came around the corner and laughed when she saw Haley dancing.

"So, what's going on here?" she asked, and began dancing herself. Only Kathy's moves were more hip-hop than showboating football player.

"We're celebrating." Haley grabbed Kathy's hand, pulled her into her office, and shut the door behind them. "I think I've convinced Larry to give me the Tyler Toys account."

Kathy looked surprised. "You? Miss I Don't Do Christmas?"

Haley was not amused. "Now you sound like Larry. I'm not a Grinch. I like Christmas. I just don't have time for all the—"

"What? The Christmas celebrations, the customs, the decorations, all the things that Tyler Toys embraces."

Haley looked around her office. "Okay, just because I don't decorate or have a Christmas tree doesn't mean I can't do Christmas. I can research."

Kathy still didn't look convinced. "You can't research Christmas spirit, it's something you have to feel. You know that, right?"

Haley snapped, grabbed one of the Christmas dolls, and waved it at Kathy. "I can do this!" The poor doll's head bobbled back and forth. "Larry hasn't given this account to Tom yet. I have the dolls. They're right here. They're mine!"

Kathy gingerly took the doll from her. "Okay, friend to friend, you know I love you, but you sound like you're twelve."

Haley glared at her.

Kathy shrugged. "I'm just saying . . ."

Haley let out a frustrated sigh. She knew Kathy was right. She was spiraling out of control. "I'm sorry. I just can't lose this account. If Tom gets this, Larry will make him partner, and who knows when I'll ever get a chance like this again. I need this now. I told my parents I was making partner and that I'd help them with the house."

"They're still trying to restore that old Victorian?" Kathy asked.

Haley picked up her phone and scrolled through her pictures until she found the one she wanted to show Kathy. It was one showing a roof with a big hole in it.

"Whoa!" Kathy looked alarmed.

"Right? I'm telling you this place is a money pit. I've already invested all of my savings, but it's the house that just keeps taking, and taking, and taking. I told my parents it would be cheaper if they'd just let me help them buy a new condo, but they love this place. It's way too big for them. It's eight bedrooms and four bathrooms. It was my great-great-grandmother's, and it's been in our family for generations. My parents' dream is to make it a bed-and-breakfast, but that dream has a hefty price tag. The latest estimate to fix everything up is three hundred and fifty thousand dollars, and who knows what else they will need to get repaired. I was planning to give the extra money I'd make with my promotion to them to help get them started."

"I'm sure that means a lot to them."

Haley scrolled through more pictures. "It does. They want this to be our family project. Not that I have the time, but at least I can help them with the money. At least that was my plan." She held up another photo for Kathy to see. It was of Haley with her parents standing in front of a beautiful grand Victorian. They were all smiling.

Kathy nodded. "Nice."

"And don't think you're getting out of helping. I already told my mom how great you are with design."

"Uh, graphic design not home design," Kathy scoffed.

Haley put her arm around Kathy. "Uh, 'tomayto, tomahto.' We'll find some way to put you to work. By the way, how are you with plumbing?"

"Plumbing?"

"Yeah, a pipe burst. They haven't had any hot water, so my parents have been staying at my place."

"Well, at least someone is," Kathy said. "You're never home. I don't even know why you keep your condo, you practically live here. All you do is work. When was the last time you even went on a date?"

Haley gave her a pointed look.

Kathy laughed. "Okay, I told you I was sorry about that guy."

The last blind date Kathy had set her up with had been a disaster. The guy had said he was taking her out for a nice dinner, but they had ended up at a juice bar where he'd told her she could order any drink she wanted as long as it was a medium, because his last girlfriend always said a large was too much. He'd spent the rest of the date talking about his ex. It was reason number 427 why Haley didn't want to waste time dating right now. She had more important things to do, like convincing Larry to give her a shot at Tyler Toys. She headed for the door.

"I'm going to go talk to Larry and get this account. Wish me luck."

"Luck," Kathy said as Haley hurried out the door.

As Haley headed down the hall to Larry's office, she saw Tom go into the break room. She figured it was the perfect chance to do a little recon on Tom's Christmas decorations and see what Larry was so impressed by.

She frowned as she got closer to Tom's office. She hated admitting it, but Tom had done a really great job. The outside of his office was covered in twinkling white Christmas lights and all the glass windows had magnificent wreaths hanging from them. The biggest wreath was on the office door. Haley leaned closer and sniffed it. Yup. The wreaths were real. Tom's office even *smelled* like Christmas!

When she peeked in, the first thing she noticed was a giant Christmas tree in the corner. It had to be at least seven feet tall! It was decorated with multicolored lights and traditional red and white ornaments that went perfectly with all the candy canes.

Haley was in awe. "He even has candy canes."

"Want one?"

Haley whipped around to find Tom standing behind her. He grinned and held up a candy cane. "I was just putting some in the break room, but you can have this one."

Of course, you were putting candy canes in the break room, Haley thought. *That's because you're a Santa wannabe pretending to be an ad executive.*

Tom waved the candy cane in front of her. He was waiting for her answer.

Haley shook her head. "No, it's okay, thanks. I'm trying to cut down on sweets."

"At Christmas?" Tom laughed. "How's that going for you?"

"Not so well." Haley fought to keep smiling. "But if I'm going to eat sugar, it's gotta be chocolate. I have to make it worth it."

Tom entered his office. "I have chocolates in here, some chocolate Santas and chocolate Christmas truffles." He held up a candy dish in the shape of a snowman.

Haley shook her head. "Thanks, but I'm good." As she continued walking, Tom called out after her.

"They're here if you change your mind!"

Haley just kept walking and muttered under her breath, "Chocolate Santas, seriously? What next?" She didn't have to wait long for an answer when she heard Christmas music coming out of Tom's office. The song was "We Wish You a Merry Christmas." She sighed, knowing the song would now be stuck in her head all day.

Not able to help herself, she hummed the song as she entered Larry's office. He was on the phone, so he motioned for her to sit down. While she waited for him, she glanced around and noticed that he, too, had his own Christmas tree. It was much smaller than Tom's, but it was still really pretty with silver ornaments and a sparkling star on top. He also had a wreath. She smelled it before she saw it. She must have missed the "everyone get a wreath" memo. She looked over at Larry's bookcase. It was twice as big as hers and made out of beautiful, rich mahogany. She estimated that he had at least three dozen Addies.

Her eyes were also drawn to his family pictures. He was the proud father of two Ivy League college students and never missed a chance to show off his daughters, Shannon and Sydney. Haley knew he'd met his wife, Ellen, in grad school when she was a free-spirited art major. He always said she was the yin to his yang.

As soon as Larry hung up the phone, Haley stood up. She was ready for round two.

Her eyes flashed with determination. It was showtime. "Larry, thank you for giving me the chance to pitch you my ideas for Tyler Toys." But before she could say more, Larry stood up.

"I don't need to hear your pitch," he said.

Haley looked stunned, then excited. "Really? So, you're giving me the account?"

"No."

Haley's smiled faded. "I don't understand."

Larry handed her a brochure he took from his desk. "You said you'd do anything to get a shot at pitching this account."

"Right . . ." Haley looked confused. "Whatever you need me to do."

"I need you to do this." He handed her a glossy brochure.

Haley glanced at it. It was for a pretty little place called Holly Peak Inn that was tucked away in the mountains. "I don't understand. You need me to go on vacation?"

Larry shook his head and smiled slowly. "No, I need you to go to Christmas Camp."

"What?" Haley sputtered, looking at the brochure again.

"For a holiday attitude adjustment."

Haley laughed out loud but stopped when she saw that he was dead serious. Her eyes grew wide. "Wait, what? You want me to go to a . . . Christmas bootcamp?!" Haley couldn't believe what she was hearing. This had to be a joke, right? So why wasn't Larry laughing? He couldn't be serious, could he? How did such a thing even exist? Her mind was whirling. She could barely focus on what he was saying.

"It's called a Christmas Camp," Larry said. "Remember three years ago when I took that vacation before Christmas?"

"Of course, it was the first time you'd taken a break around Christmas."

Larry laughed. "And that was exactly my wife's point. She was complaining that we never spent Christmas together as a family anymore. So, she signed us all up for this Christmas Camp. The girls had to cancel their ski trips. They weren't any happier about it than I was, but we all did it. We didn't have much choice. You know my wife."

Haley nodded and laughed. Ellen was relaxed and laid-back, but when she put her mind to something, watch out.

Larry went over, picked up one of his family pictures, and showed it to Haley.

Haley studied it. It was of Larry and his family posing with a snowman in front of a pretty inn. She looked closer and recognized the inn from the brochure. "This was Christmas Camp?" she asked.

"It was." Larry smiled as he remembered. "And it's one of our favorite pictures together as a family. That week we all spent at the inn changed us, in a good way. I'll always be thankful for that."

Haley looked confused. "Why? What made it so special?"

"That's something you need to find out for yourself." Larry gave her a reassuring smile. "But I will tell you this—I think it will help you if you really want to pitch the Tyler Toys account."

Haley's spirits lifted. "Wait, so does that mean if I go to this Christmas bootcamp thing, I get to pitch Tyler Toys?"

"Christmas *Camp*." Larry corrected her again.

"Right, sorry. Christmas Camp. But if I go, I get to pitch?"

Larry held up his hand to slow her down. "What I'm saying is if you go, I'll let both you and Tom pitch me your best ideas, and then I'll decide who can have the account. I'm trying to help you here, but I can't make any promises."

Haley's smile faded a little. But at least she was still in the game. She took a deep breath. She could totally do this. How bad could a little Christmas Camp be?

Larry went over to a box and pulled out one of those ridiculous Christmas sweaters people thought were so hilarious to wear. To be clear, Haley had never been one of those people. Larry tossed the sweater to her.

"And you'll need to take this with you."

Haley caught the sweater, then wished she hadn't. Her eyes hurt just looking at it. If there was an ugly sweater contest, this one would surely win first prize. It was holiday hideous. It was bright red and green and looked like a glitter gun had exploded on it. On the front, there was a giant Santa face. His rosy-red cheeks were furry, just

like the white snowballs that were dangling from the
sleeves of the sweater and lined up along the hem. It was
a Christmas mash-up of the silliest kind.

As Larry sat back down at his desk, he fired off one
more snowball. "And don't forget to bring back the
certificate."

"Certificate?" Haley's voice cracked. She was starting
to feel like she was trapped in a Christmas snow globe
that someone wouldn't stop shaking.

"Yes, the one the Christmas Camp gives you to prove
you did all the holiday activities. I want you to have the
full Christmas experience. You better get going. It starts
tomorrow."

Larry picked up his phone. Haley realized this was
her cue to leave. She fought to keep smiling and tried to
look excited.

"So, this is for a full week? There's no mini-weekend
version I could do?"

Larry crossed his arms and sat back down in his chair.
"If you don't think you can handle a week, I'll just give
the account to Tom now . . ."

Haley's eyes flew to him. "No. A week is fine! A week
is great. I can just work on the Tyler Toys campaign while
I'm there. Like you said, I'm sure it will be the perfect
place to find some Christmas inspiration."

"Great." Larry looked genuinely pleased. "Then I'll
have both you and Tom pitch me your best ideas a week
from tomorrow."

Haley smiled back at him. "I'll be ready."

Larry had already picked up his phone again.

"And, Larry . . ."

"Yes?"

Haley was no longer doing her power pose. She wasn't
trying to be a superhero. She was just being herself,

someone who was truly grateful to get a chance at making her dream of partner come true. "I just wanted to say thank you for giving me this shot. I know I'm not the obvious choice for this account, but I promise I won't let you down."

Larry smiled back at her. "I know you won't, Haley. You never do. Good luck."

As she walked out of the office, Haley let out a huge sigh of relief. She was still in the game.

But then she heard it.

It was coming from Tom's office.

Christmas music.

And this time the melody that Haley wouldn't be able to get out of her head was "It's Beginning to Look a Lot Like Christmas" . . .

CHAPTER 3

The sun was setting as Jeff Jacoby walked along the Boston waterfront, taking in all the breathtaking Christmas decorations. It was his favorite time of day. Magic hour. It was the last hour of sunlight, when the light was softer and more diffused, giving everything a golden glow. It was also the time when all the twinkling Christmas lights would turn on, transforming Christopher Columbus Waterfront Park into a magical winter wonderland.

As Jeff admired a group of the boats in the harbor that were also decked out in Christmas lights, he thought about how much his dad would appreciate all the decorations. No one loved Christmas more than his mom and dad. But now that his mom was gone—after losing a brave battle with cancer two years ago—Jeff couldn't wait to have his dad move into the city so they could spend more time together.

Jeff stopped and looked up with pride at Crane Wharf. It was a four-story gray granite building that was built back in the early 1800s. He was the architect responsible for coming up with a plan to save the wharf after it had been earmarked for demolition. Through a painstaking process, preserving the wharf's original brick walls and yellow pine beams, the landmark had been turned into luxury condos with a few longtime Boston businesses remaining on the ground floor.

Jeff looked up at the top corner unit. It was the condo he'd had his eye on for his dad. He thought it was perfect for him. It had a fantastic view of the harbor and was only a short walk from his own condo, a renovated three-story walk-up in the North End. He really believed his dad would love it in Boston—once he got used to the idea of moving. And that was the big challenge, trying to convince his dad to move.

Jeff knew it wasn't going to be easy, because his dad loved his home and business at Holly Peak Inn, tucked away in the mountains a few hours from Boston.

But like it or not, even though his dad didn't like to talk about it, the reality was that the inn was losing more money every year, and his dad couldn't afford to keep it. Now that his mom was gone, Jeff also didn't like the idea of having his dad up there all alone. He had spent the last year looking for the right person to buy the inn, but it had proved more challenging than he had planned for. The only interest had come from developers who just wanted to tear the place down, and he knew his dad would never go for that. Finally, a few months ago, he had found someone, a banker who was looking for a vacation home for his family, so it was perfect. Now all he needed to do was get his dad on board. But time was running out. The buyer needed an answer by the end of the year, and so far, his dad had done a great job of avoiding the topic. Whenever Jeff called, the only thing his dad wanted to talk about was his Christmas Camps.

Jeff knew the Christmas Camps were his dad's pride and joy. They were special weeks at the inn, between October and Christmas, that his dad and mom had created to help people find and embrace their Christmas spirit. His parents had always believed in the power of people disconnecting from their hectic lives so they could reconnect with what mattered most, things like friends, family, community, and love. During the Christmas Camp week, guests participated in all kinds of traditional holiday activities. A lot of the activities Jeff had grown up doing himself, like the mountain hike to find the perfect Christmas tree and volunteering at the local community center to put special Christmas meals together for families that needed a little extra help during the holidays.

Jeff knew putting on the Christmas Camps was a lot of work—especially now that his mom was gone, so he'd agreed to go up and help his dad. He also hoped that it would give them a chance to talk about the future, and he could convince his dad that selling the inn was the right decision.

Jeff figured his dad knew exactly what he was up to. It was hard to get anything past him. He was as smart as he was genuine and kind. But no matter what happened over this next week, Jeff would at least be able to spend some quality time with his dad. It had been a while, too long. The wharf project had consumed so much of his time, but now that it was almost finished, he could take a quick break before starting on his next project in the New Year.

Jeff took a couple pictures of the wharf with his phone to show his dad, who always liked seeing the projects he was working on. As he continued walking, he headed to his favorite street in the North End, Hanover Street. The quaint little street was one of the oldest in Boston, and home to some of the best Italian restaurants in the city. Jeff planned to drive up to his dad's first thing in the morning, but first he needed his secret weapon.

He smiled as he walked into a bakery that was decorated for Christmas. In the corner was his favorite Christmas tree, which had cookies for ornaments. Customers were encouraged to take one. The robust man behind the counter saw him and waved.

"Jeff, come on over! I have your order all ready for you!" the man said with his thick, booming Italian accent. He held up a big pastry box. "A dozen cannolis. The best we have!"

"Thanks, Mike!" Jeff inhaled deeply as he headed for the counter. He savored the smell of fresh bread just out of the oven. He always loved coming into this bakery. Mike and his Italian family owned it, and while it was famous for its cannolis, it was also popular for all kinds of other homemade Italian treats, like biscotti and tiramisu. But today Jeff was all about the cannolis because they were his dad's favorite.

Mike proudly opened the pastry box he was holding so Jeff could see inside. "I put a couple of extra ones in here for you to try," he said. "Everyone loves the pistachio at Christmas!"

"I don't know if anything can beat your amaretto ones." Jeff grinned as he took out a cannoli that had drizzled dark chocolate on top and was covered with powdered sugar. He admired it for only a second. He couldn't help himself. He had to take a bite. From the first taste, he felt transported to a foodie heaven.

He shook his head in wonder. "I don't know how you do it, but these are so amazing! I don't know if they're going to make it to my dad's!"

Mike laughed, then grabbed two more cannolis and put them into the box. "For the road. They're on me. Merry Christmas."

Jeff was touched. "Thank you. I know he's going to love these."

Mike nodded and looked pleased with the compliment. "Tell your dad he needs to come back. It's been too long!"

"I agree, and I'll tell him. Say hello to your family for me. Merry Christmas!"

"Don't forget a cookie!" Mike pointed at the tree.

Jeff grinned as he took a frosted snowman cookie off the tree and took a bite. The Christmas cookie tree ornaments never got old. They always made him feel like a kid. "Thanks, Mike!"

As Jeff stepped outside he thought about how great it would be when he and his dad could come here together all the time. There was so much he wanted to do with him once he moved to the city. But first things first. First, he had to help his dad with this last Christmas Camp.

THE NEXT MORNING, as Jeff pulled up to Holly Peak Inn, he looked around in awe. He couldn't believe all the decorations his dad had put up outside. It seemed like every year they multiplied. But Jeff knew it really wasn't the actual number of decorations that made everything so special; it was all the memories that came with them.

He looked over at the life-size wire-framed deer sculptures covered in tiny white lights. He had been five years old when his mom brought the deer home, and when he first saw them, he had gotten so upset. He thought they were Santa's reindeer, and when he couldn't find his favorite, Rudolph, because none of them had a red nose, he had worried Rudolph was lost! That night, his mom had made a red nose, put it on one of the deer, and had brought him outside to see it. He still remembered being so relieved that he had run over and hugged Rudolph. Now, all these years later, he still felt that same joy and wonder when he spotted the deer with the red nose.

"Son! You're here!"

Jeff turned around to see his dad, Ben, hurrying toward him. He looked like he had won the lottery. Jeff met him halfway, and they embraced in a big bear hug.

"Dad, it's so good to see you!"

"I wasn't expecting you for a few hours." Ben beamed back at him.

"I left early so I could avoid the traffic." Jeff put his arm around his dad. "The place looks great!"

Ben looked around proudly. "Wait until you see it at night. That's when everything really comes to life. It's magical."

"I bet. Did you buy more lights? I don't remember all of those trees having lights before."

"They're LED, the best kind." Ben grinned back at him.

Jeff laughed and shook his head. His dad never could resist buying more Christmas lights. It was one of his favorite traditions, going with the whole "the more the merrier" mentality.

Ben adjusted a strand of lights on a tree. "Son, I'm really glad you're here. We have a great group of guests for this Christmas Camp. I have a feeling this one is really going to be special, and now that you're here, it's perfect." When his dad looked at him with so much love, Jeff felt a wave of emotion wash over him. He was so thankful to still have his dad in his life. His dad meant everything to him.

Ever since his mom had passed away, Jeff had felt this

overwhelming need to protect his dad. He knew Ben had been devastated when his mom was diagnosed with terminal cancer, but he had never let her see that. For her, his dad had always stayed positive and strong, always making the most of the time they had left together. But one night, when his dad thought everyone else was asleep, Jeff had come downstairs to find him standing in front of the fireplace looking at all the family pictures and crying silent tears. Seeing this had broken Jeff's heart, but he had honored his dad's privacy and given him that time to grieve alone.

At that moment Jeff made a promise to himself that he would be strong for his dad and make him his number one priority. He broke up with the girl he was dating so he could spend any spare time he had with his dad. These last few months when things started getting really hectic at work, he'd have his dad come to Boston and stay with him.

His entire life began to revolve around his work and his dad. He told all his friends that he broke up with his girlfriend and wasn't dating right now because he didn't have the time, but the truth was, he couldn't even imagine loving someone as much as his dad had loved his mom and then losing them. He didn't ever want to feel that kind of pain. He was happy with his life just the way it was. He had a successful career and a dad he was hoping to spend more time with. His life was good. But as much as he was looking forward to spending the next week at the inn, being back at Christmas, with all the memories, was hard.

This was his mother's favorite time of year, and everywhere he looked, he was reminded of her. He missed her every single day, but especially at Christmas. She was the one who had always loved Christmas and had taught him and his dad how special it could be. She had such a big heart and had always found ways to help people. The most important thing in her life was her family, and she made sure to let everyone in her life know how much she loved them.

Sometimes Jeff missed her so much it was hard to breathe, and this was one of those times. He didn't want his dad to see him struggling, so he concentrated on getting the pastry box out of the truck.

When his dad saw the box, his face lit up. It lightened the moment and made Jeff smile, too.

"Is that what I think it is?" Ben asked, rubbing his hands together in anticipation.

For an answer, Jeff laughed and flipped open the box. Ben's excitement was contagious. "Mike says Merry Christmas!"

Ben peered into the box. "Best Christmas present ever!"

"And I got your favorite. The amaretto."

But Ben was eyeing the pistachio. "What are these green ones?"

"Oh, Mike threw a couple of those in. They're pistachio, and he says they're very popular at Christmas. I haven't tried one yet . . ."

Ben was already picking one up and taking a bite. His eyes lit up. "Yum! Pistachio, huh? These are good!" He gave an enthusiastic thumbs-up as he took another bite.

Jeff laughed. He loved how his dad was always game to try something new. He would just jump right in, heart first. Jeff, on the other hand, was the cautious one. They made a great team.

The cannoli taste testing was interrupted when Ben's

beloved golden retriever, Max, trotted over and barked. It was clear Max felt he should also be one of the taste testers.

Jeff was as happy to see Max as Max was to see the cannolis. When he leaned down to pet him, Max put his nose into the pastry box and almost got a mouthful.

Ben laughed. "You have to watch old Max. He's quick."

"Apparently!" Jeff moved the box out of Max's reach just in time.

Max wagged his tail and barked. Jeff laughed.

"Okay, I think that's our cue that it's time to get inside." Ben smiled down at Max. "I want to go over this next week with you and make sure everything's ready. Our Christmas Camp guests should start arriving any minute now. Wait until you see what I have planned for this week!"

Jeff put his arm around his dad as they walked up to the inn. It was impossible not to get caught up in his enthusiasm. When they reached the front door, Jeff smiled at the life-size elf statue that grinned back at him. He remembered how his mom had found it at a garage sale, all faded and chipped, and how they had worked together to repaint it. He patted it on its pointy little head. "How are you doing, little guy?"

Ben chuckled.

As soon as they walked into the sitting room, a woman who looked like everyone's favorite grandmother was waiting for them. She was holding a tray full of Santa mugs. A swirl of whipped cream with chocolate shavings peeked out from the rim of each mug, and there was a candy cane for a stir stick.

Jeff's face lit up when he saw her. "Laura!" He went over, took the tray from her, then set it down so he could give her a proper hug. "You look wonderful!"

"And look at you, handsome as ever." She hugged him back. "It's been too long."

"I know. It's been great having Dad come into the city, but that means I've missed seeing you, and I've also really missed your home-cooked meals. I'm always telling my dad how lucky he is to have you here as a chef. How is Geoff? Your family?"

"Everyone's great. They'd all love to see you. Can you believe Geoff and I will be celebrating our fortieth wedding anniversary?"

"Congratulations! Forty years, that's amazing," Jeff said.

Ben nodded. "What's amazing is how fast the time goes by." He walked over and handed each of them a Santa mug. "Laura made our traditional Christmas Camp hot chocolate, so we can do our traditional toast."

They all held up their mugs.

Jeff and Laura waited for Ben to make the toast.

"To our family, friends, and community . . ." Ben turned to Jeff to continue the toast.

Jeff looked honored.

"To the people we've lost but will never forget . . ." Jeff looked back at his dad to finish.

"To love everlasting. Merry Christmas," Ben said with a huge grin. "To Christmas Camp!"

CHAPTER 4

As Haley drove down a pretty, winding, two-lane mountain road, she smiled as she looked around at the picturesque winter landscape. She loved these cool, crisp, winter days when the sun came out and made the snow clinging to the treetops sparkle. She was thankful that most of the snow was on the trees and not on the ground, but when she saw the road curve ahead, she knew she'd better slow down and play it safe.

The problem was taking things slow and playing it safe wasn't Haley's thing. On a scale of one to ten, she usually had only two speeds, one or ten. One, when she was sleeping, and ten, the rest of the time, when she was barreling through life full speed ahead. But there would be no barreling ahead this time, Haley quickly learned when her tires hit a slick spot and her car started sliding.

"Oh no!" Haley's heart raced. Her instincts kicked in. She took her foot off the gas and slightly turned into the slide just like her father had taught her when she was sixteen.

It worked. Within seconds, the car had straightened

out, and she was fine. She let out a long sigh of relief as she unclenched her fingers from the steering wheel. Her heart felt like it was about to jump out of her chest, but she continued driving. It would take a lot more than a patch of ice to stop Haley in her tracks when she was going after her dream.

Still, she needed to arrive in one piece, so she slowed down. She couldn't remember the last time she'd driven when there was snow and ice like this on the road. She didn't drive much these days. She hadn't owned a car since college. Living in Boston, where public transportation was so great, she didn't need one. Plus, her company had a car service she could use for free for anything that was business related, and for Haley that pretty much covered everything.

But for this trip she'd opted to rent a car so she'd have the ability to leave the inn as soon as she was done with all the Christmas Camp activities and not have to wait and call a car service to come pick her up during the busy holiday season.

But now she was starting to wonder if renting a car was such a great idea after all. She wasn't going to lie. She enjoyed being chauffeured around and not having to worry about driving in bad weather or struggling to find a parking place or paying for car insurance. She also was one of those multitaskers who could get a lot done when someone else was driving, and she was all about being efficient with her time. And right now she was running late. She frowned when she glanced over at her cell phone on the passenger seat and saw it was already four thirty. She wanted to get to the inn before it got dark. Check-in at the inn was at noon, and the first Christmas Camp activity started at six. When she tried to speed up a little, she felt one of her wheels spin, so she had to slow back down.

Needing something to take her mind off what was feeling like an epically slow journey, she turned on the radio. The first song that came up was the song Tom was always playing in his office, "It's Beginning to Look a Lot Like Christmas" . . .

"Are you kidding me?" Haley quickly changed the station, but when only a few had good reception and all were playing Christmas music, she ultimately settled on the song "Hark! The Herald Angels Sing" . . .

A HALF HOUR LATER, when she finally saw the sign for the Holly Peak Inn turnoff, she was more than a little relieved. Her eyes widened when she saw how elaborately the sign was decorated. It was emerald green with big bold crimson letters that were covered in gold glitter, and the entire sign was impressively outlined with holly and fir tree branches. Attached underneath was a smaller sign that said WELCOME TO CHRISTMAS CAMP.

Haley shook her head. "Oh boy, here we go . . ."

Her eyes only grew larger as she continued driving and got her first look at the Holly Peak Inn. It was quaint and charming and tucked away in the woods, surrounded by majestic pine and fir trees. It had more Christmas decorations than Haley had ever seen. The entire inn was outlined with twinkling white Christmas lights and all the surrounding trees were glowing with lights in red, green, silver, and gold. There were beautiful wreaths made with real tree branches, holly, and pinecones on all of the inn's windows, with the largest one being on the front door. It was magical.

But what really had Haley doing a double take were all the life-size reindeer decorations that were lit up with white lights and strategically placed around the inn, making them look like they had just stepped out of the forest.

Her first thought was that it looked like they were just hanging out until Santa needed them for their next sleigh ride. When she spotted the reindeer with the red nose she couldn't help but smile. "Rudolph, of course," she said as she raced her car up to the front of the inn and came to an abrupt stop. "What have I gotten myself into?"

Knowing she was running late, Haley quickly got out of the car, grabbed her suitcase out of the trunk, and slung her designer black leather bag over her shoulder. Her suitcase was equally chic and carry-on friendly. Since she traveled a lot to visit her clients, she took pride in the fact that she never checked any bags, going with the philosophy that there were two kinds of luggage, carry-on and lost. She held her suitcase up high so she wouldn't get any snow on it as she made her way to the front door and quickly realized her designer boots with three-inch heels weren't the best choice for this trip. Everywhere she looked there was snow . . . and lots of it.

When a chilly gust of winter air hit her, she also realized her stylish black suede pants and sleek maroon leather jacket weren't going to cut it in this cold, but figured she'd be spending most of her time indoors.

As she got closer to the door, she saw the adorable life-size elf figurine smiling back at her. "Well, aren't you a happy Christmas camper." She laughed at her own Christmas Camp joke. Just as she was about to knock on the door, it opened, and Haley found Ben standing before her with a warm, welcoming smile.

"You must be Miss Hanson. Welcome! Merry Christmas. I'm Ben, the owner of Holly Peak Inn. Please come in and get out of the cold." He quickly took her suitcase and bags. Haley smiled at him as she followed him inside. "Thank you. I'm sorry I'm a little late. I'm not used to driving on snowy roads."

"We're just glad you made it." Ben smiled back at her. "The other guests are already settling in. You'll get a chance to meet everyone soon." Ben put down her bags and motioned for her to go into the sitting room, where Laura stood waiting for her with an adorable reindeer tray that held a colorful Santa mug with a huge swirl of whipped cream on top and a candy cane for a stir stick. Haley could already smell the hot chocolate.

Ben took the Santa mug and handed it to her. "Haley, this is Laura, our chef, who has been with us from the start—she's really more like one of the family—and this is our famous Christmas Camp hot chocolate. Everyone gets one when they arrive. The candy-cane stir sticks are my favorite," he said with childlike excitement.

Haley gave the Santa mug back to Ben and smiled at Laura. "Thank you. I'm sure it's delicious, it's just right now I'm doing this whole sugar detox thing."

Ben and Laura exchanged a surprised look.

"I'm sorry, I didn't know that," Laura said. "I didn't think you'd put anything down about having any dietary restrictions . . ."

"Oh, I didn't see that on the form," Haley said. "I went through it pretty quickly."

Ben laughed. "Giving up sugar at Christmas? That can't be easy with all the Christmas parties and holiday meals . . ."

Haley shrugged. "Honestly, I'm so busy working, I'm not on the Christmas party circuit, and I take my parents to the Caribbean for Christmas, so we don't really do the whole holiday meal thing. We usually just end up at a fish fry on the beach."

Laura smiled. "Well, we can do whatever you need, Haley. How about you and I go over the menu later tonight, and we'll make sure you're happy."

Haley looked touched. "Thank you, that's really kind, but I don't want to be any trouble. I can just work around whatever you have."

"It's no trouble at all," Ben said. "We want to make your experience here something you'll always remember. So, you just let us know what we can do, and we'll make it happen."

"Thank you. Thank you so much." Haley gave Ben and Laura a grateful smile.

When Laura walked out of the room, Haley had a chance to look around. She blinked twice. It was a lot to take in. There were Christmas decorations everywhere, in every corner, on every table. There were Christmas candles, snow globes, nutcrackers, Santa figurines, Nativity figures, the works. She shook her head in amazement. If she thought the outside of the Holly Peak Inn was decorated elaborately, it was nothing compared to the inside.

The focal point of the sitting room was a magnificent natural stone fireplace, where a crackling fire was burning brightly, casting a golden glow throughout the room, giving it a warm and cozy feeling. Next to the fireplace was a big wicker basket filled with pinecones, and above the fireplace was a beautiful wreath made of fresh pine-tree branches, holly, and pinecones, topped off with an exquisite red velvet ribbon. The wreath matched the garland that was lovingly draped across the fireplace mantel and cascaded down the sides of the fireplace, almost touching the floor. Woven into both the wreath and garland were tiny white twinkle lights, adding to the magical setting. Also, on the mantel there were red and white candles next to family photographs, and hanging from the mantel was a row of charming red velvet Christmas stockings.

Haley walked over to the fireplace to get a closer look at the wreath. She couldn't help thinking how much Larry and Tom would love it. For a moment she shut her eyes and inhaled deeply. The room even smelled like Christmas. When she opened her eyes, she saw Ben had joined her. Embarrassed at getting so swept away by it all, she turned her attention back to the wreath. "I was just thinking how much my boss would love your wreath," she said.

Ben looked up at the wreath. "Having a wreath above the fireplace was always one of my wife's favorite things," he said softly. "Before she passed away, she made me promise I would keep our tradition. I think she would have liked this one a lot, especially the pinecones . . ."

When Haley looked into Ben's eyes, she saw the love he still had for his wife, but she also saw so much sadness. She fought to find the right words. "I'm so sorry for your loss." Even as she said the words, they didn't feel like enough.

Ben gave her a grateful smile. "Thank you. She would be so happy that you're here, that all of you are here for our Christmas Camp. Christmas was her favorite time of year. She would start decorating in early October."

Haley looked around the room. "I can imagine it's quite the job putting up all these decorations."

"It is, and she was a lot better at it than I am, but I did the best I could this year."

Haley looked surprised. "You did this all yourself?"

"Laura helped and Jeff, my son, did, too, but yes, I did a lot of it myself, but that's okay. Decorating the inn brings back so many good memories. That's why we do it. Everything here has a story, a memory attached, that's what makes it so special. My wife collected decorations from all over the world when we traveled, and now we get to share all of this with our guests during our Christmas Camps."

Haley walked over to a table that was covered with Santa figurines in all shapes and sizes. "So, these came from all your travels?" she asked.

"Actually, these Santas are all gifts from our Christmas Camp guests." He picked up a Santa that stood about twelve inches high. It was made of plaster and was hand painted. It was an old-world Santa wearing a snow-white robe that had gold stars painted on it. "This was the first Santa we got from one of our first Christmas Camp guests and then we just started getting more."

He picked up another Santa that was made of glass. "This is the one your boss, Larry, gave us. I'd never seen anything like it before. It's really special, just like him and his family. That's what makes this collection so remarkable. Every one of these Santas reminds me of the guest who gave it to us."

Haley had her eye on a cute little wooden Santa.

Ben followed her gaze and picked it up and handed it to her. "You like this one?"

Haley nodded as she gently touched the Santa's face. For a second she was lost in a memory. "I think we had one like this when I was little. It looks so familiar . . ."

Ben looked into her eyes. "Do you believe?"

"What?" Haley asked as she snapped back to attention.

"Do you believe?" Ben repeated.

Haley laughed. "In Santa Claus?"

"In the magic of Christmas?"

When Ben looked into her eyes she didn't know what to say and was saved from answering when Max trotted into the room and headed straight for her. She held the Santa to her heart as she backed away quickly. Max barked, making her even more uncomfortable.

Ben petted Max. "Don't worry, he won't hurt you. He loves people. He's just wishing you a Merry Christmas."

Max barked again.

Haley didn't look convinced. She carefully put the Santa back down and slowly inched away from Max, headed for the door.

"You know, I'm actually pretty tired from the drive," she said. She kept a close eye on Max. "Would it be okay if I went to my room?"

"Of course." Ben grabbed her bags and headed up the stairs. "Just follow me."

Haley was right behind him, and when she looked over her shoulder and saw Max was sitting there watching her, she picked up her pace.

When Ben got to a room at the end of the hall, he proudly opened the door. "Here you are. It's one of our most popular rooms."

"Thank you." Haley smiled as she stepped inside, but then froze when she looked around. Her jaw dropped and her eyes grew huge.

"It's wonderful, isn't it?" Ben asked. He was clearly excited.

Haley tried to say something, anything, but she was too much in shock.

CHAPTER 5

Haley squeezed her eyes shut, and silently said to herself, *Please don't be real. Please don't be real. Please don't be real.* But when she opened her eyes, it was real all right. She was standing in an all-white Christmas angel-themed room. Angels everywhere. There were angel figurines on the dresser, on both nightstands, and on the desk. There had to be at least forty of them. There were even angel pictures on the wall and angel pillows on the bed, and she felt like all the angels, everywhere, were staring at her! It was like when she had the staring contest with the Tyler Toys dolls, only with this stare-down, Haley knew the angels were already winning. She shook her head and rubbed her throbbing temples. It was all too much. She was having a major Christmas meltdown. She knew she needed to get out of the room fast, but when she turned around, she saw Max sitting in the doorway. She was trapped.

"Is everything okay?" Ben asked. He looked concerned.

Haley forced a smile. "Uh, yes, everything's fine. I just

wasn't expecting a room quite this . . . fancy. You should really save it for someone else. I can just take a regular room."

When she took a step toward the door Max barked and looked up at her. She quickly stepped back, bumping the dresser and causing one of the angels to tip over. "Oops, I'm sorry," she said, flustered. The angel would have hit the floor if Ben hadn't caught her just in time. He carefully put it back on the dresser.

"We do have other rooms," he said.

Haley fought to hide her relief.

"We have a snowman room, a Santa room, a star room, but they're already taken. The only other room we have left is the elf room with our giant life-size elf. We call him Harry . . ."

Just the thought of a life-size elf named Harry had Haley even more freaked out. She forced herself to smile. "You know what. This room is great. I can stay here. I just didn't realize all your rooms had . . ."

"Themes?" Ben finished for her eagerly. "It's what we always do for Christmas Camp. Everyone loves it."

Haley fought to keep smiling. "I bet. Okay, then. I'll be fine in this room."

Now it was Ben's turn to look relieved. "That's great. My son will be glad to hear it. The elf room is his favorite, and I know you'll enjoy this room. You'll have all these angels to keep you company."

"Yay!" Haley said, pretending to be excited when all she wanted to do was run . . . fast.

Ben turned to leave. "If there's anything else you need, you just let us know, and we'll see you downstairs in about an hour for our first Christmas Camp activity."

Haley kept smiling and nodded. "Sounds great. Thank you." As she watched Ben leave, she went to shut her door, but there was a problem. Max. He was still sitting in the doorway looking up at her. "Time to go." She awkwardly waved her hands at him. "Come on, go!"

Max stood up and looked excited. He wagged his tail as he did a quick circle. He looked like he thought this was a new fun game.

But Haley wasn't playing around. She lowered her voice so Max would know she was serious. "Okay, time to go." When Max didn't budge, she lowered her voice even more. "Come on, I'm serious. You need to go now . . ." But when he responded by just barking and wagging his tail, she threw up her arms. "Come on! Seriously? What do I need to do?" She took a tentative step toward the door. "Okay, stay there, but I'm shutting the door. The door is shutting. It's shutting now . . ."

Max barked again. He seemed to be loving this new game, Haley not so much. Frustrated, she backed away and sat down on her bed. "Please go . . ."

Apparently "please" was the magic word because Max immediately trotted off.

Haley looked part impressed and part suspicious. As she got up and tentatively walked over to the door, she half expected Max to come running back in. But when she looked down the hall, Max was gone. She quickly closed her door and collapsed against it. She still couldn't believe what she was seeing. There were so many angels and so much white. She knew no one would ever believe it, so she got out her cell phone and snapped a few pictures. She even took a selfie with some of the angels behind her.

"Wait until Kathy sees this!" She laughed as she sent Kathy a quick text with her selfie and only one word: *HELP!*

In the selfie she looked like the kid in the *Home Alone*

movie who had his mouth wide open and was screaming. As she walked around the room eyeing all the angels, she came to a decision fast. She smiled, because she knew just what she needed to do.

Seconds later, she was running around the room picking up all the angels and stuffing them into the dresser drawers. The last angel standing was the largest one. She stood almost two feet tall and was on the chair next to the desk wearing a long white lace dress trimmed in gold. Her wings and halo were also gold and were covered with glitter. She had big blue eyes and perfect golden curls. Haley smiled as she picked her up. "I think it's time for you and your friends to go on a little vacation." In a flash, she stuffed the angel into the last drawer, until the drawer was so full she could barely shut it.

Satisfied, she rubbed her hands together as she looked around her room. She only had one thing left to tackle, the angel pillows on the bed. She had just tossed one up onto the top shelf of the closet when there was a knock on the door. When she turned to answer it, the angel pillow fell back down and hit her on the head.

"Seriously?" she asked as she picked up the pillow.

There was another knock. This one was louder.

"Coming!" she called out as she headed for the door, but when she opened it, she did a double take, because the only thing she saw was Max sitting there looking up at her. He wagged his tail and barked.

"Seriously? You're back?" She leaned down and gave Max an incredulous look. "And you know how to knock on doors?"

A sexy male laugh had her eyes shooting up just as Jeff appeared in her doorway. As she looked into his eyes she felt an instant spark and for a moment she forgot everything else as she clutched the angel pillow to her racing heart.

"You know Max is pretty smart, but I don't think he's mastered the door knock yet."

Max wagged his tail.

Haley laughed. "So, this is just a little routine you two do?"

Jeff smiled back at her. "Actually, I knocked and then realized I dropped something, although a routine's not a bad idea. What do you think, Max?"

For an answer, Max barked, quickly slid past Haley, trotted over to her bed, and lay down.

Jeff looked surprised. "I didn't know you two were friends?"

Haley gave Max a look. "Neither did I." When she looked back at Jeff, his smile had her catching her breath. She had seen hot guys before, but none of them had ever made her pulse race the way this one did. She knew she was being ridiculous and one hundred percent blamed her light-headedness on the Christmas overload and the fact that she'd skipped breakfast and lunch. Determined to regroup and act normal, Haley smiled back at Jeff and then looked over at Max.

"Actually, we're not friends," she said. But when she saw Jeff's confusion, she raced on. "I mean, I'm sure he's a great dog and all, he looks very nice, but I'm just not really a dog person." She hated how she was rambling. She decided to stop talking.

"Not a dog person?" Jeff asked. He gave her a curious look. "Sounds like there's a story there?"

Haley shook her head. "Uh, no, not really. I just didn't grow up around dogs or have any pets, so . . ."

"So, you're not a dog person," Jeff answered.

"Right, and . . ." But when Haley looked into his eyes, she again lost her train of thought.

Lucky for her, Jeff didn't miss a beat. "Sorry, I should have introduced myself right away. I'm Jeff, my dad owns the inn and runs the Christmas Camp." He held out his hand.

Haley finally let go of the angel pillow and took his hand. "Hi, I'm Haley." But when their hands touched, she felt an unfamiliar jolt. Her eyes flew to Jeff's, and he also looked like he had felt something. They both quickly let go of each other's hand. To buy herself a second to calm down, she looked over at Max, who now appeared to be sleeping, and thought to herself that she really needed to get something to eat. She rushed to fill the silence. "And just for the record, I don't usually talk to dogs, or think they know how to open doors, or anything like that . . ." As her voice trailed off, she groaned inside, knowing she was babbling again and sounding more ridiculous by the second. When Jeff laughed, it made her relax a little. She liked his laugh. It was warm and genuine and nonjudgmental.

"Well, I'm here because I have something for you," he said.

Haley's eyes lit up with curiosity. "Really? So, you're a Christmas elf bringing presents? I heard you have the elf room . . ." She stopped to look at the left side of Jeff's head and then the right.

"Uh, what are you doing?" he asked.

"Checking out your ears to see if you're really an elf." Haley fought to keep a straight face.

Jeff reached up, grabbed one of his earlobes, and wiggled an ear. "What do you think?"

Haley crossed her arms in front of her chest. "I'm reserving judgment. I'll let you know."

"A skeptic?" Jeff teased.

"A realist," she corrected, but smiled back at him. "So, what do you have for me?"

He handed her a pretty red velvet Christmas stocking with the name "Haley" embroidered on it. On the front was a beautiful angel that looked just like the angel in the white dress that had been on her dresser before she stuffed it into the drawer.

She laughed when she saw the angel. "Wow, another angel." She wisely stopped herself from saying any more.

"It goes with the angel room," Jeff said.

"Of course." She continued to block his view so he couldn't look into the room and see that she'd gotten rid of all of the angels. As she stood there she didn't realize she was nervously wringing and wadding up the top of the stocking.

Jeff was staring at her stocking. "You might want to be careful with that. You're going to need it for the week you're here."

Haley laughed. "I'm not going to be here a week!" She then noticed what she was doing to the stocking and looked guilty. "Oh, sorry about that. I can fix it."

Jeff gave her a look. "What do you mean you won't be staying the week?"

Haley tossed the angel pillow and stocking on her bed. "I mean, I plan to get all these Christmas activities done as fast as I can so that I can get back to work." When she saw the way Jeff was frowning, she hurried on. "Don't worry, I know I have to do everything to get my certificate. I just plan to crank this stuff out and get back to Boston, hopefully in a few days . . ."

Jeff gave her an incredulous look. "You do know this is Christmas Camp, right?"

Haley nodded. "Of course. It's hard to forget with all these decorations."

"Then you know this next week is all about slowing down, embracing the Christmas spirit. This is not something you *rush* to get through."

Haley laughed. "Okay, now I get it. You're not a Christmas elf, you're the Christmas Camp police." Her smiled disappeared when she saw he wasn't laughing. He was serious.

"My dad is the one who runs this place," he said. "This Christmas Camp is very important to him."

Haley smiled her best smile. She knew she couldn't afford to start off on the wrong foot. "I met your dad. He seems really great, and this camp . . . I'm sure is great, too. I just need to get in and out of here as fast as possible. I promise I won't bother anyone and I'll be outta here before you know it."

Jeff put his hands on his hips. The more she talked, the more annoyed he looked. The vibe in the room had just gone from lighthearted to tense faster than you could say "Christmas crazy."

"You make it sound like this is some kind of prison," he said.

Haley laughed. "Well, it is Christmas bootcamp, right?"

"Christmas *Camp*."

Haley fought to keep smiling. The look on Jeff's face wasn't helping. "I'm just kidding. I know it's Christmas Camp."

"But what you don't know is that my dad puts his whole heart into this Christmas Camp, to make sure the people who come, like you, have a special experience. I don't understand. If you don't want to be here, why did you come?"

Haley's smile faded. Things were going from bad to worse. She needed to turn them around fast. She took a deep breath and tried again. "Look, I'm really not a Grinch. I have nothing against Christmas. I think what your dad is doing here is great. I'm sure people love it—"

"Just not you?" Jeff asked, looking into her eyes.

Haley quickly looked away. She found it hard to think straight when he was looking at her that way—or any way, for that matter. "It's great, I just have a lot of work to do. That's my priority right now, and part of that work includes being here and doing whatever I need to do so I can pass or graduate or whatever you say so I can get that certificate . . ." She stopped talking when she noticed Jeff looking over her shoulder. She followed his gaze to her bottom dresser drawer, where one of the angels' dresses was sticking out. "Uh, I can explain," she said, having no idea how she was going to get out of this one.

He held up his hand to stop her. "Just don't. It's obvious you don't want to be here. So why are you? The truth?"

Haley gave up. Her shoulders slumped a little. She knew she had to come clean. "My boss sent me here. I'm up for a big promotion, and he said I had to come here first if I wanted to get it."

Jeff looked up at the ceiling and just shook his head.

Seeing his disapproval, she rushed on. "My boss has been here with his family and said it was amazing, so he wanted me to come and do all the activities here to help me find my Christmas spirit."

Jeff went over to her bed, picked up the stocking he had brought her, and pulled out a scroll that was tied with a pretty red velvet ribbon. He handed it to her.

"What's this?" She eyed the scroll.

"It's your schedule of activities."

When she undid the ribbon, the scroll of activities un-rolled almost to the floor. Her mouth dropped open. It looked like it would take a lifetime to complete all these activities. "This can't be right?"

Jeff smiled, but it was a smile that held a challenge. "You can see we have a pretty busy week scheduled, and it all starts in a half hour downstairs. If you're still up for it."

Speechless, Haley looked from the scroll to Jeff, and when she saw the challenge in his eyes, she stood up straighter. She assumed the position, her power hero po-sition. She would never back down from a challenge, es-pecially one that could affect her entire career. Her eyes sparkled with determination as she locked eyes with him.

"Oh, I'm up for it," she said. "I can't wait."

For a moment they just stared at each other. Neither one was backing down. Haley felt a sense of victory when Jeff looked away first.

"Then I'll see you downstairs." His expression was impossible to read. "And don't forget to bring your stock-ing." When he left, Max looked up at her then ran out the door.

"I won't!" Haley called out, determined to get the last word. She then held up her stocking and looked at the angel. "Game on!"

CHAPTER 6

A half hour later, exactly on time, Haley was about to enter the sitting room but hesitated when she saw all the people who had already gathered. Everyone was talking and laughing. There was Christmas music playing. It was all very festive and that had Haley feeling completely out of her element. She quickly sent a text to Kathy that said *911 call me in 10 minutes!* When she looked up, Max trotted over to her and gave her a look like he knew what she'd just done.

"What?" she whispered down at him. "Stop judging." Haley then saw Jeff putting another log on the fire, and when she made eye contact with him, she held up her stocking with a smug smile. But when he didn't react, her smile faded. She looked down at her phone and couldn't believe only one minute had gone by since her text. She already felt like she'd been here forever. She was seriously thinking about trying to escape when she saw Ben heading toward her. He was smiling like a kid at Christmas, and Haley couldn't help but smile back at him.

"There you are. I hope you had time to rest?" Ben asked.

Haley thought about how she'd been frantically re-arranging her room, but instead answered, "I did, thank you."

"Great, then come on in and meet everyone. We're about to get started."

As she tentatively entered the room, she couldn't help but look around in awe. Now that the sun had set, the sitting room had come alive with glittering Christmas lights, glowing candles, and a roaring fire. Even Haley couldn't deny it was cozy and magical all at the same time and that made her feel even more out of place. As she took the chair closest to the door, she concentrated on her phone, checking emails. After a couple of seconds, she peeked up to scan the group.

The first person she saw was a pleasant-looking woman in her fifties who was sitting alone. She was wearing a pretty pink sweater with pearl buttons and black pants. When the woman shyly smiled at her, Haley smiled back. Her attention then shifted to a young couple in their early twenties. They were sitting together on the couch holding hands and whispering quietly to each other. They looked very much in love.

Haley checked another email on her phone then peeked up again so she could study two teenagers who had their noses glued to their own phones, and what looked to be their dad, somewhere in his forties, sitting next to them.

Before she could look back to her phone, she caught Jeff watching her. She met his stare, and when she saw the challenge was still in his eyes, she sat up straighter, lifted her chin a little, and smiled back at him. There was no way, she thought, that she was going to let him see how out of place she felt. She knew it was crazy. She had traveled the world and worked on multimillion-dollar accounts, but being here at Christmas Camp made her feel inadequate somehow, like she couldn't live up to her surroundings.

As if sensing her nerves, Ben walked over. "Are you ready?" he asked her gently. When Haley looked up at him, she saw his eyes were filled with kindness. She gave him a grateful smile. He understood, she thought, and she nodded. "I'm ready."

He patted her on the shoulder. "You'll be fine. You just need to believe."

Haley laughed. "In Santa Claus." It was a statement, not a question.

Ben smiled back at her. "In yourself."

Before she could question what he meant, he walked into the middle of the room and addressed the group. "Hello, everyone. Welcome to Christmas Camp!" Ben had everyone's full attention, even the teenagers'. "I believe I've met everyone and that you've all met my son, Jeff, and Laura, our chef, who has been a part of our Christmas Camp family from the beginning."

Max barked and went over to sit at Ben's feet.

Everyone laughed.

"And, of course, this is Max." As Ben petted him, Max wagged his tail. "He's been part of our family since we got him as a rescue dog, and the truth is, these last two years, he's really rescued me." He looked at Max with gratitude and love. "You're a good boy, aren't you, Max?"

When Max barked again, even Haley laughed.

"We're all truly honored that you've chosen to spend this very special time of year with us," Ben said.

"This Christmas Camp was my wife and Jeff's mom's dream . . ." When his voice cracked with emotion, Jeff walked over and put his arm around him and continued for him.

"We lost my mom a few years ago," he said. For a moment his eyes filled with pain but then he continued. "It was really important to her that we carried on this Christmas Camp tradition. We do this to honor her and because of what it means to all of us . . ."

Ben nodded.

"My mom wanted to help people remember what really matters most at Christmas—spending time with your family and friends and doing what you can to give back to your community."

Ben joined in. "She knew how important it was to be grateful for all of our many blessings and to help others whenever we can. So, during this next week, we'll be doing a lot of different things to embrace and help you reconnect with your own Christmas spirit."

"Okay, sure," Haley said.

"In addition to honoring a lot of our Christmas traditions, we'll also be doing a lot of new Christmas activities, so you can create some new traditions of your own," Ben said.

The cute twentysomething guy jumped in. "That's why we're here. We need some help figuring out our own traditions."

Ben smiled as he walked over to the couple. "Then let's start with you two, Ian and Susie. I was going to have everyone go around and quickly introduce themselves."

Susie glowed when she held up her left hand and flashed a pretty, sparkly diamond ring. "We're newlyweds! I'm Susie, and this is my husband, Ian . . ." Susie laughed, looking at Ian. "I'm still getting used to saying that. My husband . . ." When she adoringly kissed Ian's cheek, he put his arm around her.

It surprised Haley how much it made her own heart ache seeing the love between the newlyweds.

Ian looked at Susie. "Susie thought it would be a good idea to come here because we could use some help in figuring out how to combine both of our family traditions at Christmas."

Susie nodded enthusiastically. "I have a large family in Maine, and we go all out at Christmas and do all the traditional stuff."

Ian laughed. "And my family's small. We do Christmas in Arizona, where our tradition is not doing any winter traditions, but enjoying the sunny, warm, beautiful desert . . ."

Haley laughed and then quickly covered her mouth. "Sorry, I can relate to that."

"So, you can see," Susie continued, "we have a lot to figure out. We want to combine both our families this year and really have a special first Christmas together."

"And we can help you do that," Ben said. "That's what Christmas Camp is all about. You've come to the perfect place."

Susie and Ian both looked relieved.

Ben turned his attention to the man with the two teenagers. The teens' focus was still on their phones. "John, do you want to introduce your family to us?" Ben asked.

"Sure." John stood up and motioned to his kids, looking like a proud parent. "This is Blake, my son, he's sixteen, and Madison, my daughter, she's fourteen, and I'm John."

"And he's a doctor," Madison chimed in. She never looked up from her phone and the way she'd said "doctor" wasn't exactly positive.

John, unfazed, like he was used to her attitude, continued. "This is our first Christmas together, just the three of us . . ."

"Since the divorce," Madison added. She was still on her phone.

John took a deep breath. "Since the divorce, I wanted to make this Christmas special, for all of us, so here we are."

"We wanted a ski trip," Blake said. He was playing a video game on his phone that kept making noises.

Madison, still texting someone, nodded in agreement.

Ian and Susie exchanged a look like they were rethinking having kids.

"But we're going to have a great time here, too," John said. He tried to look and sound optimistic, but it was an obvious struggle. When he gave Ben an apologetic look, Ben returned a smile.

Ben then turned his attention to the woman sitting alone. She was nervously adjusting a button on her pink sweater. Haley could see her hands were shaking.

"Everyone, this is Gail," Ben said. "Gail, please introduce yourself, and tell us why you're here."

Gail smiled and seemed to pick her words carefully. "Hi, I'm Gail, and I'm here because my son, Ryan, is in the military, and this is my first Christmas without him . . ." When her eyes started to well up with tears, she took a deep breath before continuing. "I'm so proud of the work he's doing to help protect our country and our freedom . . . I just really miss him, especially at this time of year. Ryan's dad passed when he was ten, and it has just been the two of us, but we always have a special time during the holidays. It was actually Ryan's idea that I come here and—"

Haley's phone rang loudly, interrupting the emotional

moment. The sound of the ring tone, "Bad to the Bone," was extra jarring. Haley looked just as surprised as everyone else. She'd forgotten she'd told Kathy to call her. She jumped up and looked at Gail. "I'm sorry." The sad look on Gail's face made Haley's stomach hurt. Her eyes flew to Jeff. He crossed his arms and looked disapproving and disappointed. "I'm really sorry. I have to get this," she said, and ran out of the room.

INSIDE HER BEDROOM, Haley felt like a caged animal, pacing back and forth talking to Kathy on FaceTime. "You should see this place, Kathy. I feel like I'm trapped in a Christmas snow globe. It's like Christmas-palooza! Everywhere you look . . . it's Christmas!"

Kathy laughed. "Oh, come on. It can't be that bad. Christmas decorations are great. How can anyone have too much Christmas?"

Haley marched over to her dresser, opened a drawer, and pointed her phone so Kathy could see all the angels piled up on top of each other. "Easy, check this out."

Kathy's eyes grew huge. "Whoa! Are those . . ."

"Angels, Christmas angels, that's right, and they're all over the place. I'm in the Christmas angel room."

Kathy doubled over with laughter. "So, let me get this straight," she said. "They gave you, of all people, the angel room, and you've put all the angels—"

"In the dresser, in the nightstands, under the bed, anywhere I could find to put them." Haley shoved the drawer closed. "And the owner's son, Jeff, caught me . . ."

"What do you mean, caught you?" Kathy was still laughing.

"He was dropping off my Christmas stocking that, by the way, has an—"

"Angel on it," Kathy finished for her.

"Exactly, and he saw one of the angels sticking out of a drawer, and now he's like the Christmas police. He's watching everything I do. You wouldn't believe this guy!" Haley was talking faster and faster, practically walking in circles now.

Kathy gave her a questioning look. "You don't usually let people get to you like this. What's going on? What aren't you telling me?" Her eyes lit up. "Wait, this guy . . . he's hot, isn't he?!"

Haley glared at her phone. "That has nothing to do with it!"

"So, he *is* hot!" Kathy shot back. "You like this guy!"

"What?!" Haley sputtered. "I don't even . . . I don't even know him!"

Kathy just shook her head, smiling.

"What?" Haley demanded.

"I think it's great. It's about time you found someone."

Haley looked at her friend like she was nuts. "I haven't *found* someone. What's wrong with you? What I've found is a crazy Christmas Camp, and I'm a hostage until I get that certificate Larry wants so he'll let me pitch the Tyler Toys account."

"But the guy, admit it. You like him, right?" Kathy asked, clearly not letting it go.

"I'll admit you're insane. I don't even know this guy. I only talked to him for two minutes, and trust me, he wants nothing to do with me. He thinks I'm the Grinch that's going to steal his dad's Christmas Camp fun."

"Then why are you getting so upset?"

"I'm not upset!" Haley yelled, then snapped her mouth shut.

Kathy laughed. "Whatever you say, Grinchy, but remember you need to play nice, do whatever you need to do to get that certificate and get back here. Tom is already putting together his pitch for Larry. You need to find your Christmas spirit fast . . ."

Emotionally exhausted, Haley stopped pacing and flopped down onto the bed. She let out a deep breath. "I know. Thanks for letting me vent. I just need to stay focused on what matters the most . . ."

"Christmas," Kathy said. It was a statement, not a question.

Haley shook her head. "No, my promotion, but if getting it means being the best Christmas Camper they've ever seen, I'm on it and—" A knock on the door interrupted her.

"I gotta go, someone's at the door . . ."

"Maybe it's Santa Claus," Kathy teased.

"Don't joke . . . it could be."

Another knock, louder this time.

"Coming."

"Good luck," Kathy said.

Haley headed for the door. "Thanks, I'm gonna need it!"

CHAPTER 7

Haley opened the door and found Jeff standing there. The fact that her heart instantly started beating faster both confused and annoyed her. When she looked up at him, she found his expression impossible to read.

"My dad sent me to check on you," he said. "Everyone's waiting downstairs."

Haley held up her phone. "Sorry, it was work calling. I had to get it."

There was an awkward silence when Jeff didn't say a word.

"But I'm ready now," Haley said.

"Okay, great." He pointed to the computer on her bed. "Grab your laptop, and let's go."

"My laptop, why?"

But Jeff was already walking away. She grabbed her computer and hurried to catch up to him. "Why do I need my laptop?" she asked.

"My dad will explain."

As Haley continued to follow him, she noticed the way he walked, without any hesitation, with a sense of purpose, like a man who knew where he was going in his life. She couldn't help but admire that about him. She also couldn't help but admire the way he looked in a pair of jeans. *Stop it!* she scolded herself, but as she tore her eyes away from him, she could still hear Kathy's voice in her head saying, *He's hot, isn't he?*

"Focus!" she commanded.

When Jeff abruptly stopped and turned around, she was horrified to realize she'd said the word out loud. She really must be losing it. She could feel her face burning with embarrassment.

"Were you talking to me?" he asked.

"No! I mean, yes. I mean, I was saying 'focus,' like what's the focus of our first activity?"

Jeff looked even more confused as he stared at her.

Haley scooted past him, so she was in front of him now, and started walking away fast. "Come on. I don't want to hold anyone up."

Jeff threw up his hands and laughed. "Now you're worried about everyone?"

When she practically ran back into the sitting room, she found out Jeff wasn't kidding. Everyone was waiting for her, and they all looked up as she entered. "I'm really sorry about before," she said, and meant it. She looked directly at Gail. "I didn't know my phone's ring tone was on. I usually turn it to silent." She held up the phone. "It's on silent right now, so I promise there won't be any more interruptions."

Gail smiled back at her. "It's okay. I understand . . ."

Ben also smiled as he walked over to Haley. "And you're right, you won't have to worry about any more interruptions."

Haley looked relieved to be forgiven so quickly until Ben held out his hand, palm up.

"Your phone," he said.

Haley smiled back at him. "I really did turn it off."

"Thank you, but I'll take it now."

Haley's smile instantly faded. She instinctively clutched her phone to her heart, already fearing where this conversation was headed. "Why do you need my phone?"

"It's part of what we do here at Christmas Camp. It's called disconnecting in order to reconnect with Christmas. I'll need your computer, too."

"What? No!" Haley looked shocked. "I need my phone and computer for work . . ."

"Don't worry, you'll get everything back at night, after all the activities are done."

Haley was now clutching both her phone and her computer to her heart.

"We had to turn ours in, too," Madison said. She did not look happy about it.

Blake nodded. He looked equally upset.

"We all did," John added.

Haley looked around the room, and everyone nodded. The last person she looked at was Jeff. He smiled at her. That same challenging smile that instantly got under her skin. She took a deep breath, and before she went ballistic, she willed herself to calm down. She thought about what Kathy had said, how Tom was already working on his Tyler Toys pitch and how she needed the certificate from this Christmas Camp so Larry would give her a shot at the account. She didn't have a choice. Reluctantly, she handed both her computer and her phone to Ben. She watched as he put them into a big box that was wrapped up like a Christmas present.

"You won't regret this," he said.

Haley turned her back and walked away. "I already do," she mumbled under her breath.

Max, who was standing next to Ben, heard her and barked.

She gave him a look that said, *Give me a break.*

Ben picked up the box and gave it to Jeff then faced the group. "Okay, who's ready for the first activity?"

Susie's hand shot up.

"Perfect!" Ben beamed at her. "You can be my helper."

Haley looked over at the teenagers. They rolled their eyes. She knew how they felt.

Seconds later, Susie was helping Ben hand out miniature scrolls that matched the bigger scrolls that had been in their stockings listing all their activities. Ben also passed out snowman pencils.

Haley gave her pencil an incredulous look. She'd never seen a snowman pencil before.

"Here's what we're going to do," Ben said with excitement. He held up a scroll and a snowman pencil. "Before we head into dinner, I would like each of you to write down a Christmas wish and put it in your stocking."

"I wish I had my phone," Blake muttered. Madison and Haley both heard him and nodded in agreement.

Ben continued: "Don't worry. No one will see your Christmas wish. This is just for you. So write down what you really wish for most."

Haley watched everyone start writing. She looked at her scroll and drew a complete blank. She didn't have a Christmas wish. She didn't make wishes at Christmas or ever. She believed in making things happen, not just wishing for things to happen.

"What? You don't have a Christmas wish?"

Startled, Haley looked up to find Jeff standing over

her. Before she hit him with a sarcastic comeback, she reminded herself that she needed him on her side if she was going to get that certificate. She needed to stop fighting him and find a way to get him on her side. So this time when she smiled at him, she really tried to make it look like she meant it.

His eyes narrowed. He looked . . . suspicious.

"You know," she started, still smiling, "there are so many things to wish for that I just want to be sure to pick the right one . . ."

"I'm surprised getting out of our Christmas Camp isn't top on your wish list."

Haley wanted to agree with him but remembered her new strategy. "I think we got off on the wrong foot . . ."

He looked surprised.

"I think your Christmas Camp is great. I really do. Everyone here is going to have an amazing time."

"But just not you?" Jeff asked.

Haley looked him in the eye. "Honestly, no. But please understand, it's nothing against Christmas Camp. I'm just not here on vacation, I'm here to work, so I really need to do all the activities as fast as possible to make my deadline. My entire future is riding on this."

"Well, maybe you can do both, have fun and work," Jeff said. "Trust me, I understand. I work a lot, too, but I also really look forward to doing this every year. Things get so crazy at work, and this gives me a chance to disconnect and spend some time with my dad. When I go back down to Boston I always feel better."

Haley knew she'd only feel better after she won her competition with Tom, and got her promotion. The problem was, she knew it wasn't going to be easy; because Tom was such a brownnoser, she figured he was probably helping the intern put up the tree. Or worse, he'd gone out and bought his own real tree, knowing that's what Larry really wanted. She knew the longer she spent at Christmas Camp the more time Tom would have to show Larry he was the better person for the Tyler Toys account.

"Is everything okay?" Jeff asked. He was watching her closely.

Haley realized she'd been staring off into space. "Sorry. I was just thinking about . . ."

"Work?" Jeff finished for her.

Haley laughed. "See, you already know me so well. Okay, enough about me. What about you? You said you work in Boston? What do you do?"

"I'm an architect."

Haley looked impressed. "Do you design buildings or homes?"

"Both, but I actually specialize in restoration projects. I'm doing a condo project right now down on the waterfront . . ."

"The one at Crane's Wharf?"

"Yeah, you know it?" Now it was Jeff's turn to look impressed.

"I do. I also live in Boston and that's where my parents' favorite seafood restaurant was until it got torn down for the renovation."

"You mean the Crab Shack?"

"Yes, that's the one." Haley smiled at him. "They've been going to it for years, and they were really bummed when it shut down . . ."

"Well, you'll have to tell them it's only shut down temporarily. We're restoring it, too. We're planning to bring it back as soon as we reopen everything. It's a Boston institution. We couldn't get rid of the Crab Shack."

Haley nodded enthusiastically. "That's what we've been hoping for! I can't wait to tell them. They're going to be so excited." She automatically reached for her phone and then remembered it had been taken away. Her smile faded a little.

"Don't worry, you'll get your phone back tonight," Jeff said.

Haley wiggled her empty fingers. "I know. It's just so weird not having it. It's like it's become a part of me. I know that's so wrong and sounds a little weird, but . . ."

"That's how you feel."

She nodded. "It is. I clearly need phone therapy."

Jeff laughed. "Well, you're getting Christmas Camp therapy. I hear that's the next best thing."

Haley squeezed her wiggling fingers together. "Okay, then, lucky for me, but as soon as I get my phone back, I'm calling my parents. They could use some good news right now."

"Is everything okay?" Jeff asked, looking concerned.

"Oh, they're okay, but the Money Pit isn't."

"The Money Pit?"

"Yeah, I call it the Money Pit, but my parents, the eternal optimists, call it"—she made air quotes—"a vintage Victorian." She sighed. "It's our family home. It was my grandmother's and now it's a family project. Or more like a never-ending renovation project that is trying to bankrupt us all."

Jeff nodded, understanding. "Renovations can get really expensive, but in the end, you'll have a piece of family history that you've preserved. And that's priceless."

"I don't disagree with you, but running out of money before it's done is a real concern. There's so much red tape to make sure things are historically correct and that means more delays, and time is money. I know this is what you do full time, but for me it has been really frustrating."

"I guess I like the challenge. That and being able to take something that has been forgotten and bring it back to life."

Haley looked surprised. "That's what my parents say. I think they'd be much better off in a nice new condo, but they love the Money Pit."

"The vintage Victorian."

"The Money Pit."

Jeff laughed just as his dad walked up.

"Haley, do you have your Christmas wish ready?" Ben asked.

"She's working on it," Jeff answered for her.

"Wonderful. Everyone else has done theirs, so whenever you're ready . . ."

Haley looked around and felt guilty when she saw the rest of the group waiting for her. Again. "Sorry. Just give me a sec." Making sure Jeff and his dad couldn't see her, she pretended to write something down then quickly rolled up the scroll before anyone could see that she hadn't actually written anything on it. "Done," she said as she proudly held up her scroll, and then followed everyone else and tucked her scroll into her stocking.

"Okay, great," Ben said. "Dinner is in an hour. In the meantime, relax and make yourself at home, and don't forget to wear your Christmas sweaters to dinner."

Jeff gave Haley a questioning look. "If you need to borrow a sweater for tonight, we have a few extra around here."

Haley jumped up. "I'm good, but thank you. I've come prepared."

"Good to know," Jeff said. He smiled when he looked into her eyes, and for a moment she was unable to look away. *Why do you have to be so good-looking?* she thought. She knew he was the kind of guy who could totally be a distraction, and right now she couldn't afford to get sidetracked, by him or anyone else. She just had to figure out how to balance making sure she kept him as her ally while still keeping him at arm's length.

"I'll see you later," she said as she headed out.

"I'll look forward to seeing you—and your sweater," Jeff answered.

Haley was still smiling when she walked into her bedroom. When she caught one of the angels in a picture on the wall giving her a knowing look, she marched over to it. "Stop judging. I'm not going to let him distract me." She took the picture down and put it in the closet. "I'm here to work. That's my focus." She felt better saying the words out loud. Looking at the other angel pictures still on the wall, she said, "You're either with me or you're not, and if you're not, you're in the closet." She looked at each picture, one by one, and seemed satisfied. "Okay, then, let's do this. Those of you who are left can be my cheering squad. Christmas Camp, here I come!"

CHAPTER 8

A couple minutes later, Haley was back downstairs. She was starving. Hoping to find a little snack before dinner, she peeked into the kitchen and saw Ben. He smiled at her.

"Haley, hi. Come in."

"Hi, thanks." Haley looked around the kitchen as she entered. It was a true chef's kitchen with all the latest appliances and, of course, Christmas-themed objects everywhere. There was a collection of Santa Claus mugs hanging from a line of red hooks in the corner, and they matched the giant Santa Claus cookie jar. There were also pretty green glass jars filled with candy canes and gumdrops and red and green M&M's. Even the reindeer fruit bowl followed the Christmas theme with shiny red and green apples. But it was the snowman platter of Christmas treats that really grabbed her attention and had her mouth watering. On the platter there was dark chocolate fudge, white chocolate-dipped pretzels, red and green Rice Krispies bars, and delightfully decorated sugar cookies. She couldn't help herself. She walked over to the platter to get a closer look and saw there were sugar-cookie Christmas trees with emerald-green frosting and Red Hot candies for Christmas ornaments. There were stars with white frosting and silver sprinkles, and snowmen cookies with all white frosting that had faces carefully drawn on with black frosting and a tiny dab of orange frosting for the carrot nose. There was even a Christmas angel sugar cookie. Haley knew she shouldn't be surprised. The angel was exquisite. It was also covered in all-white frosting and outlined in sparkling gold, making it almost too pretty to eat . . . almost . . .

"You're welcome to have one," Ben said. He walked over to join her. "They're really something, aren't they? Laura does an amazing job."

"These look better than what I see in our bakery by my office. She's really talented." Haley's fingers itched to take a cookie, but instead she clasped them tightly together.

"Laura loves to bake. We've been really lucky to have her all these years. Here, please try one."

Haley sadly shook her head. "No, thank you. I'm trying to be good."

Ben picked up another tray of cookies. This time the cookies were on a Rudolph platter. He brought them over to her. These cookies were much simpler. They were round with white frosting, and they were covered with finely crushed candy canes.

"If you're cutting back, and you're only going to allow yourself one thing, you need to try these," Ben said. "You can't come to Christmas Camp and not taste one of our famous sugar cookies."

Haley laughed. "Are you sure you're not in sales? What makes them so special?"

Ben picked one up and took a bite, shutting his eyes and savoring the taste. Haley's stomach growled. "These are from my grandma's famous secret sugar-cookie recipe. Now we call them Christmas Camp sugar cookies. Laura makes everything else, but I make these myself."

"Really?" Haley looked impressed.

Ben nodded. "They're simple to make, nothing fancy, but I promise you, you've never had a Christmas cookie this good. So, when you're ready to splurge, this is what you want to splurge on. Are you sure you don't want to try just one?" Ben held up the tray of cookies to her. They were so close she could smell the peppermint of the candy canes.

Haley, not trusting herself, took a step back. "It's a slippery slope. I'm a sugarholic, so once I have one, I won't be able to stop, so I better not." She eyed the fruit bowl but didn't look too excited about it. "Maybe I can just have an apple."

Ben instantly picked up the bowl and brought it over to her. "Of course, you know what they say. An apple a day keeps the—"

"Doctor away," Haley finished for him.

"No, the Grinch away."

Haley laughed. "Well, then I better have an apple for sure." She picked up a shiny green apple and took a bite. It was tasty, crisp and tart, but now all she wanted were the sugar cookies. When she looked back at them longingly, she noticed the chalkboard Ben was getting ready to write on.

On the top it said 14 DAYS TO CHRISTMAS.

Haley shook her head in disbelief. "I can't believe Christmas is only two weeks away. I still have so much work to do."

Ben stopped to look at her. "You know, Haley, the

whole idea of being here for our Christmas Camp week is to take some time out to really celebrate the holiday and what matters most at Christmas."

"But what if work is what matters most to me?" she asked.

"Then I would say I am very glad to have you with us at Christmas Camp," Ben replied. He gave her a kind smile as he picked up a piece of chalk and wrote the word "merry" on the chalkboard. "Every day I'll be putting up a new word as our theme for the day . . ."

"So, today's theme is merry?" Haley asked.

"Exactly."

"Merry as in, whooo-hoo, it's Christmas . . ." She held up her hands in celebration.

Ben laughed. "Sure, it can mean that. 'Merry' means anything that brings you joy and happiness. 'Merry' is about doing things that make you laugh and smile so you just feel happy . . ."

Haley nodded. Happy was good. She was about to take another bite of her apple when she spotted the box Ben had put all their phones and computers in. Her eyes lit up as she walked over to it and peered inside. When she saw her phone, it was like seeing an old friend. She reached in and picked it up. "You know what really makes me happy?" she asked as she smiled playfully at Ben. "My phone makes me very happy. You could even say it makes me feel *merry*."

Ben laughed.

"So, does that mean I can use it?"

Ben came over and gently took the phone from her. "Why don't we work on finding some things that make you merry besides your cell phone."

"But my cell phone makes me so happy—I mean so merry!"

When Ben laughed at her pleading look, she had to laugh with him.

"Come back tonight after we're done with the activities, and I'll give everything back to you, same thing every night. Deal?"

Haley hesitated. "Deal."

"Trust me, you will thank me for this."

Haley gave him a look like she wasn't so sure, but she did love his optimism and enthusiasm. When Ben held out his hand she gave him her phone. He then gently guided her away from the box of temptation. She sighed as she looked at it over her shoulder, thinking, *So near and yet so far.*

"You know we have some wonderful books in the library you might enjoy," Ben said.

Haley took the hint. "Okay, you win."

Ben gave her a fatherly pat on the back. "No, Haley, actually you win. You'll see."

"Okay, I'm going to go before I break down and have one of those cookies." She took another bite of her apple, but it didn't even come close to satisfying her sugar craving. As she headed for the library, she remembered when she was little, making sugar cookies with her mom at Christmas and how they'd had matching snowman aprons. She must have been about five the first time her mom let her put all the ingredients into a big red bowl and taught her how to crack eggs. But her favorite part had been using the Christmas cookie cutters and frosting and decorating the cookies. She remembered her favorite cookie cutter was a Christmas angel and how she would decorate the angels with white frosting and gold sprinkles just like the ones Ben used. She laughed at the irony of it all. She hadn't thought about making Christmas cookies for years.

As she walked into the library, she was still smiling, remembering, but when she saw all the books, her jaw dropped. There were hundreds of them. It was one impressive library for such a quaint little inn. The room wasn't that big, but the hand-carved wood bookshelves were floor to ceiling and took up every inch of the wall.

As Haley walked along one bookcase, she saw all kinds of books, from glossy new hardcovers to vintage classics and paperbacks. In the corner, there was a little table with a half-finished puzzle on it. The puzzle was of a beautiful Christmas tree set up in a quaint town square. Looking at it, she felt like she'd been there before. It had that timeless, could-be-anywhere feeling about it.

As she walked past the back bookshelf, she gently ran her hand across the books. Reading had always been one of her favorite things, but she couldn't even remember the last book she'd read. She knew she'd downloaded several recently that her clients had written, but she'd had her intern read them for her and give her a quick synopsis.

As she pulled an old well-loved book off the shelf, she took a moment to feel its weight before opening it up, shutting her eyes, and inhaling deeply. She'd always thought there was nothing like the smell of an old book. To her, this one smelled a little like vanilla with a musky hint of coffee. It triggered memories of all the hours she had spent at the library growing up, because money had been so tight her parents could rarely afford to buy her books. Her life changed the day her father gave her her first library card. The library had opened up the whole world to her. It was the one place where it didn't matter how much money you had; you could travel anywhere, be anyone, and learn anything. Books became her escape, and the library, her happy place. She inhaled one more time . . .

"So, this is what they mean when they say someone always has their nose in a book."

Haley spun around as Jeff walked into the room. Embarrassed, she quickly put the book back.

"Please, by all means, continue with what you were doing," he said. "The books are here to be enjoyed. Have you found one that you want to read?"

Haley spun around. "Not yet. There are so many to choose from. I can't believe how many you have, and some of these look really old."

Jeff joined her, carefully took one of the older books off the shelf, and opened it to the copyright page. "They are. Like this one was written in 1936. I found it at one of the renovations I was doing. That's actually where a lot of these books came from. You'd be surprised how many people just leave them behind . . ."

Haley frowned as she studied a group of old books. "Really? That seems so . . ."

"Sad . . ."

Haley looked back at him. "Yes. Sad. I feel like books are a part of your history, your story, they help make you who you are, so to just leave them behind doesn't seem right somehow."

"I agree and that's why I always bring them back here, so they'll have a new home. Guests enjoy them, and you never know what you're going to find."

Haley smiled as she watched Jeff rearrange some books on the shelf and thought, first he saves old homes and now he saves abandoned books, it was almost impossible not to like this guy. But then she shook herself mentally. She was getting distracted again. She needed to find something and move on. When she wandered over to a stack of colorful books on the desk, Jeff joined her and picked one up. "These are just some from our Christmas collection," he said.

Haley's eyebrows rose. "You actually have a Christmas collection."

"Of course. You can't come to Christmas Camp and not read a Christmas book."

Haley immediately snapped to attention. "Wait, is this one of our activities? How many do we have to read?"

Jeff laughed at her seriousness. "Don't worry. It's not one of the activities on the list. I was just saying most people enjoy reading them while they're here. It helps them get into the Christmas spirit. But maybe we should add it to the list. It's not a bad idea."

Haley's eyebrows rose. "Well, just wait until next year. I think that list is long enough already."

Jeff handed her a book. "Just in case you find the time. I think you might like this one."

Haley looked down at it and laughed. "*An Angel's Christmas*? Seriously, you're giving me another angel. I'm on angel overload right now . . ."

"You can never have too many angels," Jeff said.

"I think that's a matter of opinion." Haley smiled. "Let's just say I have more than I can handle at the moment." She picked another book off the pile. It was a beautiful Christmas decorating book. She flipped through the pages, admiring the photographs of gorgeous homes and beautiful settings for Christmas parties. "Actually, I might be able to use something like this for research for my Christmas campaign."

"Is that what you're working on? A Christmas campaign?"

Haley's eyes instantly lit up when she started talking

about work. "It's a Christmas toy campaign for the Tyler Toys company. They're about to expand internationally, so it would be a huge account, and I'm trying to land them as a new client."

"You work in advertising?"

"I do. I'm a brand specialist."

Jeff arched an eyebrow.

"That means I work with companies and brands to help strategize the best ways to present themselves to their customers. I help them get their message out about who they really are, to really connect with their customers. That's what makes a successful business."

"You sound like you love what you do."

Haley nodded, smiling. "I really do. It's an honor and a huge responsibility to take people's dreams, the companies they've worked hard to create, and help them be successful. And if I can get this Tyler Toys company to come on board at our agency, my boss will make me a partner."

Jeff looked impressed. "Wow, that's really something."

Haley looked into his eyes and saw he was being completely genuine. There was no judgment. "Thank you. That means a lot. It has been a long journey. I started off representing small mom-and-pop businesses, which I loved because I could see how I was really making a difference . . ."

"And now?"

"Now I've moved up, and I'm representing some of the largest companies in the country. I usually specialize in travel and hospitality."

"But now you're trying to work with a toy company?"

"I know it's a little out of my lane, but my boss said I needed to land one more huge account and this would be it. So that's why I'm here. Tyler Toys is all about Christmas tradition, so bring on the inspiration."

"Then Christmas Camp should be the perfect place for you."

Haley laughed. "And now you sound like my boss. But I hope you're both right, because I only have about a week to put this Christmas campaign together, and my entire career is riding on it."

"Well, I've been doing a traditional Christmas my whole life, so let me know if you have any questions. You might call me a bit of an expert," Jeff joked. "And I'm happy to help."

"Thank you." Haley gave him a grateful look. "I might take you up on that."

Jeff went through the pile of books and picked out four, stacked them up, and handed them to her. "Here, I think these might help in your research."

Haley laughed when she saw the book on top was *A Christmas Angel*. "So, you're not giving up with this angel book, huh?"

"I don't give up easily."

When he looked into her eyes, they shared a smile, and Haley realized she was doing it again, getting distracted, so she quickly headed for the door. "I better get to work. I'll see you at dinner."

BACK IN HER ROOM, as she was getting ready for dinner, Haley looked at herself in the mirror and cracked up. She was wearing the Santa Christmas sweater Larry had given her, and it was on a whole new level of ridiculous. It was so ugly, it was pretty amazing. If there was an ugly-Christmas-sweater contest tonight, she'd be winning it.

She looked around at the angel pictures on the wall and modeled her sweater. "No judging or laughing, any of you, or you'll all end up in the closet." She glanced over at the angel book Jeff had given her to read. "And that goes for you, too!

"Okay, let's do this." She headed for the door, and when she opened it, she almost tripped over Max, who was sitting there waiting for her. "Whoa, sorry," she said as she grabbed the wall to keep from falling. When she looked at Max closer, she burst out laughing. "Wow! What happened to you?"

Max was wearing his own Christmas sweater, which featured a bunch of crazy cats wearing Santa hats. He barked when Haley couldn't stop laughing.

"I'm sorry," she told him. But when she looked at him again, she couldn't stop laughing. "Okay, you win," she said. "Your sweater is worse than mine. Cats with Santa hats, you poor thing."

Max turned around in a circle, like he was modeling his sweater for her. He then trotted off down the hall. She was still giggling as she followed him. When he reached the dining room, he sat and waited for her to catch up. "What?" she asked, looking down at him. "Oh, I know. You're too embarrassed wearing that to go to dinner alone? You need some reinforcements?"

Max wagged his tail.

"Okay, let's do this. Maybe no one will notice me if they're too busy checking out your crazy Santa cats."

Unfortunately for Haley, that wasn't the case, because as soon as she walked into the dining room, everyone stopped talking and then started laughing. The loudest laugh came from Jeff.

"Hey! Come on now," she shot back at them all. "Don't laugh at me. Look at Max. He's wearing cats! Santa cats, or cats in Santa hats, whatever. I almost look normal compared to that."

Everyone just laughed louder when Max barked. Even Haley couldn't help but join in as she took the last seat at the table, sitting between Jeff and his dad.

"Your sweater is the sickest thing I've ever seen," Madison said. She was still laughing.

"Madison," her dad said in a stern voice. He gave her a warning look.

"What? That's a good thing," Madison said. "Right, Haley?"

Haley threw up her hands. "Yeah, it means I have the *best* worst sweater here . . . I think?"

Everyone laughed again. She gave Jeff a grateful look when he handed her a glass of wine.

"You might need this," he said in a teasing voice.

"Ya think?" She laughed and took a sip. "But what about poor Max. I mean, come on, Ben, how could you do that to the poor guy? Cats? Really?"

Ben held up his hands in mock innocence. "It wasn't me."

Laura smiled as she went around the table and poured more wine. "It was me. I'm the guilty one. But Max loves it, don't you, Max? He always likes to be included."

Max barked.

When Haley looked at Laura's sweater, she started laughing again. Her stomach was starting to hurt from laughing so much. "Wow, Laura, your sweater is so perfect for you."

"Thank you." Laura held up her arms and turned around slowly so everyone could see. There was no denying her sweater was perfect—perfectly adorable. It had a giant gingerbread boy and gingerbread girl on the front. They were holding hands and were elaborately decorated with all kinds of colorful buttons, ribbon, and glitter.

When everyone clapped, Laura took a little bow. "Wow, thank you again." She laughed. "I actually made it myself. I make a new one every year."

"Every year?" Haley asked incredulously. "Why do you need a new one every year?"

"Because we have a lot of repeat guests that come to our Christmas Camp weeks, and they look forward to seeing what I'll come up with next."

"And she even takes requests," Ben said proudly.

Haley was about to take another sip of her wine but froze. "Requests?"

Gail was fascinated as well. "What do you mean, requests?" she asked. Her own sweater was pretty spectacular. It had a giant penguin wearing a Santa hat, and the Santa hat lit up.

Laura pointed at the gingerbread boy on her sweater. "This year's sweater, for example, was a request. One of our guests last year, a little ten-year-old boy, Tommy, asked me if I could make a gingerbread sweater like the gingerbread cookies I made him when he celebrated his birthday with us. I told him I would make one for next year, and he could come back and see it."

"Did he?" Haley asked.

"He sure did," Ben answered for her. "They were here just a couple of weeks ago, and you should have seen little Tommy's face when he saw Laura's sweater. He was so excited."

"He was even more excited when he found out she made him one, too," Jeff added.

Haley looked at Laura like she was a superhero. "Wow, that's really cool."

"So cool," Madison agreed.

"That's really wonderful," Gail joined in. A second later Gail's penguin's Santa hat lit up.

Ben looked at Laura with pride. "That's what we try to do here, help people create special memories."

"Okay, enough about me. Please, everyone, eat your dinner before it gets cold." Laura sat down next to Madison. "I hope you like it. We have Ben's favorite honey-baked ham, a roasted baby-beet salad, garlic mashed potatoes, roasted spring vegetables, and fresh-baked buttermilk biscuits."

"And be sure to save room for dessert," Ben said. "Laura makes the best pies."

Laura smiled. "We have several you can choose from: berry, pumpkin, pecan."

Haley's eyes were huge as she took in all the food. "This all looks amazing. So much better than the vending machine dinners I've been eating."

Madison looked fascinated. "You can get dinner out of a vending machine?"

"If you call a granola bar dinner, yes," Haley answered. She looked at Madison's sweater and laughed. "Now, that's one creative sweater you're wearing."

Madison's face lit up. Her sweater was brilliant in its simplicity. It was all white with a big red velvet bow attached. "I figured I'm the Christmas gift. I'm a big present."

Blake laughed. "One I would return."

Madison glared at him. "Better than yours; whatever it is, at least you nailed the ugly part."

Blake grinned as he looked down at his sweater. It was black with a red-and-white-striped pole on the front and the word "north." "My North Pole sweater is dope."

"You're a dope," Madison shot back at him.

"Guys, come on. It's Christmas," John said. He gave them a hopeful look. "Can you try to be nice to each other?" His own sweater had a giant reindeer on the front whose antlers stuck out about six inches.

"We *are* being nice," Madison said. She took another helping of beet salad.

"We're just kidding around, Dad. It's what we do," Blake said as he piled more mashed potatoes onto his plate.

When John, pretending to be frustrated, dropped his head into his hands, his forehead hit his antlers, and everyone laughed. Jeff's laugh was still one of the loudest, so Haley looked him up and down and just shook her head as she buttered another biscuit.

"I don't know if I'd be laughing so much if I were you, elf boy," she said as she pointed at Jeff's sweater. On the front of it there was a hilarious-looking long-haired elf whose hair was hanging off the sweater. "Let me guess," Haley said. "That's Harry the elf."

Jeff puffed out his chest proudly. "It sure is! And this is one of my favorite sweaters."

Laura laughed as she passed more ham to Ben. "It really is. We keep trying to get him to buy something new . . ."

"But he won't," Ben added. "He's very loyal."

Jeff smiled smugly. "And that's a good thing. And, Dad, I wouldn't talk if I were you. You've been wearing that sweater for—I don't know, how many years?"

Ben smiled proudly. "It was your mom's favorite." He passed the ham to Jeff.

Jeff laughed. "Oh, I know. She's the one that got it for you, along with the rest of the outfit.

Haley covered her mouth to keep from laughing as she looked at Ben's sweater. It basically looked like Santa's suit. It was red with a black belt around the middle and white fur trim, and clearly, it had been well worn and well loved.

"I can go get the hat and beard out if you want," Ben offered.

Jeff waved his hands and laughed. "No, no, this is fine."

Haley looked over at Ian and Susie. So far they were the only ones who had escaped the teasing. They were busy enjoying their meal and laughing at everyone else. They wore sweaters that matched. Susie was wearing a girl moose that had ornaments hanging from its antlers, and Ian was wearing the boy moose, on whose head was a Santa hat, and both sweaters said MERRY MOOSE-MAS!

"So, what's with the moose?" Haley asked them.

Ian rolled his eyes. "She's from Maine," he answered, as if that explained everything.

Susie gave him a look. "So, what would you want us wearing? A sweater with a giant cactus on it because you spend Christmas in Arizona?"

"No," Ian said. "I wouldn't want us wearing sweaters like this at all. We'd be in Arizona wearing bathing suits for Christmas."

Susie looked at Ian like he'd said they should be wearing straitjackets. "And now you can see why we needed to come here." She looked at the rest of the group. "We're going to need a Christmas miracle to figure out a compromise."

"Well, you've come to the right place," Ben said, smiling at them.

"So, who wins the ugly-Christmas-sweater contest?" Madison asked. "I'm voting for Haley's."

"Thanks. I think," Haley said. "I'm voting for Max. I mean, come on. He has Santa cats."

Max barked. He clearly looked excited to be in on the competition.

"Actually, here at the Christmas Camp the whole idea of wearing the sweaters is just to have some fun, be a little silly, and laugh. I think we all did that, don't you?" Ben asked Madison.

Madison smiled. "I know I laughed. A lot."

"Me too," Haley said. "I don't know when I've laughed so hard."

"Then it was a success," Ben said. He looked pleased as he got up and started clearing away the dishes. Jeff joined him.

Haley gave Laura an impressed look. "Wow, you've trained them well."

Laura laughed. "I wish I could take credit, but actually, Ben and Jeff had been clearing the table long before I got here."

"My mom taught us." Jeff smiled, remembering.

"The rule in our house was whoever cooked didn't have to wash. Everyone else cleared and cleaned," Ben added.

"We do that at our house, too," Susie said. "Ian's the far better cook. But that's okay. I'm fine with cleaning up as long as he's cooking me great meals. We make a great team."

Ian kissed her on the cheek. "We sure do, babe. Now we just have to agree on what to make at Christmas."

"Yeah," Susie said. "There is that." She held up her empty wineglass. "More wine, please."

Everyone laughed.

John looked at his two teenagers. "I think we need to start doing this deal of who cooks doesn't clean at our house."

"Uh, Dad, first someone would have to actually cook because takeout doesn't count."

John pretended to look confused. "Wait, what? Why not?"

Madison and Blake both laughed.

"I love takeout," Haley jumped in. "I'm coming to your house."

"You're welcome anytime," John said.

When Ben returned from the kitchen, he stood at the end of the table, rubbing his hands together. It was clear he was up to something. Haley didn't have to wait long to find out what.

"So, now that everyone's done with dinner, are you ready for your next Christmas Camp activity?" he asked.

Haley's smiled faded. She hadn't realized there was another activity after dinner. She was hoping to get some work done before she went to bed, and she was already exhausted. But by the look of excitement in Ben's eyes, it was clear he had more Christmas Camp fun in store for them.

CHAPTER 9

The group had now gathered in the sitting room and was looking at Ben expectantly, waiting to find out what was happening next. He walked over to the fireplace and took down a red velvet stocking with white fur trim.

"In every Christmas Camp, one of our traditions is playing Christmas Camp Charades on the first night," Ben said. "We've found it's a great way for everyone to relax and have some fun and get to know each other better."

Susie jumped up. "I love Christmas charades! I play every year with my family."

Haley looked over at her. "Great, then you're on my team."

Ben looked around the room. "Okay, since we already have some teams forming here, how about we do the girls against the guys?"

Haley looked over at Jeff, who gave her a look that was a challenge. She stood up and walked over to Susie. "I think that's a great idea. Come on, Gail and Madison.

Let's show them some girl power. We're going to crush this."

Ben's eyes widened. "Well, I don't know about anyone *crushing* anything; this is just a friendly little game of charades . . ."

But the look Haley gave Jeff didn't say *friendly,* it said, *You're going down!* She got her team in a huddle and put her arms around them. "Okay, girls, we've got this. Susie, you'll be our coach. What advice do you have?"

Susie looked a little scared by Haley's intensity. "Um, I'd just say, have fun!"

When Gail and Madison nodded their agreement, Haley jumped in. "Have fun and win. We definitely want to win . . ."

Ben laughed at Haley's enthusiasm. "Okay, sounds like the girls are ready to go. So, here's how it's going to work. Inside this stocking are the names of some Christmas songs, and you'll each draw one name and that will be your song for the charades . . ."

"Got it!" Haley said, eager to get going. She was already eyeing the stocking Ben was holding.

"And here's a little twist," Ben added. "Both teams are going to go at the same time and whatever team guesses the correct song first, wins. Any questions?"

"Nope, we're good," Haley said, answering for everyone. She clapped her hands several times. "Let's go. Come on, team!"

Haley's team looked slightly afraid of her.

Ben held the Christmas stocking out to Gail. "Okay, Gail, why don't you draw first?"

Gail put her hand inside the stocking and pulled out a folded piece of green paper. Unfolding it, she read what was written on it. "I got a good one," she said.

"Yes!" Haley high-fived her.

"Okay, just remember, don't show anyone," Ben said. He then continued around the whole group, and everyone drew their song from the stocking.

Haley was the last to pick. When she pulled out the remaining little piece of paper, she read it and laughed.

"Problem?" Jeff asked. He watched her closely.

Haley hid her paper from him. "Nope. I'm good. I'm ready. Let's do this."

Ben smiled back at everyone. "You heard Haley, it's time to start. Son, why don't you go first for the guys, so you can show everyone how it's done. Who wants to go first for the girls?"

Haley jumped up. "I do!"

Everyone laughed when Haley went over to Jeff, and they went toe-to-toe and playfully stared each other down.

"You're sure you want to go first?" Jeff asked. "I thought Susie was the expert here?"

"She is, but we have a strategy," Haley said. "Don't we girls?"

"Uh, sure," Susie answered. But she looked clueless, like she had no idea what Haley was bragging about.

"Okay, then let's do our first round." Ben held out his hand. "Please give me your songs and let me remind you of the rules. This is charades, so there's no talking, but when someone guesses the right word, you can point to your nose, like Santa would, to let them know they guessed it right . . ."

Haley pointed to her nose then pointed to the girls and then kept repeating the motion over and over again.

Jeff laughed. "What are you doing?"

"I'm practicing," Haley said proudly. "Because I know my girls are going to be guessing all the right words. Right, girls?"

"Right!" Madison said, pointing back at Haley.

Everyone laughed.

Haley pumped her fists into the air and bounced around like a boxer in a ring. "Okay, come on. Let's go!"

Jeff looked amused at her showboating.

Ben stood between them and took Haley's hand then Jeff's. "Okay, if everyone's ready?"

"We're ready!" Susie said.

"Then let the Christmas Camp charades begin—right now!" As soon as he let go of their hands, both Haley and Jeff started running around trying to get their team to guess their song.

"Come on, Jeff!" Ian shouted.

"Come on, Haley," Susie fired back.

Haley thrust her hand up to the ceiling and pretended to be singing.

"The Statue of Liberty," Susie guessed.

"'Singing in the Rain,'" Gail jumped in.

Ben laughed. "Remember these are *Christmas* songs."

The guys' side wasn't doing much better. Jeff was motioning like he had a huge stomach and was over at the fireplace, pointing at the chimney.

"A chimney guy? A chimney sweep?" Ian guessed.

Ben laughed. "We're looking for Christmas songs. Keep guessing, teams."

Haley started leaping through the air, flapping her arms. She looked like . . . a crazy person wearing an ugly Christmas sweater.

Jeff, watching her, stopped what he was doing and burst out laughing.

Now Haley had made a circle with the fingers of both hands and held it over her head as she continued to leap across the room.

"It's a bird," Madison said.

"It's a plane," Blake chimed in.

"It's super Haley," John finished.

Everyone laughed.

"Wait, wait! I got it!" Madison jumped up, waving her arms around. "She's an angel!"

Haley victoriously shot both fists into the air then pointed at her nose and then to Madison.

Meanwhile, Jeff grabbed a pillow off the couch and stuffed it into his shirt, giving him a big belly.

"'Baby, It's Cold Outside'?" John guessed.

Jeff shook his head and kept motioning to his belly then threw his head back like he was laughing and mouthed the words "ho, ho, ho . . ."

"Santa Claus!" Ian shouted. "You're Santa Claus?"

"Yes!" Jeff shouted back at him.

Haley threw a pillow at Jeff. "No talking!"

He threw it back at her. "You're talking!"

Ben stepped between them. "Both of you, stop talking. Keep going, teams."

"Okay, okay, you're Santa Claus," Ian said.

Haley started to panic. She jumped in front of the girls to get their attention and then started leaping around the room while Jeff ran over to the fireplace again and kept pointing at it and then back to him.

"Okay, everyone, you're so close. Keep going!" Ben was just as excited as everyone else.

Haley did one more leap and then stopped to hold her hand up to the ceiling and pretend she was singing, like an opera singer. Jeff was back at the fireplace.

Gail and Ian guessed the correct answers at the same time.

"'Hark! The Herald Angels Sing'!"

"'Here Comes Santa Claus'!"

"Yes!" Haley shouted out in victory and then ran over

to give Gail a big hug while Ian and the guys also celebrated. Ben came over, took Haley and Jeff's hands, and held them up in victory.

"We have a tie!" Ben shouted.

"I want a rematch," Jeff demanded in a teasing voice. He smiled when he looked at Haley. "Not bad for a rookie," he told her.

"Oh, I'll take you on any day, Santa." Haley pointed at her nose and then back at Jeff.

As they were laughing Haley realized she couldn't remember when she'd had so much fun, and for the first time she thought maybe Jeff was right. Maybe she could do her research at Christmas Camp for her Tyler Toys pitch and still have a little fun. Still, she knew her number one focus had to be work. She ran over to the fireplace, took down her stocking, and removed the Christmas Camp activities list. After she dug around and found her snowman pencil, she proudly marked Christmas charades off her to-do list. "One more activity completed," she said proudly. "I'm going to get all this stuff done in record time." But when she looked up and saw Jeff watching her, she noticed his smile had faded. She pretended it didn't bother her and turned her attention to her team. "Who's up next?"

"I am!" Susie waved her Christmas song pick in the air.

"Oh, you're going down," Ian said. He joined her in the center of the room. He was bouncing around like a boxer.

Susie rolled her eyes but was laughing.

"Oh, this should be good," Blake said.

"Real good," Madison agreed. "And we're next."

"You're on!" Blake pointed to his nose and back at his sister.

Haley and Jeff flopped down on the couch at the exact same time. They looked at each other and laughed.

"I'm exhausted," Haley said.

"Being an angel isn't easy."

"You can say that again." She laughed. "But it was fun trying."

"Really?" he asked.

"Really," she said, feeling surprised that she actually meant it.

Ben walked over to Susie and Ian, took both of their hands, and raised them in the air. "Okay, everyone, get ready for round two!"

"You got this, Susie!" Haley yelled.

"Come on, Ian!" Jeff countered.

"Ready, set, go!" Ben dropped both their hands and round two started with Ian looking like he was playing a drum.

"'Little Drummer Boy,'" Jeff shouted.

"Yes!" Ian shot his fist into the air.

"Hey, no fair!" Haley turned to Jeff. "You probably already know all the songs we're doing!"

"And you're just figuring that out now?" Jeff asked.

When Haley playfully swatted him with a pillow, Madison, Susie, and Gail joined in and pretty soon he was under a full pillow fight attack. Haley laughed so hard she had to hold her stomach. When she looked over at Ben, he was smiling at her.

"Are you feeling *merry*?" he asked her.

At the same moment when Haley nodded, Jeff hit her over the head with a pillow.

There was more laughter, and when Haley looked at Ben, she really did for the first time in a long time understand the "merry" in Merry Christmas. And then it hit her, an idea for her Tyler Toys campaign. She hurried over to Ben. "This has been so much fun," she started.

Ben didn't miss a beat. "But?"

"But"—Haley fought to find the right words—"I was thinking, hoping, that I could maybe turn in a little early?"

"Of course. I know it's been a long day," Ben said.

Haley smiled her best smile. "And since I'm done for the night, do you think I could get my phone and computer?"

"To help you rest?" Ben asked, looking her in the eye.

Haley squirmed. Clearly, she thought, she wasn't going to be able to fool Ben. Unfortunately for her, he was as smart as he was kind, so she didn't even try to pretend. "I do have some work I need to get done, so I thought it better to start now before I get too tired. The charades gave me an idea . . ." But as Ben continued to look into her eyes, she forgot what she was about to say. It was like he was looking into her soul, and she was afraid of what he might find. So, she looked away first and was surprised when he took her hand and gave it a gentle squeeze.

"I'll go get your things and be right back. I hope you enjoyed your first night at Christmas Camp?"

Haley felt a wave of guilt over Ben's genuine concern and kindness. "I did," she assured him quickly. Even though all she wanted to do was mark everything off the to-do list and get back to Boston as soon as possible, if she was honest with herself, there was something about being at Holly Peak Inn that made her feel things she hadn't felt in a long time. Like what it was like to sit with family around a dinner table and share a meal and joke around and play games. Lately, she'd spent so much time at work and working from home, she'd forgotten how to have the kind of fun that didn't involve making money for her clients.

As Ben disappeared to get her things, Jeff walked up to her and gave her a questioning look. "Is everything okay?"

Haley avoided looking into his eyes. She was already overheating from her bulky sweater and playing charades, and she knew looking at him would only make it worse. "I'm just feeling a little tired, so . . ." As she struggled to find words, she nervously fiddled with one of the Christmas ornaments hanging from her sweater, and accidentally knocked it off. When she and Jeff reached for it at the same time, their fingers touched, and their eyes met. The spark between them was undeniable, and they both looked confused by it and stood up. Jeff had the ornament, so he handed it to her.

"Here you go. I'll see you in the morning." He walked back to join the group before Haley could say anything.

She was relieved when Ben appeared holding her computer and phone.

"Here you go," he said. He handed her everything.

"Thanks, Ben." She saw Gail and the girls watching her. They looked disappointed. She started to feel a little guilty, but she had already turned on her phone and saw she had six missed calls. She'd had her fun, now it was time to pay the piper and get back to work. As she headed up the stairs, she didn't realize Max was following her until she was halfway to her room. When she stopped, he stopped. "What are you doing following me?" she asked.

Max barked, wagging his tail.

Haley stared down at him and shook her head. "Sorry, all I'm doing is work; go back and hang out with everyone else."

Max tilted his head and looked adorable.

Haley looked away, thinking Max was just another distraction she didn't have time for. But a couple seconds later, she realized he was following her again.

"Seriously." Haley looked over her shoulder and rolled her eyes. "Okay, whatever. It's your house." But when she entered her room, she left Max standing outside. "Sorry, time for me to get to work."

Max barked again as Haley shut her door. She stood inside her room and waited about thirty seconds, then slowly opened the door and peeked out. Sure enough, Max was still sitting there. He wagged his tail. His eyes were hopeful.

Haley let out a long sigh. "Fine, you can come in, but only for a few minutes." When Max ran into her room, she would have sworn he was grinning.

CHAPTER 10

As Haley sat on her bed with her computer on her lap, she FaceTimed with Kathy on the phone.

"Finally, you call back," Kathy said. "I've left you like four messages and was starting to wonder if you got abducted by Santa Claus."

"Close, I was playing Christmas charades against a Santa Claus, but that's a whole different story. What's going on?" Haley looked closer at Kathy. "And where are you?"

"I'm at the Christmas party, our company party. Remember?"

Haley fell back onto the bed and looked up at the ceiling. "That was tonight?"

"Yup, do you like my outfit?" Kathy held the phone back so Haley could see that she was wearing a pretty red satin dress.

"Is that new?" Haley asked.

"Yup." Kathy grinned back at her. "I splurged. It's Christmas. I deserve it." She brought the phone closer to her and was now looking at Haley. "But wait, the bigger question is, what are you wearing? Is that . . . no!"

"Oh yeah, it's a Christmas sweater, an ugly one." Haley held her phone back so Kathy could see better.

Kathy started laughing. "That's from the ugly-Christmas-sweater campaign we shot last year."

"Yup, Larry gave it to me before I left because, of course, you can't come to Christmas Camp without an ugly Christmas sweater."

"Of course," Kathy agreed, still laughing.

Max barked. He was sitting on the floor next to Haley's bed, looking up at her.

"What was that?" Kathy asked. "A dog?"

Haley sat back up and held out her phone so Kathy could see Max. "That's Max. The Christmas Camp mascot."

"Oh my God, is he wearing a Christmas sweater, too? And are those . . . cats?!"

"Yup, they're cats. Everyone had to wear a sweater, even poor Max."

"But wait, you don't even like dogs . . ."

"It's not that I don't like them . . . I just don't like hanging around them."

Kathy laughed louder.

"You know what I mean," Haley said. "I'm just not used to them, that's all."

"So why is this one in your room, then?"

"He followed me and wouldn't leave."

Kathy's eyes grew huge, and she covered her mouth with her hand. Clearly, she was laughing again. "Wow, this place is really getting to you. A Christmas sweater, a dog, what next?"

Haley rolled her eyes. "I don't even want to think about it. Update me on what's happening at work."

"Well," Kathy started, but then stopped when someone walked up to her. Haley could see it was Tom. He looked into the phone.

"Hey, Haley, Merry Christmas. We're missing you here at the Christmas party."

"I bet," Haley grumbled.

"What was that?" Tom leaned closer to the phone. "I couldn't hear you."

"I said . . . I bet it's a great party."

Tom nodded. "Oh, it's a great party. I even found some Christmas carolers to perform. Larry loves them."

Haley forced a smile. "Well, don't let me keep you from having fun. Enjoy the party."

"Good night." Tom waved before he took off.

Kathy brought the phone closer to her face and whispered, "Sorry about that, he just walked over, but that's why I've been trying to call you. Tom's going all out with Christmas twenty-four/seven! He volunteered to help with the Christmas party, and I have to say, it really is the best party we've ever had."

"Uh, not helping," Haley said. She gave Kathy an annoyed look.

"Sorry. Okay, I didn't just call because Tom's killing it at this party. I called because he's also killing it with his Tyler Toys pitch."

Haley jumped up and started pacing around her room. "What do you mean? I've only been gone a day, how much could he have done?"

"Well, you know how Tyler Toys wants a traditional campaign but also something unique and special?"

"Yes, I know. Why do you think I'm here at this Christmas Camp, where Christmas tradition was born?"

"Well, Tom got ahold of a bunch of Tyler Toys' old Christmas campaigns over the years, and he's using them to create this whole vintage Christmas theme. It's pretty brilliant, I have to say. It checks off all the boxes. It's nostalgic and heartwarming and honors Tyler Toys' past and—"

"Enough, I get it." All of Haley's confidence and bravado was starting to slip away. Her shoulders drooped, and her head hung low. "This isn't good."

"I know, that's why I wanted to give you a heads-up, but I know you can come up with something even better! You're Haley Hanson; you got this!"

But Haley didn't feel like she had anything. Earlier, downstairs, she'd thought maybe for her Tyler Toys pitch she could do something with Christmas games, like Christmas charades, but now she knew she really needed to up her game if she was going to outdo Tom's vintage theme. When it came to tradition, she thought, how could she beat vintage? Deflated, she sat back down on the bed. "Kathy, I gotta go. Have fun at the party."

Kathy peered into the phone. "You okay? You don't look so great."

Haley didn't feel so great, but she summoned a half-hearted smile. "I'll be fine. I just need to get to work and come up with something better than Tom's genius vintage idea."

"I know you can do it!" Kathy gave her a thumbs-up. "I mean, you're at Christmas Camp. If you can't find some Christmas inspiration there, you can't find it anywhere, right?"

Haley nodded. "Sure, if only it were that easy. Go have fun. Keep an eye on Tom for me, and I'll check in tomorrow." She watched as someone came up and wrapped a sparkling silver garland around Kathy's neck.

Kathy laughed. "Okay! Will do! Have fun at Christmas Camp!"

When Haley hung up, having fun was the furthest thing from her mind. What she felt was scared as she worried about losing the Tyler Toys pitch and her promotion. When Max came over, put his head on her lap, and looked up at her with his big brown eyes, she would have sworn he looked sympathetic. It made her feel better, less alone, and as she stared off into space, lost in thought, she didn't even realize she had started petting him.

A few minutes later Max ran over to her door and barked.

Haley sighed. "So now you want to go, Max? You really should make up your mind." When she got up and opened the door, he ran out. As soon as she closed the door she yanked off her crazy Christmas sweater, went to the closet, and grabbed her favorite baby-blue cashmere hoodie. She snuggled up inside it and immediately felt better. Some people had comfort food, she had comfort clothes. She went back over to her bed, sat down with her computer, and brought up a file titled *Tyler Toys Campaign Ideas*. The page was blank. She stared at the screen for several seconds. She had nothing. Feeling a crushing sense of defeat, she dropped her head into her hands. "What am I going to do?"

Max answered her. He barked twice outside her door.

"Are you kidding me? That's it. I'm telling Ben to come and get you. Enough is enough." Haley marched over to her door, yanked it open, and found Max sitting there holding his leash in his mouth. It was a red leash with green fringe—Christmas themed, of course.

Max dropped the leash at her feet.

As much as she wanted to be angry, it was pretty hard when she looked at Max and saw him wagging his tail. She looked over at her laptop on the bed and thought maybe some fresh air would help clear her mind. At this point, it certainly couldn't hurt, and she was willing to try anything. "Okay, a short walk, but that's it. I have to get back to work." When Max barked his approval, Haley grabbed her coat.

IT WAS ONE of those cold and clear winter nights when the sky was filled with more stars than you could ever count. But Haley had her eyes focused on the ground not the sky. She was watching where she was walking in her high-heeled boots, trying to make sure she didn't fall as she carefully followed Max around to the back of the inn.

"It's a beautiful night, isn't it?"

Haley's eyes shot up as she rounded a corner and saw Jeff. She shivered, but not just from the cold. It was seeing Jeff that was messing with her senses again. She was almost annoyed as she watched him walk toward her, because somehow he managed to look handsome even all bundled up in his winter coat, hat, and scarf.

"Is it?" Haley laughed a little as she ran her hand back and forth along the sleeve of her lightweight leather coat trying to warm up. "All I noticed was the cold."

Jeff gave Max a surprised look. "I didn't think you were a dog person."

"I'm not," Haley said, also looking down at Max. "I'm not really sure how this happened. He just showed up at my door with his leash . . ."

"That's his favorite trick." Jeff laughed.

"Oh, really?" When Haley gave Max an accusing look, he just wagged his tail.

"You might not like dogs, but old Max here seems to like you," Jeff said.

Haley looked from Max to Jeff. "It's not that I don't like them. I've just never really been around them. I always wondered what it would be like to have a dog, but I travel too much. It wouldn't be fair to them. I don't even have any plants, unless you count a cactus. I haven't watered it for a year, but I think it's still alive." When Max tugged on his leash, Haley continued walking, and Jeff joined her.

"So, no pets, or plants, or anything else?" Jeff asked.

She shook her head. "Nope, it's just me. There's no husband or kids . . . much to my parents' distress. They want grandchildren."

"And you want?" Jeff asked.

When Haley answered quickly, there was no doubt in her voice. "A career I can count on, so I can have a safe and solid future."

"Can you ever really guarantee that you're safe? I mean, things happen, life changes . . ."

"And that's why it's so important to have a plan and make the right choices to protect yourself as much as possible."

They walked a few more steps in silence.

"What about you?" Haley asked, looking up at him. "Wife, kids, dog, picket fence, the whole nine?"

He smiled back at her. "My dad would love that . . ."

"But?"

"But, unfortunately, no to all of the above. I guess in a way I'm like you. My job keeps me busy, and any spare time I have I spend with my dad. He asks me every week if I've met anyone special. He's a hopeless romantic. But right now he's my number one priority, making sure he's okay."

Haley looked up at him, seeing the pain in his eyes. "I'm really sorry about your mom."

"Thank you." Jeff took a deep breath. "I know my dad misses her so much. He tries to act strong for me, but I know."

"And I'm sure he knows how much you miss her, too."

When Jeff looked up to the sky, she could see his sadness. It made her heart hurt for him.

She wished she could say something helpful, but she'd never experienced that kind of loss and couldn't even imagine that kind of pain. When she shivered again, Jeff wrapped his scarf around her neck. "Here, we can't have you freezing on your very first night."

Surprised and touched, Haley looked into his eyes. She was so close to him she could feel his breath on her cheek. She touched his hand as he finished adjusting the scarf. "Thank you."

He smiled back at her. "You're welcome."

When Max barked up at them, they both quickly looked away.

"It looks like someone is impatient for his walk," Jeff said. He smiled down at Max.

Haley handed Jeff Max's leash. "Do you mind taking him? I'm afraid these boots aren't going to take me very far, and I should really head in and get some work done."

"No problem."

Haley gave him a grateful look. "Thank you. Good night."

Max barked as she walked away.

She laughed and looked over her shoulder. "Good night, Max."

CHAPTER 11

When Jeff walked into the library, he was still trying to thaw out from his walk with Max. The temperature had dropped below ten degrees, and the wind had picked up, making it feel even colder. When he saw his dad in the corner moving around some big boxes that were marked as Christmas decorations, he hurried over to help.

"Here, Dad, I got it." Jeff took a box from Ben, accidentally brushing his hand.

"Your hands are freezing," Ben said.

Jeff put the box down and began rubbing his hands together. "I know. I went outside for a minute but then ran into Haley. She was walking Max."

Ben chuckled. "So, Max is up to his old tricks?"

"Apparently."

"He always knows how to pick a softie."

Jeff laughed. "I'm not so sure I'd call Haley a softie."

"Really. Why not?"

Jeff shrugged. "I don't know. She doesn't strike me as someone who can be easily persuaded to do something she doesn't want to do. You know she's only here because her boss made her come."

Ben nodded. "I know."

Jeff looked surprised. "You do?"

"Yes. Larry, Haley's boss, talked to me about it. He's a good man. He's been up before with his family. He sent Haley here to try to help her—"

"Yeah, to win some big toy account. Trust me, she takes the term 'workaholic' to a whole new level. Work is all she cares about."

"Sounds like you're making a pretty big assumption about someone you hardly know," Ben said as he picked up another box of decorations.

"No, she told me herself. I'm not assuming anything," Jeff said. "She said she was married to her job and seemed pretty happy about it."

"Well, you're working all the time, too," Ben said. "You're always telling me you're not dating because you don't have any time. Does that mean you only care about work?"

Jeff gave his dad a look. "No, of course not. You know I care about you. I care about a lot of things."

"Well, there you go. I'm sure Haley cares about a lot of other things, too. You shouldn't be so quick to judge." Ben walked over to the window and looked out. "The wind is really picking up. I'm going to go outside and check on the decorations and make sure they don't blow over."

Jeff stopped his dad as he was heading toward the door. "Dad, I'll go. Trust me. It's brutal out there, and I already have my stuff out."

"Well, you need some better gloves."

"I'll go grab some." Jeff watched as his dad went back

to the window. "Don't worry. I'll make sure everything's fine."

"Hey, come look." Ben waved Jeff over. "It's snowing. There's nothing better than having one of our Christmas Camps when it's snowing."

Jeff joined his dad at the window. Ben smiled at him. "I love the snow."

"I know you do."

"Your mom used to always say that each snowflake was—"

"A Christmas kiss," Jeff finished for him. He smiled, remembering. "So, she always said that the more snow we had . . ."

"The more love we had." Ben put his arm around Jeff. "So, bring on the snow."

Jeff affectionately put his arm around his dad. "Bring on the snow."

As they stood side by side, father and son, watching the snow fall, the scene outside was magical. Delicate snowflakes danced in the wind, swirling around tree branches that were sparkling with snow, swaying back and forth like a winter wonderland orchestra being conducted by a maestro.

"I miss her," Ben said softly. He was still watching the snow.

"I do, too," Jeff said. When he watched his dad, he didn't know what was harder: missing his mom or watching his dad miss his mom. It just all hurt. A lot. He turned away from the window, needing to think about something else, anything else. So, when he saw a pile of boxes in the corner, he walked over to get a closer look.

"What are all these boxes for?" he asked.

Ben turned around. "They're all the decorations for

the Christmas trees. I'm getting them ready for tomorrow. I know there are more, I just can't remember where we put them. I thought they were in the attic, but I can't find them." He shook his head. "I don't know what's wrong with my memory these days . . ."

"It's probably because you're exhausted from doing so much," Jeff said. He looked worried. "After I check on the reindeer outside, I'll go look for the other boxes. You just need to take a break. You've been going nonstop."

Ben was already walking toward the door. "Son, I'm fine. I'm going to look again right after I check in on Ian and Susie. One of the snowman lights in their room isn't working."

Jeff met Ben at the door. "But I can do that, too, Dad. Really, please, let me help. That's why I'm here."

Ben gave Jeff an affectionate pat on the back. "You're here so we can spend time together. I have everything under control. Don't you worry about a thing."

"But I do worry," Jeff said. "You used to have Mom help you and now you're trying to do everything alone. It's too much. This is why you really need to move to Boston . . ."

Ben's smiled faded a little. "We agreed not to talk about that right now."

"But, Dad . . ."

Ben held up his hand to stop him, frustrating Jeff.

"We have to talk about this sometime," Jeff said. "You can't avoid it forever."

"I didn't say forever. I just said not right now."

Before Jeff could say anything more, Ben left the room.

Discouraged, Jeff walked back over to the window and looked at the snow, missing his mom more than ever. After he walked back to the boxes of Christmas decorations, he opened one up and pulled out a beautiful string of silver stars. For a moment he shut his eyes, and he could see his mom and dad working together hanging the stars on their Christmas tree. He didn't want to open his eyes. He wanted to keep living in that memory forever. If it hadn't been for a gust of snow blowing up against the windowpane, he wasn't sure how long he would have stood there remembering, but instead he headed out to do what he'd promised his dad. He needed to go check on the reindeer.

Twenty minutes later, he carried one of the reindeer into the kitchen. "Don't worry. I'll fix you up in no time," he said to the reindeer, who had a crooked leg. "The wind really did a number on you, but it's nothing I can't fix."

He disappeared, and when he returned a few minutes later, he had his toolbox with him. It took him only a few seconds to straighten out the reindeer's leg. Standing the reindeer up on the counter, he made one more adjustment and stood back to admire his work. "Perfect."

Then he grabbed a screwdriver out of his toolbox and started going around checking cupboard doors until he found one that was a little loose. He went to work fixing it and was just putting the screwdriver back and reaching for the drill when Laura walked in.

Her eyes grew wide when she saw him with the drill. "Do we have a problem here?"

Jeff smiled back at her. "I just found some loose cupboard doors that needed tightening." Before he could attack the door with the drill, Laura touched his arm gently.

"What's wrong?" she asked.

"Just fixing the door," Jeff said as he powered up the drill again.

Laura gave him a look. "The door is fine. You're not. What is it? What's wrong?"

"I'm fine," Jeff said. He tried to laugh off Laura's concern, but she wasn't buying it. Looking him in the eye, she held out her hand for the drill. He hesitated a moment, then sighed, and reluctantly gave it to her. He never could fool her. Not when he was a kid and not now.

"So, what's really going on?" she asked, setting the drill down on the counter. "I've known you since you were a kid, and whenever something was wrong, you'd always try to fix something. So, what is it this time?"

Jeff ran his fingers through his hair and took a deep breath. "My dad. I'm worried about him."

"How so?"

"This inn, the Christmas Camp, he can't keep doing it all alone, and he's losing money . . ."

"Have you talked to him about it?" Laura asked.

Jeff dragged his fingers through his hair. "I've tried. I just tried again a few minutes ago, but he never wants to talk about it." He looked around the kitchen at the aging refrigerator and stove. "This place is getting older and so is he. He's using his savings to keep this place going, and at his age, he should be putting money away for retirement. I found him a great condo in the city, in my neighborhood, so we could be closer, and I could spend more time with him, but he won't even talk to me about moving."

"Because he loves it here," Laura said.

"I know," Jeff said. "But he could love it in Boston, too, if he'd just give it a chance. Everything changed when my mom died, but he's still trying to live their dream. He won't accept reality. We have to sell this place . . ." He stopped talking when he saw how sad Laura looked. He realized selling the place didn't just impact his family; it would impact her family as well. She'd worked at the inn for as long as he could remember. He reached out and took her hand.

"Laura, I'm sorry. Here I am talking about selling the place, and I know this is your home, too."

"It's okay, don't worry about me. I'll be fine. The truth is, my husband has been wanting me to retire for the last five years. He wants to move somewhere warm like Florida or Arizona. He's tired of our cold, snowy winters. I haven't wanted to go because I didn't want to leave your mom and dad. You are all like family to me . . ."

"And you know, we've always felt the same way about you," Jeff said. "And I'm so grateful you stayed on after my mom passed away. My dad couldn't have kept this place running without you."

"I wanted to help in any way I could. Your mom was like my sister. I miss her every day, but especially at this time of year." Laura touched her heart. "This time of year I feel even closer to her. I'm sure your dad would have a hard time leaving. All his memories are here. I'm sure what you've found for him in Boston is very nice, but . . ."

"But?" Jeff asked.

"I just can't imagine him anywhere but here. I'm sorry, that's probably not what you want to hear . . ."

Jeff put his arm around her. "I always appreciate your honesty. You know I'd hate giving this place up, too, but I have to look after my dad's future and make sure he's going to be okay, and I can do that better if he's in Boston. I've already found a buyer for the inn, and it's a good offer, but he needs to make a decision before the end of the year."

Laura shook her head. "You don't have a lot of time."

"I know." Jeff picked up the drill again. "That's the problem."

Laura looked at the drill. The worry was back in her eyes.

"Don't worry." Jeff laughed. "I'm putting it away. Your kitchen is safe."

"For now." Laura looked relieved. She gave him an affectionate pat on the back. "You're a good son. Your dad loves you very much, and I know he's so glad you're here."

Jeff smiled at her. "I'm glad I'm here, too. There's a lot of activities coming up this next week, and I'm going to make sure everything goes as planned. Dad always works so hard on putting these Christmas Camps together, and if I can convince him to move to Boston, this will be the last one, so I want it to be really special for him. Nothing can go wrong."

"What could go wrong?" Laura asked, surprised. "I think your dad has everything under control."

"But he can't control the guests and what they do," Jeff answered. He looked worried.

"Ah, don't you mean one guest in particular?" Laura gave him a knowing smile. "I saw you outside walking with Haley and Max. Is there a problem?"

Jeff opened a drawer and shut it again, making sure it was working smoothly. Laura put her hand over his. "Jeff?"

Jeff shut the drawer. "I don't know. I just know she's not here for the right reasons, and I don't want her attitude to impact the other guests or upset my dad. Does that make sense?"

Laura nodded. "You're trying to protect your dad, like you always do, but are you sure you need to in this case? Haley doesn't seem like the kind of person who would ruin Christmas Camp."

"She might not mean to," Jeff said. "But I don't know. I just don't know." He sounded stressed.

Laura went over and picked up a plate of the special

Christmas Camp cookies and held it out to Jeff. He took a cookie and gave her a grateful look.

"Do you know what I think?" Laura asked. "I think everyone's here for their own reasons. It doesn't really matter why Haley's here. It's Christmas and Christmas Camp is for anyone and everyone. Maybe she needs to be here more than anyone else, and it's our job to help make sure the time she does spend here is special. So, I'd say if you really want to help your dad, then you'll help Haley in any way you can, just like you'd help the other guests. You know he gets his happiness from seeing his guests happy."

Jeff nodded. Laura was the voice of reason. Maybe he had been too quick to judge. There was just something about Haley that made him uncomfortable. He was usually really good at reading people, but he couldn't figure her out and that made him nervous.

"You're right," he told Laura. "I'll keep an eye on her."

Laura gave him a sharp look.

"I mean I'll keep an eye on her to see if I can help her in any way. She said she needs to learn about Christmas traditions for this project she's working on, and we certainly have a lot of Christmas traditions around here."

"We certainly do."

"So I'll see what I can do for Haley and the other guests. I just want to help my dad over this next week in any way I can."

"You just being here is a blessing and that's helped already," Laura said. "He's been so excited about spending time with you and doing this Christmas Camp together. It's going to be a good week. I just know it. Try to relax and enjoy this time with your dad. I know that's what he wants more than anything. And if you ever need to talk to anyone, you know I'm always here for you."

"Thank you. That means more than you know."

Laura gave his hand a little squeeze. "And be nice to my kitchen. I don't want to come back here and find the refrigerator torn apart."

Jeff laughed. "Oh, come on now, that was one time a long time ago. You're never going to let me live that one down, are you?"

"Not a chance." Laura was still smiling as she left the kitchen. "And don't eat all the cookies," she called over her shoulder.

It was too late. Jeff already had a second cookie in his mouth.

CHAPTER 12

As the sun rose over the spectacular snow-covered mountain ridge, it cast a golden glow on the Holly Peak Inn. Some of that sunlight was streaming through the blinds of Haley's bedroom window, but she didn't see it. She was snuggled deep beneath her covers, sleeping soundly until she was jarred awake by Max's bark. She quickly shut her eyes and dove back down under her duvet only to be interrupted again by another bark. "Please make him go away, please make him go away . . ." she whispered.

But Max barked again.

Haley groaned and with her eyes still shut reached around until she found her phone on the nightstand and brought it with her underneath the covers. She opened one eye and saw it was only six thirty.

Max barked twice.

"Seriously?" Frustrated, she threw off her covers, jumped out of bed, and yanked her door open to find Max staring up at her with loving eyes. In his mouth was his leash. He dropped it at her feet.

"Come on! It's six thirty in the morning!"

Max barked again.

"Shhh! You're going to wake everyone up!"

When Max looked like he was about to bark again, she stopped him by opening the door even further. "Okay, come in, but just stop barking . . ."

Max grabbed his leash and happily trotted in.

Haley was not so happy. She grabbed her bathrobe and put it on. "What am I going to do with you?" She stared down at Max.

For an answer, he dropped his leash at her feet again.

Haley sighed and headed for the closet, where she quickly threw on some black pants and a pretty pink silk blouse, not even bothering to button it all the way. She put on her boots and grabbed her coat. When she caught her reflection in the mirror, she cringed. Her hair was sticking up all over the place. She ran a quick comb through it, but it didn't do much good. As she headed for the door, she grabbed the scarf Jeff had loaned her and wrapped it around her head and neck.

As she headed down the hallway Haley didn't hear anyone else up yet. "Of course they're not up," she whispered to Max. "Everyone else is sleeping, like I should be."

Max wagged his tail.

When they got to the front door, Haley attached Max's leash to his collar. "Okay, we're going to make this fast," she told him. But when she opened the front door, she took a quick step back. "Whoa! Where did all this snow come from?"

The front walkway, which was usually clear, was covered in almost three inches of snow. In fact, there was snow everywhere. Haley looked down at her boots. They were stylish black leather riding boots, but there was no way they could handle all this snow. She gave Max an apologetic look. "Sorry. I'd never make it out there in these."

But Max wasn't giving up. He ran over to a pair of winter snow boots that were lined up by the door, grabbed one, and dragged it over to Haley.

"Hey, what are you doing?! You can't just steal those." Max barked.

"Shhh! Okay, fine. I guess I can borrow them for a second."

Max spun around in circles, wagging his tail.

Haley quickly slipped off her boots and put on the snow boot Max had brought her. It was several sizes too big. She gave Max a look. "Hey, pal, if you're going to steal boots for me, next time find some my size?" She put on the other boot and felt like she was walking in snow-shoes. They were huge and awkward, but she figured they would at least keep her feet dry. This time when she opened the door, she was ready for the snow but was completely caught off guard by an icy gust of wind that almost took her breath away.

"Max, you so owe me for this. Let's make it quick." Shutting the door behind her, Haley saw the life-size elf figurine grinning back at her. "I don't know what you're grinning about because it's freezing out here." She barely had time to zip her coat all the way up before Max took off in a run, plowing through the snow, pulling the unsuspecting Haley along with him.

"Whoa. Wait. Hold on!" she yelled after him, but Max was running full speed now. He was clearly excited to be playing in the fresh snow. "Max, wait!" Haley couldn't believe it when he actually listened to her and stopped. She finally caught her breath, but only for a second before she saw that Max was running back toward her. Her eyes grew huge. "Oh no! No, no, no, no, no . . ." She frantically tried to back away but stumbled over her too-big boots and fell backward into the snow, landing on her butt just as Max ran up and started licking her face. "Eww! Stop that." She tried to cover her face but ended up falling flat on her back. Max looked like he was loving all of this. He was standing over her, panting and wagging his tail.

"Everything okay down there?"

Haley looked up, but Jeff blocked her view of the sky. He was laughing. Embarrassed, she struggled to get up but began to slip again until he grabbed her around the waist. They were so close you could see the cold vapor of their breath mingle. When Haley realized she had grabbed Jeff's arms to steady herself, she quickly let go.

"Sorry, thanks for . . ."

"Saving you?" Jeff laughed.

"Yeah." She held up one foot. "I blame it on the boots. I'm not usually so klutzy."

"You did grow up in Boston, right? Aren't you used to the snow?"

Haley laughed. "You'd think I would be, but I've lived in the city for the last ten years. I pretty much just go from my apartment to work and don't have to deal with all this . . ."

"Snow?"

"Exactly. I should have packed a little better. I didn't have a lot of time. I guess I wasn't thinking. I just threw in a pair of jeans, a couple of shirts and sweaters, but nothing that could really handle this kind of cold or being outside for very long. I should have brought a hat, gloves, and obviously some better boots."

"Well, at least you have a scarf." Jeff smiled at her.

Haley touched the scarf and laughed. "You mean your scarf." She quickly started taking it off. "Here, let me give it back to you."

Jeff reached out and put his hand over hers. "No, keep it. You need it more than I do."

The touch of Jeff's hand sent a warm jolt through her. Their eyes locked. They both looked a little confused. When he took his hand away, Haley fumbled with his scarf. "Are you sure? I don't want to steal your scarf."

"Well, you've already stolen my boots, so why not?" Jeff teased.

Haley's eyes flew to her boots. "These are yours?! I'm sorry. It's Max's fault . . ."

Jeff's eyebrows rose. "Really?"

Haley nodded, totally serious. "He saw them and brought them over to me, because I wasn't going to take him out in my boots."

"So, you're blaming Max?"

Haley's chin shot up. "Trust me, he's not as innocent as he looks."

Jeff laughed. "Oh, I know. He can be quite clever."

"Exactly!"

When they both looked at Max, he innocently wagged his tail.

"So, I'm guessing it's also his fault that you're out here so early?" Jeff asked.

"It is!" Haley's eyes narrowed as she looked at Max. "He wouldn't stop barking, and I didn't want him to wake everyone up. I figured he had to go out, if you know what I mean, and when you gotta go, you gotta go."

Jeff laughed. "I actually took him out a half hour ago."

Haley stared down at Max. "Really?"

"Getting people to take him for walks is his favorite trick."

"And apparently, I've been tricked twice now." She handed Jeff Max's leash. "Well, here you go. You can have him. I'm gonna head back in and get warmed up."

"Good idea, because we're leaving at nine sharp for our next activity. We're all meeting out front."

"Got it," Haley said as she walked away. But unfortunately, she didn't get very far before she realized that walking anywhere in Jeff's boots was going to be challenging.

"Watch your step, the snow's pretty slick," he warned.

Too late. Haley had already slipped again and had just barely caught herself before going down. "I'm good. I got it," she yelled back over her shoulder, trying to hide her embarrassment.

When she finally made it to the front door, she looked at the grinning life-size elf again. "Just be thankful you're up here and not out there in the snow," she said as she opened the door and hurried inside. She slipped off Jeff's boots but found the melted snow from them was already causing a puddle on the floor. "Oh no, what a mess." She took off for the kitchen.

As she hurried into the kitchen, she found Ben at the chalkboard changing the Christmas countdown to thirteen days to Christmas. He looked surprised to see her. "You're up early." Then he noticed she was only wearing thin nylon socks. "You know we have slippers for you in the room."

"Oh, I know. Thank you. I was just outside, and I borrowed Jeff's boots. I just came in bringing a bunch of snow. It's all melting. I'm looking for something to clean it up. Do you have any paper towels or a rag? Oh, and this whole thing is Max's fault." Haley was talking a mile a minute.

Ben tried to hide a smile. "Max's fault?"

"Oh yeah, it's all on him."

Ben nodded. "Okay, I'll take your word for it, but don't worry. I'll take care of everything. It'll only take a second to clean up. We actually have some towels in the front closet by the door. But what were you doing wearing Jeff's boots? They have to be way too big for you."

"Oh, they are. That's why I'm covered in snow." When Haley held out her arms, more snow fell from her coat. She was literally dripping, and another puddle formed on the floor. "But really, I can clean up my own mess . . ."

Ben was already grabbing some paper towels. "No, what you need to do is go upstairs, take a warm bath or a shower, get warmed up, and come down here and have breakfast. You have a big day ahead of you."

Haley looked confused. "I thought we were decorating a tree today."

"You are."

"Oh, good. For a minute there, I thought we were doing something hard."

Ben chuckled. "Go on up. I'll take care of everything else."

Haley gave him a grateful smile. "Thank you! A shower actually sounds great." As she headed out of the kitchen, she noticed the word for the day on the chalkboard was "joy," and couldn't help thinking about how joyful it would be to be sitting on a nice warm sunny beach in the Caribbean, wiggling her toes in the sand instead of in her soggy socks.

A HALF HOUR LATER, after a long hot shower, Haley felt like a new person. While she was blow-drying her hair, she heard a knock on her bedroom door.

"Max, if that's you, I'm not falling for any more of your tricks!" she shouted at the door.

"Haley, it's me, Laura."

Haley hurried over and opened the door. "Sorry about that. Hi, come in . . ."

Laura held up a neat pile of clothes. "I brought you a little something Jeff thought you might need. Some winter clothes." She held up a pair of boots. "And some snow boots." She handed the pile to Haley. "He said you didn't have a lot of winter gear with you and that this might help."

Haley looked surprised and touched. She held up a cute red hat and gloves. There was definitely a red theme going on. "Where did you get all this?"

Laura gave her a gentle smile. "They were his mom's . . ."

Haley's eyes flew to Laura. She tried to hand everything back. "I couldn't . . ."

"Please, he wants you to have them. So does Ben. You can borrow them while you're here."

"But it doesn't feel right wearing her things . . ."

Laura smiled. "Grace would have loved it. She was one of the most generous people I've ever known. We also have a coat downstairs for you. I put it in the closet. It's the red one."

"Red again." Haley laughed a little.

"It was Grace's favorite color."

"For Christmas?" Haley asked.

"Exactly." Laura smiled.

Haley held up the boots. "This is all because I borrowed Jeff's boots this morning to take Max for a walk."

"Ah, you're the one Max conned into another walk, huh? I heard him barking this morning."

"Yeah, he got me. But he's not going to fool me again. I'm onto him now."

Laura laughed. "Well, with all this, you should be set for the rest of the week. The boots are a size eight. Will that work? I think Grace also had some nines . . ."

"I'm actually an eight, so these should be perfect. Thank you again."

"You can thank Jeff. It was his idea. I'll see you downstairs for breakfast."

After Laura disappeared down the hall, Haley looked at all the clothes. She was touched by Jeff's thoughtfulness, and grateful, because she really had come unprepared.

When her phone rang, she ran over to where it was lying on her bed and saw it was her mom calling on Face-Time. Her mom rarely called this early in the morning, so she answered quickly. "Mom, is everything okay?"

Haley's mom didn't look like things were okay at all. "Not exactly," she said. "Honey, we need your help."

CHAPTER 13

Haley sat down on her bed. "Mom, what is it? Is it Dad? Are you okay?"

Haley's mom looked guilty. "Honey, I'm sorry. I didn't mean to scare you. Your dad and I . . . we're fine. It's the house . . ."

Haley groaned. "The Money Pit?"

"The Victorian," her mother corrected her. "We had some pipes freeze and burst and now we're trying to find a plumber because we already have some flooding that's freezing. We need to get someone out here right away, and our usual guy is out of town and so is our backup guy. Then your dad remembered that friend of yours, that helped us last summer . . ."

"Michael?"

"Yes! Michael, that was his name. Do you think you could call him and see if he's available to help us. We need to get someone out here right away. It's supposed to get even colder tonight, and we don't want any more pipes to burst."

Haley started pacing around her room, "Michael's in

Florida right now, but I'll see if he can recommend someone else."

Haley's mom looked relieved. "Honey, that would be wonderful. I hate to bother you when I know how busy you are with work. We just didn't know what else to do . . ."

"It's okay, Mom. I'll get on it right now, and I'll call you back as soon as I find someone. You have the keys to my place, right? You can just stay there if you need to."

"We have them. Thank you. So, maybe we'll see you tonight . . ."

"I'm actually not there right now. I'm up in the mountains . . ."

"With a client?"

Haley looked at the angel picture hanging over her dresser. "Not exactly, but I'm here hoping to land a new client. I'll tell you all about it when I get back. I gotta go make some calls for you. I'll call you back as soon as I can."

"Thank you, honey. I love you."

"I love you, too, Mom."

As soon as Haley hung up, she called her friend Michael, praying he could help.

AN HOUR LATER, when Haley walked into the kitchen, the only thing she was wearing that was her own was her designer jeans. Everything else, all of it red, was what Jeff had loaned her.

When Laura saw her, she nodded her approval. "It looks like everything fits."

Haley quickly modeled her outfit. "It does. Thank you again. This is great. So much better than what I brought." She looked around. "Where is everyone?"

Laura pointed at a Santa clock on the wall. It said it was twenty minutes after nine.

"Oh no! I forgot! We were all supposed to meet at nine out front. Did I miss everyone?"

"Not everyone," Laura said. "The rest of the group went ahead to stay on schedule, but Jeff waited for you."

Haley's smile faded. "Oh boy. I'm in trouble, aren't I?"

Laura gave her a look that said she kind of was. "He doesn't really like it when people are late."

Haley took a deep, calming breath. "Okay, wish me luck."

"Good luck," Laura called after her.

Flying out the front door, Haley immediately found Jeff leaning against his truck, looking impatient. Seeing her, he checked his watch.

"I know, I'm late. I'm sorry . . ." She rushed up to him. But instead of responding, he just walked to the passenger side of his truck and opened the door. He wasn't smiling.

Haley hopped in. "I can explain, and thank you for all the clothes." She pulled her borrowed coat's collar closer around her neck. "These are really great."

As Jeff got into the truck, she continued.

"I'm late because my parents called with an emergency."

Jeff's expression instantly switched from annoyed to concerned. "Are they okay?"

"Thankfully, they're fine, but the Money Pit isn't—"

"The Victorian?"

"Right. Apparently, a bunch of pipes burst, and they couldn't find a plumber. I had a friend they were hoping could help, but I couldn't get ahold of him, and I've been frantically calling around, trying to find someone who can get out there today."

"Don't they have a general contractor who can find someone for them?"

"No, that's the problem. They're doing a lot of the restoration themselves to keep costs down, and every time we've tried to find a contractor, it's been a nightmare. They've either quit halfway through a job or just don't show up at all. Right now we're on our own. So when something like this happens, it's all hands on deck. I finally found someone but had totally forgotten about the time. I really am sorry."

"Of course. I understand. Family first."

Haley gave him a grateful smile.

"Where do your parents live?"

"About an hour outside of Boston."

"I could give you the names of some good contractors I've worked with if that would help?"

Haley gave him a grateful look. "That would be amazing. Thank you. I would feel so much better if they had someone they could trust, and once I get this new promotion, I'll be able to afford to hire someone to work with them." She stopped talking. She looked a little embarrassed. "I'm sorry. I don't know why I'm telling you all this . . ."

"Maybe because you know I can help. All this is in my wheelhouse."

Haley nodded. "That must be it."

"So, you're good to go now?"

Haley put on her seat belt. "Yes, I'm good to go. We're heading to town to get a Christmas tree, right?"

Jeff started the truck and gave her a smile. "The Christmas tree part is right."

As JEFF'S TRUCK followed a pretty, winding mountain road Haley looked around, confused.

"I thought we were going to get a tree?"

"We are," Jeff said, keeping his eyes on the road.

"But isn't town the other way?"

"It is." He slowed down and turned off onto a one-lane dirt road that was now covered with snow.

"So, then what are we doing? I didn't see four-wheeling on our activities list."

"You'll see." Jeff turned up the radio. It was playing the Christmas song "Hark! The Herald Angels Sing." He smiled at her. "Hey, listen, they're playing your song."

Haley gave him a look. "Very funny." But then it did get funny when he started to sing, or at least try to.

"'Hark! The Herald Angels Sing. Glory to the new-born King!'"

Haley laughed and cringed a little.

"What?" he asked with mock surprise. "You don't like my singing?"

"Um, let's just say, don't quit your day job."

"Okay, let's hear you do better." The look he gave her was a challenge.

Usually Haley was up for any challenge, but not one that involved singing. She knew she could never win a singing competition unless it was for the worst voice. So she shook her head. "Trust me. No one wants to hear me sing."

Jeff grinned. "Oh, come on, you can't be that bad."

"Oh yes, I can!"

"Who cares how you sound. It's Christmas. Everyone sings at Christmas."

"Clearly not everyone . . ."

Jeff laughed. "Okay, but you're missing out." He continued to sing along. "'Joyful, all ye nations rise. Join the triumph of the skies . . .'"

As he continued singing, Haley looked out her window and tried not to laugh. But when she glanced around and all she saw were huge fir trees, she was confused.

"Where are we?" she asked.

"We're almost there," Jeff said. Then he started singing again.

A few seconds later they'd come to the end of the road; several other cars were parked, but there were no people in sight. That's when she spotted a sign that said FIR FOREST TRAILHEAD.

Haley's eyes grew huge. "We're not going . . ."

"Are you ready for some hiking?"

"Hiking . . ."

They both said "hiking" at the same time, but while Jeff was smiling, Haley was not.

CHAPTER 14

Haley watched Jeff jump out of the truck, but was in no hurry to follow him. Even after he came around and opened her door, she just sat there staring at him.

"Is this really where we're getting a Christmas tree?" she asked, looking around, noticing they were in the middle of nowhere.

"It is! Come on, let's go. We're already running late." He waited as Haley got out, then closed the door and happily grabbed a saw out of the back of the pickup.

Haley's jaw dropped. "We're seriously cutting down our own tree?"

"Is there any other way?"

"Uh, yeah, how about buying one that's already been cut down. That's what most people do," Haley answered.

"Where's the fun in that?" When Jeff started walking toward the trailhead, she rushed to catch up to him.

"Let me guess, this is one of your Christmas traditions?"

"Yup, every year we cut down our own tree. This was one of my favorite parts of Christmas when I was little."

"And now?"

He grinned back at her with childlike enthusiasm. "Still a favorite part. You'll see. Everyone at Christmas Camp loves it."

"So, everyone else is meeting us here?"

"No, they're actually about twenty miles farther up the road, but since we're running behind, this spot will have to do."

"So, wait, they're getting another tree? Why do we need two?"

Jeff laughed. "Two? You're all getting your own tree."

"What? That's crazy," Haley said. "Why does everyone need their own tree?"

"For our next activity: decorating."

"We couldn't all just share one tree?"

Jeff shook his head. "This way everyone can decorate their trees the way they want and have them in their room. Then, when you leave at the end of the week, my dad always donates the trees to our local community center for people who need a little extra help and can't afford to buy their own."

Haley looked surprised and impressed. "That's really nice. I'm sure the families really appreciate that."

"They do, and they look forward to getting our trees, so let's go find you a good one!" As he started down the trail, he slipped a little and instantly checked behind him to make sure Haley was okay. "Watch it right here. It's a little slippery."

Haley treaded carefully. "Thanks for the heads-up. Now I see why you loaned me these boots. How far do we have to go?"

"Not that far at all."

Ten minutes later she stopped to catch her breath. "How much farther do we have to go?"

"You okay?" When Jeff turned around to check on her, he found her standing with both hands on her hips, but she wasn't doing her superhero pose; she was doubled over catching her breath.

"Apparently, I need to ramp up my cardio," she said.

"I've been walking pretty fast. I can slow down. My legs are a lot longer than yours."

Haley stood up straight again. "I'm good. I just needed a second. I'm not used to hiking in the snow."

"But it's beautiful out here, isn't it? And the smell, that's my favorite part." He inhaled deeply.

Haley followed his lead and inhaled as well. "It smells like . . ."

He held his arms up to the sky. "Christmas. It smells like Christmas."

She laughed. "Yeah, I guess it does. These are fir trees, right?"

Jeff nodded. "Most of the ones you see here are Fraser firs. There are also some Douglas firs."

"Which one's better?" Haley asked.

"It's not a matter of one being better than the other," he answered. "They're just different, but both make great Christmas trees. A Fraser fir is, botanically, a true fir tree, whereas a Douglas fir is more of a fir-tree cousin."

Haley laughed. "How do you know this?"

Jeff smiled. "I worked for the Forest Service during college." He walked over to a Fraser fir. "Here, let me show you something."

Haley joined him by the tree.

"Take off your glove and feel how soft the needles are." Jeff took off his own glove and lightly ran his fingers over a group of needles. Haley took off her glove and did the same.

"It *is* soft," she said. She ran her fingers over it again and was surprised.

"This is a Fraser fir. See how the pinecones are sitting upright on the branches?"

Haley nodded.

"That's one of the ways you know it's a Fraser fir." Jeff motioned for her to follow him as he walked past several trees and stopped in front of one. "See the pinecones on this tree, how they're different?"

Haley leaned in for a closer look. "They're facing down, not up."

"Exactly." He smiled. "And that's one of the ways you know that this one is a Douglas fir. You can also tell by the way the needles are shaped and how they grow on all sides of the branches. Our Fraser fir over there has two-toned needles that are dark green on the top and almost silver underneath, and the branches are really sturdy, so they're great for heavier ornaments. They both make great Christmas trees, because they can handle the heat inside a house."

"For how long?"

"Sometimes up to a month if you make sure to keep giving them fresh water."

Haley looked impressed. "Wow, you're like a Christmas-tree guru! I had no idea about any of this."

Jeff started walking off, looking around. "And I haven't even told you about the balsam fir or the blue spruce or—"

Haley caught up to him and grabbed his arm. "Stop! I'm having a Christmas-tree overload here."

They both laughed.

"Then we better get going so you can pick out your tree," Jeff said as he continued walking toward a group of trees up ahead.

Haley follow him. "Wait, did you say I have to pick out a tree?"

"Of course. It's your tree. So which one speaks to you?"

She looked at him like he was crazy. "If any of these trees start *speaking* to me, I'm outta here!"

"Okay, then do it your way. Pick however you like, but you'll need this." When he tried to hand her the saw, she backed away fast.

"I don't know how to cut down a tree. Do I look like a lumberjack?"

When Jeff studied her from head to toe, Haley tried not to squirm.

"You look more like a lumber jill. Now here, take the saw."

She stubbornly shook her head. "You know the activity list said we were getting a tree, it didn't say anything about cutting down a tree."

"Surprise!"

Haley wanted to hit him over the head with the saw.

"But, hey, if you can't handle it, that's fine," he said. "You just won't get to mark this activity off your list."

Haley's mouth dropped open. "And that would mean I wouldn't get my certificate . . ."

Jeff shrugged, clearly enjoying himself.

Haley was not amused. She grabbed the saw out of his hands and marched off. When she was just a few feet ahead of him, she looked around. "Okay, what one do you want me to cut down?"

Jeff chuckled. "Oh no, this is all you. Your tree, you decide."

"Seriously, I don't care. Just pick one." She was running out of patience fast.

"That's not how it works."

They stood staring at each other for several seconds. Neither of them was backing down. "Look, you're making this harder than it has to be," Jeff said. "Just pick any of the trees right here. Pick the one that reminds you of Christmas. They're all perfect."

Haley looked around and frowned. "That's the problem," she said. "They're all too perfect." When she started zigzagging around a bunch of trees, Jeff followed her. Finally, she spotted a little tree tucked away in between two larger ones, and her eyes lit up. "That one! That's the one I want!"

Jeff walked over to a beautiful six-foot Douglas fir. "She's a beauty all right."

"No, not that one. That one!" Haley pointed to the funny-looking Charlie Brown Christmas tree that was right next to it. It was only about three feet high and had a crooked trunk, and there were fewer than a dozen branches that stuck out every which way. As far as Christmas trees go, it was one hot mess.

Jeff laughed and gave her an incredulous look. "This is the tree you want? This isn't a Christmas tree. It's just something that's popped up here."

Haley stubbornly marched over to the funny little tree. "You said all the trees here are Christmas trees and that I could pick any one I want."

"I know but—"

"Well, this is the one I want." When she locked eyes with him, he just shrugged.

"Okay, it's your choice. Have at it."

When Haley realized he meant for her to start sawing the little tree down, her confidence faded, but she refused to let him see she was nervous. So she got down on her hands and knees, sinking in the snow, and was fighting to lift up some branches so she could get the saw to the tree trunk when Jeff started helping by holding up some branches.

"Here, does this help?" he asked.

She nodded and crawled closer to the tree. She was getting covered in snow, but she didn't care. She was determined to complete this activity so she could mark it off her list. She wasn't about to let some Christmas tree stand in the way of her promotion. But when she finally got the saw to the little tree trunk, she had trouble making the saw glide back and forth.

"Here, let me show you how to do it," Jeff offered.

Part of Haley, the stubborn part, wanted to cut down the tree without his help, but the other part of her, the part that was getting numb from the cold, gave in and handed him the saw.

"You need to grab the handle of the saw like this." He showed her. "And keep your index finger right here, along the top of the handle, because it will help you guide where you want the saw to go. Here, you try it."

When he handed her back the saw, she eagerly tried to do what he said but still had a hard time until he helped position her hand correctly. When their eyes met she gave him a grateful look, and for that moment she didn't feel cold anymore as a rush of heat filled her body.

"Okay, I think I've got it," she said, and quickly turned her attention back to the tree. She held the saw like Jeff had showed her and tried again, and this time it worked. A smile lit up her face as she looked back at him. "I'm doing it! I'm sawing down a tree. Whooo-hoo!"

"Great job! Keep at it, you've got a long way to go," Jeff said in an encouraging voice.

"But I'm doing it!"

"You're doing it." He laughed.

When the tree started to get a little wobbly, Jeff came over and held it upright. "Keep going, I've got it. I won't let it fall down."

"You better not! I'm almost there, I think." Haley, excited, picked up her speed. "Okay, are you ready?"

"Ready!"

"Done!" Haley said as she made the last cut.

"Got it!" Jeff held the little tree up in the air.

"We did it." Haley grinned.

"You did it." Jeff smiled back. "Nice job." He handed her the tree. "Here you go!"

Haley proudly took it. It didn't weigh very much, because it was so scrawny, but to Haley, in that moment, it was the best Christmas tree she'd ever had.

CHAPTER 15

Later that afternoon, everyone gathered in the library around a bunch of boxes that were overflowing with Christmas decorations. Haley looked around in awe. There were boxes of Christmas lights in all shapes and sizes. There were multicolored lights and all-white lights. There were strings of just green lights and red lights, gold lights, and silver lights.

As she walked around, she also found boxes filled with different kinds of beautiful garlands, from the traditional silver glittery kind to others in gold, green, and red. There were even strands of garland that were hot pink. But the real showstoppers were the fancy garlands that mimicked real tree branches. Some already had little twinkly lights added to the branches and were decorated with everything from red ribbon and bows to poinsettias and pinecones and holly berries. Some of the garlands had colored beads woven through the branches along with Christmas ornaments. There was also a box filled with real holly branches and a stack of Christmas wreaths, waiting to be decorated.

Then there were the Christmas-tree ornaments, hundreds of them, separated by color and theme. Haley walked over to one of the boxes and was surprised to see dozens of different kinds of train ornaments. In another box, she found all kinds of different Santa ornaments, and in the box next to it, she discovered nautical-themed ornaments, including everything from sailboats to starfish.

When Ben joined her, she was practically speechless. "Wow!" was the one word she could get out.

Ben chuckled. "It's really something, isn't it? Grace loved her ornaments. We've been collecting them for years."

"That's really cool." Haley picked up a cute little red caboose from the train box. It looked vintage. "How old is this one?"

Ben smiled and looked nostalgic. "That one's probably about fifty years old. It was mine when I was little. My parents used to give us a new ornament every year, starting with the year we were born, so when we grew up and moved out, we'd already have some Christmas traditions to take with us."

"And you took your trains?" Haley asked.

"I did." Ben lifted a train engine out of the box. "And it's a tradition I continued with Jeff. He has his own box here somewhere."

Haley looked over at Jeff. He was looking through another box with Ian and Susie. She smiled, seeing how happy everyone looked as they discovered new Christmas treasures in different boxes.

Ben stepped out to the center of the library to get the group's attention. "Okay, everyone, are you ready for your next Christmas Camp activity?"

"We're ready," Susie answered enthusiastically, and kissed Ian's cheek.

Ben continued: "So, I heard you all found some wonderful Christmas trees today."

"We did!" Susie answered again. "Our tree is incredible, right, babe?"

Ian laughed. "Well, if incredible means huge, yeah, sure, it's incredible and incredibly heavy to lug out of the forest."

Susie laughed. "Don't mind him, they don't do a tree in Arizona . . ."

"We get a Christmas cactus and we put it on a table and put presents underneath it," Ian said proudly. "It works."

Susie's smile faded. "I can't even imagine not having a Christmas tree, a real Christmas tree." Susie took a deep breath. "We need to get a real tree at home, not just a Christmas cactus."

Ian nodded but didn't look convinced.

"Our tree's pretty cool, too," Madison said as she wrapped some of the hot-pink garland around her neck.

"That's because you got your way, and we got the tree you wanted." Blake gave his sister an annoyed look.

"You liked it, too, right, Dad?" Madison asked.

John looked torn between his two kids. "I thought they all were great, and I'm just thankful to have one."

When Madison gave Blake a satisfied look, he just rolled his eyes and turned his attention back to a box of nutcrackers.

Haley hid a smile watching the teenagers be teenagers. Growing up as an only child, she'd never had a sibling to argue with, or for that matter, to hang out with, and watching Blake and Madison, she definitely saw the pluses and minuses. She also couldn't help but feel a little sorry for poor John, who looked like he needed a break. She walked over and joined him.

"How's it going?" she asked.

John pointed at his two kids, who were still arguing. "Teenagers, what do you do?"

Ben also joined them. "It can be a tricky age. I remember when Jeff was sixteen."

John looked over at Jeff, who was helping Susie untangle a bunch of Christmas lights. "Well, that's encouraging because your son turned out pretty great from what I can see. At the very least, you survived to tell the story."

Haley laughed.

Ben gave John a reassuring pat on the back. "And your kids will, too. They have a wonderful dad who cares about them, and that's the most important thing."

John looked over at Blake who was now holding up two nutcrackers, trying to scare Madison with them, and it was working. John shook his head and turned back to Ben. "You know, lately I haven't felt like a very good dad. Being a doctor, I'm on call twenty-four/seven. I've realized these past few years I've been putting my patients first, because they needed me, but now I realize my kids need me, too, especially after the divorce. It's been hard trying to figure out how to do this first Christmas together. I've missed so many Christmas activities with them over the years, I don't even know where to start . . ."

"Well, you're starting here, right now, at Christmas Camp," Ben said. "You've already taken the first step by coming here. This is the place for families to come together and reconnect. It's going to get better. You'll see."

John glanced over at Madison, who was laughing as she draped pink garlands around Blake's neck that Blake was quickly yanking off. "I sure hope so," he said, and smiled at Ben. "And I'm very grateful we're here with you, with everyone." When John looked at Haley she gave him a reassuring nod.

"I think Ben's right: it'll get better," she said.

They both watched as Ben joined Jeff and Susie and in no time had untangled the lights they were struggling with.

"I guess we all have our Christmas issues." John laughed a little.

"We sure do," Haley agreed.

Ben picked up a box of lights and looked around the room. "Okay, everyone, let's get started. I don't know yet if you've seen the theme of the day, but today's theme is 'joy.' The kind of pure joy and happiness you had as a child when you hadn't a care in the world. I'm hoping, as you all decorate your trees, that you find some of that joy again."

"That's the next activity on our list—decorating, right?" Haley asked.

Ben nodded and held his arms wide. "You can see we have enough here to decorate the entire forest, so each of you can go around and see what you can find that brings you joy." He pulled a fistful of candy canes out of a box. "Christmas decorations can bring back wonderful memories."

Jeff pulled a pretty crystal icicle from another box. "Or they can help you create some new memories and traditions," he said, and smiled at his dad.

Ben nodded. "The important thing is to always remember there's never any right or wrong way to decorate your Christmas tree as long as it brings you joy."

"I love this!" Susie said.

"You love everything about Christmas," Ian chimed in.

"True." Susie laughed.

John looked around the room. "Where's Gail?"

"She said she needed a little break," Ben said.

"She told me that decorating the tree was her favorite

thing to do with her son," Susie said. "So this is probably pretty hard on her. I could go check on her."

"Let's give her the time she asked for," Ben said. "Sometimes all we need is a little time alone."

Susie nodded, but still looked somewhat concerned.

"We have a lot to choose from, so please go ahead and get started," Ben said.

Blake had already dived into the box of nutcrackers and was holding one that was almost two feet high. Excited, he looked around for something to crack. He grabbed his sister's hand with the nutcracker's mouth.

"Hey, knock it off!" Madison yanked her hand away just in time.

When Blake laughed, John gave him a warning look. "Blake, come on, help us pick some things out."

"I already have," Blake said, holding up the nutcracker. "There's a whole box of these. We need to put them up all over the room."

Madison looked horrified. "What?! No! They're creepy-looking!"

"They're cool! Right, Dad?"

Madison pulled on her dad's sleeve. "Dad, tell him no!"

John covered his face with his hands for a second before facing his dueling teenagers. "Okay, guys, it's like this: we're a family, so we all have to agree on how we're going to decorate. That's how it works. So, Madison, what's your idea for decorations?"

Madison marched over to a box and pulled out another hot-pink garland strand and some matching hot-pink Christmas lights.

Blake's eyes grew huge, and not in a good way. "Dad! Pink! Come on!"

Haley was watching the whole thing and struggled not to laugh.

John turned to his son. "Blake, what were you thinking for decorations?"

When Blake held up the nutcracker again, John took it from him. "Besides the nutcrackers?"

"I don't really care. I just want the nutcrackers," Blake insisted stubbornly.

"Okay, then." John smiled at his two children. "Blake, you can have your nutcrackers, and Madison, you can have your pink-themed Christmas tree, and we'll all be one happy family."

"Dad!" both kids protested in unison. They were clearly not experiencing any Christmas joy.

Haley turned her attention from John and his family to Jeff, who was busy going through a box of sparkling silver star ornaments. She then looked over at Ben, who was helping Ian and Susie go through another box. She slowly inched toward the door. She knew this was her chance to leave without anyone seeing her. When she got to the door, she gave one more quick look around the room to make sure the coast was clear. When she saw Max looking at her, she held her finger up to her mouth. "Shhh," she whispered to him, and then silently slipped out. She needed a break from the Christmas overload.

As she was heading down the hall to her room, she stopped outside Gail's door when she thought she heard someone crying inside. She hesitated for a moment and then continued walking, but she only got a few steps before she turned around, walked back to Gail's room, and knocked softly.

"Gail, it's me, Haley."

A few seconds later, when Gail opened the door, Haley could see tears in her eyes. As Gail quickly tried to brush them away, she also tried to smile. "Hi," she said in a quiet, sad voice.

Haley kept smiling, not wanting to make her feel uncomfortable. "I just wanted to let you know we're all downstairs picking out decorations for our Christmas trees. I thought maybe you'd want to join us?"

Gail looked touched. "Thank you, Haley, that's very sweet of you, but I'm just feeling a little . . . tired right now."

"Okay, I understand," Haley said. When something sparkly caught her eye, she looked past Gail into her room and saw that it was decorated in a star theme.

"Ah, so you have the star room?" she asked. "It looks very pretty."

Gail opened the door wider so Haley could get a better look. "It really is beautiful. Would you like to come in and see it?"

"I would love to." Haley followed her into the room. The walls were painted a soft baby blue with little silver stars, and the ceiling was sapphire blue, like the night sky, with white stars. The star theme continued with a canopy of tiny white twinkling lights above an all-white bed covered with silver star pillows.

"Wow," she said as she took it all in. "This is really magical. I feel like I'm outside looking up into the sky."

Gail nodded, picked up one of the star pillows, and held it to her heart. "Ben said he gave it to me because he says the stars in the sky are the people we've loved and lost, watching down on us, protecting us."

Touched by Gail's words, Haley looked up at the ceiling. "That's really beautiful."

"Isn't it?" Gail looked up at the ceiling, too. "I'd like to think my husband is up there watching over our son, Ryan."

"I'm sure he is," Haley said softly, and then noticed a Christmas tree in the corner. It stood about five feet high and was perfectly proportioned. She walked over to study it closer. She touched the needles and recognized it was a Douglas fir. "I like your tree."

Gail smiled. "It *is* a pretty one, isn't it? Ben helped me cut it down."

"Oh, really?" Haley smiled back. "Because Jeff made me cut my own down. He said it was one of the Christmas Camp rules."

"Then I guess I got lucky." Gail smiled again.

"I think you did." As Haley looked at the tree her face lit up. "Wait, I have an idea. Can you give me a second, I'll be right back, okay?" She was already headed for the door.

"Okay . . ."

Haley ran down the hall and didn't stop until she was back in the library, where she headed straight for Jeff.

He looked surprised to see her. "I thought you'd snuck off to your room to do some work."

"No, although that's not a bad idea—I have so much work to do—it's not why I left." She looked around. "Where is that box of silver stars you had before?"

Jeff walked over to a box and picked it up. "This one?"

Haley's eyes lit up. "Yup, that's the one! Can I borrow it?"

When she held out her hands, Jeff placed the box in them.

"Sure, here you go. It's all yours."

"Thanks." Haley grinned at him then hurried out the door.

A minute later she was knocking on Gail's door. This time Gail answered right away. "You're back . . . that was quick." She looked at the box with curiosity. "What do you have there?"

"It's for you." Haley handed her the box, then waited for her to look inside and see all the star ornaments. "I thought these would be perfect for your tree and that you might like some help decorating."

Gail's eyes filled with tears of gratitude. When she looked up at Haley, she nodded and whispered softly, "Thank you," and then opened the door so Haley could come in.

About an hour later, the two of them were putting the finishing touches on the tree. Gail stood back and admired their work.

"Haley, thank you so much for this."

Haley joined her by the tree. "You're welcome. I haven't decorated a Christmas tree in a long time, but I have to say, even though I'm biased, this tree is one of the prettiest I've ever seen."

Gail put the last star on the tree. "It really is beautiful."

"I can come back tonight when I get my phone back and take a picture of you with the tree if you want to send it to your son."

Gail smiled. "I would love that. Thank you."

A knock on the door surprised them both.

"Apparently, I'm very popular tonight." Gail laughed as she headed for the door. When she opened it, Laura was standing in the hallway holding a tray with two Santa mugs and some sugar cookies.

"I thought you girls might like a little snack."

When Gail opened the door wider so Laura could come in, Haley's eyes immediately focused on the sugar cookies. They were the round ones with white frosting and crushed pieces of candy canes.

Laura put the tray down on the dresser. "I brought you our famous hot chocolate and our Christmas Camp sugar cookies that are made from a secret recipe . . ."

"Ben's grandmother's recipe," Haley added.

Laura smiled. "That's right. Ben thought you might like to try one or two . . ."

As she looked at the cookies, there was nothing Haley wanted to do more, but she willed herself to be good. She just wished being good didn't feel so bad. It didn't make it any easier to watch Gail take a bite of one of the cookies, looking like she was in heaven.

"These are incredible." Gail studied the cookie like it was a treasure. "Haley, you have to try one."

But when Laura held out the tray to her, Haley clasped her hands behind her back and shook her head. "I can't. Remember? I'm trying to cut back on sugar. They do look amazing, though. Too amazing . . . that's the problem."

Laura laughed. "Well, I'll leave them right here in case you change your mind."

"I won't," Haley said. "I'm very disciplined when I set my mind to something. But thank you."

Laura looked at the tree they were decorating. "Gail, your tree is looking wonderful. I love what you've done with all the stars. It's so perfect with the room."

"Isn't it?" Gail said, glowing. "It was all Haley's idea, and she has been helping me. I couldn't have done it without her."

Haley blushed. "I haven't done that much."

Gail walked over and gave Haley a hug. "Yes, you have. More than you know."

As they hugged, Laura flashed Haley a grateful smile and mouthed the words "thank you."

"Well, it looks like you girls still have some work to

do, so I'll let you get back to it. If you need anything else, you know where to find me."

"Thank you, Laura. That was very thoughtful of you to bring us up a treat," Gail said.

"You're welcome." Laura smiled back at them. "Enjoy. Have a good night."

After Laura left, Gail took another bite of her cookie and studied it like she was trying to figure out the secret of its flavor. "Um, these really are so good. Are you sure you don't want to try one?"

Haley shook her head and forced herself to look away from the cookies.

"Okay, but surely you can have some hot chocolate? I had some earlier. It's not very sweet. They use dark chocolate and not a lot of sugar. I think you're allowed a little something. To celebrate our decorating success."

Gail handed her a Santa mug, which Haley took, not wanting to hurt her feelings. Gail then held up her mug for a toast, and Haley joined her. "To our beautiful tree, new friends, and new Christmas memories." She smiled as she looked into Haley's eyes.

Haley smiled back and continued the toast. "And to joy, Ben's theme word of the day. I think we nailed it!"

Gail laughed and so did Haley as they clinked their mugs together.

CHAPTER 16

The outdoor Christmas lights at the Holly Peak Inn glowed brightly against the night sky, casting colorful reflections on the fresh snow.

Inside, Haley was cuddled up in a chair in the sitting room, sipping hot chocolate out of a Santa mug while staring into the crackling fire. Her computer was open on her lap, but the page on the screen that said *Tyler Toys Campaign Ideas* was still blank. She looked up when she heard Jeff come in.

"Working?" he asked.

"Your dad said it was okay. We're officially done with all the Christmas Camp activities for today, so I'm not breaking any rules."

Jeff laughed. "It's okay. I believe you."

Haley sighed and put down her hot chocolate. "Sorry, I'm just a little on edge. I'm running out of time to come up with an amazing toy campaign, and so far this is all I have." She picked up her computer and turned it around so Jeff could see the blank screen.

He raised his eyebrows. "So, you're having trouble?"

"That would be an understatement."

"I'm sure something will come to you," Jeff said as he walked over and put another log on the fire. "So how does your tree look with all the star decorations?"

Haley looked confused for a second. "Oh, those weren't for me. They were for Gail."

"Gail? I thought they were for your tree. What did you end up choosing as your theme, then?"

"I haven't decided yet."

Jeff frowned. "So you haven't decorated your tree at all?"

"Not yet. It's still outside. I told your dad I'd do it before I go to bed. I wanted to try to get some work done first. I just don't understand." Haley dragged her fingers through her hair. "Coming up with creative campaigns is what I do best, and here I am surrounded by everything Christmas, but still nothing has come to me."

"Maybe you're just trying too hard."

"What do you mean?"

"I mean maybe you're forcing yourself to come up with Christmas ideas instead of just experiencing Christmas and letting the ideas come naturally."

"There's nothing about a traditional Christmas that's natural to me. That's why I got sent here in the first place. No offense."

"None taken," Jeff said. He was still working on the fire. "I'm just saying you probably need a break. Inspiration usually hits when you're not trying so hard to find it. Right now you're surrounded by Christmas, so maybe you should just relax a little and take it all in." He picked up her empty Santa mug. "So, you finally tried our famous hot chocolate. What did you think?"

Haley smiled. "It was good. It was really good."

"So, it was worth the calories?"

Haley nodded. "Totally."

"Laura will be glad to hear it. I'll let you get back to work. Good luck."

"Good night," Haley said as she watched Jeff leave and then turned her attention back to her computer. She put her hands on her keyboard and started typing.

Tyler Toys Santa mugs . . .

She stopped, looked around the room, glanced over to the table where Ben had left his Santa collection, and started typing again.

Tyler Toys Santa collection . . .

She spotted a snow globe and continued typing.

Tyler Toys snow globes . . .

Her hands stopped moving on the keyboard. She stared at the screen, frustrated that her only ideas were boring clichés. She needed something fresh, fun, and new if she was going to compete with Tom. But when still nothing came to her, she shut her laptop and stared up at the ceiling. That's when she realized how tired she was. She shut her eyes for a moment but then opened them quickly. She'd almost forgotten. She'd promised Ben she'd decorate her tree tonight. She still needed to mark that activity off her list.

Groaning, she forced herself to get up and put on her winter wear. "All right, let's make this quick," she said as she hurried outside and headed straight to the back of the inn where she'd left her little tree. She was just picking it up when Ben came around the corner. He was carrying a snow shovel, and by his rosy cheeks and heavy breathing, you could tell he'd been working hard.

He smiled when he saw Haley but looked a little confused. "Haley, what are you doing out here with Jeff's tree? He should be bringing that in himself."

Haley laughed. "This isn't Jeff's tree. It's mine."

"Really, that's your tree? The one you picked out to-day?"

Haley held it up proudly. "Yup, it sure is."

Ben looked surprised. "Sorry, I thought it was Jeff's. He picks out a tree just like that every year."

Now it was Haley's turn to look surprised. "What? Really?"

Ben nodded. "He's been doing it since he was a kid. He says all the other trees are too perfect."

"Seriously? That's what I always say, too. When I was growing up, my family didn't have a lot of money, and one year, when I was about ten, we couldn't afford a tree. I, of course, didn't understand. So I went around the neighborhood until I found a big tree branch I could reach, and I tore it off. I took it home and wrapped the bottom in a blanket so it would still fit in the tree stand and then I decorated it for Christmas."

Ben smiled knowingly. "A Charlie Brown Christmas tree."

"Exactly. After that Christmas, we never had a perfect tree again, even when we could afford one." Haley shook her head, remembering. "We'd go to a tree lot, and I'd see a funny little tree like this one. I'd always feel sorry for it, thinking no one would ever take it home."

"So you got it and took it home."

She nodded. "You know I haven't thought about that in a long time . . ."

"It sounds like a wonderful tradition," Ben said. "I'm glad you're honoring it while you're here."

"I guess I am." She looked at her little tree. "I haven't had a Christmas tree in years. I've been so busy traveling around during the holidays, I never bother to get one anymore. Now I just need to figure out how to decorate it."

"I'm sure something will come to you. I look forward to seeing it when you're done."

"Wish me luck," Haley said.

"I wish you joy . . ."

Haley smiled as she went inside. After she dropped the tree off in her room, she went back downstairs to the library and started looking through the boxes of decorations, searching for some inspiration. She found a box of pretty birds and a decorative bird's nest, obviously meant for a nature-themed tree, but while they were cute, they weren't really for her. In the next box she opened, she found a bunch of adorable little elf ornaments and picked one up. It was dancing. She wiggled her own arms around like she was dancing but then put the ornament back in the box and picked up another. This elf was licking a red-and-white-striped lollypop. "Ah, so you like sugar, too?" She laughed. She put that elf back and decided to try another box. In this one she found some stunning crystal snowflakes. When she held one up to the light, it cast sparks of light all around the room. It was beautiful, but it still didn't seem right.

She was about to give up when she saw a little box standing all alone in the corner. She went over, picked it up, and brought it back to the table. As she got a closer look, she wrinkled her nose. It smelled musty and looked very old. There was yellowed string wrapped around it that she carefully untied. When she opened it the first thing she found was a lot of tissue paper that had also yellowed over the years. The paper surrounded another box that was covered in white velvet. She took it out and set it on the table. "So, what do we have here?" she asked, intrigued. When she opened the lid and looked inside, she found about a dozen tiny white-and-silver angel ornaments. She laughed and shook her head. "More angels? Seriously?" But when she looked closer, she saw they were exquisite. When one of the angels glowed in the light, she knew they belonged in her room, on her tree, with her.

"Okay, you're coming with me," she said as she picked up the box and headed for her room. "I have some of your friends waiting for you."

A few minutes later, as she sat on her bedroom floor next to her little Christmas tree, she carefully took one of the angel ornaments out of the box and looked for a place to put it. She picked one of the highest branches and tested the ornament's weight before she tried hanging it. It was perfect. Haley smiled and picked up another angel. "Now, where should you go?"

Just as she was trying to figure out where to hang her next angel, Max came trotting in. Apparently, she hadn't shut her door all the way.

He sat down next to her and sniffed the angel.

"She's pretty, isn't she?"

Max barked and wagged his tail while watching her.

"Shhh! You can only stay if you behave yourself."

Max immediately lay down and looked up at her with his big, brown, innocent eyes.

Haley struggled not to smile and then turned her attention back to decorating. As she put another angel ornament on her tree, she didn't even realize she had started humming "Hark! The Herald Angels Sing" . . .

WHEN JEFF WALKED into the library, he found his dad in the corner decorating a beautiful Douglas fir. It stood about six feet high and was perfectly shaped.

Ben smiled when he saw him. "Son, come over and join me. I could use some help."

"It looks like it." Jeff laughed. "I think this tree is even bigger than the one you picked out last year."

"It might be a little bigger, but what can I say? It spoke to me."

"And, of course, you always listen."

"It would be rude not to." Ben grinned as he put another ornament on the tree.

Jeff was still laughing. "You know the trees we put in here, that always have our homemade family ornaments, are my favorite."

"Mine too." Ben took another ornament out of its box and held it up proudly. It was a picture framed with Popsicle sticks of Jeff when he was little. He was adorable. "Remember this one? You made it in fifth grade."

Jeff laughed as he took the ornament from his dad and gave it a closer look. "Seriously, Mom kept everything."

"She sure did. She used to say that every single ornament held a special memory."

"That's why it would always take you two so long to decorate. Every time you took out a new ornament, you would reminisce about it," Jeff said, handing the Popsicle picture frame back to his dad.

As Ben found the perfect place for it on the tree, he turned back to his son. "If I remember right, you always loved to help."

Jeff smiled, remembering. "You and Mom would tell me that I was in charge of decorating all the lower branches, because those were the ones I could reach . . ."

"Oh, that wasn't the only reason . . . I also didn't want to have to lean over and strain my back!"

They shared a laugh.

"So, who's going to do the lower branches this year?" Jeff asked, picking up a funny-looking pinecone with a felt Santa hat on it and two pieces of black felt glued on for the eyes.

"Guess." Ben grinned back at him.

Jeff laughed. "I was afraid you were going to say that." He had to kneel down on one knee to get low enough to put the pinecone on one of the lowest branches.

"Well, if you'd just give me some grandkids, we could pass the tradition on to them," Ben said, giving him a pointed look.

Jeff looked up. "I think you're putting the cart before the horse, or as you would say, the reindeer before the sleigh. I'm not even dating anyone, so don't hold your breath on the grandkids."

Ben chuckled. "Anything can happen at any time, especially at Christmas."

Jeff laughed and stood up. "Whatever you say, Dad."

Ben handed him another ornament. It was a simple silver star made out of tinfoil and covered with gold glitter. "I forgot about these stars we made that Christmas."

"I think we made about a dozen of them and took them to the community center."

"But Mom made sure we kept a few to always remember . . ."

"And now we *are* remembering."

Jeff handed the star to his dad. "Here, you put this one up."

Ben nodded as he took the star, looked for the perfect place to put it, and reached up high to place it next to one of the white twinkling lights so the light reflected off the foil.

"Nice." Jeff patted his dad on the back. "I gave Haley a box of star ornaments today. I thought they were for her tree, but she apparently gave them to Gail."

"I know," Ben said. "Laura told me. She also told me that Haley stayed and helped Gail decorate her tree, knowing how Gail always decorated with her son. That was a very kind thing of her to do."

Jeff looked surprised. "I didn't know she helped Gail. I thought she just gave the stars to her."

"No, she stayed and helped her decorate, and Laura said Gail was very grateful."

"Huh."

"You're surprised?" Ben asked.

"I guess I am," Jeff answered. "I just know Haley is all about getting everything done here as fast as she can so she can get back to work. I just wouldn't expect her to be helping anyone else."

"I also saw the tree she cut down." Ben gave Jeff a knowing look. "It looked familiar."

Avoiding the look, Jeff picked up a candy cane and put it on the tree. "Yeah, she did a good job cutting it down."

"She made an interesting choice," Ben said.

Jeff avoided his dad's pointed look. "She just picked the smallest one because cutting it down involved the least amount of work."

"Actually, she told me, since she was little, she has picked funny little trees like this, because she wanted to make sure they got a good home. Sounds like someone else I know . . ."

"Dad . . ."

"I'm just saying that maybe you two have more in common than you think."

Jeff laughed loudly. "What, Haley and I? I don't think so. Haley only cares about one thing. Work. She doesn't care about any of this stuff. She wouldn't even be here if she didn't have to be."

"People can change . . ." Ben said as he picked up an old-fashioned clothespin angel ornament. It was made out of white paper and lace. He handed it to Jeff.

"You know I love the way you always see the best in everyone, but I wouldn't expect too much of a transformation from Haley. I don't want you to be disappointed. Christmas Camp can't change everyone."

Smiling, Ben watched as Jeff put the angel ornament on the tree, and it glowed in the light. "I believe that at Christmas Camp, anything is possible."

Jeff shook his head. His dad's optimism was relentless. "Okay, but after camp, remember, you promised we're going to have a serious talk about the future because *I believe* that unless you plan on Santa Claus bringing you a big bag of money, you're going to have to sell this place, and it will be the best thing for you. You'll see . . ."

But when Ben just continued decorating without saying a word, Jeff knew he'd upset him. But he also knew his dad was in denial about his finances, and it was his job to protect him.

THAT NIGHT, SNUGGLED in bed, Haley looked over at her tree. The angel ornaments were glowing in the moonlight. The tree was a little lopsided and some of its branches were sagging from the weight of the angels, but she thought it was perfect, and for the first time in a very long time, she felt it. Joy. Just like Ben had said she would. She fell asleep smiling.

CHAPTER 17

As the sun came up over the mountains, its golden glow lit up the Holly Peak Inn and the snow-covered trees.

The first thing Haley saw when she opened her eyes was her Charlie Brown Christmas tree decorated with the angel ornaments. She loved her little tree. Throwing off the covers, she jumped out of bed and was just starting to get dressed when she heard Max bark outside her door.

"Hold on, Max. I'm coming!"

This time when she opened her door and saw Max sitting there with his leash in his mouth, she was ready for him. She already had on her coat, hat, and scarf. As she bent down to pet him, she noticed he was wearing a new Christmas sweater. This one was red with green stripes. "Well, look at you in your new sweater. This one is much better than the one with the crazy cats. Okay, let's go!"

Max was so excited he practically dragged her down the hallway. When they went out the front door, Haley was hit in the chest with snowball.

"Hey!" she shouted as she looked around, surprised.

That's when she spotted Blake and Madison, both with snowballs in their hands. She gave them a warning look. "Don't even think about it!"

Madison laughed. "Sorry, I was trying to get my brother."

Blake took advantage of the distraction to pelt Madison with two snowballs.

"Whoa! Wait! That's not fair!" Madison threw a snowball at him but missed.

"Do you need some help?" Haley asked her.

"Please!" Madison said, and then got hit in the leg with another snowball. "Hurry!"

Laughing, Haley quickly put Max back inside the house. "I'll come back and get you in a second. Just hang on. Madison needs some help." She then ran back to Madison, expertly made two snowballs, and fired them at Blake. They were both direct hits, landing square on his back, sending snow everywhere.

He whirled around. "Hey!"

"Nice shot, Haley!" Madison grabbed some more snow and ran to hide behind a tree.

"No fair," Blake complained. "It's two against one!"

All of a sudden Haley got pelted in the back with a snowball. When she spun around, she saw Jeff grinning at her. He was holding another snowball and coming right at her.

"Run, Haley, run!" Madison shouted from behind the tree.

Haley took off running just as another snowball hit her in the leg.

"Nice one!" Blake ran up to Jeff, and they high-fived.

When Susie and Ian walked out the front door, Madison started waving her arms at Susie. "Susie, over here! It's the girls against the boys. Hurry!"

"Wait, what?" Susie looked confused until one of Blake's snowballs hit her in the stomach. "Seriously?" she said, glaring back at Blake. "Oh, you are so going down!" She grabbed some snow, ran up to Blake, and stuffed it down the neck of his coat.

"No!" Blake laughed and squirmed, but it was too late.

Ian laughed. "I should have warned you. My wife has three brothers who taught her how to fight back. She annihilated me the first snowball fight we had."

"Then get over here, Susie! Hurry!" Haley yelled.

But just as Susie ran over to join the girls, a snowball hit her in the back. She froze and turned slowly, and when she saw it was Ian who was standing there grinning back at her, she gave him a look that had him running in the other direction.

"Come on, girls, let's get 'em!" Haley shouted.

For the next five minutes, they battled in an epic snowball fight, girls against boys. Both teams were pretty evenly matched until John came outside and joined the guys. His first snowball hit Madison.

"Dad! How could you!" Madison gave her dad a look.

"All's fair in love and snowball fights. Love you, honey!" John hugged his daughter, but when she squirmed out of his embrace, grabbed some snow, and rubbed it into his hair, it was his turn to look shocked.

"Seriously, Madison? To your own dad?"

"All's fair in love and snowball fights! I love you, too, Dad!"

Everyone laughed.

"Hey, what's going on out here?" Ben asked as he walked through the front door.

Everyone turned to look at him then looked at each other. When Jeff nodded, they all pelted him with snowballs.

"Wait! What?" Ben dodged as many snowballs as he could, but the one Jeff threw smacked him on the chest. "Son, you know better than that!"

A second later Ben was running toward Jeff with two snowballs in his hands.

Jeff started backing away. "Dad, you wouldn't."

But Ben looked like he, indeed, would . . . happily.

"But we're family," Jeff pleaded in a teasing voice.

"But all's fair in love and snowball fights, right, Dad?" Madison asked gleefully.

"She's right," John said. "Sorry, buddy, you're on your own here."

Ben picked just that moment to throw his first snow-ball at Jeff.

Jeff expertly dodged it and was celebrating his victory when he got a surprise hit in the back.

"What?!" When he spun around, he saw Haley doing her own victory dance before she ran up to Ben and they gave each other a high five.

"Nice job, Haley!" Ben put his arm around her, and they both grinned at Jeff, who was still trying to brush all the snow off him. "Okay, everyone, let's all go clean up and get some breakfast because we have a big day ahead of us."

As they headed in, Jeff caught up with Haley. "Teaming up with my dad, huh?"

"Oh yeah." Haley smiled. "I know a winner when I see one." She winked at Ben, and he winked back before she gave Jeff a victorious look, laughed, and ran inside to get Max for his promised walk.

A FEW HOURS LATER, Ben led the group into the town's modest-looking community center, where Haley noticed a sign on the door that read HOLIDAY VOLUNTEERS

NEEDED. She looked at Gail, who was walking alongside her. "I guess we're the volunteers."

"I guess we are," Gail said. She smiled at Haley. "I'm really looking forward to this. My son, Ryan, and I used to volunteer every year at our local food pantry. It's one of our favorite family Christmas traditions."

"That's a great tradition," Haley said. "What did he think about the picture we took of you with your Christmas tree?"

Gail's smile faded a little. "I haven't heard back from him yet. I know he's really busy. He has a high security job in the military, and he's always traveling to remote places, so he's not always able to reach out, but I'm sure I'll hear from him when he can."

"He sounds like a great son," Haley said.

Gail's eyes lit up. "He really is. We've always been really close. He's been so worried about me this year, being alone at Christmas . . ."

Haley put her arm around Gail. "But you're not alone. You're here with all of us."

Gail gave her a smile and put her arm around her. "You know what? You're right, and I'm thankful for that. Now, let's go see how we can help here."

Haley and Gail and the rest of the group followed Ben to a table covered with food. The food was separated by category. There were turkeys, boxes of mashed potatoes, canned yams, cranberry sauce, stuffing mix, and pumpkin pies.

Ben picked up an empty box to pack things in and smiled at the group. "Okay, everyone, here's what we're going to do. We're going to fill up these boxes with the Christmas dinner supplies you see here on the table. They're for families who need a little extra help this year, so we are going to make sure they have something special for Christmas."

Blake picked up a frozen turkey. "Does everyone get one of these?"

"Blake, put that down." John took the turkey from his son.

"It's okay," Ben said. "Blake has just volunteered to do the turkey."

Madison laughed, pointing at Blake. "I always said you were a turkey!"

Blake playfully held the turkey up to Madison's face, "Why don't you give it a kiss?"

Madison backed away and gave him a look. "Funny."

Ben laughed. "Actually, Madison, your brother has an important job. He's in charge of making sure every box here gets a turkey."

Madison grabbed a pumpkin pie. "Then can I do the pie? Every family needs a pie, right?"

"Absolutely," Ben said. "Pie is one of the best parts of Christmas dinner."

"Totally," Madison agreed. "My favorite part."

"Mine too," Haley agreed. "Sometimes at Christmas all I'd eat was the pie—"

"Then I'm coming to your house," Madison said.

Everyone laughed.

"Okay, everyone, team up, and let's get going. We have a lot of meals to put together and a lot of families counting on us," Ben said. "Let's pair up and keep working."

Haley walked over to Gail. "Since it sounds like you're the expert and have done this before, I'm staying with you if that's okay?"

Gail laughed. "Of course it is, and you'll be an expert, too, in no time."

"Fantastic." Haley eagerly picked up a pie.

Gail gently took it from her. "But the pie goes in last. We don't want to get it smooshed."

"Oh, of course." Haley picked up the frozen turkey. "So, I'm thinking this little butterball is the one that goes in first . . ."

"And you'd be exactly right. Just put it in one of those plastic bags so when it starts to thaw out, it won't get everything else all gooey," Gail said.

"Good tip. See, you *are* the expert. I knew I picked the right table." Haley followed her lead as Gail picked up a box of mashed potatoes and a can of cranberry sauce and put them both in the box. Next, when she grabbed a can of yams, so did Haley. Haley was literally copying Gail's every move, and they worked together perfectly.

After a couple of minutes, Gail gave Haley a look of approval. "You're a great student."

Haley laughed. "I always was an overachiever."

Gail smiled back at her. "Seems like you still are. I heard you telling Jeff you work in advertising."

"I do," Haley said proudly. "I'm a brand specialist."

Gail gave her a questioning look.

"Don't worry." Haley laughed. "No one's really sure exactly what it means. Even my parents get confused and just tell people that I come up with cool ad campaigns."

"Like television commercials?"

"Sometimes, but it can be any kind of campaign— newspapers, magazines, radio, online, social media . . ."

"So, you come up with the ideas for the campaigns?"

Haley nodded. "I do. It's one of the things I love the most, although right now I'm really struggling to come up with an idea for a Christmas toy campaign."

"I'm sure you'll come up with something wonderful," Gail said.

"I'm trying to. I just need to stay focused," Haley said. When she saw Jeff walking toward them, she knew he was her number one distraction.

WHEN JEFF GOT to their table, he looked impressed. "Wow! Looks like we have a couple of pros here."

Haley nodded toward Gail. "She's the genius in this operation, I'm just the muscle." She held up a turkey for emphasis but it slipped out of her hands. "Oh no!" She tried to grab it but missed. It would have crashed to the floor if Jeff hadn't caught it at the last minute.

Gail covered her mouth, but you could tell she was laughing.

"Okay, so I'm not the muscle, I'm the klutz," Haley said, laughing, too.

Jeff carefully handed her back the turkey. "Can I trust you with this?"

Haley looked down at the turkey. "I can't make any promises. It's kind of slippery, right?" She looked to Gail for support.

"It *is* slippery," Gail agreed. "Let me get it." She then took the turkey from Haley and handed her a towel to wipe her hands.

"Thanks," Haley said.

"Gail, it looks like you've been working hard here," Jeff said. "Why don't you take a break with the rest of the group. Everyone's getting some coffee. I'll fill in for you here."

Gail smiled back at him. "That sounds wonderful, Jeff. Thank you."

"Hey, what about me? Don't I get a break?" Haley asked.

"I think you need to redeem yourself first," Jeff teased. "Unless you're not up for it?"

Haley saw it again, the challenge in his eyes. Even if he was teasing, she could never resist a challenge. She stood up straighter. "Fine, but I'm telling you, I have the canned yams and mashed potatoes down to a science."

Jeff and Gail exchanged a look and a laugh. "Good luck," Gail said to Haley.

As Gail left to join the group Haley looked up at Jeff, who was already putting a turkey into a new box. "So, check this out," she said as she picked up a box of mashed potatoes and used it as a tray for a can of yams, a can of green beans, and a can of cranberry sauce. When the cranberry sauce started to wobble, she quickly grabbed it with her other hand. "Pretty impressive, right?"

"You definitely have skills." Jeff laughed.

"Right!" Haley smiled back at him.

"And I was just kidding before. If you want a break, go for it."

Haley kept packing her box. "I'm good, but thanks. So, how long have you and your family been doing this?"

Jeff had to think about it. "Wow, for as long as I can remember."

Haley watched as he quickly finished up his box. "That's really nice. Gail says it's her family tradition, too. Just imagine if every family that could helped out just a little bit, it could really make a big difference."

"I agree," Jeff said.

They shared a smile as they both reached for the same can of yams. When their hands touched, their eyes met and Haley felt the pull between them. It was stronger than ever. This both scared and frustrated her. She pulled her hand away quickly and concentrated on putting another turkey in a bag, but she felt like Jeff was still looking at her.

"There's something I want to show you," he said. "I

thought it might give you some inspiration for your work project."

When Haley heard the word "work," she gave Jeff her full attention.

"You game?" he asked.

She eagerly smiled back at him. "Lead the way."

It didn't take long for Haley to figure out where Jeff was taking her as she followed him up to the front of the community center, where there was a huge nine-foot Christmas tree. Almost every inch was covered with sparkling white twinkle lights. The only other things on the tree were simple white paper angels.

"This is the community's angel tree," Jeff said as he looked up at the tree fondly.

Haley stepped back so she could see the very top. "Wow, there has to be at least two hundred angels on this."

"Probably closer to three hundred," Jeff said as he stepped closer, took an angel down from the tree, and showed it to Haley. "Check this out." On the angel was written *Bobby, 7, Toy Truck*. "Kids get to make their Christmas wish, and we get to help parents make their children's wishes come true."

As Haley watched him put the angel in his pocket, she found it impossible not to like him. He was obviously a good guy. He cared about helping people, he cared about his dad, and she knew he even cared about all of the guests at the Christmas Camp. The fact that he cared was a big problem, because she knew she was starting to care about him.

"So, are you ready?" Jeff asked.

Haley turned around and saw he was holding some white paper and a pair of scissors. He handed them to her. "We can always use some more angels."

"I can do that," she said. She was grateful to have something besides the way he was making her feel to concentrate on. As she started cutting out an angel, she reminded herself that all she needed to do was focus on work. *Work, work, work, and only work,* she chanted in her head. And that's when she accidentally cut off her angel's wings.

CHAPTER 18

Oh no!" Haley's hand flew to her mouth as she scrambled to pick up the angel's wings.

Jeff was instantly by her side. "What happened? Are you okay?"

When Haley, with a guilty look on her face, held up her angel in one hand and the wings she had just cut off in the other, she saw Jeff fight back a laugh.

"It's okay," he said. "We have lots of paper. Here, try again."

"I'm not very good at this," Haley said, meaning much more than just cutting out angels. What she was really thinking was that she wasn't very good at handling the feelings she was starting to have about him. She'd never felt like this before, so she was pretty much clueless. What she did know was that she didn't like not being able to control her feelings. It seemed like the more she told herself not to let Jeff distract her, the more he was getting under her skin. She knew she needed to pull herself together fast. She just wasn't sure how. Just like she was struggling with her Tyler Toys pitch, she was struggling to figure out how to handle the Jeff situation. Without even realizing it, she had started to cut out another angel.

When she looked up, she saw that Jeff was watching her. He was smiling. "I have faith you'll figure it out."

Haley almost dropped the scissors. For a moment she felt like he had read her mind, but then quickly realized he was just talking about having faith in her angel. She was saved from saying anything when another volunteer, a pretty girl in her midtwenties, walked up carrying a Christmas basket.

"Merry Christmas! Can I interest you in a few treats?" she asked, revealing that her basket was filled with baked goods and candies. She was smiling and batting her long eyelashes at Jeff without even acknowledging Haley.

Haley's eyes narrowed as she watched the girl flirt.

"We also have coffee and some soft drinks over in the corner if you need some caffeine," the volunteer continued, still smiling at Jeff. "And there's also a great bar across the street. I'll be there in about an hour if you'd like to grab a drink . . ."

Annoyed, Haley put herself between Jeff and the cute volunteer. "I'll take a candy cane," she said, making it impossible for the volunteer to continue to ignore her. But when the girl quickly gave Haley the candy cane and went back to ogling Jeff, Haley snapped . . . literally snapping her candy cane in two, ripping off the wrapper, and putting a piece of the candy cane into her mouth.

This instantly caught Jeff's attention. "I thought you weren't doing sugar?"

Haley couldn't answer because she was devouring the candy cane, crunching away, so she just smiled and grabbed another candy cane and two cookies out of the basket. She was about to grab something else when the volunteer backed away.

"I better go and stock up," the volunteer said, and then gave Jeff a hopeful look. "Maybe I'll see you at the bar later?"

When Jeff said, "Maybe," Haley stuffed a cookie into her mouth and then quickly walked to the other side of the angel tree so Jeff wouldn't see how annoyed she was. She was mostly annoyed with herself. She wasn't used to feeling jealous, and she didn't like it one bit. She was taking another bite of the cookie when Jeff caught up to her.

"You okay?" he asked.

She finished her bite of cookie. "Yeah, why?" she asked as she wiped some cookie crumbs off her face.

He looked at the other cookie and candy cane she was holding. "Uh, no reason, I guess."

Haley handed him a cookie.

He laughed. "No thanks, nothing compares to our Christmas Camp cookies, but I'll take the candy cane if you're offering it."

For a moment it didn't look like Haley wanted to but then finally gave it to him.

"Thanks." He grinned at her. "They're my favorite."

Haley looked surprised. "Mine too. Ever since I was a kid."

When Jeff smiled and their eyes met, Haley's heart beat faster. She quickly turned away and looked up at the angel tree and that's when inspiration struck.

"I got it!" she said, looking back at Jeff. "You know, maybe there's a way I can use this angel tree in my Tyler Toys pitch. The toy campaign I'm working on . . ."

"How so?"

"I'm thinking Tyler Toys could partner with a program

like this and donate some of their toys to children, making their Christmas wishes come true."

"I love that!" Jeff looked impressed. "That could have such a positive impact on so many children."

"Right? That's what I'm thinking, and it would be good for the Tyler Toys brand, too. They're a family-owned company, and they're all about giving back."

Jeff looked really excited. "I think you're onto something here."

"Me too!"

Jeff looked like he was about to hug her but stopped himself. Instead he handed her his candy cane. "Here, take this! If the last candy cane gave you this idea, who knows what this one will do. I don't think you should ever give up sugar again!"

"Maybe you're right." Haley laughed as she took Jeff's candy cane, unwrapped it, and popped it into her mouth.

When Ben appeared, both Jeff and Haley were still laughing.

"There you two are," he said. "We've been looking for you. I should have known I'd find you here at the angel tree. What do you think of our tree, Haley?"

Haley looked at the tree and couldn't stop smiling. "I think it just gave me a brilliant idea for work, so I love it."

Ben chuckled. "Work? That wasn't exactly the reaction I was looking for, but I admire your enthusiasm."

"She really did come up with a great idea, Dad," Jeff said, and then smiled at Haley.

Ben smiled, too. "Okay, then, awesome. I want to hear all about it, but right now we're about to start loading some of the boxes into the trucks for delivery. I was looking for some help."

"You got it," Jeff said.

"I can help, too," Haley joined in.

"That would be great. We still have a few boxes that need finishing; if you want to help Gail with that, she's right over there at the table where you started."

"Sounds good," Haley said. "I'll see you guys later, and thanks, Jeff, for showing me the angel tree."

She was still smiling when she joined Gail.

Gail noticed the change instantly. "Someone looks pretty happy. What happened?"

"I think I just got a great idea for my Christmas toy campaign," Haley said as she put a can of cranberries into a box.

"That's wonderful," Gail said.

Haley smiled and nodded. "It's just an idea at this point, but it's a start. I'll take it."

Gail packed up the last box. "I think this does it. Let's take these over to the guys to load up."

After they delivered the last boxes, Haley and Gail watched the guys set up an assembly line to pack them all in the truck.

"They really know what they're doing," Haley said, impressed. She was watching Jeff load up one of the last boxes when he turned around, saw her, and smiled. She blushed a little and smiled back. When she then realized Gail was watching her with a knowing look on her face, she turned to face her. "What?" she asked.

Gail just smiled. "Nothing. It just looks like you and Jeff are getting along really well. He's a nice young man and he's single."

Haley's mouth dropped open. "It's not like that . . ."

"Why not?" Gail asked. "He's also very good-looking. I'd say he's quite a catch."

Now Haley was really embarrassed. "There is nothing going on between Jeff and me. If anything, he's just making sure I'm doing all these Christmas Camp activities. He thinks he's the Christmas Camp police or something . . ."

"I'm sure he's just trying to make sure everything goes smoothly, knowing how important this is to his dad."

Haley nodded. "I know. I'm just saying, that's all that's going on."

"Well, I think it's a shame," Gail said. "A nice girl like you and a nice guy like him, both of you single . . ."

Haley held up her hands to stop her. "Okay, enough. Now you're starting to sound like my mom. She's always wanting me to find someone and settle down."

"And you don't want to settle down?"

Haley shook her head. "Honestly, what I really want is to get this promotion at work, and once I do, I'll have even less time for . . ."

"A personal life?" Gail asked.

Haley nodded. "Exactly, and on that note, if we're wrapped up here, I really should get back to the inn and start working on this idea I have."

"What about dinner?" Gail asked. "We're on our own tonight, and everyone's getting something in town. I thought maybe we could have dinner together and then do a little last-minute Christmas shopping. I saw this really cute gift shop in town that I wanted to stop by. What do you say?"

"I really don't need to do any Christmas shopping," Haley started, but then seeing the hope in Gail's eyes, she didn't have the heart to disappoint her. "But I guess I do have to eat . . ."

Gail's face lit up. "Wonderful. Let's go."

All of a sudden Haley got an idea. "Okay, but can you wait a minute? I just need to run back inside really quick."

"Sure."

"Great. Thanks. I'll be right back!" Excited, Haley

ran back into the community center and over to the angel tree. She stood on her tiptoes, took one of the angels off the tree, and then ran back to where Gail was waiting.

"Okay, now I'm ready," she said. "Let's go."

As Haley and Gail walked down the beautifully decorated main street, Gail kept stopping to admire all the pretty Christmas decorations. The window of the ice cream store, designed to look like an old-fashioned ice cream parlor, was surrounded by red and white twinkling Christmas lights. Painted on the window was a winter wonderland scene with an adorable Frosty the Snowman. Above Frosty was written CHRIST-MAS SNOWBALL ICE CREAM. Gail grabbed Haley's hand when she saw it.

"Oh, let's go try the snowball ice cream," she said as she pulled Haley inside.

"This is your idea of dinner?" Haley laughed.

"You know what they say, 'Life's short, eat dessert first!'"

"What?" Haley gave her a look. "Who says that?"

"I do!" Gail said. Laughing, she headed straight for the sales clerk and ordered them both two scoops of the snowball ice cream.

A few minutes later, they were back outside, walking down Main Street, eating their snowball ice cream cones.

"Okay, I admit it. This is really good!" Haley said as she licked some ice cream that was dripping onto the cone.

"Told you," Gail said, and touched her ice cream cone to Haley's like she was making a toast. "Merry Christmas!"

"Cheers!"

"Now we better go get some real food to eat. I don't want to corrupt you, too much," Gail said.

"Uh, too late," Haley said. She held up her almost finished ice cream cone. "I've been trying to give up sweets, but obviously that's not going to happen hanging out with you."

Gail pretended to look hurt. "Are you calling me a bad influence?"

"Absolutely!"

Gail smiled back at her. "Well, I want you to know I don't feel a bit guilty. It's Christmas, and it's the one time of year you're allowed to splurge."

"Says who?" Haley asked, already knowing the answer she was going to get.

"Says me." Gail laughed and then pointed to a cute pizzeria. She linked arms with Haley. "How do you feel about a sausage and pepperoni pizza?"

Haley laughed. "Actually, I'm more of a Canadian bacon and pineapple girl. And wait, now you want to get pizza? Are you sure you're not a teenager?"

"This time of year I feel like a teenager," Gail said, beaming. "There's always something about Christmas that makes you feel like a kid again, don't you think?"

Haley shrugged. "I've never really thought about it."

"Well, I say we go get pizza, and look, there's a candy store next door. I bet they have Christmas fudge."

Haley held her hands over her ears. "I'm not listening . . . fa la la la la la, la, la, la, la."

"Well, at least you're singing Christmas songs now."

Haley laughed as they headed into the pizza place. "You're impossible."

"And you're the best for coming out with me tonight," Gail said. "Thank you for being a friend. I really needed this."

Haley was touched. "You're an easy person to hang out with. Even if you are . . ."

"A bad influence?" Gail finished for her.

"A bad influence," Haley agreed.

They both continued laughing as they walked into the restaurant and heard "Deck the Halls," the same song Haley had been humming seconds ago.

"It looks like we found the right place," Gail said with a huge grin on her face.

"Because of the Christmas music?"

"No, because of that . . ." Gail stopped and pointed over to a table where Jeff was sitting with Susie and Ian. "Let's join them."

Haley didn't have time to answer, as Gail was already heading over to the table.

The cozy pizza place was decorated with vintage Christmas decorations. There was a fireplace burning in the corner, and the wood tables were decked out in red-and-white-checkered tablecloths. Susie waved when she saw Gail.

"Gail, Haley, come on over! We just ordered enough pizza for an army."

"Because we couldn't agree on what kind to get," added Ian. "I always like pepperoni—"

"And I love a veggie pizza," Susie jumped in.

Jeff stood up and moved over to another chair, making room for Gail and Haley to sit down together. "And I ordered Canadian bacon and pineapple," he said.

Gail laughed and pointed to Haley. "Well, that's perfect because Haley was just saying that was her favorite. Right, Haley?"

"I was," Haley said, catching Gail's smug look.

Jeff held out the chair next to him. "Then, Haley, you sit over here by me, and we'll share my pizza."

Susie held out the chair next to her for Gail. "And you sit right here, and you can share mine."

"Sounds perfect." Gail smiled at all of them as they sat down. "I'm ready for round two."

"Round two?" Susie asked. "Where did you guys go before this?"

"The ice cream place," Gail said. She licked her lips. "It was wonderful. We tried their new Christmas flavor. What was it called again, Haley?"

"Snowball, and it had these little pieces of peppermint in it. It was pretty amazing."

"So you both had a scoop of ice cream a few minutes ago?" Ian asked incredulously.

"No, of course not," Gail answered.

Ian looked relieved.

"We had two scoops!" Gail laughed. "You always need to have two."

Haley threw up her hands. "Don't look at me. It was all her idea."

Everyone laughed.

"And now I'm ready for pizza," Gail said.

Haley shook her head. "I'm telling you, she's really sixteen." She looked around. "Where are our other favorite teenagers?"

"Blake wanted Mexican," Ian said. "So did I, but . . ."

"But you also wanted to have dinner with your lovely wife," Susie finished for him.

"What she said." Ian laughed, but was shaking his head no.

Everyone laughed, and then all eyes were on the two waiters walking toward them with three giant pizzas.

Haley's eyes grew huge. "Whoa! That's a lot of pizza."

"Told ya! Good thing you two came when you did," Susie said.

When they put the Canadian bacon and pineapple

pizza in front of Jeff, he smiled at Haley. "Are you ready for this?"

Haley's mouth was already watering. She was, all of a sudden, starving.

"So ready!"

Jeff cut the first piece and handed it to her. "Here you go. You're going to love it."

When Haley took a big bite, a string of cheese slid onto her chin. She laughed and reached for her napkin, but Jeff was faster. He leaned over and gently wiped the cheese off for her. Surprised by the gesture, she looked up and their eyes met. For a moment Haley could hear her heart beating, and it was beating fast. This time it was Jeff who looked away first, and when he did, Haley caught Gail watching them and gave her a warning look. But Gail still had that knowing smile on her face when she bit into her first slice of pizza.

After they finished dinner and were leaving the restaurant, Jeff pointed over to his truck. "I'm heading back to the inn now if anyone wants a ride."

He looked at Haley, but she quickly looked at Gail. "We still have some shopping to do, right, Gail?"

Gail nodded and looked very pleased. "We sure do." She linked arms with Haley. "Would anyone else like to go Christmas shopping?"

"I would," Susie said. She was about to join the girls when Ian grabbed her arm. "Oh no, you don't. You promised no more Christmas shopping if I brought you up here."

"But . . ." Susie pleaded.

"Don't even try." Ian laughed and then kissed her on her cheek.

Susie smiled back at him. "Okay, you win. This time."

Ian smiled back at her. "I'll take any win I can get."

Everyone laughed.

"Okay, we better get going," Gail said. "I'm not sure how late the shops stay open."

"Usually until eight during the holidays, so you should have a good hour," Jeff said.

"Power shopping, here we come," Gail said. She laughed as she pulled Haley toward some shops.

Haley looked back over her shoulder at Jeff and mouthed the word "help."

He laughed and mouthed the words "good luck."

CHAPTER 19

As Gail headed down Main Street, she was obviously a woman on a mission. Haley had to hurry to keep up with her, and it didn't take long to see where she was headed.

Gail pointed to an adorable gift shop named Wish Come True and hurried over to it.

"Haley, this is the gift shop I was telling you about. Isn't it a sweet little shop?"

"It certainly has a lot of Christmas decorations," Haley said. There were lit-up Christmas trees on either side of the front door, which was painted a Christmas red and was highlighted by a big beautiful wreath made out of fresh fir-tree branches, holly sprigs, and pinecones.

Haley inhaled deeply as she admired the wreath. "I think this was made using Douglas-fir branches. It has that almost sweet, citrus smell."

Gail looked impressed. "You know your Christmas trees."

Haley laughed. "Only the ones I learned about when I had to cut mine down."

"With Jeff?" Gail smiled. She was giving her that look again.

Haley grabbed her arm. "Let's go see what they have inside."

As soon as they entered the store, Haley smelled cinnamon and they could hear Christmas music playing. As she looked around, she saw they were surrounded by floor-to-ceiling Christmas decorations. "Wow, everyone around here is really into their Christmas decorations," she said.

"Isn't this magical?" Gail did a slow circle, taking everything in. "I know I'm going to find some great gifts here." She grabbed two shopping baskets and gave one to Haley.

"What about you? Do you have anyone left on your list to get Christmas gifts for?"

"Me?" Haley shrugged. "I'm done. I just do gift cards. It's a lot easier and less trouble."

"Really?" Gail seemed surprised. "I love buying Christmas gifts. I mean, don't get me wrong. I won't go out and buy a bunch of things just because it's Christmas. I only buy gifts if they have a special meaning. But I really think there's something special about finding someone the perfect gift. It means you really know who they are and what they might like."

"But what if you don't really know what someone will like?" Haley asked.

"That's really the point, isn't it?" Gail answered. "You should know your friends well enough to know what they like. Plus, it's the thought that counts. I would rather get something small and thoughtful than something that someone just bought and gave me to mark me off their list. A friend once gave me some smoked salmon, which would be a lovely gift if I wasn't allergic to it."

Haley laughed. "You never told her you're allergic?"

"Of course I did, years ago, and several times since, but obviously this is the Christmas gift she gives everyone. So, you see what I mean. If you're going to give a gift, it should be a thoughtful one."

"Not one that makes you break out in hives."

Gail laughed. "Exactly."

"I guess that's why I give gift cards to my parents and friends, because at least I know what stores they like, and then they can go and pick out their own gifts," Haley said. "I've been giving my mom a Starbucks gift card for the last ten years. She goes there every day for her caffeine fix."

Gail nodded. "That's thoughtful, because you know it's something she likes. But I think it's also nice to give an actual gift, something that lasts, that someone can keep for a memory. I know those are the gifts that mean the most to me."

Haley walked over to a table displaying some pretty vintage Christmas music boxes. She picked up the one that had Santa and a little girl on it. When she turned it on, it played "Silent Night." She smiled and looked at Gail. "This is my mom's favorite Christmas song."

"It's beautiful. It's one of my favorite songs, too. It's such a classic."

Haley continued to study the music box. "It's nice, and she really does love anything vintage."

"Do you think she'd like it better than her Starbucks gift card?" Gail asked in a teasing voice.

Haley laughed and put the music box down. "Probably, but then you don't know my mom and her caffeine. That's a love you don't want to mess with." After they shared a laugh, she looked back at the music box and picked it up again. "But I do think she would like this, don't you?"

Gail nodded. "I think she'd love the fact that you were thinking of her when you saw it and bought it for her, and every Christmas she could put it out and remember that."

Haley smiled, thinking about Gail's words. "Okay, you've convinced me. I'm getting it. Are you sure you don't work here? You're a really good saleswoman. Now, besides wrecking my diet, you're a bad influence on my bank account."

Gail laughed. "It's only money. Let's go spend some more." She pointed at a table of snow globes. "Look at those little treasures."

"Wait!" Haley suddenly remembered the angel she had taken from the angel tree at the community center. She took it out of her pocket and showed it to Gail. "Because you're the expert shopper, can you help me with this?"

"Sure, what do you have there?" Gail looked with curiosity at the angel Haley was holding.

"One of the angels from the tree at the community center," Haley said. She turned the angel over to read the writing on it. "It says, 'This Christmas wish is for a little five-year-old girl named Anna who says she wants a baby doll.'"

Gail touched her heart. "That's so sweet. Every little girl should have a baby doll. I see a toy section over in the corner. Let's go see what they have."

As they headed to the corner of the little store, Gail had to stop several times to admire different Christmas decorations, including a table of Christmas candles. She made sure Haley smelled every scent they had from holly berry to pine tree and gingerbread to cinnamon stick. When she couldn't decide which candles she liked best, she gave up and decided to get one of each.

By the time they finally made it over to the toys, Gail's shopping basket was overflowing. "I think I need another basket." She laughed. "This one is getting pretty heavy with all these candles."

Haley quickly took the shopping basket from her. "I got it."

"No, it's okay. I'm fine." Gail tried to grab the basket back, but Haley wouldn't let her.

Haley smiled at her. "It's not a problem. Besides, I need your help picking out this baby doll. I don't have a clue. So, pick one out that you think five-year-old Anna would like."

They both stood in front of a long line of toys, taking it all in. They weren't your usual run-of-the-mill toys. All of them were thoughtfully curated and displayed in different Christmas themes. On the top shelf, there were cute stuffed animals, mostly reindeers and Santas and even a Grinch. Haley laughed and pointed it out to Gail.

"If my best friend Kathy could see this, she would get it for me for sure."

"The Grinch?" Gail asked surprised. "You like the Grinch?"

"No, it's more like she calls me the Grinch. Actually, probably everyone at work calls me that." Haley picked up the Grinch and looked into his eyes. "It's my nickname because I don't really celebrate Christmas."

"When you say you don't celebrate—"

"I mean I go to the Caribbean every year and take my parents so I can avoid all the usual Christmas chaos. I work with a client we have there, and my parents relax. We all love it, but it's certainly not your traditional Christmas."

"So, you're not a Grinch. You don't hate Christmas." Gail took the Grinch from her, put it back on the shelf, and took down a stuffed Santa. She gave it to Haley. "I think this reminds me more of who you are."

Haley laughed loudly. "Santa? What?" She looked at the Santa and gave it back to Gail. "I think sniffing all those candles has gone to your head."

Gail laughed and hugged the Santa. "No, I'm serious. Look at you. You're here right now in the toy section of this store because you're making a little girl's Christmas wish come true." She handed Haley the Santa. "So, I'd say that definitely makes you closer to a Santa than a Grinch."

Haley stared at the Santa. "I don't even know what to say."

"I do." Gail took the Santa back from Haley and put it in her basket. "Merry Christmas; my gift to you so that you'll always remember this time."

Haley laughed. "No, Gail, really, you don't need to do this." She took the Santa out of Gail's basket and put it back on the shelf. "Really, I don't need the Santa."

Gail grabbed the Santa again. "Everyone needs a Santa."

Haley couldn't help but laugh.

Gail put the Santa in her basket and held it away from Haley so Haley couldn't take it out again. "I told you when you find the perfect gift for someone, you really need to get it. This Santa will always remind you of who you really are. Who you really can be . . ."

Haley gave up. "Okay, if that's what you want to do . . ."

"It is. Now, let's find that baby doll for Anna." She walked over to a glass shelf where a bunch of adorable dolls were lined up. One in particular caught her attention. "Look at this one. She's really sweet."

When Haley got closer, she couldn't believe it. Gail was holding a Tyler Toys doll. The exact same doll she herself had in her office back at work, the same one she'd lost the staring contest to.

"Wait, I know that doll!" Haley said. "It's a Tyler Toys doll."

"It is," Gail agreed. "It must be this year's Christmas doll." She admired the doll's cute red velvet dress. "When I was growing up, this was the one thing I always asked Santa for. I've saved a lot of my dolls in case I have a granddaughter. The Tyler Toys dolls always bring back so many good memories. Do you know them? Did you have any growing up?"

Haley laughed. "Oh, I know them all right. You know that Christmas toy campaign I was telling you about that I'm working on? It's for Tyler Toys, the company that makes these dolls."

Gail looked impressed. "They're one of the largest toy companies in America."

"I know, and that's why getting this account is so important to me."

"Because of the Christmas tradition and all that Tyler Toys stands for?" Gail asked.

"No, because they're a huge company, and they would be one of our biggest accounts, a real moneymaker for us," Haley said. "If I can get the account, then I get my promotion."

"Oh, I see." Gail looked a little disappointed as she went to put the doll back on the shelf.

"Wait." Haley stopped her. "Do you think Anna would like this doll?"

Gail's smile was back. "I do. I think any little girl would love to get this doll. I know how much I loved my first doll."

"Well, that's good enough for me." Haley put the doll

in her basket. "My basket is getting pretty full. Is there anything else you want to check out?"

Gail looked around, and when she spotted some crystal snowflake ornaments hanging in the window, she gave Haley a hopeful look.

Haley laughed. "Okay, we can look at the ornaments, but that's it. We're running out of room."

Gail was already making a beeline for them. "Don't worry, they're small!"

Haley laughed as she followed her.

Ten minutes and a dozen crystal snowflake ornaments later, they were finally at the register when this time it was Haley who spotted something across the store. It was a table of exquisitely painted ceramic Santa figurines.

"I'll be right back," she said, and hurried over to the Santas. There was one in particular that had caught her eye. He stood about seven inches tall and had the look of an old-world Santa. He had a long gray beard and bushy eyebrows that framed gentle-looking eyes. He was wearing an emerald-green cloak with gold stars, and he was holding a miniature Christmas tree that reminded Haley of her own little tree. When she picked up the Santa, she saw it was signed and dated by the artist. She smiled and walked back over to the register with it and told the cashier, "I'll take this, too."

CHAPTER 20

By the time Haley and Gail were done with their shopping and back at the inn, a light snow was just starting to fall. As they passed the life-size elf by the front door Gail patted him on the top of his head.

"Hello, little guy, looks like some snow is coming."

Haley gave her a look. "Why is everyone always talking to that elf?"

Gail turned to her and smiled. "I think the question you should be asking is why aren't you talking to him? It's Christmas Camp, and he's part of it. Where's your Christmas spirit?"

Haley laughed. "I'm working on it." She wasn't about to admit that she, too, had been talking to the smiling elf, but she didn't think in her case it had anything to do with having Christmas spirit.

Just as they were heading inside, Jeff appeared and held the door open for them. He hurried to help when he saw all their shopping bags. "Looks like you girls have been busy."

"Oh, you have no idea," Haley said. She pointed at Gail. "This one here is quite the little shopper."

"And proud of it," Gail said. "And if I remember right, you found a few things, too."

Haley nodded. "I did. She's a bad influence on me."

"Like eating ice cream for dinner?" Jeff asked.

"Exactly." Haley smiled back at him.

Once they were inside, Gail held out her hands. "I can take those now."

Jeff felt the weight of them. "Are you sure? I can take them up to your room."

Gail gave him a grateful look. "Thank you, but I'm good. That's one of the rules of Christmas shopping. I can only buy as much as I can carry."

"Or as much as your shopping partner can carry," Haley added.

"We really did make a great team, didn't we, Haley?" Gail asked. She looked tired but happy.

Haley nodded. "We sure did."

Gail gave her a quick hug. "I'm going to head upstairs and call it a night. Oh, and Haley, I know Anna's going to love that doll. Have a good night, you two. Thank you for everything."

After Gail left, Jeff gave Haley a questioning look. "So, you bought a doll?"

Haley pulled the Tyler Toys doll out of the bag and showed it to him. "I did, and this isn't just any doll, this is a Tyler Toys doll."

"Okay." Jeff still looked confused.

"And this is Anna." Haley dug around in her pocket and found the angel she had taken from the angel tree.

Now Jeff looked really surprised. "From the community center?"

Haley nodded.

He looked into her eyes and smiled. "That's really nice of you. You're making a child's Christmas wish come true."

Embarrassed by the way he was looking at her, Haley quickly put the doll back in her bag. "The doll is made by the company I'm trying to win over as a client, the big Christmas toy campaign I've been trying to work on." The way he was studying her made her squirm a little. She felt he could see right through her.

"So, you're saying you bought that doll for Anna as part of your research for work."

"That's right," Haley said, trying to sound like she meant it.

"Really?" He smiled at her. It was obvious he didn't believe her.

Haley didn't blink. "Really."

"Well, that's good to hear, because I have some more research for you."

Haley kept a smile on her face as she mentally prepared herself for the trap she'd just laid for herself. "What kind of research?"

Jeff held out his hand. "Come on, I'll show you."

Haley looked into his eyes and saw that familiar challenge. "Okay, but this better be good." As she put her hand in his, she hoped this wouldn't be something she'd regret. When Jeff opened the front door, she gave him a surprised look. "We're leaving right now?"

"Don't worry." He held the door open for her. "We're not going far."

As she followed him outside, she quickly saw he wasn't kidding about not going far. He stopped about twenty feet from the door. Only then did she realize he was still holding her hand. Slowly withdrawing it, she felt instantly cold as the warmth she had felt from his touch was gone.

Jeff looked up at the sky. The snow was coming down faster. Haley followed his gaze, and within seconds, she was wiping snowflakes off her cheeks. When he leaned over and brushed some snowflakes off her face, she could only stare back at him. "It's really starting to come down," he said softly. Haley, not trusting herself to speak, just nodded.

Jeff turned his smiling face up to the sky. "I love it when it's like this. When the snow starts falling, and everything gets quiet . . ."

Haley wasn't looking up anymore. Instead she was watching Jeff enjoy the snow. She held out her hands and watched some snowflakes swirl around in the wind before disappearing when they touched her skin. Then she rubbed her hands together to warm them up.

Jeff noticed and frowned. "We need gloves. Don't go anywhere, I'll be right back."

Haley laughed as he ran back into the house, and she glanced over at the elf by the door. "Like where would I go?"

Seconds later Jeff was back, tossed her a pair of gloves, and put on his own as well. "You're going to need these."

Haley put them on. "So, when are you planning to tell me what we're doing? You said this was something that would help me with work. How can standing out here in the snow help me?"

Jeff laughed a little. "I'm not going to tell you how it will help you, I'm going to show you." And with that, he put both arms up into the air, spread his legs out wide, and then fell backward into the snow.

Haley's hands flew to her mouth. "What are you doing? You're crazy."

Jeff was laughing as he moved his arms and legs back

and forth, making a perfect snow angel. "Come on. Your turn."

Haley shook her head, laughing. "You're crazy!"

"Come on . . ."

Haley looked at him, her hands on her hips. "This is not on the Christmas Camp activities list."

Jeff continued to move his arms and legs. "No, but I bet it will help you with work."

She tilted her head as she looked at him. "How?"

"Think about it. You're trying to come up with a Christmas toy campaign, right?"

"Right . . ."

"So, if you're trying to come up with ideas for a toy company, you need to think like a kid, right?"

Haley nodded. "Yes, but even when I was a kid, I didn't like making snow angels. I always got a lot of snow inside my coat, and it wasn't a good experience."

Jeff laughed. "Sounds like you need to replace that memory with a better one. Come on, Haley, what are you afraid of?"

"Besides making a fool of myself or breaking something when I try to do this?"

Jeff sat up but was careful not to mess up his angel outline. "It's snow. It's soft, and no one is watching. You just need to let go and fall back. Have some faith."

"Ha! Easy for you to say! You obviously do this all the time."

Jeff laughed. "I actually don't, but that's not the point. I'm just saying, try. Trust me. You'll love it. I thought you were the kind of girl who was up for anything? You're not afraid of making a little snow angel, are you?"

Haley's mouth dropped open. There he was again with his challenge, and here she was falling for it. Again. But she couldn't help herself. "Fine." She threw up her hands. "I'll try it. But I swear if I get snow down my back again . . ."

"It's just snow." Jeff laughed. "Come on, let's go. Just hold out your arms and fall back into the snow. You're making it way harder than it is. Remember research. You're doing this for work. How much do you really want this toy account?"

That did the trick. With a look of pure determination, Haley planted her feet shoulder-width apart then raised both arms to the sky. She shut her eyes then opened them and quickly looked behind her to see where she was about to fall.

"You got this," Jeff said. "Just fall."

Haley squeezed her eyes shut.

"I'll count you down," Jeff said. "One, two . . ."

But before he could say "three," Haley had already let herself fall back. She didn't open her eyes until she'd landed perfectly in the snow. "I did it." She laughed. She looked over at Jeff, and they were so close, their fingers could almost touch.

"You did!" He smiled back at her. "Now make the angel."

Haley watched as he started moving his arms and legs again, and she did the same thing. She couldn't stop laughing. "I don't know what's wrong with me," she said.

"It's called having fun," Jeff said. "Maybe you forgot how?"

She laughed again. "Maybe, but not anymore. I wish Larry, my boss, could see me now, or my friend Kathy, or anyone, because no one would believe I'm doing this."

"So, how does it feel?"

"Besides wet and cold?" Haley asked. Then she smiled. "Actually, it feels pretty good." She moved her arms and legs as she looked up to the sky. The snow was coming down faster, so it was getting harder to see. When she tried to wipe some snowflakes out of her eyes, she just got more snow in her face from her gloves. She sputtered when some snow got in her mouth, and laughed.

"Are you getting cold? Are you ready to go in?"

Haley nodded. "I think I'm ready. But wait, how do I get up and not wreck my angel?"

"Hold on. I'll help you." Jeff carefully sat up and held out both hands to her. "Just sit up and take my hands, and keep your feet where they are. I'll pull you up."

Haley looked embarrassed. "No, it's okay. I can do it." But when she tried to get up, she started to slip backward.

Without saying a word, Jeff just walked over, stood in front of her, and held out both hands.

Silently, she took them, and when he pulled her up, she was standing so close to him that she could feel his breath on her cheek. When their eyes met, the spark was there, stronger than ever. Haley held her breath, because it looked like he was about to kiss her. She didn't move. She didn't want to move. She must have closed her eyes, because when she opened them, Jeff had stepped back and was brushing some snow off himself, not looking at her. She was so confused. She'd wanted him to kiss her, and she'd thought he'd wanted to kiss her, too. Her mind was whirling like the snow.

"Let's get inside," he said, snapping her back to reality. He was already heading for the door.

As she hurried to follow him, she looked back at their angels. They were perfect. They were so close together their wings were almost touching.

As soon as they stepped inside, Haley saw Laura waiting for them with her tray of hot chocolate. "I saw you outside making snow angels. I thought you might need to warm up a little."

Jeff took one of the Santa mugs and handed it to Haley. "Laura, you read our minds. Thank you so much."

"Thank you," Haley said. She enjoyed a long, satisfying sip.

"This is another tradition we have," Jeff said. "Having hot chocolate after making snow angels."

"Is he making this up?" Haley asked Laura.

Laura shook her head and smiled back at her. "No, it's true. Snow angels and hot chocolate always go together."

"See," Jeff said as he held up his Santa mug for a toast. "Cheers to snow angels."

When Haley looked into his eyes, she saw something that had her wondering if he was talking about the snow angels they had just made or if he was calling her a snow angel. "Cheers," she said as she clinked her Santa mug to his.

AFTER SHE TOOK a long hot bath, Haley snuggled up in her robe and walked to her bedroom window. The snow was still coming down fast, making it hard to see. So she got closer and pressed her nose against the cold glass. She wanted to see if the snow angels were still there, but all she could make out was a faint outline. Disappointed, she turned back, picked up her laptop, and got comfortable in bed. She was ready to work but was having a hard time concentrating.

Her mind kept going back to making the snow angels with Jeff and that moment when it seemed like he was about to kiss her. Remembering, she picked up the angel pillow and hugged it to her heart. She didn't know how she should feel about it. Relieved that it hadn't happened? Disappointed that it hadn't happened? She was getting more confused by the second.

"Stop it!" she scolded herself out loud. "You need to focus on work!"

With a look of determination, she brought up her work emails and started catching up on them. She was making some progress until she read an email from Kathy, who had some updated intel on Tom's Tyler Toys campaign and how much Larry was loving what he was seeing. That email was followed by one from Larry checking in on her, asking how she was enjoying Christmas Camp and saying how he was looking forward to seeing her pitch for Tyler Toys in a few days, and that he was expecting great things.

"Great things?" She groaned. "Great things? All I have are a few ideas, and I don't even know what to do with them." She took a deep breath. She knew she'd never be able to come up with anything creative if she was in panic mode. Forcing herself to feel more positive, she sat up straighter and started writing down a few words.

Wishing Tree / Angels / Presents for Kids / Snow Angels???

She stared at the screen for several more seconds, but when nothing came to her, she dropped her head into her hands and rubbed her throbbing temples. She was a bundle of nerves and stress, and she couldn't sit still any longer. She jumped out of bed and started pacing around the room.

"Okay, so far I have an angel tree, angels, dolls, toys, more angels, what else? What else do I have?" She looked around the room and locked eyes with the angel in the picture above the dresser. She hurried over, yanked open the top drawer, and saw all the angels she had hidden away. She took one out and smoothed her wrinkled dress.

"Maybe I shouldn't have hidden you all away," she said to the angel. "Maybe that was bad Christmas karma or something. So, I'm officially saying I'm sorry." She started putting all the angels back where she had found them. She knew she was being a little crazy, but so far nothing else had worked, and at this point she was willing to try anything and everything. When she was finally done, she stood back and surveyed her work. All the angels were staring back at her. Only this time they didn't freak her out. This time they actually gave her some hope.

She then walked over to the stack of Christmas books next to her bed. She hadn't touched any of them yet—she hadn't had the time, but she quickly found the one she was looking for, *An Angel's Christmas*, the one Jeff had given to her. She opened it up to the first page and started reading.

"Okay, angels, let's see what you got. Bring on the inspiration."

CHAPTER 21

A brilliant sunrise cast a warm golden glow across the entire mountainside and Holly Peak Inn. It looked like the start of a picture-perfect day.

Haley was in bed sleeping peacefully when all of a sudden she heard a bark. She turned over and tried to go back to sleep, but there was another bark. This time she knew exactly what was happening, covered her head with her pillow, and whispered, "Please go away, please go away . . ." but when she heard Max bark again, even louder this time, she threw off her covers and sat up. "Seriously, Max?"

For an answer, Max barked twice.

As she climbed out of bed, she looked over at the angels on her dresser. "Okay, angels, to be clear, this was not the kind of inspiration I was looking for."

A FEW MINUTES LATER, as Max walked Haley around the inn, it was clear who was in charge. And it wasn't Haley. She practically had to run to keep up with Max, who was having way too much fun in all the fresh snow. As they rounded a corner, she saw Susie and Ian walking her way.

"Good morning!" Susie called out, and waved cheerfully.

"Good morning," Haley answered as she joined them.

"Looks like Max has found a friend," Ian said, bending down to pet Max.

"I don't know about that." Haley laughed. "But for some reason, he thinks I'm the one that's supposed to walk him in the morning."

"So, he's basically training you?" Ian asked.

Haley laughed. "Apparently."

"Have you been in the kitchen to see the word of the day yet?" Susie asked, looking excited. "'Sharing.' We think it has something to do with cooking, because we saw Laura getting out all kinds of things in the kitchen."

Haley's smile faded. "Oh, I hope not. My cooking skills are limited to using a microwave. I better go find out what's going on. I'll see you guys inside." Max had already taken off for the kitchen, dragging Haley behind him.

As soon as they entered the kitchen, Haley saw Laura taking a fresh batch of cookies out of the oven. She inhaled deeply. "I knew I smelled cookies! Susie said the word for the day is 'sharing,' so I hope you'll be sharing those cookies with us."

"I'll go one better than that," Laura said. "I plan to teach you how to make these cookies for yourself."

Haley's smile faded a bit.

"It's our first Christmas Camp activity today. Do you want to be first up?" Laura asked.

Haley took a deep breath. "Sure, if it means I get to mark something else off our list. But I'm warning you, I don't cook."

"Good to know," Laura said.

Haley looked relieved.

"Because we're not cooking, we're *baking* . . ."

Haley's smile was now gone.

"And here, you're going to need this," Laura said. She tossed Haley a red apron that said CHRISTMAS CAMP on the front.

Haley laughed as she slipped the apron over her head and struggled with the strings, trying to figure out how to put it on correctly. "We're going to need a Christmas miracle if you're expecting me to make anything edible. I burn toast. I'm just saying."

"I have complete faith in you, Haley."

"I'm glad someone does." Haley looked down at her apron and realized she'd put it on backward. "See!" She pointed at her apron. "This is what I'm talking about."

Laura laughed as she walked over to help her. "Well, lucky for you I'm pretty good at all of this, including getting an apron on right." She took off Haley's apron and put it back on correctly, tying the ties for her. "See, now you're all set. Are you ready?"

Haley gave her a teasing look. "The question is, are *you* ready for Hurricane Haley?"

Laura laughed loudly. "Hurricane Haley?"

"Yeah, just something my mom called me once when I was little and tried to make a milk shake and forgot to put the lid on the blender . . ."

Laura laughed. "Okay, we'll keep you far away from the blender."

AN HOUR LATER, covered in flour, Haley was proudly taking her own batch of sugar cookies out of the oven. She was grinning from ear to ear because they looked perfect.

"I can't believe I did it!" she said. "Finally, a batch I didn't burn!"

Laura clapped her hands. "I told you you could do it! How does it feel?"

"Actually, pretty good! I have to admit this was a lot more fun than I thought it would be, but that's only because I had your help. But the real test is how do they taste?"

"Let's try one," Laura said. "Just be careful; they're still really hot, but that's when I like them the best." She got a spatula out, carefully scooped up one of Haley's cookies, put it on a little reindeer Christmas napkin, and handed it to her.

Haley tested the cookie's temperature with her finger. "It doesn't seem too hot."

"Then let's try it." Laura scooped up another cookie for herself.

They both took a careful bite at the same time. Haley's face lit up. She was getting more excited as she chewed. "These are really good!"

Laura nodded her agreement. "You did an excellent job!"

"I'll be the judge of that . . ."

Both of them turned to see Jeff walk into the room. He was sniffing, and his eyes went straight to Haley's cookies. He looked impressed and surprised. "You made these, Haley?"

"She sure did!" Laura said proudly.

"With a lot of help," Haley added quickly.

"May I try one?" Jeff asked.

"Of course," Laura said. "Let us know what you think."

Jeff took his time taking a bite and tasting the cookie. He looked at Haley then back at Laura.

"Well?" Haley asked, anxious to get his feedback. "Do they pass the Christmas Camp test?"

When he frowned, her smile disappeared. "What's wrong? I just tried one. I thought it was good . . ."

"You know, I'm not sure," Jeff said. "I better try another one so I can figure it out."

When he went to grab another cookie, Laura swatted his hand away. "Nice try." She looked over at Haley. "You have to watch this one. He has all kinds of tricks up his sleeve when it comes to getting more cookies."

Haley, hands on her hips, looked at Jeff. "I can see that."

Jeff shrugged and gave her an innocent look. "Did Laura tell you the secret behind our secret Christmas Camp cookies?"

Haley looked from Jeff to Laura. "No . . ."

"Jeff, you go ahead and tell her. It's your family secret," Laura told him.

"Okay," he said. Even though he had a very serious look on his face, his eyes were smiling. "You already know that the recipe for our Christmas Camp sugar cookies has been in our family for generations."

Haley nodded, eager to hear more.

"It's a secret recipe. So, the rule is that anyone we share the recipe with, like our Christmas Camp guests, has to agree that they will only share it with people they love, keeping our Christmas tradition alive. So, can you do that?"

"I can." Haley laughed a little, even though Jeff was still looking very serious. "And since I never bake, your secret recipe is very safe with me, trust me." She started taking off her apron. "This was a really cool activity, Laura, thank you for having so much patience with me." When she tried to hand her the apron, Laura just smiled and shook her head.

"Oh, you don't think you're done yet, do you?" she asked.

Haley looked confused. "I made the cookies . . ."

"But now you need to decorate them," Laura said as she picked up one of the cookies. "We can't leave them like this." She pointed at Haley's apron. "And I think you're going to want to put that back on. I've set up a lot of decorating supplies in the dining room. Follow me."

"Decorating supplies?" Haley looked curious as she followed Laura into the dining room. When she saw everything, her jaw dropped. Laura wasn't kidding. The entire dining room table was covered with bowls of colored frosting. There were also small glass containers filled with red, green, silver, and gold sprinkles, and a large muffin tin where each cup was filled with a different kind of candy. There were M&M's, Red Hots, gumdrops, Froot Loops, red and green minimints, Hershey's Kisses, and dark, white, and milk chocolate shavings and sprinkles. There was also a big bowl of tiny marshmallows and one filled with tiny crushed pieces of candy canes, and a pile of even more candy canes on the table.

When Jeff took some M&M's, Laura playfully swatted away his hand. "Hey, you know the rules, no eating the decorations."

"Unless you're doing the decorating," Jeff finished for her, grinning like a little kid.

"Exactly." Laura smiled back at him. "So, that means you can help Haley decorate her cookies."

"Wait, what?" both Haley and Jeff said at the same time, and then laughed.

Haley looked embarrassed. "I'm sorry, I just meant, I'm sure Jeff has more important things to do than help me decorate cookies."

But Jeff was already sitting down. This time he was

popping marshmallows into his mouth. "Actually, I don't. And if I may say so myself, I'm a pretty good decorator."

Haley sat down next to him. "Really?" she asked in an unbelieving voice. "Does that come with your restoration work?"

"It does." He grabbed some gumdrops and popped them into his mouth. "I have a great eye for detail."

"Oh, really?" Haley locked eyes with him.

"Really," he said, his mouth full of gumdrops.

Haley couldn't help but laugh.

"Okay, you two, time to get serious. We have a lot of cookies to decorate," Laura said. "I'm going to get the cookies so you two can get started, and Haley, keep an eye on this one for me and make sure he doesn't eat all the decorations."

Jeff popped another gumdrop into his mouth and grinned at Haley.

Haley fought back a laugh. "I think you're giving me an impossible job, Laura."

As Laura exited the dining room, Jeff was already reaching for more marshmallows. Haley swatted his hand away. "You heard Laura: more decorating, less eating of the decorations."

Laura reappeared just in time with a big tray of cookies. She had brought the round sugar cookies Haley had just made as well as some of her own specialties—sugar cookies in the shape of Christmas trees, stockings, and stars. "This should keep you two busy," she said as she put the tray down.

Haley's eyes grew huge. "We don't have to decorate all of those, do we?"

Laura laughed. "Don't worry. I'm going to round up some of the rest of the crew to help you while they're taking turns baking their own cookies."

Haley let out a sigh of relief.

"I can't wait to see what you two come up with," Laura said as she was leaving the room.

Once she was gone, Haley turned to Jeff. "Is this really one of our activities?"

He nodded.

Her eyes narrowed. "Now what are you eating?"

Jeff just shrugged innocently and continued chewing as he handed her a bowl of frosting.

CHAPTER 22

Jeff picked up one of the stars and handed it to Haley. "You heard Laura. She's expecting great things from us."

Haley laughed and handed the star back to him. As she watched him she realized it was happening again. She was having fun. Not wanting to think too much about what that meant, she picked up one of the round sugar cookies. "Well, if you're wanting to see great things, then I better start with basics. Now, if I remember right, with these Christmas Camp cookies, all I need to do is add some white frosting and some of those candy-cane pieces, right?"

"So, you *have* been paying attention," Jeff teased. "You're right, but it's not just any frosting. You haven't tried one yet. One that's been decorated?"

Haley sighed. "I swear, between you and Gail, I might as well just forget about cutting back on sugar. I've been trying to be good."

Jeff frowned. "But being good is so bad, especially at Christmas. Here, let me show you." Taking the round sugar cookie from her, he grabbed a knife and dipped it into a bowl of creamy frosting. "One of the secrets is we always use cream-cheese frosting, not just ordinary white frosting for our Christmas Camp cookies."

"Why is that?"

"Because cream-cheese frosting was my grandpa John's favorite. He loved carrot cake, mainly because of the cream-cheese frosting so he didn't see any reason why we shouldn't also put the same frosting on our Christmas cookies, and he was right! Wait until you try it."

Haley held out her hand for the cookie.

Jeff laughed. "Not yet! We haven't even put the other secret ingredient on."

"Seriously?" Haley threw up her hands and fought to keep from laughing. "How many secret ingredients do you have in these things?"

"Uh, that would be a secret."

This time Haley didn't even try to hide her laugh. "Okay, so show me."

"The trick is to not be stingy with the candy-cane pieces." He picked up the container of crushed candy-cane pieces. "The more you can fit on the cookie the better, just don't pile them on top of each other. You need to spread them out, just like this." When he held up his cookie, Haley could see that almost every inch was covered with the cream-cheese frosting and the candy-cane pieces, without one candy-cane piece overlapping.

"Nicely done," she said.

"Thank you." Jeff puffed up his chest, joking around. "I'm sorta the superhero of Christmas cookies."

"Wait, wait. Is that even a thing?" Haley laughed.

Jeff started laughing, too. "I don't know. I just made it up. But it could be. It should be. Anyway, now you can try the cookie. See what you think." He held out his perfectly decorated cookie for her.

Determined to look at the cookie and not into his eyes, Haley inched closer, took a small bite, and shut her eyes, enjoying the way the peppermint flavor added to the taste of the rich cream-cheese frosting. She smiled a slow, satisfied smile.

Jeff was watching her closely. "So, you like it?"

Haley gave him a look. "Does anyone *not* like these? They're amazing. Wow!" She took another bite and looked like she was in heaven.

Jeff seemed pleased with her response. "Everyone loves them, so I'm glad you do, too. We have a reputation to uphold and all."

Haley laughed. "Of course you do, but I don't think your secret Christmas Camp cookies have much competition. I've never tasted anything as good. But now we have a big problem."

"What?" Jeff asked, looking concerned.

"My sugar addiction is officially back, so you better hide these. Otherwise, I can't take responsibility for my actions."

Jeff laughed. "I'll warn Laura."

"You better," Haley said as she took another bite.

Jeff smiled, watching her. "You know I can still remember the first time I decorated cookies with my mom. I was probably around six or seven. She put out all these same bowls on this same table, just like we have here, and she let me do whatever I wanted. There weren't any rules or any wrong ways, she just told me to decorate from my heart." When he picked up a bowl of frosting, he smiled, remembering. "So, I ended up with this cookie that was piled so high with frosting you couldn't even eat it."

"Because . . . ?" Haley asked.

"Because I *really* loved frosting." Jeff laughed. "So, once I got as much frosting as I could onto the cookie, I was so proud, and I gave it to my mom to try."

Haley covered her mouth with her hand. "Oh no."

"Oh yes, and you know what? She took the cookie from me like it was the best cookie she had ever seen, and then somehow she managed to take a bite and told me she loved it. I still remember how excited and proud I was."

"Sounds like she was a wonderful mom."

"She really was . . ." As Jeff's voice trailed off, Haley could see the sadness in his eyes. So she picked up a cookie, put a huge mound of frosting on it, and handed it to him. "Your turn."

Jeff, his eyes still sad, looked confused when he saw all the frosting. "What do you want me to do?"

Haley handed him the bowl of frosting and the knife. "You know what to do."

Jeff finally got it and added even more frosting to the cookie until it had so much frosting it was about to break. "Yup, this looks like how I remember it. Now what?"

"Uh, take a bite."

Jeff shook his head. "No way. I'll be in a sugar coma for a month."

"But I thought Christmas Camp was all about traditions. This is your tradition, so go for it. Come on. What happened to your Christmas spirit?"

Jeff laughed. "Okay, here it goes." When he took a big bite and got frosting all over his face, Haley couldn't stop laughing.

When he passed the crazy-frosting cookie to her, she quickly shook her head and backed away. "Oh no, this is your family tradition not mine. This is all yours, frosting boy. You leave me out of it."

"Really? You're going to leave me hanging?" He gave her a mock-serious look. "My mom tried it when I made it."

"Oh no, you did not just bring your mom into this. Have you no shame?

"Fine." Haley made a face, took a big bite, and got more frosting than she did cookie, with most of the frosting covering her nose. "Eww!" she exclaimed. The more she tried to wipe it off, the more frosting she got all over her face.

Laughing, Jeff grabbed a napkin. "Hold still, let me get it."

"It's going up my nose."

This just made Jeff laugh harder. "Come on, I'm trying to help you. Just sit still . . ."

Finally, Haley stopped wiggling around and let Jeff help her. In a few seconds, he had gotten most of the frosting off her face. "You know you're supposed to eat it, not inhale it."

"Funny," Haley said. She was still rubbing her hand over her nose, making sure all the frosting was gone.

Jeff took her hand. "You're good. You look great."

For a second Haley's heart stopped as Jeff held her hand and looked into her eyes. The look was back, she thought. It looked like he wanted to kiss her. Not wanting to risk disappointment a second time, she pulled away and stood up. Flustered, she struggled for something to say and quickly picked up a container of gold sprinkles. "We're almost out of these."

"We are?" Jeff looked confused. The container was almost full.

"Well, I mean we're going to be, because gold sprinkles are my favorite, so I'm going to get some more. I saw some in the pantry earlier. So that's where I'm going. To the pantry . . ." Haley knew she was babbling but couldn't shut up, so she rushed off to the kitchen. When she got into the pantry, she shut the door behind her and put both hands up against her racing heart. *Breathe,* she told herself. *Just breathe.* She wasn't sure what was going on. Maybe it was just all in her head, and Jeff didn't feel the same things she was feeling, but she knew whatever it was, she had to pull herself together. She only had a few days left at Christmas Camp. She was so close to getting everything she ever wanted. Right now what she needed was sprinkles. She just needed to find the sprinkles. She knew she had seen them earlier when she was making the cookies.

So she retraced her steps and found the flour and sugar and that's when she spotted something else for the first time. A box wrapped like a Christmas present was on the bottom shelf. It looked familiar. She pulled it out to get a closer look. Her eyes widened when she realized it was the same box Ben had put all their computers and cell phones in. She opened it up, and sure enough, it was filled with all their electronics.

Excited, she dug through the box looking for her computer and phone. This was exactly what she needed to get back on track. Work had always calmed and centered her, and she knew she'd feel a lot better and a lot more in control if she could just quickly check her email and make sure there weren't any fires she needed to put out.

But when she turned on her phone, saw she had six missed text messages, and the last one from Kathy said *911* and to call back immediately, she panicked. It was only ten in the morning. She couldn't wait all day to call Kathy back. They only used the *911* text when it was a real emergency. So she peeked outside the pantry to make sure the coast was clear and was about to call Kathy when she heard someone enter the kitchen.

"Oh no," she whispered as she stuffed her phone into her apron and rushed to put the box back. She took a deep breath and hurried out of the pantry, fully expecting to see Laura, but instead found Max. He was sitting in her path, staring at her like he knew what she had done. She pointed a finger at him and then to her lips. "Shhhhhh."

"Hey, did you get lost in there? Do you need some help?" Jeff's voice called out from the dining room.

"Coming!" Haley fought to compose herself and walked into the dining room smiling.

"Everything okay?" Jeff asked.

Paranoid, she overcompensated by laughing. "Everything's great."

"So where are the sprinkles?"

Haley looked down at her empty hands but refused to panic. "You know I couldn't find them, but I just remembered I told Gail that I would bring her some . . ." She desperately looked around for something, anything, that could help with her lie. Her eyes landed on a plate of cookies. ". . . Cookies. I told her I'd bring her some cookies. So, I'm gonna go and do that, and I'll see you later."

"But we haven't even started decorating yet," Jeff called out after her.

Haley didn't answer and just picked up her pace. By the time she got to her room, she was already calling Kathy on FaceTime. Kathy picked up almost immediately. She looked stressed out.

"Finally," she said. "I've been trying to call you all morning."

Haley looked into the phone, equally stressed. "I'm

sorry. I know. But they take away our phones in the morning. So, what's going on? I only have a few minutes. I stole my phone, and I can't get caught."

"So you haven't checked your emails this morning either? You didn't get Larry's email?" Kathy asked.

Haley started pacing around her room. "No. I haven't gotten anything, yet. So, what's going on? Just tell me."

"The Tyler Toys pitch just got moved up. You have to pitch the day you come back to work."

"What? That's impossible. I'll never be ready."

"It has something to do with the Tyler Toys execs. I don't know the whole story but knew you'd want to know. Look, just send me everything you have now, and I'll get started putting the storyboard together for you and pulling any other visuals you need, videos, or images. Just tell me what you want."

Panicked, Haley stopped pacing. "I can't send you anything because I don't have anything yet, except a few ideas . . ."

"What? What do you mean you have nothing?" Kathy asked, looking freaked out. "What have you been doing there this whole time? You're at Christmas Camp; isn't this place supposed to give you all these great ideas?"

"Well, yeah, in theory, but I've been so busy with all these Christmas Camp activities they make you do. I mean, Jeff had me chopping down my own Christmas tree, and we had to make snow angels last night, and I just snuck away from him downstairs, where we were decorating Christmas cookies . . ."

Kathy's eyebrows arched. "Wait, Jeff, the hot guy, the owner's son? The one you like?"

"I don't like him!" Haley glared into the phone.

This had Kathy looking even more suspicious. "You so like him. Oh no, what have you done?"

Haley collapsed onto her bed, fell back, and stared up at the ceiling. "I haven't done anything. I don't know. It's a big mess." She grabbed an angel pillow and put it over her face.

"Does he know how you feel about him?"

Haley pulled the pillow away. "*I* don't even know how I feel about him. It might just be all this sentimental Christmas stuff that's getting to me. But I promise you, nothing has happened."

"Yet," Kathy said.

"Yet," Haley agreed. "I need help, Kathy, I really do. Forget about Jeff. I need help with this campaign pitch. I don't know what I'm going to do."

Kathy took a deep breath. "Okay, we just need to calm down. I'm sure you're just tired and freaking out. I know it's hard to come up with a brilliant idea when you're so stressed out, and whatever is happening with this guy, I'm sure, isn't helping."

"I told you," Haley said, her voice full of determination. "Nothing's happening with Jeff. I won't let it."

"Okay, good. So look," Kathy said. "You still have a couple of days. I've seen you create entire campaigns in a few hours. You got this. Just try to relax, and stay away from anything or anyone who is stressing you out, and if this Jeff guy is a distraction—"

"I know, I need to stay away from him."

"Exactly, and you know I'm all about romance and hot guys, but as your friend, I'm telling you, you've worked too hard to let anything get in your way of this promotion. So, you know what to do."

Haley stood up. "I do." She assumed the position. Her superhero power-pose position. "Thanks for the pep talk. I got this. I can do this, and I will do this! The Tyler Toys account is mine."

Kathy grinned into the phone. "Now, that's the Haley I recognize! Go get 'em!"

"I'm on it!"

"Oh, and you've something on your nose; it looks like . . ."

Haley wiped her nose again. "Frosting . . ."

A knock on the bedroom door interrupted them. Haley covered her mouth with her hand and then whispered, "I gotta go. Someone's at the door . . ." She then held a finger to her lips so Kathy wouldn't say anything, waved, and hung up quickly.

"Haley, it's Jeff . . ."

She frantically stuffed her phone back into her apron pocket and hurried to get the door. She tried to act as normal as possible when she opened it and saw Jeff standing there.

"Hey, what's up?" she asked. She hated that her voice sounded a little too high.

Jeff looked concerned. "Is everything okay?"

She faked a smile. "Everything's great."

He held up a plate of cookies. "You said you needed to take cookies to Gail, but you didn't take any, so I brought these up for you."

Haley quickly took the cookies and put them on her dresser. "Thanks."

Jeff peered inside her room. "Were you just talking to someone? I thought I heard someone else?"

Haley could feel herself start to sweat. She shook her head. "No, no one's here. Just me." She grabbed the plate of cookies. "I should get these to Gail. Thanks for—" But before she could finish, her phone rang. She froze. She then turned around slowly to face Jeff, and the incredulous look on his face made her cringe. Without a word, she gave him the plate of cookies, reached into her pocket, and took out her phone. It was Kathy calling back. She quickly turned it off and looked back up at Jeff. "I can explain . . ."

She was fully expecting Jeff to be furious, but when she looked into his eyes, it was much worse. He didn't look angry. He looked disappointed. Before she could say anything more, he had already started walking away. Haley hurried to catch up to him. She held out her phone.

"I really can explain. It was a work emergency. See! Look at my text, right here. It says 911. I was in the pantry looking for the sprinkles when I found my phone and thought—"

Jeff stopped and turned around. "And thought what? That you'd just take it and then lie about it? If you had a real work emergency, you could have just told me. You're not in jail here, but instead you just lied about it. What else are you lying about? Why should I even believe this story? Maybe you've had your phone all along."

"No! I haven't, really. I just got it, and here, you can take it back. I don't need it anymore. You can put it back in the pantry or wherever."

When Haley saw Jeff look at her like he was really disappointed, she felt worse. She held out her phone again. "Here, please take it." This time he took it and, without a word, walked away.

CHAPTER 23

Jeff eyed the drawer in the kitchen that was next to the sink, and ten seconds later, he had taken it out and was putting it on the countertop with five other drawers he'd already removed. He still couldn't get out of his head the way Haley had looked him in the eye and flat-out lied to him when he'd asked her if she had been talking to anyone. He didn't know if he was more upset or disappointed, but either way, he didn't like the feeling. He grabbed another drawer just as his dad walked in.

Ben did a double take, seeing all the drawers on the counter. "Oh no, what's wrong?"

Jeff held another drawer in his hands that he had just taken out. "Nothing's wrong. I'm just fixing your drawers."

"But there was nothing wrong with my drawers."

"Actually, they were sticking again," Jeff said as he pulled another drawer out, but this time Ben stopped him before he set it on the counter.

"The drawers are fine." Ben took the drawer and put it back where it belonged. He slid it open and slid it shut.

It didn't stick a bit. "So, why don't you tell me what's going on before you take apart the rest of my kitchen?" Ben sat down at the kitchen table and pulled out another chair for Jeff.

Jeff reluctantly sat down. Ben picked up a plate of sugar cookies and offered one, but Jeff shook his head. Ben frowned, "Okay, out with it. It has to be pretty bad if you're passing up cookies."

"It's Haley," Jeff said. "I found her in her room with her phone. She'd snuck it out of the pantry, and she was making work calls. She lied about it at first, and then she tried to make up a bunch of excuses. Now I have no idea what to believe and what not to believe."

"So, you're upset that she lied to you?"

"That and that all she cares about is work. When she first showed up for Christmas Camp, it was clear she didn't want to be here, that she had to come because her boss sent her, but I thought—"

"That she was starting to come around and find her Christmas spirit?" Ben asked.

Jeff, looking upset, stood back up and walked over to the drawers again. "Yes, I really thought she was. I mean we made snow angels, and she took an angel off the Wishing Tree at the community center, and she bought a little girl a doll. She seemed to really be embracing what Christmas Camp is all about, or at least I thought so, but now it just looks like it was just a big act. I don't want her messing up your last Christmas Camp."

Ben looked confused. "What do you mean my *last* Christmas Camp?"

Jeff started tightening another screw on one of the drawers. "Dad, we talked about this. We've done the books together, twice. The numbers don't add up. It's costing you almost twice what you make to keep this place running. I know it's hard, but it's time to sell the inn. I've found you a great buyer, but they can't wait much longer for your answer."

Ben walked over to his son and looked him in the eye. "I told you I didn't want to talk about this or any other business until after our Christmas Camp. We're telling our guests that they need to relax and enjoy the season, but here you are talking about work. It's sounds like you're doing the same thing as Haley. So, maybe you shouldn't be so quick to judge her."

Jeff, upset, looked back at his dad. "That's not fair. You can't compare me to her."

"Is judging Haley fair? She made a mistake. Did she say she was sorry?"

Jeff didn't answer right away. "It doesn't matter . . ."

"But it does. People come here for all kinds of reasons, and it's not our place to pass judgment, it's our place to try and help them as much as we can. So, maybe Haley needs some extra help. What we need to focus on is how to make sure everyone, including Haley, has a special experience here. That's all I care about right now. Do you understand that?"

Jeff met his dad's questioning look. "I understand, and I'm sorry. I didn't mean to upset you. I just want what's best for you."

Ben put his arm around him. "I know you do, but right now what's best for me is having you here and the two of us enjoying this time with our guests."

Jeff nodded. "I know, but your rules are for a reason . . ."

"I'll talk to her," Ben said.

Jeff gave his dad a look, knowing he had a heart as big as the North Pole. "Okay. As long as you're happy, whatever you want to do. I'll let you handle it. I have to run into the city anyway. I just got a call that the wharf project I'm working on needs another permit and we have to get it before Christmas. But I'll be back first thing in the morning. Just call me if you need anything."

"I will," Ben said. "And don't worry. I have everything under control here. Just drive safe, and we'll see you first thing in the morning. We have a big day tomorrow, so I wouldn't want you to miss it."

"I promise I won't." Jeff gave his dad a quick hug as he headed out the door. "Don't get into any trouble while I'm gone."

"Me, trouble? Never!"

"Right . . ." Jeff laughed as he left the kitchen. His goal was to drive to the city and get back to the inn as fast as possible. Christmas Camp would be wrapping up soon, and he wanted to be ready to have the tough conversation with his dad about selling the inn. He would respect his dad's wishes to wait until after Christmas Camp to talk business, but that was only a few days away.

When he passed the sitting room and saw Haley talking to Ian, Madison, and Blake, he felt conflicted. When he first met her, he'd thought he had her all figured out, that she was a workaholic who only cared about her job. But over the last few days, he'd actually enjoyed spending time with her. She was smart, funny, stubborn, and caring all at the same time, and there was no denying she was beautiful or that there was just something about her that made him want to know more.

But after Haley's phone stunt today, his guard was back up. She had lied to him. Maybe he'd been right about her all along. Honestly, he didn't know what to think, and the fact that he couldn't figure her out bothered him. He just knew that right now he needed to concentrate on his dad and getting the inn sold before the end of the year.

BEN WAS IN the kitchen finishing up a cookie when Haley peeked her head in. She had decided that coming clean was her best bet, and hoping he didn't react as negatively as Jeff had.

She knew she shouldn't have lied to Jeff about taking her phone. She'd just panicked. She realized it was no excuse for her behavior. Now all she wanted to do was own up to her mistake and apologize to Ben, and hopefully, salvage at least their relationship, as she had obviously blown up any friendship she was starting to have with Jeff.

When Ben saw her, he smiled and waved her in. "Haley, I was just thinking about you."

She walked in with a guilty look on her face. "I'm guessing Jeff already told you, but I wanted to tell you myself how truly sorry I am. I respect the rules you have here, I really do. I know you just have them to help your guests with this whole experience, and I'm not going to make excuses for why I did what I did. I just want to apologize and promise that it won't happen again. I was hoping I could also find Jeff and try to explain better and apologize . . ."

"Jeff's actually headed into Boston today. Some work came up. He won't be back until tomorrow morning," Ben said.

Haley was trying to hide her disappointment when Max trotted in with his leash in his mouth. Ben took it from him and smiled up at Haley.

"Let's go for a walk."

After they got on their winter gear, Haley followed

Ben and Max outside. Ben took her around the back of the inn, through a trail in the woods, to a pretty scenic spot she hadn't seen before. She looked around, taking in all the snow-covered trees and pristine snow. "I didn't know this was here."

Ben smiled as he pointed to a cedar bench and headed over to it. While everything else was covered in snow, it had been cleared off. "It's one of my favorite places. This is where I'd always come with Jeff's mom when we needed a little break. It's close enough to the inn but still feels like we're miles away, don't you think?"

"I do," Haley answered. "It's perfect."

When they sat down on the bench, Max lay down at Ben's feet.

"Max loves it here, too," Ben said, petting Max.

Haley smiled at them both. She then looked around and took in a deep breath, soaking up the peacefulness. "I really am sorry about the whole thing with the phone. I know Jeff is so mad at me."

Ben gave her hand a reassuring squeeze. "Don't worry. You apologized. He'll come around. He's just really worried about me, and he probably overreacted."

Haley gave him a concerned look. "What's wrong? Are you okay? Is everything okay?"

Ben nodded. "I'm fine, but Jeff still worries. Ever since his mom died, he has been overprotective. He doesn't like me being up here running the inn all alone. He wants me to sell. He even has someone lined up to buy this place."

Haley looked surprised. "You want to sell the inn?"

Ben turned to admire the breathtaking mountain range and shook his head. "I can't even imagine selling all of this. This is my home. I love it here. This is where all my memories are. I know it's hard for Jeff, because some of those memories make him sad, but for me, it's different. Those memories make me feel closer to her. It's like she's here with me, and it's comforting."

"Well, if you love it here, why does he want you to sell?"

Ben sighed. "Because I'm losing money. It's getting more expensive every year to run the inn, and the Christmas Camps have always been a labor of love, not a moneymaker. Jeff's mom and I didn't care when we started the Christmas Camps because we loved doing them so much. We were just going to do the one when we started, but one turned into two, and now ten years later, it has turned into ten weeks of Christmas Camps between Halloween and Christmas. Our Christmas Camps have become a tradition for a lot of families."

"But if they're so popular and you're selling out, doesn't that bring enough money in?"

Ben shook his head sadly. "I'm afraid it doesn't. It's just not enough to break even anymore. We'd need more rooms, a lot more rooms . . ."

They sat in silence for several minutes and then all of a sudden Haley jumped up. "I know how to get you more rooms!"

"I can't afford to build."

"No, you wouldn't need to build," she said. "You can franchise your Christmas Camp."

"What?" Ben asked, confused. "How would that work?"

"If you franchised the Christmas Camp concept to other hotels and resorts around the country, and even around the world, the money from that would help pay to keep your inn and Christmas Camps running. Anyone who did your Christmas Camp would pay a licensing fee, and you would get a cut of their profits. With all your experience, you would be like a Christmas Camp expert, a consultant who could help other properties put together their own Christmas Camps. Does that make sense?"

Ben's eyes lit up. "So I would have more rooms by partnering with other hotels and resorts, and I would get a percentage of anyone who came for their Christmas Camps?"

"Exactly!" Haley was pacing back and forth in front of Ben and Max, getting more excited by the second. "And since you do this every year, I'm sure other inns and resorts would also want to do their Christmas Camp's every year and have it be part of their tradition for their guests. So you would have a built-in revenue stream coming in year after year that would only continue to grow as more Christmas Camps were held."

Ben stood up. His face was full of hope. "And I could still stay up here at the inn and do our Christmas Camps like always?"

"Absolutely! You'd be the flagship."

Ben shook his head in amazement. "You actually think this could work?"

Haley took his hand and looked into his eyes. "I don't think, I know. This is what I do for a living, remember? I help companies build their brands."

"But I don't have a brand," Ben said.

Haley laughed. "Actually, you do. Your Christmas Camps help people celebrate Christmas, honoring old traditions and creating new memories; that's your brand. That's who you are. A brand is something that makes your business unique and special, and successful brands answer a need and you're doing that with your Christmas Camps. You're helping people who need it to slow down and appreciate what really matters most at Christmas. Isn't that what your brochure says? I know it's why my boss sent me here. There are a lot of people who need your Christmas Camp, Ben, and this way you can help even more people."

Max barked and looked up at Haley as he wagged his tail.

Haley laughed. "See, even Max agrees!" When she petted Max, he wagged his tail even more.

"And you know how to do this?" Ben asked, his voice filled with hope.

Haley nodded. "I do. I just helped another resort client do it with a yoga retreat, and now they're cashing in. So, I know we could do the same thing with your Christmas Camps. What do you say?"

Ben looked nervous but excited. "Well, we'd have to move fast. Jeff needs to give the buyer he found an answer before the end of the year."

"I can put together a quick proposal for you to check out and see what you think," Haley said. "It'll be easier to understand when you see everything written down on paper."

Ben looked around at his property then back at Haley. "Okay. Show me what you can do."

LATER THAT NIGHT, as a soft snow fell, the outside of the inn looked magical. There was only one light still on, and through the window you could see the shadow of two people in the library.

Inside, Haley and Ben were huddled over Haley's laptop. The clock on the wall showed it was almost eleven o'clock.

"Okay, there you go," Haley said. "I just sent you an email with the Christmas Camp proposal I've been showing you, outlining potential profits and a timeline to make everything happen for next year, so now you'll have a copy."

"And you think we can be ready by next October?" Ben asked. "Because that's when we usually start the Christmas Camps."

"Absolutely. You already have the concept and a proven track record. Let me show you some ideas I have for the website we could set up."

But when Haley opened another file and turned her computer around so Ben could get a better look, he saw the time on the computer and gently shut her laptop.

"Hey, what are you doing? We aren't done yet." She tried to open her laptop again but he stopped her.

"But we *are* done," Ben said as he looked into her eyes. "Did you see how late it is? I'm sorry. I completely lost track of the time. I guess I'm just so excited about this all possibly working. You've used all your free time to work on it with me." He gave her an apologetic look. "I really am sorry. I shouldn't have gotten carried away. You're not here to work."

"But I love doing this, and it didn't interfere with any of our activities."

Ben smiled at Haley. "I know, and I really do appreciate it, but we can do this later, after the Christmas Camp. You shouldn't be working while you're here."

Haley frowned. "But I love this idea, and you know I love working . . ."

Ben chuckled. "Yes, I do know that, but, Haley, if you want to help me pitch my Christmas Camp to other people, how are you going to do it if you haven't really experienced it for yourself?"

Haley opened her mouth to say something but then closed it. She gave Ben a shrewd look. "Oh, you're good. You're *really* good."

Ben laughed. "I have to be to keep up with you. I thought you were only going to show me one quick idea tonight, and we've been working for several hours. So, we need to put this all away for now. I'll look over everything you just sent me. I promise. But for now, I want you to enjoy the little time you have left here. That's really important to me, okay? So, do we have a deal?" He held out his hand.

Haley took it, and they shook. "Deal."

"And for now, let's just keep this between us," Ben said.

"You don't want to tell Jeff?" Haley asked.

"Not until I know if it's something I can really do. He and I also agreed not to talk business until Christmas Camp wraps up."

"Got it. Whatever you say," Haley said. "I'm just excited that this is a way for you to keep your inn and the Christmas Camp legacy."

"Me too," Ben said. His voice was full of gratitude. "And then you would be making my Christmas wish come true."

Haley touched her heart as she smiled back at him. Helping him reminded her of how she had helped small businesses when she had started working at the agency. That feeling she got when she knew she was really making a difference in someone's life.

Ben picked up her laptop and gave it to her. "So let's turn in. We have a big day tomorrow. Thank you again, Haley, for all your work."

"I'm happy to do more—"

"After Christmas Camp." He gave her a gentle push toward the door.

Haley smiled back at him. "Okay, you win. After

Christmas Camp, but you know that's just a few days away . . ."

Ben laughed. "I know."

Haley smiled as she left the room. "I'll see you in the morning."

CHAPTER 24

The next morning as the sun peeked over the mountains, Haley was already up and dressed. She hummed her Christmas song, "Hark! The Herald Angels Sing," as she opened her door. She looked around and was surprised not to see Max waiting for her. As she headed down the hall, she continued looking around for him.

"Okay, where are you, Max?" she whispered, not wanting to wake anyone up. When she popped her head into the kitchen, she didn't find Max, but she saw the latest word for the day on the chalkboard was "wonder," and the Christmas countdown had been changed to 10 DAYS TO CHRISTMAS. "Huh," she said, looking around. "Well, right now I *wonder* where you're hiding, Max." But she didn't have to wonder for long. Her next stop was the sitting room, and that's where she found Max sleeping by the fireplace.

"There you are, Max. Come on, boy, let's go. Time for your walk." When she held up his leash, he came running over. As they headed out the front door, she saw Jeff's truck drive up. "Oh boy. Here we go. Wish me luck," she said to Max as they walked toward the truck. When Jeff got out, Haley saw he was wearing sunglasses, which made his expression impossible to read. She fought for a smile and tried to remain optimistic. "Good morning," she said.

"You're up early?" Jeff gave her a questioning look then turned his attention to Max. "I suppose this is your fault?"

For an answer, Max barked and wagged his tail.

Haley laughed. "Actually, I woke *him* up this morning; right, Max?"

Max wagged his tail as he looked up her.

Jeff's eyebrows rose. "Really?"

"True story."

"Let me guess, you were working?"

Haley's smiled faltered a bit. "Actually, I did get some work done already, but it's such a beautiful morning I wanted to do our walk early, when it's so peaceful."

Jeff nodded, but still didn't look convinced.

"And about work," Haley started.

He held up his hand to stop her. "You don't owe me any explanations. Like I said, I'm not the Christmas Camp police. It's not for me to judge, and I apologize that I got a little carried away yesterday."

"And you had every right," Haley interrupted him. "I know you just want this camp to go well for your dad, and so do I. So, from now on, I'm all in. I'm going to be the best Christmas Camp guest you've ever seen."

Jeff took off his sunglasses and gave her a suspicious look. "Seriously?"

Haley laughed. "Seriously, I'm going to be a perfect angel for the rest of the week. I mean, I *am* in the angel room. Some of that has to rub off at some point, right?" She didn't have time to hear his answer because Ben walked out the front door.

"Son, great, you're back, just in time to help me get everything ready for our next activity."

"Which is sledding," Haley said proudly. "I checked the list. Is there anything I can do to help?"

"You're doing it," Ben said. "I know Max loves his walks with you. Then join the rest of us for breakfast, and we'll head out. I want to get an early start."

"We're not sledding here?" Haley asked, looking around.

Jeff laughed. "Oh no. We have a favorite sledding spot, don't we, Dad?"

Ben patted Jeff on the back. "We sure do. It's a nice little hill, you're going to love it, Haley."

As HALEY STOOD with the rest of the Christmas Camp gang at the top of a huge sledding hill, she looked more than a little freaked out. "I thought you said this was a nice *little* hill. What happened to the little part?" she asked Ben and Jeff.

Jeff laughed. "This one is little. You should see the one we usually go to at Eagle Peak."

"Uh, no, thanks. This one looks big enough, actually too big . . ."

"You're not afraid, are you?" Jeff asked in a teasing voice.

"Of course not," Haley shot back. "It's just I'm more of a city girl than a sledding girl."

"When was the last time you went sledding?" Ben asked.

Haley had to think about it. She actually couldn't re-member ever sledding down a hill like this. Her only sledding memory was of sitting on a trash-can lid that her dad had tied a rope to and being pulled around their driveway. She might have been four or five years old. When she realized Ben was still waiting for an answer, she shrugged. "I honestly can't remember ever going sledding like this."

Ben looked at the collection of different sleds he brought with them and picked up a red plastic toboggan. "Then you can have this one, Haley. It's perfect for a beginner."

Blake laughed. "We had one of those when we were little, didn't we, Madison?"

Madison laughed. "We did! Don't worry, Haley, it's super easy to use. A baby could do it."

Everyone laughed but Haley. Right now she was feeling like a big baby because when she looked down the hill, she felt only one thing. Fear.

Ben pointed to all the different kinds of sleds. "Okay, this is what I have for all of you today, depending on your sledding skills. Did you all see our inspirational word for the day?"

"It's 'wonder,'" Susie chimed in as she excitedly grabbed Ian's hand and swung both their hands in the air.

"You're crazy." Ian laughed.

Susie kissed him on the cheek. "Crazy about you and Christmas!"

Haley laughed. "That sounds like a bad country song."

Gail joined in on the fun. "It does!"

This just got Susie more wound up, and she started to dance and sing. "I'm crazy about you and Christmas, you and Christmas. I'm crazy about you!"

"Okay, babe, that's enough." But when Ian tried to grab her hand to stop her, she just pulled him into dancing with her.

"Help! I have a Christmas-crazy wife!" Ian called out.

Everyone laughed.

"This is great," Ben said. "I'm seeing the wonder already! Okay, so today's theme is wonder, and it's all about remembering how you felt at Christmas when you were a child."

John smiled at his kids. "It wasn't that long ago for you guys."

"Dad!" Madison exclaimed, embarrassed. "We're teenagers now. We're not little kids!"

When John turned to Haley and whispered, "Don't I know it," she had to fight back a laugh.

Ben held up his camera. "And I'm going to be taking some pictures of everyone, so be sure to smile."

"My dad, the paparazzi," Jeff joked, and winked at his dad.

"I just want to be sure I get photo approval before you post anything about me," Madison said, adjusting her hat and scarf.

When Ben looked confused, John came to the rescue. "She means if you post any pictures of her on social media, like Facebook or Instagram, she wants to be sure she likes them first."

Ben gave Madison a reassuring look. "I promise you, I won't be posting anything anywhere."

Madison looked confused. "Then why are you even taking pictures?"

John rolled his eyes. "Teenagers, what can you do?"

Everyone laughed again.

Still laughing, Ben picked up a vintage wooden sled that had steel blades and wood strips on the top. There was also a horizontal wooden piece at the front of the sled, tied to a red rope, to help you navigate. "So, who wants to use this little beauty?"

Ian looked at Susie. "Don't even think about it. That one looks older than we are and hard to steer."

"You're right about this one being an oldie but goodie, Ian," Ben said. "She's one of the first sleds ever made. One of my favorites, but this one does take a little skill and—"

But before he could finish, Gail had walked up to him. "I'll take it."

Everyone looked surprised and impressed.

"Are you sure?" Ben asked.

Gail looked at the sled with confidence. "Oh, I'm sure. I was quite the sledder in my day, and this is what we'd always use. Old school is the only way."

Ben handed the sled over with a smile. "That's the spirit!" Next, he picked up a giant inner tube and looked over at John, Blake, and Madison. "I was thinking this one might be big enough for all of you. If you think you can handle it?" He said the last part looking at the kids.

Blake, excited, ran up to him. "Oh, we can handle it. Right, Dad?"

"Absolutely," John said. "Right, Madison?"

Madison looked a little nervous but nodded.

"Okay, then, show us what you can do." Ben handed the inner tube to Blake. Everyone watched as the family piled on.

"What if I fall off?" Madison asked.

"Just hold on to me," John answered. "Are you guys ready?"

Blake pumped his fist into the air. "Ready."

When John gave the sled a push, Madison screamed and Blake and John laughed. Within seconds, they were flying down the hill.

"Whoa!" Madison squealed, laughing.

"Whooo-hoo!" Blake hollered.

"Hold on!" John shouted back at them, and moments later, they were all laughing as they raced down the hill.

Before anyone knew what was happening, Gail was on her sled and had taken off. "I'm going to catch you guys!" she called after John and the kids.

"Go, Gail!" Haley yelled as she watched Gail skillfully navigate her sled and start catching up to the inner tube.

Ian and Susie were the next up. They grabbed a two-person toboggan and also started flying down the hill.

"I love Christmas!" When Susie threw her arms in the air, she almost fell off the sled, but luckily Ian grabbed her.

Haley, Jeff, and Ben were the only ones left at the top of the hill. Still holding her toboggan, Haley didn't look like she was going anywhere.

Jeff took it from her and smiled. "You ready?"

When her eyes grew huge, Ben snapped a picture of her.

"Hey, wait." Haley laughed. "I'm gonna need photo approval on that one."

"I'll give you anything you want after you get down this hill," Ben said.

"Do I have to?" she asked, sounding like she was Madison's age.

Jeff smiled back at her. "You want that certificate, don't you?"

"Of course, but . . ."

"No buts, come on, let's go," Jeff said. "I'm an expert. You're safe with me."

Haley very much doubted that, in more ways than one, and when she saw Jeff put the sled down and run it back and forth a couple of times in the slick snow, her heart skipped a beat.

Jeff sat down on the back of the sled and patted the spot in front of him. "Come on, Haley, you can do it."

Haley shook her head. "You go ahead. I'll stay up here and help Ben."

"I have everything under control, Haley. You go ahead. You can do this. Jeff is an excellent sledder. You're in good hands," Ben said.

Jeff patted the space on the sled in front of him again. "Don't worry; I'll do all the work. You just have to sit here and enjoy."

But all Haley could think of was that she'd rather be getting a root canal. She took another step back.

Jeff locked eyes with her. "You said you were all in for the rest of Christmas Camp. What were your exact words? That you were going to be a *perfect angel* and an ideal guest from now on . . ."

Haley's jaw dropped. He was using her own words against her. When she looked at Ben for some help, he just smiled.

"This is one of our activities," Ben said. "Don't you want to experience everything so you truly understand what Christmas Camp is all about, like we talked about last night . . ."

Haley knew what he was getting at. She threw up her hands in defeat. "Okay, but I swear, if I break my neck, you two are going to have to explain it to my boss and my parents."

"Deal," Jeff said, patting the space in front of him again.

Haley's smile faded. The space on the sled was tiny, meaning she was going to have to be snug up against Jeff, and that thought was just as scary as flying down the hill. As she got on the sled, she tried to sit toward the front so she could keep their contact to a minimum.

"You can lean back on me," he said, when she continued to sit up, stiff as a board.

"I'm good. Thanks." Her voice sounded high and thin. She wanted to blame the cold air, but she knew it had more to do with feeling Jeff's warm breath on the back of her neck in the spot where her scarf had slipped, and she had a tiny bit of exposed skin. She hurried to adjust her scarf, but when she struggled to fix it, Jeff came to the rescue. He leaned forward so his cheek was almost against hers.

"Better?" he asked.

She could only nod, not trusting herself to talk. She was shaking but not from the cold. To steady herself, she grabbed the front of the toboggan with both hands.

"Are you ready?" Jeff asked.

Haley squeezed her eyes shut. "No, but okay. Go." At this point she just wanted to get it over with. She didn't know what she was more afraid of, being this close to Jeff or the hill looming in front of her.

"Hey, Dad, can you give us a little push?"

"You got it, son, but first, smile!"

When Jeff put his arm around her, Haley looked up at him, surprised, and that's when Ben snapped the photo. Seconds later, she felt the sled moving . . .

"Off you go! Have fun!" Ben shouted. As they picked up speed, Haley held on for dear life. When they hit a bump, she screamed, and Jeff held her tighter.

"I got you, don't worry," he hollered in her ear.

She was screaming and laughing at the same time, and Jeff was laughing right along with her.

"Isn't this great!" he shouted.

Haley couldn't answer because she was still screaming. When she finally stopped, the laugher kicked back in. Racing down the hill was both thrilling and terrifying. True to his word, Jeff was an excellent sledder, and when they hit a big bump and almost tipped over, he protected her, pulling her closer to him. She laughingly grabbed his arm and realized she didn't feel scared anymore. She felt safe. As they came closer to the bottom of the hill, for a moment she let herself lean back so she could feel the heat of Jeff's body. She shut her eyes and just let herself feel the exhilaration that was only partly due to the sledding. When they finally came to a stop, she opened her eyes.

"So, what did ya think?" Jeff asked as he got up from the toboggan and held out his hand to help her up. "Great, right?"

Haley took his hand and looked into his eyes. "It was amazing." Again, she wasn't just talking about the sledding. "Let's go again!"

Jeff laughed and grabbed the sled. "I knew you'd love it."

As they walked over to join the rest of the group gathered at the bottom of the hill, Haley couldn't remember a time when she'd had more fun. She now felt the wonder Ben had been talking about. It was intoxicating, and she wanted more. She couldn't wait to see what was next.

CHAPTER 25

After another fun-filled hour of sledding, the whole gang was exhausted and ready for a break. Haley touched her rosy-red cheeks. They were numb from the cold. Her face actually hurt from smiling and laughing so much.

As the guys helped Ben load up the sleds, Ian was high-fiving everyone. "This was so cool. Thank you, Ben. Best activity ever."

"Even better than hanging out at the pool in Arizona?" Susie asked in a teasing voice.

Ian came over and gave her a quick kiss. "Even better than that. I think we need to make this one of our new traditions together."

Susie looked overjoyed. She gave him a big hug. "I love that. Let's add it to our list."

Blake eyed the inner tube they had been using. "Dad, can we make this one of our new traditions, too?"

"Yeah, Dad, that would be great!" Madison said.

John looked surprised but pleased. "We sure can. We can even get an inner tube just like this one."

"Awesome!" Blake high-fived his dad, and Madison did the same.

John looked over at Ben and gave him a thumbs-up.

When Gail came over to join Haley, she was also in a wonderful mood. "I don't think I've laughed this much in a long time," she said.

Haley smiled back at her. "That's exactly what I was thinking. And you weren't kidding. You're definitely the sledding queen. You had some serious moves out there."

Gail chuckled and looked proud. "Thank you. Call it years of practice." She put her arm around Haley. "It looked like you and Jeff were having a great time, too . . ."

Haley laughed. "You're not giving up, are you?"

"Never," Gail whispered as Ben walked up to them.

"What are you two ladies whispering about? Should I be worried?" he asked. He smiled back at Gail.

"About us?" Haley feigned innocence. "Never."

Ben laughed and snapped a picture of them.

"Hold on," Haley said. "Ben, you've been taking pictures all day. We need one with you in it. Can I have your camera for a second?"

"Sure," Ben said as he handed her his camera and put his arm around Gail. "How about one of the two of us?"

As Haley took the picture, she didn't miss the way the two of them smiled at each other. "Got it. Now let's get one of all of us?"

"Can you do a selfie with that big camera?" Gail asked.

"I bet I can. You might be the sledding queen, but I'm the selfie queen. Let's give it a try. Okay, everyone scooch in so we're all close enough together. Everyone get cheek to cheek. Okay, ready? Everyone say 'sledding!'"

"Sledding!" Gail and Ben said at the same time as Haley snapped the perfect selfie.

Jeff laughed when he saw what they were doing and came over. "I can take a real one for you."

Haley pretended to be offended. "I'll have you know my selfie was perfect. We're good."

Jeff laughed.

"But let me get one of you and your dad."

When Jeff put his arm around his dad, you could see how much love they shared. It touched Haley's heart. She took the picture and handed the camera back to Ben.

"Okay, time to head back to the inn," he said.

Haley rubbed her hands together. "Okay, What's next on the list? I'm ready!"

Jeff laughed and looked at his dad. "Looks like some-one's finally getting with the program."

"If you mean the Christmas Camp program, remember I'm all in," Haley said.

"Really?" Jeff gave her a look. "Okay, we'll see about that." He turned to Ben. "Dad, we'll meet you back at the inn."

Ben nodded. "Sounds good."

As Ben and Gail walked off together, Haley looked up at Jeff. "So, what is this you want to show me?"

A HALF HOUR LATER Haley was hiking with Jeff through the woods when they came to a spectacular scenic over-look with a magnificent view of the snow-covered moun-tain range.

Haley looked around in awe. "This view is amazing . . ."

Jeff smiled as he looked toward the mountains. "I al-ways come up here when I need to clear my head and slow down."

"I can see why," Haley said, taking a deep breath.

"The locals call it Star Peak, because it's a great place

to see the stars at night. My dad proposed to my mom right here, right before Christmas."

"Really?"

Jeff nodded. "And every year after that, on the anniversary of his proposal, they'd come up here and find a pinecone to bring back to the inn."

Haley looked confused. "A pinecone? Why?"

"When he proposed, he put the ring in a pinecone, gave it to her, and said it was his Christmas wish for them to build a home up here in the mountains and be together forever . . ." As Jeff's voice trailed off, Haley could see the sadness in his eyes, and it made her own heart ache. She wanted to say something, to offer him some comfort, but when no words came, she reached out and touched his arm.

"I'm sorry."

Jeff smiled through his pain. "Thank you. You know I am thankful that they got a chance to move here and live their dream for a little while. I just wish they'd had more time together. You should have seen them. They were best friends. They helped each other be better people, and they were happiest when they were together. They had the kind of love everyone wants . . ."

"What kind is that?" Haley asked, genuinely wanting to know.

"The kind that makes you a better version of yourself. The kind you can count on no matter what."

Haley walked to the edge of the overlook and stared out at the horizon. She tried to think if she had ever felt love like that and realized she had not. She'd always had her career, and that had been enough, but now she wasn't so sure.

"And you think that kind of love is what everyone wants?" she asked.

"I do," Jeff said as he joined her. "My parents showed me how powerful that kind of love is. If you have that kind of love, you have everything."

"So, was that their Christmas wish?" Haley asked. "Love?"

Jeff nodded. "And I can't think of a better one, can you?"

Haley didn't know what to think. She'd never made any kind of Christmas wish before, and she wasn't sure if she was ready to start now.

When she didn't immediately answer Jeff gave her a questioning look. "You disagree?"

Haley shrugged. "I just don't think love is the be all and end all. You said if you have that kind of love you have everything, but my parents had that love and it didn't pay the rent. We really struggled, and it was especially hard this time of year, at Christmas."

Jeff looked at her like some pieces of the puzzle were finally fitting together. "So, is that why you don't like celebrating Christmas?"

"Probably. I've always thought of Christmas as something to get through, not something to celebrate." She took a deep breath. "My parents always tried so hard to make it special for me, but even when I was little, I knew what a strain it was, that they didn't have the money. We couldn't afford Christmas trees and presents and all the decorations. I know my parents felt bad for me, so I acted like I didn't care, and over time I really did stop caring."

Jeff shook his head. "That had to be so hard on you and your parents."

"It was," Haley said. "When Christmas came all my friends would be excited, but I couldn't wait for it to be over. That's why when I was finally making enough money to give my parents any kind of Christmas they wanted, we all agreed to spend it in the Caribbean, and instead of focusing on the holiday, we'd just make it a vacation. None of us have the best memories of Christmas, so this is just easier." She stood up straighter, lifted her chin a little higher, and turned her gaze to the view. She didn't want to look up at Jeff. She didn't want to see the pity in his eyes. She was embarrassed by what she'd just told him. She rarely told anyone about her past. Even Kathy didn't know how bad her Christmases were growing up.

After a few moments of silence, Jeff finally spoke, and Haley was surprised that she didn't hear any pity in his voice. It was quite the opposite. He sounded impressed.

"Your parents are very lucky to have a daughter like you," he said.

Surprised, she looked up at him. "Why do you say that?"

"Because look how much you love them. Even growing up, you put their needs in front of yours. You were a child who worried about her parents at Christmas when no child should have to bear that burden. That's real love."

All of a sudden a wave of emotion caught Haley off guard. She turned away from Jeff so he couldn't see how she was fighting off tears. It was like all the years of sadness and pain she had felt at Christmas and had buried so deep inside were now rushing to the surface.

To buy herself some time to pull herself together, she walked over to a pine tree. As she bent down to pick up a pinecone, she thought about what Jeff had said about what love really is and should be.

"Are you looking for your Christmas wish?" Jeff asked softly as he moved closer to her.

She looked down at the pinecone she was holding, still struggling with her emotions. "I guess I am." She showed him the pinecone. "How does this one look?"

Jeff took the pinecone, studied it, and then studied her. "I'd say it was perfect."

When their eyes met, she saw he wasn't teasing. She stood up, turned her back to him, and took another deep breath. Her emotions felt raw. So much was running through her head.

When Jeff stood up and joined her, she saw that he, too, had picked up a pinecone.

Haley fought for something to say. "So, what do we do with these now?"

"Bring them back to the inn and make a Christmas wish."

"That's really how it works?"

"It's my family's tradition. We do it every year."

"So, wait, all those pinecones in the basket by the fireplace . . ."

Jeff nodded. "That's right. They're all Christmas wishes from over the years."

Haley smiled, thinking of all the things at the inn that had a special meaning. The decorations weren't just from some fancy department store. They all had memories attached to them. The sadness she had felt at reliving her Christmas memories was fading. She was hoping they were getting locked away again in a safe place where they couldn't hurt her. She looked at the pinecone in her hand. "I've never wished on a pinecone before . . . or anything, for that matter."

"Do you believe in Christmas wishes?" Jeff asked.

She took a deep breath. "I would like to believe. I really would . . ." When he smiled back at her, it warmed her heart and gave her hope.

"I think that's a great start," he said. "We'll make a believer out of you yet." They stood together taking in the view. "We should probably be heading back."

Haley nodded and then looked up into his eyes. "Thank you for bringing me here."

"I'm glad you enjoyed it," he said. "I mean, I know it's no Caribbean beach or anything, but it's someplace that's special to me."

"I can see why. Being up here, in the mountains, in the snow, with all the trees and beautiful scenery . . . it really is a magical winter wonderland," Haley said. "It's like a Christmas dream."

"But your parents really like going to the Caribbean, right?"

"Yeah, I mean, I think so. They've never said they didn't like it . . ." Her voice trailed off as she realized they'd never really talked about it. All they'd said was that they wanted to spend time with her.

CHAPTER 26

When they got back to the lodge, Haley headed up to her room. Halfway up the stairs, she stopped and backtracked to find Jeff where she'd left him in the sitting room. He was putting the pinecone he had picked up at Star Peak into the basket of pinecones by the fireplace.

"Jeff?"

He looked up, surprised to see her.

"I wanted to ask you . . ." She struggled to get the words out. "I mean, you can say no. It's okay. I'd totally understand. I was just thinking, hoping, that maybe . . ."

"Haley, what is it?"

She took a deep breath. "Sorry. Okay. I know we have another activity tonight, and we'll probably get our phones and computers back pretty late . . ."

"So?" Jeff asked.

"So, I was just wondering if I could borrow my phone for two minutes. I wanted to call my parents. It's not a work call, I promise, and I totally understand if . . ."

But Jeff was already heading out of the room.

Haley covered her face with her hands. She'd ruined it

again. But before she could beat herself up any more, he was back, and without a word, he handed her the phone.

"Thank you," she said. "I'm just making the one call. I'll bring it right back. I promise . . ."

Jeff slowly smiled. "I believe you."

Haley looked into his eyes. "Thank you."

"For the phone?"

"And for believing me." She turned and hurried up to her room, where she called her parents on FaceTime.

When her mom answered, she looked concerned. "Hi, honey, is everything okay?"

Haley laughed. "Why do you always assume something's wrong when I call?"

Her dad popped into the picture. "Because we know how busy you are with work, and you don't have a lot of time to call us. So, is everything okay?"

Haley smiled back at them. "Everything's fine . . ."

"Oh, then I bet you're calling to make sure we got our plane tickets for the Caribbean," Haley's mom said. "Don't worry, they just came, and we're all set. We can't wait to see you! Your dad even has new swim trunks."

Haley laughed. "That's great. I'm actually calling because I had a quick question . . ." When she hesitated, her mom and dad leaned in, trying to see her better.

"What is it, honey?" Haley's mom asked.

"You're sure everything's okay?" her dad added.

Haley smiled so her parents could see everything was fine. "I promise, everything is fine. I just wanted to ask you guys about going to the Caribbean for Christmas. I know we always go. It's what we do . . ."

"So you can work and we can still all be together," Haley's mom jumped in.

"Right," Haley said. "But you guys like going to the Caribbean for Christmas, right?"

Haley's mom and dad exchanged a quick look.

"Honey, as long as we're with you at Christmas, we're happy," her mom said.

"We know how busy you are," her dad added.

She glanced around her room, saw all the angels looking back at her, and knew what she needed to do.

"Well, what would you say if we changed things up this year? How about we just stay home and celebrate. We could get a tree, make cookies . . ."

"Really?" Haley's mom looked like she was about to cry.

Haley's dad put his arm around her. He looked equally excited. "That sounds wonderful, honey. We would both really love it."

Haley's mom nodded enthusiastically. "We would. We really would . . ."

"We can't wait to have you home," her dad said. "We've missed you."

Now Haley was fighting back her own tears. "I love you guys . . ."

"We love you, too," said her parents in unison.

Haley kissed her fingers and touched the screen. "Bye. I'll see you soon." She was still smiling after she hung up and ran back downstairs. But when she entered the sitting room, Jeff wasn't there anymore, but Ben was. When he saw her phone, he looked surprised.

"It's not what you think," she said, rushing over to him and handing it to him. "Jeff said I could borrow it to call my parents."

Ben looked concerned. "Is everything okay?"

Haley smiled. "Everything's good. Really good, actually. We're going to celebrate Christmas at home this year and my parents seem really excited about it; and honestly, I am, too. It'll be a nice change."

Ben looked very pleased. "So, you'll actually be celebrating Christmas this year?"

Haley nodded. "I guess it will be this year. Do you know where Jeff is? I wanted to tell him. He's the one who actually gave me the idea to talk to my parents about it."

"I think Blake and Madison roped him into taking them into town. They wanted to try that ice cream place you and Gail went to."

Haley tried to hide her disappointment. "I guess I'll just tell him later."

"I bet Laura could use some help in the kitchen with dinner if you're up for it?"

She laughed. "I'm not sure how much I can help but I'll go see if there's anything I can do."

It TURNED OUT Haley was worth more in the kitchen than she thought as Laura put her to work peeling potatoes and cutting up vegetables for a homemade turkey vegetable soup. What was even more surprising to Haley was that she enjoyed helping. She felt a real sense of accomplishment learning how to make something from scratch. She was just finishing up with the soup when Jeff came into the kitchen looking for a snack. When he reached for a sugar cookie, Laura swatted his hand away.

"Dinner is almost ready," she scolded him.

Haley laughed. "And didn't you just take Blake and Madison for ice cream?"

Jeff gave her an incredulous look. "Really? You're selling me out after I let you use your cell phone?"

Now it was Laura's turn to look surprised. She turned to Haley. "He let you use your cell phone? Even when it's totally against the rules? Rules he loves to enforce," she said. She gave Jeff a teasing look.

Haley played along. "You know it really was pretty

shocking considering he is the Christmas Camp police and all . . ."

"You two are hilarious," Jeff shot back at them. He then looked quite pleased with himself as he held up a sugar cookie he'd managed to get his hands on. He was about to take a big bite when Laura snatched it away and gave him an apple instead.

"Wait, what!" He tried to grab the cookie back, but Laura was too quick.

Haley laughed. "You know what they say, an apple a day keeps the—"

"—Christmas spirit away!" Jeff finished for her. "I want my cookie!"

Laura and Haley laughed.

AT DINNER THAT NIGHT, everyone looked afraid when Laura told them Haley had made the soup, but Jeff stuck up for her.

"Hey, I've tasted it myself, and let me tell you, it's pretty good."

Haley smiled at Jeff. "Thank you. Laura and I might let you have dessert after all."

Jeff laughed. "I'm easily bribed with treats."

"You and Max, good to know," Haley said.

Everyone laughed.

At the end of the meal, Ben stood up and raised his glass of wine. "Let's all toast Laura and Haley for a delicious dinner. To another special holiday meal."

As everyone lifted their wineglasses, the teenagers lifted their water glasses.

"Cheers!" Ben said as he clinked glasses with Gail, Susie, Ian, John, Jeff, and finally with Haley. Looking into her eyes, he said, "Nice job. I think you're starting to find—"

"My unknown cooking skills?" Haley finished for him.

Ben smiled at her. "That too." He then addressed the rest of the group. "And that brings us to our next Christmas Camp activity Laura's going to help us with."

As he sat down Laura stood up. "First of all, thank you. You're all so wonderful to cook for because you're so appreciative . . ."

"We love your pie!" Madison grinned at her.

"We really do!" Blake agreed.

Everyone laughed and nodded in agreement.

"And your cookies!" Jeff added. "Even when you try to hide them from me." When he gave Haley a pointed look, she just feigned innocence.

Laura blushed a little at all the praise. "I'm so glad you enjoy everything. You know Christmas is a time when family and friends get together to share a meal. The food we eat becomes part of our Christmas traditions."

Ben stood back up. "And that's why you're all going to help Laura put together a special Christmas menu for tomorrow night since it will be our last night and meal together."

Haley's smile faded a little. She knew she should be relieved that Christmas Camp was almost over and she could get back to work, but instead she felt . . . sad.

She told herself it must just be because she still hadn't figured out her Tyler Toys campaign pitch, and she was just stressed about work. But as she snuck a peek at Jeff, she knew that wasn't the only reason for her sadness. There was no denying she felt something for him. What exactly that was she wasn't sure, and it scared her to think about it too much. She had told him more about her past than she had told most people, and she knew that had to mean something; she just wasn't sure what.

Laura picked up a pen and notepad. "So, let's get

started. Madison and Blake, what are some of your favorite things to have for Christmas dinner?"

Before the teenagers could answer, their dad jumped in. "Madison loves the dinner rolls. When she was little, that's all she wanted to eat." John smiled, remembering. "And Blake loves sweet potatoes."

"Dad! I don't eat rolls anymore. They have too many carbs!" Madison gave her dad a look like she was wondering what was wrong with him.

"And I like mashed potatoes now. Not sweet potatoes," Blake said.

John's smile faded. Now he looked apologetic. "Oh, okay, sorry. Good to know. Scratch the rolls and sweet potatoes; we'll buy some mashed potatoes this year."

Madison laughed. "Dad, you don't *buy* mashed potatoes, you have to make them."

John's eyes widened. "Got it. Of course, we'll make them."

Laura gave him a look that said, *Hang in there,* and then turned her attention to Susie and Ian. "What about you two? What are some of your favorite Christmas dinner dishes?"

"My family always has turkey," Susie said with a smile.

"And we usually do Italian. Lasagna or baked ziti," Ian added.

Susie shook her head. "But you're not Italian."

"But that's our tradition."

Susie and Ian looked at each other like they still had a lot of things to figure out.

"Who's next?" Laura asked.

Gail raised her hand. "I always make a special cranberry sauce for my son. It's his favorite."

"And my mom makes the best pie," Susie jumped in.

Excited, John looked at his kids. "And our favorite pie is apple, right?"

"Pumpkin!" they said in unison.

"I give up!" John said in mock despair and dropped his head into his hands.

"Apple's *your* favorite, Dad, not ours," Blake said.

John lifted his head. "Well, see. I even forgot that!"

When the teenagers laughed, John joined them.

Laura turned her attention to Haley. "Okay, Haley, what about you?"

Haley looked at Jeff and at Ben before answering. "Well, honestly, I haven't really done the traditional Christmas dinner in a while . . ."

"What about when you were little? Do you remember anything from then?"

Haley tried to think and then remembered one time when her mom had made stuffing. They hadn't had a turkey, but they'd had the box stuffing. "Stuffing! We had stuffing," she said proudly.

"Stuffing, perfect. Do you like it with gravy from the turkey?" Laura asked.

"I think we probably had gravy from a can, if we had any at all," Haley said. "But I'm sure gravy from the turkey would be great."

"I love turkey gravy," Gail said.

"Me too," Susie said, and then looked at Ian. "Don't worry, you can put the gravy on your Italian food."

Everyone laughed.

"Okay, it sounds like we have our Christmas menu!" Ben said. "I know it's been a long day, so everyone, you're on your own. We won't have any more activities tonight. You can take some time to relax and enjoy one of your last nights here, and yes, Haley, that means you can have your computer and cell phone."

Haley tried to look innocent. "I didn't say a thing."

"But you were going to." Jeff smiled at her.

"Am I that predictable?" she asked.

"Yes!" everyone said at the same time.

When Haley laughed, everyone laughed with her.

A FEW MINUTES LATER she was pacing around her room talking with Kathy on FaceTime.

"So, you'll be home in two days. We definitely need to celebrate," Kathy said while doing a little celebratory dance.

Haley forced a smile. "Sounds good."

Kathy gave her a suspicious look. "What's wrong? You should be dancing around, too. You're almost out of your Christmas jail sentence."

"It hasn't been that bad . . ."

Now Kathy looked really intrigued. "What? What do you mean it hasn't been that bad? That place is Christmas twenty-four/seven, and you don't do Christmas. It's that guy, isn't it? The owner's son? You said you were staying away from him, concentrating on work. What happened?"

"Nothing . . . everything. I don't know," Haley said, looking more confused than ever.

Kathy took a deep breath. "Okay, at least tell me you're done with your Tyler Toys pitch, because Tom finished yesterday, and I hate to say it, but from what I've seen, it's pretty amazing."

Haley looked out her window and watched Jeff playing with Max.

"Haley, are you still there?"

"Sorry. I'm here."

"So, what are you doing to beat Tom?" Kathy asked.

When Haley looked away, Kathy's eyes grew huge. "You're still not done? But you have your pitch in just a few days . . ."

"I know!" Haley shouted into the phone then immediately looked apologetic. "I'm sorry. I don't know what's wrong with me. I've never had such a hard time coming up with a campaign pitch. I have some time to work right now, so I'm going to put something together. You know I work best under pressure."

"Okay, but if you want me to put together a storyboard for your pitch, you're going to need to start sending me some of your ideas. Anything. Tonight. Or else I won't be able to get it done."

"Got it. I promise I'll send something tonight. I have some ideas, I just need to pull everything together."

"Okay, well, don't let me keep you. Go to work! Text me once you've sent it."

"Thank you. I'm on it. Talk soon." Haley hung up and with a look of determination sat down on her bed, opened up her laptop, and brought up the file of Tyler Toys campaign ideas. With her fingers posed over the keyboard, she squeezed her eyes shut and willed herself to come up with a fabulous idea.

But when after a few minutes nothing came to her, she stood up, went back to her window, and looked outside, where Jeff and Max were still playing. "Go back to work," she told herself. "You need to come up with something. Anything." She marched back over and picked up her computer, and this time she sat down at the little desk. She moved an angel so her laptop would fit on it. "Okay, let's do this." She sat up straight and forced herself to smile, but when still nothing came to her, she stared forlornly at the angel. "I need help."

She jumped up, went to her closet, and took out the shopping bag that had the Tyler Toys doll that she'd bought for Anna. She put the doll next to the angel, stood back, and stared at them. "Okay, you two. Help me come up with something amazing for this Christmas pitch. It needs to be traditional, heartfelt, authentic, magical, and charming." Haley picked up the Tyler Toys doll and the angel. "It needs to be a love story to Christmas." As soon as she said the words out loud, her face lit up. She had an idea! Excited, she quickly sat back down at the desk and put the angel and Tyler Toys doll next to each other again. When her fingers started flying over the keyboard, she knew she was onto something special. She didn't even realize she had started humming "Hark! The Herald Angels Sing" . . .

SEVERAL HOURS LATER, when Haley finally pulled herself away from her laptop, she wandered into the sitting room looking for Ben but found Gail sitting by the fireplace knitting a red scarf.

"That's really pretty," she said, admiring the work.

"Do you knit?" Gail asked.

Haley laughed. "I wish I had time to knit. I don't even have time to order a scarf online."

"I'd be happy to show you how if you're interested. It's really easy and relaxing."

"Thank you, that's very sweet. I'm actually looking for Ben. Have you seen him?"

"I think he's in the library."

"Great. I'll try to catch up with him. Enjoy your knitting!"

A minute later, when she peeked her head into the library, she found Ben putting away some books.

"Gail said I might find you in here . . ."

"Haley, what can I do for you? You're all done with work already?" Ben's eyes twinkled. It was clear he was teasing her.

"How did you know I was working?"

"Because that's what you do with any free time you have."

"Okay, true, but I was working on my Christmas toy pitch and it is all about Christmas, so that should make things better."

Ben laughed. "Whatever you want to tell yourself. So, what can I do for you?"

Haley held out her hand. In her palm was the pinecone she had found at Star Peak earlier.

Ben looked surprised when he saw it.

"It's from Star Peak. It's a Christmas wish pinecone," she said.

Now Ben looked even more surprised. "That's where Jeff took you earlier?"

She nodded. "You seem surprised?"

"I am. Star Peak is our special place. As far as I know, he's never taken anyone there before."

"Really?"

"But I'm glad he took you."

Haley handed him the pinecone.

"What's this? I thought this was your Christmas wish pinecone."

"It is," Haley said. "And my Christmas wish is for you to get your wish. You're always helping all of us, and I wanted to give you something, whatever it is that you wish for."

Ben looked touched. "That means a lot to me, Haley. Thank you." He gave her an affectionate pat on the back. "It looks like you might have found it . . ."

"What? The pinecone?" Haley asked, confused.

"No." Ben smiled back at her. "Your Christmas spirit."

CHAPTER 27

When Haley got back to her room, she saw someone was waiting for her. Max. He was sitting patiently with his leash in his mouth and wagging his tail. Haley couldn't help but laugh. "Okay, you win. We'll go for a quick walk." When she bent down to pet him and put on his leash, he caught her off guard and happily licked her face. She jumped back. "Eww, come on, not the face!" As she wiped her cheek with the back of her hand, she kept her eye on Max. "That was sneaky! Don't be trying it again. We don't have that kind of relationship."

Max barked, wagged his tail, and started to trot down the hall, dragging his leash behind him.

"Hold on, I'm coming." Haley hurried to catch up to him.

As soon as they walked outside, the icy, cold night air took Haley's breath away. She bundled up even more, wrapping Jeff's scarf around her neck. She was going to hate giving it back to him. It was always so cozy and warm and had become the favorite part of her borrowed winter wear. As Max pulled her around to the back of the inn, she was surprised to find Gail standing alone looking up at the sky.

"Hi there," Haley called out. "I thought we were the only crazy ones to be out here tonight. The temperature has really dropped."

Gail smiled when she saw her. "It really has. I think they said it's going to get down to around five degrees tonight."

"I guess that means it's too cold to snow. I hope it stays that way so we don't have any trouble driving home in two nights when Christmas Camp is done."

Gail gave Haley a sad look. "I can't believe the week has gone by so fast."

Haley nodded. "I know. My work deadline keeps reminding me of how fast it's really going."

"How are you doing on that?" Gail asked.

Haley smiled a little. "I think I've come up with my pitch. I'm sending it in to my friend Kathy tonight. She's our graphic designer, and she'll help pull everything together in time, I hope."

"Do you think your time here at Christmas Camp has helped?"

"Definitely," Haley answered without thinking about it, surprising herself. She looked back at the inn. "I'm actually going to miss it here. I would have never thought that barely a week ago when I arrived."

Gail laughed and looked down at Max. "I think Max is really going to miss you when you go, too."

Haley bent down to pet Max, but when he tried to lick her face again, she gave him a stern look. "We talked about this, Max. Don't even think about it."

Gail laughed. "See how much he likes you."

"He only likes me because I keep taking him on his walks."

"I think it's more than that," Gail said. "Dogs know a good person when they see one."

Haley covered both of Max's ears with her hands. "Don't tell him. I don't want it going to his head, but the truth is, I think I'm actually going to miss him." She took her hands away from Max's ears and gave him a quick hug. "You're a good dog, aren't you, Max?" Max licked her face before Haley could stop him. "Seriously?" She threw up her hands. "I take back everything I just said, especially the part about you being a good dog."

When Max just wagged his tail more, Gail laughed. "Thanks, you two, for cheering me up."

Haley was instantly concerned. "What's wrong?"

Gail waved off Haley's worry and tried to smile, but Haley noticed that her smile didn't quite reach her eyes. "I just haven't heard from my son, Ryan. I know I shouldn't worry. He has a pretty high security clearance in the military, and he's always traveling somewhere on some mission, so I know he can't always call or email, but still . . ."

Haley put her arm around her. "It's hard. I can't even imagine." She looked up into the sky. "But he has a lot of people watching out for him, right?"

Gail smiled a little as she followed Haley's gaze up into the sky. "He does. You're right. Thank you for reminding me."

Haley shivered. "It is really getting cold out here. Should we head in?"

Gail zipped her coat up even higher. "I think I'm going to stay a few more minutes."

Haley took off Jeff's scarf and wrapped it snuggly around Gail's neck. "Then you're going to need this until you finish the scarf you were knitting."

"Oh, thank you," Gail said, snuggling up in the scarf. "But that scarf is going to be a Christmas gift."

"Nice gift," Haley said.

"I hope so." Gail admired the scarf Haley just gave her. "This is a lovely scarf."

"It's not mine. Jeff let me borrow it."

When Gail smiled a knowing smile, Haley raised her eyebrows. "There's that look again," she said. "I know what you're thinking, about Jeff and me."

"There's a Jeff and you?" Gail's smile grew.

"What? No." Haley rushed to correct herself. "I just meant . . . Oh, forget it. My brain is frozen. I'm heading in. Why don't I leave Max with you to keep you company." She handed Gail the leash.

"Great idea. Thank you," Gail said as she looked down at Max. "And you can lick my face all you want."

Haley shook her head. "Max, you are the most spoiled dog I've ever known. I'll see you guys inside." As she headed back to the inn, the night air seemed even more biting. Out of habit, she went to cover up with Jeff's scarf. When she remembered she'd given it to Gail, she missed it, just like she knew she was going to miss a lot of things at Christmas Camp.

When she got inside she went looking for Ben. She had a few quick follow-up questions for him about the franchise. She was about to head into the library when she heard Ben and Jeff inside, having what sounded like a heated conversation. She didn't want to interrupt, so she turned to go, but when she heard Jeff say her name, she stopped. She knew she should just keep walking, that this was none of her business, but when she heard him say her name again, she couldn't help herself. She went around the corner so they couldn't see her but she could still hear them.

"Haley told me you took her up to Star Peak," Ben said.

"I did. We just took a quick trip. She needed some inspiration for work."

"I think it must've helped. She brought me her Christmas wish pinecone and said her wish was for me to have my wish."

Haley peeked around the corner to see Jeff's reaction and was pleased to see that he looked impressed.

"Wow, that was nice of her," he said.

"It was very thoughtful," Ben said. "And we all know what I'm wishing for this year . . . a way to save the inn."

Jeff looked frustrated. "Dad, you know that's not possible, but what *is* possible is to sell this place for a good price and start a new chapter with me in Boston. I know we said we weren't going to talk about this until after Christmas Camp, but we only have one more day, and we're running out of time. Just let me show you something."

Haley watched as Jeff walked over to the desk, picked up a manila envelope, and handed it to his dad.

"What's this?" Ben looked like he wasn't sure if he wanted to really know.

"Open it up and see," Jeff said.

Ben pulled out some photographs, and Jeff quickly came around so they could look at them together. "We just took the pictures for our waterfront condos. They're going up on the website now. Aren't they great?"

Ben looked impressed. "They are. You did a wonderful job of preserving the old wharf but still creating something modern that people will want to live in."

"People like you, I'm hoping."

When Haley saw Ben's smile fade, she felt bad for him and for Jeff.

But Jeff just kept talking excitedly. "The corner condo is available. I thought after the Christmas Camp is over

we could go and look at it together. There's a great swimming pool and a gym, and it's only about a mile from me,
so you could even walk to my place. We can spend a lot
more time together."

Haley leaned back against the wall. She couldn't watch
any more. It was too hard for her to see Jeff looking so
excited about having his dad move to Boson when she
knew that wasn't what Ben planned to do at all and that
she was now part of that plan.

In bed that night, she tossed and turned. She kept
thinking about how tomorrow would be her last day at
Christmas Camp and her last day with Jeff. Before she
closed her eyes the last thing she saw was the angel on
her dresser glowing in a stream of moonlight coming
through the window.

THE WEATHER COOPERATED for the last day of Christmas
Camp at the Holly Peak Inn. The sun was sparkling, and
there wasn't a cloud in the sky.

Unable to sleep, Haley had gotten up with the sunrise.
She had already showered and dressed and was putting
the final touches on her Tyler Toys campaign pitch. Sitting next to her on the bed was Max. He was sprawled
out watching her work. She had let him jump up on the
bed because he had looked so sad when he came into her
room. It was like he knew she was leaving. Haley glanced
over her Tyler Toys pitch idea one more time and then
looked at Max. "I did it! And it's good! Really good." She
attached the proposal to her email to Kathy, and with a
flourish, she pressed send.

"Done," she said as she petted Max. "I did it. It might
have taken me until the very last minute, but I finally
came up with a campaign that I know Tyler Toys will

love, and now I can just spend this last day relaxing and enjoying whatever happens at Christmas Camp."

She picked up her phone and texted Kathy: *Sorry it's late. See if you can work a Christmas miracle.*

The only response she got back was the shocked emoji.

Haley laughed. She knew Ben would be proud of her. She was finally able to give one hundred percent to her last day at Christmas Camp.

"Max, let's go get some breakfast," she said. Max jumped up and ran to her door. He waited for her, and when she was ready, they walked down the hall together.

When they entered the kitchen the first thing Haley noticed was the chalkboard. The Christmas countdown now said nine days to Christmas, and the word for the day was "inspiration."

"Well, I'm inspired to find something to eat. What about you?" she asked Max.

He barked his approval.

She looked around and finally found his treats inside—what else?—a cookie jar that looked just like Max, only this dog was wearing a Santa hat. She was just giving Max his treat when Laura walked in.

"Good morning, Haley and Max," Laura said in her most cheerful voice. "Have you two come in to volunteer to help me make breakfast?"

Haley looked at Max, and they both looked at Laura. "I don't know about *making* breakfast, but we're both hungry, so I thought we'd get a little snack."

Laura went to the refrigerator, took out a carton of eggs, and handed them to Haley. "The sooner we make breakfast, the sooner you two can eat. How does that sound?"

Max answered with a bark.

"Max has spoken," Laura said. She gave him another treat. "So, let's get going."

A few minutes later, when Jeff walked in, Haley was whipping up eggs like a pro. When she looked up at him she had a proud look on her face.

Jeff looked impressed. "Wow, first Christmas cookies, then soup, and now breakfast. Who knew you were such a whiz in the kitchen."

"Certainly not me." Haley laughed. "But when you have an excellent teacher like Laura, it's hard not to learn something. Still, you might want to hold off on the compliments until after you taste it."

Jeff walked over and peeked into Haley's bowl to see how she was doing. "I have faith in you. I'm sure it will be great."

Instead of making one of her usual jokes, Haley decided to just take the compliment with a smile.

When Jeff went to grab a cinnamon roll that Laura had just frosted, she batted his hand away and gave him an apple.

Instead of arguing with her, he took a big bite. "So, Haley, I heard from the contractor I recommended for your parents, and he said things are going really well."

Haley smiled back at him. "Yes, thank you so much. They emailed me the same thing this morning. We're all truly grateful."

"I'm really glad it's working out," Jeff said.

"It actually might be working out too well."

"What do you mean?" he asked, taking another bite of his apple.

"Well, now that my parents have found a contractor they can trust, they want to do even more renovations."

"And that's a bad thing?"

"That's an expensive thing," Haley answered. "And I

haven't gotten my promotion yet. It's also a lot of time and work."

"The best things usually are," Jeff said as he met and held her gaze.

For a moment Haley forgot what she was doing and whipped her eggs too hard, sending some of the mixture flying out of the bowl. "Whoa!" She snapped back to attention and scrambled to clean up the mess. "Sorry about that. Obviously, I'm still a rookie here. I don't think the Cooking Channel will be calling me anytime soon."

"Lucky you have a job you love, right?" Jeff asked.

"Right," Haley agreed. "And I finally finished my Christmas toy campaign pitch. I can't wait to get back to Boston and show my boss. He's going to love it."

"Then this should get you your promotion, which I'm guessing is your Christmas wish."

Since it was a statement not a question, Haley decided not to answer. Then she remembered she'd never written down a Christmas wish to put in her stocking. It had been their first activity at Christmas Camp, and she hadn't done it. Now she knew she needed to.

She walked over to Jeff and handed him the bowl of whipped eggs. "I'm deputizing you to be Laura's new assistant. I think we'll have a much better chance of actually getting breakfast made before dinner if you help her."

"Wait, what?" Jeff looked from Haley to Laura.

"Oh, wait, and you'll need this." Haley took off her apron and put it around his neck. When their eyes met she smiled and he smiled back. It was a moment that gave her heart hope. She put both of her hands on his chest to smooth the apron out and fought hard not to show the jolt of attraction that went through her when she touched him. As she stepped back, she saw Laura was watching them. She had the same smile on her face that Gail always had, that all-knowing smile, and seeing it made Haley even more self-conscious.

"So just like that you're outta here? Leaving me with *this*?" Jeff looked down at his apron.

Haley laughed. "Yup, just like that." She snagged a cinnamon roll.

"Hey!" he called out. "How come she can have one?"

Laura laughed. "Because she's our guest."

Jeff held up his hands. "And what am I?"

Laura went over and gave him a kiss on the cheek. "You're family. Now help me get breakfast ready."

Haley laughed as she left the kitchen. She was heading up to her room when she heard the teenagers outside. When she opened the door to see what was going on, she saw Madison, Blake, and John making a snowman. John waved her over. "Haley, come help us."

Grinning, Haley grabbed her coat, hat, mittens, and boots and joined them a minute later.

"So, what do you think of our snowman, Haley?" Madison asked proudly. "Isn't he the coolest snowman you've ever seen?"

"Well, I don't know about that . . ." Haley said, pretending to be serious. "I'm going to have to check it out." As she started to walk slowly around the snowman, she caught John's eye and winked. What she saw was pretty impressive, but she wasn't about to admit it to the kids yet.

The snowman stood about five feet tall. He had four sections to his body instead of the traditional three. The head was perfectly shaped and had two round eyes made out of rocks and a mouth made out of smaller rocks. He was grinning ear to ear, literally, as they had also added ears, making them out of leaves. For his arms, there were tree branches—one pointing up and one pointing down—making him look like John Travolta in *Saturday Night Fever*. Haley kept a poker face as she completed her circle around the snowman. "Hmm . . ." she said as she looked closer at the eyes.

"We're not done with it yet," Blake said. "We're still going to do eyebrows."

Haley fought to keep from laughing. "I think eyebrows would definitely add something."

John walked over to Blake. "And you know what else it needs?"

"What?" Blake asked.

John took Blake's hands and pulled off his gloves.

"Hey! I need those!" Blake tried to grab them back from his dad but it was too late. John was already putting them on the snowman's branch arms.

Madison was cracking up until John came over and stole her scarf.

"Wait, not my scarf!"

"Yup," John said, and then put the scarf on the snowman. He was looking pretty pleased with himself until Haley snuck up behind him and stole his hat.

"Wait, what!" John tried to stop her but it was too late. "I need that!"

Haley laughed as she twirled the hat around her finger.

"Hey, it's important to wear a hat when you're out in the cold," John said in his very doctorlike voice.

"Is that so, Dr. John?" Haley asked in a voice that had both teenagers cracking up. "That's really good to know, because it's even more reason why our snowman needs a hat."

Haley tossed the hat to Blake, who quickly put it on the snowman.

"It's perfect," Madison said.

"So cool," Blake agreed.

Everyone was laughing when Laura opened the front door. "Who's ready for waffles?"

Both teenagers took off like a shot and were inside before Haley could even answer. She looked over at John. "Wow, they must really love waffles!"

John laughed. "Oh, they do, and they've already told me how much they're going to miss all of Laura's great cooking." He gave Laura an appreciative look. "It really has been great, Laura. Thank you. My idea for breakfast is usually cereal or frozen waffles. You have definitely spoiled them."

Laura smiled back at him. "I'm glad they like my cooking, but I think what they really like the most about being here is spending time with you."

"I agree," Haley said. "When they first got here, remember how upset they were about getting their phones and computers taken away, and now here you all are making a snowman. Not many teenagers do that anymore, and it looked like they were really having fun."

John nodded. "I think they have been having fun. They've even made their own activities list, like the one we have here, that they want to do at home. This trip has really showed me how fast they're growing up and how we need to spend as much time together as a family as we can. I feel like the time has just gone by so fast, and I've already missed so much."

"I've been starting to feel that way, too," Haley said.

"Well, it's never too late to make a change," Laura said.

"Actually, about that," John said, looking at Laura. "I was going to ask you if you could maybe give me a few quick cooking lessons?"

Laura smiled warmly at him. "So you can make waffles?"

"That and mashed potatoes so I can make the kids their favorite things on Christmas, or at least a few of the things."

"I would love to help you," Laura said.

CHAPTER 28

At breakfast Haley gave Blake and Madison a run for their money on how many waffles they could eat. After everyone was done Ben got the entire group, including Max and Laura, to meet outside.

Blake immediately went over to the big snowman and added some more snow to his big belly.

Madison laughed. "What, did he have too many waffles, too?"

Blake laughed with her. "Good one."

Ben laughed, too, as he held up a pretty wicker basket that had a plush red velvet bow on top. "Okay, everyone, let's get started," he said. "Jeff and Laura and I are all going to be handing out these baskets. I know you've all seen the theme for today is inspiration . . ."

"I love that theme," Susie said.

"Me too," Gail chimed in.

Ben smiled at them both. "I'm glad, because this is our last day together and I want everyone to use their inspiration for our final activity here at Christmas Camp."

Haley felt her smile fade. She knew she should be excited. This is what she'd waited for, to finally be done with Christmas Camp, but as she looked around at the rest of the group she saw that everyone felt the same way she did. Sad.

When Ben noticed their expressions he stopped passing out baskets. "Everyone, there's no need to be sad . . ."

"But we've really loved it here," Susie said, taking Ian's hand.

"We really have," Ian agreed.

"And that's why we need to celebrate and make the most of our last day together," Ben said. "So, who is ready to celebrate?" He held up a basket.

"I am." Madison ran up and took the basket.

"I am, too," Gail said, and took another basket.

"Me too," Haley said as she took her basket.

After everyone had a basket and was smiling again, Ben continued. "So, for our last activity together, I want you to walk around and explore. You can go on a little hike or stay close to the inn, whatever you'd like to do, but your assignment is to gather up some things from nature that inspire you."

"Because today's word is 'inspiration,'" Susie chimed in.

"Exactly." Ben smiled back at her. He then picked a pinecone up off the ground, put it in Haley's basket, and gave her a little wink. "Find things that mean something to you. That connects with a memory or something that you like that you might want to make a new memory with. Just take your time and explore outside. You can also go inside the inn, and see what speaks to you . . ."

Haley whispered to Jeff, "It must run in your family—you guys speaking to nature. First the Christmas trees, now this."

Jeff laughed. "Careful, spend more time here, and things will start speaking to you, too."

"Oh no. I'm not going to let that happen." Haley laughed. "One of us here has to stay sane."

"So, what are we going to do with everything after we find stuff?" Madison asked.

"We're all going to make Christmas-tree ornaments out of what we've found that inspires us."

Blake looked confused. "But we already decorated our trees," he said.

Ben pointed over to where a new six-foot Christmas tree was leaning against the side of the inn.

"We have one more Christmas tree to do . . . together."

"Another tree?" Blake asked. "Where are we going to put it? I don't think there's any more room."

When Ben gave the teenager a look of disbelief, Jeff laughed.

"Oh, there's always room for more Christmas, right, Dad?"

Ben nodded, smiling at Blake. "When you all leave tomorrow, we're taking your trees to the community center. But this tree that we'll all be decorating together will stay here. So after you're all gone, we will still have something to remember you all by."

Gail looked genuinely touched. "That's so nice." She shared a smile with Ben.

"It really is," Susie said. "I love this last activity!"

"You love everything about Christmas!" Haley, Ian, and John all said at the same time. Everyone laughed when Susie just held out both hands.

"And what's wrong with that?"

Ian kissed her on the cheek. "Nothing, honey, absolutely nothing."

Susie grinned at him. "I'm glad you're finally coming around to see it my way."

There was more laughter.

"Okay, everyone, we better get started," Ben said. "Laura's going to put some decorating supplies out in the dining room for you, so you should have everything you need to create your ornaments."

Haley looked a little nervous. "What if you're not very . . . crafty?"

Ben gave her a reassuring look. "Don't worry, Haley. Whatever you do doesn't need to be perfect; it just needs to come from your heart and mean something to you."

Haley looked over at Susie, who was already picking up pine needles off the ground, and then walked over to Gail. "I have no idea what I'm going to make, do you?" she asked.

Gail shook her head. "Not yet, but I'm just going to walk around and see what speaks to me."

"Oh no." Haley laughed. "Now it's rubbing off on you, too. The whole nature-speaking-to-you thing."

Gail gave her a wise smile. "Well, maybe you should try it."

"Try what?" Haley asked.

"Listening to what nature says to you."

Jeff joined them. "But that would mean she would have to stop talking first."

While Haley pretended to be offended, Gail struggled to hide a laugh. Max chose that moment to trot over and bark, making them all laugh.

"Well, Max is speaking to me, but I'm not sure how I'm going to make him into an ornament."

Max barked again.

———

SEVERAL HOURS LATER Haley walked into the dining room to find Blake and Madison sitting at the table working on their ornaments. She quickly saw that Ben hadn't been kidding. Laura had pulled out all the stops covering the table with all kinds of decorating materials. There were bowls of popcorn, cranberries, and lots of colored paper, scissors, tape, glue, and glitter.

When Blake and Madison both grabbed the popcorn bowl at the same time there was a brief tug-of-war.

"I need the popcorn," Madison said, pulling the bowl her way.

"I had it first," Blake said, pulling it back his way.

After some popcorn spilled out of the bowl, Haley stepped in to referee. "Okay, guys, hold on. I'm sure there's enough popcorn for everyone."

"No, there's not," Madison said stubbornly. "For what I'm making, I'm going to need this whole bowl. And now there's hardly any left . . ."

"That's because you ate it all," Blake said, pulling the bowl toward him.

Haley took the bowl away from them. "Okay, I'll tell you what. I'll go make you some more popcorn. Just hang tight."

When she got to the kitchen she headed straight for the pantry, figuring that was her best bet for finding the popcorn, but when she looked around on the shelf, she found everything but popcorn. There was flour, sugar, baking soda, baking powder, and a big box of dog biscuits. When she moved the box of biscuits, Max barked, startling her. She whipped around and found him sitting in the doorway. "Let me guess," she said. "You want a treat?"

When he barked again, Haley laughed, picked up the dog biscuit box, and gave him a treat. That's when she saw the bag of popcorn that was behind the box. "And look, you helped me find the popcorn. You're a good, dog, Max." He wagged his tail even more when she tossed him another treat. "Now, how are you at making popcorn?"

She looked skeptical as she picked up a bag of popcorn kernels. The only popcorn she'd ever made was the microwave kind. Still, reading the instructions, she didn't think it sounded too hard. "So I just need a pan and some oil. How hard can it be?"

Max barked his encouragement.

Ten minutes later, when she was standing over the stove with a saucepan of burning popcorn and kernels were flying all the over the place, she realized making popcorn wasn't as easy as she'd thought. When Jeff walked in, she gave him a pleading look as she held out the popcorn pan that was still sending popcorn flying. "Help!"

"Whoa . . ." Jeff laughed as he took the pan from her and placed it in the sink. "What happened?"

Haley was scrambling around trying to pick all the popcorn kernels off the floor. "I think I put too much popcorn in, or maybe too much oil, or I was trying to cook it too hot . . ."

"Or you used too small of a pan?"

Haley looked at the pan. "Yes, definitely too small of a pan."

"And the lid?"

"Oh yeah." Haley rolled her eyes. "A lid would have been helpful. Clearly, I didn't think this through. I was just trying to hurry and get the kids some popcorn."

Jeff laughed. "So it was for a good cause."

"Exactly."

Jeff took a fancy popcorn popping machine out of the cupboard. "This might help."

Haley nodded. "Of course you have one of those."

Jeff grinned back at her. "Of course. But you know what? Not everyone does, so let me show you the other way."

"No, really, it's okay. Let's use the popcorn machine."

But it was too late. Jeff was already putting the machine back and pulling out a bigger pan. "This should do the trick."

Haley handed him the popcorn bag. "Okay, let's see what ya got."

They shared a smile.

A few minutes later, after Jeff had talked Haley through making two more batches of popcorn, both of which turned out flawlessly, they took the two bowls into the dining room for the kids.

"Here you go," Haley said. "Sorry for the delay. I had a little incident in the kitchen."

"I thought I smelled something burning," Blake said.

Haley shook her head. "Don't ask."

"Awesome! Thank you!" Madison took her bowl from Haley and gave her a grateful look. "Have you started on your ornament yet?"

Haley picked up her basket. It was covered with a red napkin. "Not yet. I'm still looking for that inspiration."

They all looked up as Laura walked in. "Madison and Blake, it looks like you two are hard at work." She then looked at Haley and Jeff. "And I see you two have been in my kitchen."

Haley jumped up. "I'll clean up the mess. It's my fault."

"And I helped," Jeff added.

"It's not a problem," Laura said. "I can clean it up, but would you mind running into town for me? I'd like to add some roasted chestnuts to the dressing I'm making for our Christmas meal tonight."

"Of course not," Jeff said.

"And why don't you take Haley with you," Laura suggested. "Maybe she'll find some inspiration for her ornament." She smiled at Haley, and that all-knowing look was back. "Have fun."

IT WAS A beautiful afternoon as Haley and Jeff walked down Main Street. All the snow on the sidewalks had been shoveled, making it easier for last-minute Christmas shoppers to do their power shopping. When Haley passed a cute couple loaded down with bags struggling to take a selfie, she stopped.

"Here, let me take the picture for you," she offered.

The cute couple gave her a grateful smile. The girl handed over her phone. "Thank you! I was trying to get all the Christmas decorations in behind us, but my arm just wasn't long enough."

Haley positioned the camera just right so it would include all the decorations they wanted. "Okay, are you ready?"

"Ready," they both said.

"Say 'Christmas!'"

"Christmas!" they said together, and started laughing. That's when Haley snapped the picture. When she looked at her handiwork, she was pleased. The picture was adorable. She handed the camera back to the couple. "Here you go."

"Thank you so much," the girl said. "Merry Christmas."

"Merry Christmas." Haley smiled back at them before they continued down the road.

Jeff turned to study her.

"What?" she asked, when she saw the way he was looking at her.

"You just continue to surprise me, that's all."

"In a good way or a bad way?"

He looked into her eyes. "In a good way."

Haley could feel herself blush, so she quickly changed the topic. "So, where are these famous chestnuts you keep talking about?"

"Right up there," Jeff said as he pointed at a street vendor.

A few minutes later, as they walked back to Jeff's truck, he held a bag of chestnuts out to her. "Try one."

Haley shook her head. "That's okay."

"You don't like them?"

"I actually don't know."

"What? You've never had roasted chestnuts at Christmas?"

Haley laughed at his amazement. "Let me guess. It's another one of your traditions?"

"You bet it is. Now you have to try one."

She gingerly put her hand into the bag, pulled out a warm chestnut, and took a tiny bite. Her face registered her surprise. She took a bigger bite. "It's actually really good."

"I told you. Just wait until you try it in Laura's dressing. You're going to love it."

Haley took in the charming scenery as they continued walking. "Talking about loving it . . . my parents would love this place. It's like something out of a Christmas card."

"I thought they loved the beach at Christmas?"

"Well, actually, I think they're more excited to stay home this year and do a regular Christmas."

Jeff looked surprised. "You mean a traditional Christmas? You're doing that?"

Haley nodded and smiled, remembering how excited

her parents had been. "I thought we'd change things up this year."

"Well, there you go again," he said.

"What?"

"Surprising me."

Haley couldn't help but smile as she popped the rest of the chestnut into her mouth.

"Seriously, I think that's really great, and I hope it's a very special Christmas for you," Jeff said. "You deserve a special Christmas."

When Haley looked into his eyes and saw how sincere he was, it made her heart melt.

"But I have one important question for you. Will you be doing snow angels?"

She laughed. "I don't know about that. At this point I'm just hoping we don't have any more pipes burst."

"If you get into any trouble, you can always call me. I've been told I'm pretty handy around the house."

"Really? Even a Money Pit? Because this one can be a beast."

"Hey, I'm the restoration guy, remember. I like a challenge." When he looked into her eyes, she wasn't sure if he was talking about the house . . . or her.

She looked away quickly. "You better be careful, I might take you up on that offer."

Jeff smiled at her as he held out the bag for her to take another roasted chestnut. "I hope you do."

Haley laughed as she took a chestnut. She couldn't remember a time when she'd felt this happy and hopeful.

CHAPTER 29

Back in her room at the inn, Haley was just about to tackle her ornament project when there was a soft knock on her door. She opened it to find Gail standing there.

"Hi," she said. "What's up?"

Gail held up her basket. "I was hoping you could help me with my ornament. I need another set of hands."

Haley opened her door wide. "Absolutely, come on in." When they sat down on the bed, she turned to Gail. "So, what can I do to help?"

Gail pulled some twigs out of her basket and some tinfoil. "I was hoping you could hold these twigs for me while I wrap them in tinfoil."

"Sure, that's easy."

Gail started wrapping up the twigs. "So, I saw you and Jeff making snow angels several days ago."

Haley laughed. "Yeah, that was crazy. I haven't done that in—forever."

"It looked like you were having fun together," Gail said, and her knowing look was back.

Haley shook her head. "You have to stop with the look. It's not like that. I mean, he's a great guy. Look how much he loves his dad, and he's smart and funny and kind and—"

"And you like him," Gail finished for her.

Haley groaned and fell back onto her bed. "And I like him. Now what am I going to do. This was not part of the plan."

"You know what they say, life is what happens when you're making other plans."

Haley sat back up. "But I don't have a life beyond work, and that's really been okay . . ."

"Until now?" Gail asked.

Haley nodded. "I mean, honestly, I don't know what I mean. I'm just confused. You know I'm really good at my job. I'm confident about that. But when it comes to a relationship—that's a whole different story."

"Maybe you're overthinking it. You just need to trust your feelings." Gail gave her hand a little squeeze. "Just let yourself feel what you feel without trying to figure it all out right now."

"So, you're basically saying to just slow down and feel. That's exactly what Ben said I needed to do about being here at Christmas Camp, so I could find my Christmas spirit."

"And has it worked?"

Haley nodded, looking thankful. "I think so . . ."

Gail put her arm around her. "I think so, too."

ABOUT AN HOUR LATER everyone gathered at the dining room table. Haley sat between Gail and Jeff. Everyone had their baskets in front of them with their ornaments inside. When Jeff tried to lift Haley's red napkin to peek at her ornament, she playfully swatted his hand away. "It's a surprise."

Ben overheard her and laughed as he stood up. "So, is everyone ready to reveal what they've made? I know Haley's been keeping hers a big secret."

Madison jumped up. "I'll show mine!"

"Great," Ben said as he sat back down. "Okay, Madison, show us what you've made and tell us what inspired you."

Madison gave her brother a grateful look when she held up her ornament. It was about the size of a tennis ball, made of popcorn and cranberries. "I wanted to make a Christmas ornament that could go outside, for all the birds, so they can have a Christmas meal, too."

Susie clapped her hands. "I love that!"

"So do I," Gail said. "I want one of those for my house."

John looked at Madison with such pride and love. "That's really beautiful, honey, the ornament and the idea. Great job."

Madison was beaming from all the praise. "Blake helped."

John looked surprised. "Really? You two worked together on it?"

"It was her idea, I just helped with the glue."

"So it was a true team effort," Ben said. "Now that's the Christmas spirit. Nice job." He turned to Susie and Ian. "Okay, Susie what do you have?"

Susie smiled at her husband. "Well, Ian and I also worked on our ornament together."

"I wanted something natural," Ian said.

"And of course, I wanted a little bling," Susie added.

"Of course," Ben said.

Everyone laughed.

Ian kissed Susie on the cheek. "But we found a way to compromise and not just on making the ornament."

Susie smiled back at him. "Being here this last week really showed us that now that we're married, we need to have our own Christmas traditions. We, of course, want to respect our family traditions, as different as they are, but we now know it's all about having balance."

"And compromising," Ian added.

"And compromising," Susie agreed.

"I have faith that you two will find a way to honor all your traditions, old and new, this Christmas," Ben said.

"Thanks to you and this Christmas Camp." Susie smiled back at Ben. "So, here's our ornament. It will always be a reminder of our first Christmas together."

When she held up their beautiful ornament everyone could see that it was a pinecone covered with gold glitter.

"A little bit of nature," Ian said.

"And a little bit of bling," Susie added.

Ian kissed her on the cheek.

"Very nice!" Ben said.

"I want one of those at my house, too," Gail chimed in. "It's beautiful."

"Okay; so, Gail, you're up next. Show us your ornament," Ben said.

Gail smiled as she held up a lovely little star made out of twigs and tinfoil. She looked over at Ben. "Thank you for inspiring me, Ben, and for putting me in the star room and sharing how special stars are in our life. It's a true gift you've given me, one I'll never forget, and I'm very grateful."

Haley took it all in. When she saw how Gail's heartfelt words touched Ben, she knew there was the potential for something very special between them. She glanced over to Jeff and saw he was smiling and watching them, too.

"Okay, Dad, it's your turn," Blake said. "What did you make?"

All eyes turned to John. He looked a little embarrassed. "You know I'm not great with arts and crafts . . ."

"But you made something, right?" Madison asked, looking concerned.

John nodded. "Ben said to make something from your heart, that inspired you, so that's what I did, or at least tried to do."

When he held up his ornament, there was a collective "Awww . . ." It was a paper heart. On one side, there was a picture of Blake, and on the other side a picture of Madison. Madison and Blake looked touched.

"Where did you get our pictures?" Madison asked.

"I always carry them in my wallet," John answered. "You guys are always with me, even when we're not together. I love you both so much. I hope you always know that. And I promise this is a new start for us. I'm going to spend less time at work and more time with you—"

Before he could finish, Madison gave him a hug.

"I love you, Dad." Her voice cracked with emotion.

Blake high-fived his dad. "That's cool, Dad. Thanks."

Ben looked over at Haley. "Okay, we saved you until last, Haley. Show us the ornament you made and tell us what inspired you."

Haley laughed nervously. "Well, mine's pretty basic compared to all of yours."

"Come on, show us what you've got," Jeff said in a teasing voice.

Max barked. He was sitting at Haley's feet looking up at her.

"See, even Max wants to see!" Madison said.

Everyone laughed.

"Okay, okay . . ." Haley slowly took off the red napkin that had been hiding her ornament and held up a long red velvet ribbon that had dog biscuits tied to it. When one fell off, Max gobbled it up.

"Merry Christmas, Max." When Haley laughed, everyone laughed with her.

Ben watched Haley closely. "And what inspired you to make this for Max?" he asked.

As she looked down at Max and petted him, all of a sudden she felt a flood of emotion. "I guess what inspired me was that Max never gave up on me even though I tried to ignore him when I first got here, because I've never really been around dogs."

"But he wouldn't let you ignore him," Jeff said.

"No, he wouldn't. No matter what I did, he just kept showing up."

"That's kind of how Ian was with me," Susie said. "He wouldn't take no for an answer and just kept showing up."

Ian's eyes grew wide. "Are you calling me a . . . dog?"

Everyone laughed again.

Susie kissed him. "No, I'm calling you the love of my life. Someone who I know, no matter what, will always show up."

Haley continued to pet Max. "And I get it now. Why people love their dogs so much. Because they love you back no matter what, right, Max?" Max licked her hand. She whispered to him, "I'm going to miss you."

But Jeff heard her and whispered back to her, "He's going to miss you, too." When Haley looked into his eyes, she saw only kindness and understanding, and it made her care for him even more. She didn't even want to think about how much she was going to miss him.

"Okay, time to move into the siting room," Ben said, getting everyone's attention. "We have a Christmas tree to decorate."

As the group gathered around the tree, Blake looked impressed. "Wow, the tree looks even bigger in here," he said. "And we only have a few ornaments . . ."

"Oh, we're not just decorating with the ones we've made," Ben said, pointing to three boxes in the corner. "Those are ornaments our other guests have made over the years. So, we always put them up, too, so every year we get more and more."

"You're going to need another tree," Madison said.

"Oh, please, don't give him any ideas," Jeff said with a laugh.

"I think it's a wonderful tradition," Gail said. She smiled at Ben. "I can't wait to be part of it."

When Haley looked over at Jeff, their eyes met and held for a moment before she got out her ornament and looked for a place on the tree to put it.

"Then let's get started," Ben said. "I'll go put on some Christmas music."

As Haley walked around the tree looking for the perfect spot for her ornament, Jeff joined her.

"How about I help you with that," he said, taking her ornament and putting it up on a high branch. "This way your new friend, Max, won't be able to get it. You wouldn't believe how resourceful he is."

Haley laughed. "Oh, I would believe it. Thank you. That's perfect."

"Your ornament is pretty perfect, too," Jeff said. "I know Max thinks so."

They looked over and saw Max lounging by the fireplace, watching them.

"Even though I know you didn't want to be here, I'm really glad you came," Jeff said.

When Haley looked into his eyes, she forgot to feel guarded and scared. She just felt happy. "I'm really glad I came, too." Jeff moved closer to her, never taking his eyes off of her, and her heart beat faster.

"You know, we both live in Boston," he said. "And when my dad moves there, he'll have Max, so you should really come and visit the two of them. I know they'd like that."

"And what about you?" Haley asked boldly. "Would you like it?" She couldn't believe she'd asked exactly what she was wondering out loud, but at the moment she felt hopeful, like anything was possible.

Jeff smiled a slow, sexy smile. "I would. Very much."

Ben interrupted the moment with another announcement. "And now it's time for the presents," he said, getting everyone's attention.

"Presents? I didn't know we were doing presents?" Susie said, looking concerned. "I don't have anything for anyone. Ian, you should have let me go shopping."

"It's okay," Ben interrupted her. "We're not exchanging presents This is just a little something I have for all of you. Another tradition. I'll go grab them. They're in the library."

"I can get them for you, Dad," Jeff said.

"Great, thank you, son. They're in a box on my desk. Just bring in the whole box."

"I'm on it," Jeff said. "I'll be right back." When he smiled at Haley, her heart raced faster. She hugged herself a little and couldn't stop smiling. She already felt like she'd just been given the best gift in the world.

CHAPTER 30

Jeff walked into the library, smiling and humming "We Wish You a Merry Christmas." He was feeling thankful that this Christmas Camp had been such a huge success. He'd wanted his dad's last one to be special, and this one was. He also was feeling thankful for Haley and how she made him feel. He felt like his heart was finally opening up again, and that's something he hadn't felt since his mom had passed away. It was like the heaviness was finally lifting, being replaced by hope. He didn't know what his future with Haley held, but he knew he wanted to find out.

When he saw the box of presents, he quickly picked it up and accidentally knocked a file from the desk on the floor. Haley's Christmas Camp proposal landed at his feet. As he went to pick it up he saw her name on it. Confused, he quickly flipped through the proposal. His smile disappeared. He couldn't believe what he was seeing. He didn't want to believe it.

He shook his head in disbelief. "I should have known . . ."

As soon as Jeff walked back into the sitting room with the box full of presents, Haley knew something was wrong. He didn't look at her. His body was rigid, and his jaw was clenched tight.

She hurried over to him. "Is everything okay?" When she touched his arm, he moved away, and when she looked into his eyes, they were cold and hard. It took her breath away. Before she could ask him what was wrong, Ben came over and took the box from him.

"Here we go," Ben said happily, and started handing out presents. Each present was beautifully wrapped and topped with a red velvet bow.

"Go ahead, everyone, you can open them." He handed John a present. "This one is for the whole family."

"Thank you." John smiled back at him.

"Can I open it?" Madison asked eagerly.

"Sure," John said, and handed her the present.

Within seconds, Madison was ripping off the paper and opening a box. She took out a pretty framed photograph. It was a picture of her dad, her brother, and herself when they were all sledding. In the picture, the smiles on their faces showed how happy they were.

"This is great!" Madison said, showing her dad and brother.

"Cool," Blake agreed.

"Very cool," John chimed in. "Thank you so much, Ben. This is our first family photo together this Christmas and a wonderful way to remember our time here."

"I'm so glad you like it. I always find that photographs are the best memory keepers, and nowadays everyone's taking pictures in their phones and not as many people are printing them up. So, this way you have one."

As everyone else opened their own sledding pictures,

there was a lot of laughter and reminiscing. Haley was about to open her present when Jeff walked over to her.

"I need to talk to you," he said. His voice barely concealed how upset he was.

Haley immediately put down her present. "Okay."

"Not here," Jeff said. "Come with me." As he turned around and left the room, Haley quickly followed him. He didn't say a word until they entered the library and then he shut the door behind him. When he turned to face Haley, she was startled because now he wasn't trying to hide his anger. It was all over his face.

"What happened?" she asked. "Just tell me."

He walked over to the desk and picked up the Christmas Camp proposal. "What's this?" he asked. As he locked eyes with hers, his question seemed more like an accusation.

Haley was surprised to see her proposal. "Your dad told you?"

"No. No one has told me anything. That's the problem. I just found it by accident."

When she saw the anger in his eyes, she struggled to find the right words, but he didn't wait for her.

"This looks like you're trying to sell my dad on some franchise idea for his Christmas Camp. Is that why you're really here? You came here to try to get my dad as one of your clients?"

"What? No . . . It's not like that!"

"So, this franchise business wasn't your idea?"

Haley could feel herself start to sweat. "Well, yes, it was my idea, but . . ."

Jeff gave her an incredulous look. "I am not going to let you take advantage of my dad."

Now it was Haley's turn to get angry. "I would never do that! I'm trying to help him so he can keep doing his

Christmas Camps. That's what he really wants, not to move into the city into some condo . . ." She realized she'd gone too far when she saw the way Jeff was looking at her, like she was the enemy.

"The only person you're trying to help is yourself!" He threw the proposal on the desk.

Haley flinched. His words cut through her like a knife.

"I don't know why I thought any different," he said. His voice was filled with a mixture of anger, hurt, and disappointment. "I mean, you made it very clear when you came. You said you were only here for work. I just didn't listen, or I thought you'd changed. My mistake, a big mistake. Congratulations. You might have fooled my dad, but you haven't fooled me."

When he stormed out of the room, Haley just stood there, in shock, with her heart breaking.

HALEY WAS IN her room packing when she heard a knock on the door. She rushed over to get it, hoping it was Jeff so she could try to explain, but it was Ben. Her shoulders slumped, and her head dropped.

"Are you okay?" he asked, looking upset and concerned. "I apologize for anything my son might have said or done."

Haley reached out and took his hand. "You don't need to apologize for anything. I'm just so sorry he found out like this and jumped to all the wrong conclusions. You know I was only trying to help you, right? I wasn't trying to drum up more business and get you as one of my clients . . ." Her voice cracked. It hurt her even saying the words. When Ben gave her a hug, she finally let the first tear fall. "I really am sorry. I was only trying to help . . ."

"Of course you were!" Ben said, gently patting her on the back. "I know that, and once Jeff calms down, he'll see it, too. He's just so overprotective of me right now, and he's been working so hard to get me to sell this place. I'm sure it was just a big shock to see the proposal."

He stood back and looked into Haley's tear-filled eyes. "This is all my fault. Not yours. I guess I should've told him from the start. I just didn't want to say anything until I was sure it would work. You have to know I am so thankful to you for finding a way to save the inn, to save our Christmas Camps. You know that, right?" When Haley just stood there and looked miserable, he gave her another hug. "It's gonna be okay. I'm sorry I got you in the middle of all this."

"Don't worry about me. I worry about you. This was my idea, and now I'm coming between you and Jeff. It's the last thing I wanted to do . . ."

"I know that."

"Really?" Haley asked in a small shaky voice. "Because I swear I was only trying to help you . . ."

"I know. It's going to be okay. I'll talk to Jeff. Don't you worry about anything."

Haley nodded but still looked depressed and heart-broken.

"Everyone's downstairs asking where you are, because we're about to do our Christmas dinner. You can't miss that. It's the best part of our week together, and Laura worked really hard and even made your stuffing. So, do you think you can come down and join us?"

Haley couldn't even imagine going down and facing Jeff, but she didn't want to let Ben down. She owed it to him at least to show up. "Just give me a second to wash my face and put myself back together, and I'll be right down."

Ben smiled at her. "Good girl." He squeezed her hand. "It's going to be okay. It's our last night together with everyone. Let's make it a good one. Everything else will work itself out. I promise."

A few minutes later, when Haley entered the dining room, the first thing she noticed was that Jeff's chair was empty. She was both relieved and disappointed. As she sat down, she learned that he had gone back to the city because something last minute had come up at work, but he'd wished them all a Merry Christmas. Everyone was disappointed but understood, everyone but Haley, who knew it wasn't really work that had him going back to the city. It was her. Gail gave her a concerned look.

"Are you okay?" Gail whispered to her. "I saw you and Jeff leave to go talk and then he looked pretty upset when he left to go to Boston."

Haley just gave Gail a sad look. "It's a long story. I'm sure everything will be fine." But even as she said it, she knew it wasn't true. She didn't know if it would be fine at all. She shivered thinking how Jeff had looked at her. His look hadn't been the kind that gave you much hope of anything ever being fine again, and that's what hurt her heart so much.

When Laura brought out a beautiful turkey, everyone clapped, and Haley forced herself to concentrate on the meal and not let anyone else see her sadness. When Max came to sit by her and put his head on her lap, it almost made her cry again. She knew he was trying to give her comfort. He always seemed to know just what she needed.

After Laura put down the turkey, Ben stood up. "Laura, we all want to thank you for all your hard work on this special Christmas meal and all our meals this last week. You put the joy, the inspiration, and the wonder in every meal we ate, and please know how grateful I am for that."

"We all are," John said, and everyone nodded in agreement.

"And for this meal, we know you've worked hard and made all our favorite Christmas dishes," Ben said. "And that is a wonderful gift you've given us."

Laura smiled at them all. "Thank you, Ben. You all know it has been an honor and my privilege to get to know you this last week, and when it comes to this last Christmas meal, I can't take all the credit. I had some help." She motioned over to John. "John made the mashed potatoes, from scratch."

Blake and Madison looked shocked. "No way," Blake said, looking at his dad.

"Yes, way." John laughed. "With the help of Laura, of course. She also taught me how to make her famous waffles, so we can have those Christmas morning."

Madison's face lit up. "Really? That's awesome, Dad. So cool."

John gave Laura a grateful look. "We need to thank Laura and Ben and Christmas Camp. I think we've all learned a lot this week."

Ben picked up his glass of wine, and all the adults followed. "To finding your Christmas spirit! Merry Christmas, everyone."

"Merry Christmas." They all toasted each other.

Haley fought to keep smiling. She put her wineglass down. When she saw Max looking up at her, she smiled back at him and was sure he understood. He always seemed to understand.

THAT NIGHT IN BED, she couldn't sleep. The moonlight was coming through her window, and it made all her angel decorations look like they were glowing. She got out of bed. She knew what she needed to do.

She put on her robe and quietly went downstairs, where she found Max sleeping by the fire. He looked up when she came into the room and wagged his tail. "Shhh," she told him. "Go back to sleep." For once, he listened to her, and put his head back on his paws and shut his eyes.

As Haley tiptoed over to the fireplace, she had her eye on one thing. Her stocking. After she carefully removed it from the fireplace, she sat down on the couch and took out the Christmas wish scroll she was supposed to write her wish down on her first day at Christmas Camp. On that day she had left it blank. She unrolled the scroll and also found the angel pencil in her stocking.

Max looked up at her.

"I know what I want to wish for now," she told him.

He wagged his tail.

CHAPTER 31

The next morning, the last morning at the inn, as Haley and Max took their traditional sunrise walk, Max didn't pull her along as he usually did. Instead, he walked by her side. As the wind picked up it felt like the temperature was dropping quickly. She shivered and looked down at Max. "I think it's time to go in."

Max sat down and looked up at her. He wasn't moving.

"I know," she said. "I'm going to miss our walks, too." When she bent down to pet him, she also gave him a hug. "Thanks for being my friend." This time when he licked her face she let him, because he was licking tears that she couldn't stop from falling.

A few minutes later, when they walked into the kitchen, Haley got one of Max's treats and gave it to him, and he perked up instantly. She wished it was that easy for her. When she looked over at the chalkboard she saw the Christmas countdown had already been updated. It now said LAST DAY OF CHRISTMAS CAMP! 8 DAYS TO CHRIST-MAS, and the word for the day was "love." Seeing it just made Haley's heart hurt more and she knew it was time. She couldn't stay any longer. She needed to go home.

A FEW MINUTES LATER, when she came out of her room carrying all her bags, Max was waiting for her. Seeing him just made it harder. She put down her bags and got down on one knee so she could give him another hug. "Now, you be a good dog," she said, determined to lighten the mood, "and some fashion advice. Don't be wearing any more crazy Christmas Camp sweaters."

Max barked.

She smiled back at him. "I am going to miss you, Max."

When she got downstairs she ran into the rest of the group putting on their coats and getting all bundled up.

Ian gave her a surprised look. "You're leaving?"

"But we're about to take our Christmas trees to the community center," Susie added.

When Haley gave Ben a look, he nodded and she knew he understood. She managed a smile. "I got a call from work and I really need to get back," she said. "Plus, the weather doesn't look great outside, so I want to get going before it starts snowing . . ."

Ben went over, got Haley's stocking from the fireplace, and handed it to her. "This is to remember us by." He also picked up the present she had left unopened last night. "And don't forget your present."

Haley gave him a hug. "Thank you. Thank you for everything."

"We'll talk after Christmas about our idea," he said. "For now, just go enjoy the time with your family."

"I'm going to miss you," Gail said. "Thank you for helping to make my time here so special."

Haley went and gave Gail a hug, too. "I'm going to

miss you, too. I'll be keeping you and your son in my thoughts and prayers. I hope you hear from him soon . . ."

"I'm sure I will." Gail smiled back at her.

Haley looked at the rest of the group. "I'm going to miss you all. It really was great meeting everyone."

Max barked.

When everyone laughed Haley was grateful, because she felt like she was about to cry. Once again Max had saved her. She looked down at him fondly. "And of course I'll miss you, too, Max. Even though I'm looking forward to sleeping in."

When everyone laughed Haley knew it was her chance to escape without breaking down. "I better get going . . . Merry Christmas, everyone!"

"Wait, don't forget your certificate!" Ben said. "Your boss will be wanting this." He handed her a scroll that was tied with a red velvet ribbon.

Haley couldn't believe she'd completely forgotten about it. It was the whole reason she'd come, but now everything felt so different, including the things that had mattered so much before.

"Are you ready for your work pitch?" Ben asked.

"I am," Haley said. "And we'll talk soon about our project. Very soon. Good-bye, everyone . . ." She grabbed her bags and hurried toward her car. She didn't dare look back. She didn't want the others to see the tears in her eyes. When she heard Max bark, the first tear fell. She quickly threw her bags in the trunk and got into the car, tossing her certificate onto the passenger seat. She was still holding the Christmas present Ben had given her. She put it down but then picked it back up again and decided to open it. Inside she found a wonderful framed picture of her and Jeff sledding. They were laughing and looked so happy. She didn't even realize she was crying until a tear dropped onto the picture, landing on Jeff's face, and slid slowly down the glass.

She put the picture down next to her certificate and started the car. She just wanted to get home, back to her real life, back to work, where she belonged.

CHAPTER 32

As night fell on the Holly Peak Inn a howling wind whistled through the trees and the snow started to fall.

Jeff found his dad in the sitting room giving their new Christmas tree some fresh water. "I just heard from Gail; she got home safely and so did Ian and John, so everyone's good. They left early enough to beat the storm."

"What about Haley, did you check on her?" Ben asked.

Jeff gave his dad a look.

"Son, I told you. I'm the one who asked her not to say anything about the franchise idea. You shouldn't be mad at her. She was just trying to help . . ."

"Help herself get a new client," Jeff said as he added another log to the fire.

"She was trying to help me, help us. This Christmas Camp is your legacy as well as mine. Can't you see that?"

"What I see is that this franchisee idea is too risky. I don't want you using the last of your savings on a gamble and getting your hopes up and getting hurt . . ."

"Are you sure you're not worried about yourself getting hurt?" Ben asked. "Isn't that the real reason you're so upset? I saw the way you and Haley were together."

"Dad . . ."

Ben walked over to the fireplace and joined his son. "Wait, hear me out. We lost your mom, but that doesn't mean we should be afraid to love again. Don't you think your mom would want us to be happy?"

"Of course," Jeff answered.

Ben took the photo of the three of them off the fireplace mantel and handed it to Jeff. When Jeff looked at his mom his heart ached. He missed her so much. He missed what they were like as a family, and most of all he missed the love he always felt when she was around. "I know Mom would want us to be happy, but she wouldn't want us making bad choices . . ."

"You think Haley was a bad choice?" Ben asked.

When Jeff didn't answer, Ben walked over to his Santa collection, picked up a new Santa and a Christmas card, and handed them to him.

"What's this?" Jeff asked, looking at the Santa.

"A present, a Santa for my Santa collection. Read the card . . ."

Reluctantly, Jeff read the card out loud. "'I believe. Thank you for helping me open my heart to Christmas and to love. Merry Christmas. Haley.'" Confused, conflicted, he looked up at his dad.

"People can change," Ben said. "I told you, anything is possible at Christmas . . ." He took the Santa and carefully put it back with the rest of his collection. "The question is, do you believe?"

THE NEXT DAY, back in Boston, Haley hustled down the street, texting on her cell phone. This time when she got to her office and saw the Santa ringing his bell next to a sign that asked DO YOU BELIEVE? she stopped, put her phone away, and got out some money to donate.

"Merry Christmas!" the Santa said. "Do you believe?"

"With all my heart," Haley answered back. "Merry Christmas." As she entered her office building she took a deep breath. This was it, her big day, the day she was pitching Larry her Tyler Toys Christmas campaign idea and she had never felt more confident or sure about anything in her life. She knew exactly what she needed to do.

When she got to Larry's office, the first thing she did was hand him the crazy Christmas sweater he'd given her. "Merry Christmas," she said.

"Wait." Larry gave her a look. "I gave you this. Are you re-gifting?"

"I guess I am," Haley said, and smiled back at him. "And I also have this." With a proud swagger she handed him the Christmas Camp certificate she had worked so hard for.

Larry looked impressed. "You really did it."

Haley put her hands on her hips and assumed the position, her power-pose, superhero position. "I did."

Larry sat back in his chair and crossed his arms in front of him. "Okay. You held up your end of the bargain and I'm holding up mine. I'm ready to hear your pitch. Where's your storyboard? I know Kathy put one together for you . . ."

"About that," Haley said as she sat down.

"You're sitting down?" Larry looked confused. "You never sit down . . ."

Haley picked up a nearby snow globe and shook it, and then smiled as she watched the snow fall. "I've been thinking a lot about the Tyler Toys account and what's best for the company, and I think Tom should be the one to pitch it."

Larry stood up from his desk. "What? Wait, I'm sure I didn't hear you right . . ."

Haley smiled and stood up, too. "No, you did. I'm giving Tom the account to pitch if that's okay with you. I already talked to him about some of the ideas I had that he could incorporate into his pitch if he wanted. Like my idea about having an angel tree and having Tyler Toys help make children's Christmas wishes come true and some other ideas."

"But you wanted this account so much. You said it meant everything to you."

"It did," Haley said.

"And you even went to Christmas Camp for a week— *you,* someone who doesn't even like Christmas, just so you could get this pitch. I don't understand what happened?"

Haley put down the snow globe. "It wasn't that I didn't like Christmas. I think I just forgot what matters most at Christmas. I told you about the idea I came up with to help Ben franchise his Christmas Camps?"

Larry nodded. "And I think it's a great idea."

"That's the account I want to work on. Tom can have Tyler Toys."

"But the Christmas Camp account is just a mom-and-pop start-up."

Haley nodded. "I know, and that's where my heart is. If I learned anything at Christmas Camp, it's that at the end of the day you have to follow your heart or you're not really living your life; you're just going through the motions."

"Are you sure?" Larry still looked stunned. "What made you change your mind?"

Haley smiled confidently. "I'm sure, and Christmas Camp made me change my mind. I've realized I'm so busy rushing to get ahead in my career that I've been missing some of the most important things in life: my family, spending time with my friends, love . . ."

Larry smiled slowly, walked over to Haley, and held out his hand for her to shake. "Congratulations," he said.

Now it was Haley's turn to look confused. She took his hand. "For?"

"For finding the balance between your career and your personal life. That's what's going to make you a great partner here."

Haley's mouth dropped open. "What? You're still promoting me?"

Larry looked into her eyes. "You earned it, Haley. Merry Christmas."

BACK IN HER office Haley was putting the last of the decorations on a little Christmas tree she had just bought. It was another Charlie Brown Christmas tree and it was adorable in its own funny way. The tree had a theme. All the decorations were angels, just like her room back at Christmas Camp.

As she admired her work she picked up the Christmas stocking Ben had given her and pulled out the little Christmas wish scroll. She opened it up and read her Christmas wish out loud.

"My Christmas wish . . . is love."

Just as she put the scroll back into her stocking Kathy breezed in and looked around in awe. "Whoa. Look at you. I can't believe you've done all this decorating so fast. Who are you and what have you done with my Grinchy best friend?"

Haley laughed, reached for a present underneath her little angel tree, and gave it to Kathy.

Kathy looked surprised. "Wait, this isn't the gift card you usually give me?"

Haley smiled back at her. "That's right. I thought we'd start a new tradition."

Kathy opened the present and her face lit up. She held up a beautiful crystal angel ornament. "It's beautiful. I love it! Thank you!" She gave Haley a quick hug, then noticed the new picture on her desk and picked it up. It was the picture Ben gave her of her and Jeff sledding at Christmas Camp.

"Well, this explains so much," she said, looking at the picture. "You look . . . happy."

Haley nodded. "I was."

"You still haven't heard from him?"

Haley's smile faded. She shook her head. Her heart hurt just thinking about Jeff.

Larry walked in. "Ben, from the Christmas Camp, is here to see you."

Haley's face lit up. "Ben's here? He didn't tell me he was coming into the city . . ."

"Well, he's in the conference room, waiting for you," Larry said as he left her office.

"Thanks!" Haley practically ran out the door to the conference room. When she raced inside her smile faded a little when she saw Ben was alone.

He stood up. "It's just me, sorry."

Haley quickly hid her disappointment and gave him a hug. "I'm so happy to see you. I'm just surprised. I didn't know you were coming into the city."

"It was a last-minute decision, so I thought I'd stop by and surprise you and take you out to dinner to celebrate. Larry just told me you gave up the big toy account you wanted so you could have more time to work with me.

You didn't need to do that, Haley. I know how much that big account meant to you . . ."

"Not as much as you and Christmas Camp mean to me," Haley said, giving his hand a squeeze. "I'm really excited about working together."

"So am I. So let's go celebrate. I'm taking you to a great place for dinner," Ben said as he guided her out the door, not giving her a chance to protest.

As she passed him she noticed he was wearing a red scarf. "That looks like the scarf Gail was knitting . . ."

Ben smiled proudly. "It is. She gave it to me as an early Christmas gift."

Haley arched her eyebrows. "I know she was working very hard on it. You're very lucky."

Ben touched his scarf and looked smitten. "Yes, I am."

CHAPTER 33

A half hour later Haley was completely confused when Ben stopped his truck outside a cute little house that was beautifully decorated for Christmas. There were white twinkling Christmas lights and an adorable snowman out front.

"Where are we?" she asked as they got out of the truck and she looked around. "I thought you were taking me to dinner?" But before she could say another word, the front door of the home opened and Gail appeared. "Surprise. Merry Christmas!" she said, holding both arms out wide.

"What?" Haley looked from Gail to Ben. She couldn't believe it, and then her eyes grew even wider when she saw Susie, Ian, and John all come out the door, too.

"Surprise!" Susie said.

"Merry Christmas!" John said.

Haley covered her mouth with her hand. "What? All of you are here?" She looked behind John. "Are the kids here, too?"

"They're here," John said. "They're in the back room

watching a Christmas movie they actually agreed on. It's a Christmas miracle."

"No, it's Christmas Camp," Susie said.

"Same thing." John laughed.

While everyone laughed Haley was still looking and hoping for one more person to come out the door, but no one came. She looked at Ben. "So everyone's here?"

"Except Jeff," Ben said. "I'm sorry."

To hide her disappointment Haley gave him a hug. "Best surprise ever. Thank you. Thank you so much."

"Come on, everyone, let's get inside, it's cold out here," Gail said as she hustled everyone in. Haley hurried over to give her a hug.

"What a great surprise," she said.

"It was all Ben's idea. It turns out we all live within an hour of each other, and he thought since you had to leave the inn so quickly, why not have one more great night. Plus, I needed help decorating my tree. I wasn't going to decorate this year, but Ben thought I should . . ."

"And I agree with him one hundred percent," Haley said. "So let's see this tree."

As they walked into Gail's home Haley looked around and smiled. The little house suited Gail perfectly. It was cute and cozy, and the focal point when you walked in was a fireplace that had a nice fire crackling. On the mantel she saw a picture of Gail's son, Ryan. He was in his military uniform and looked very handsome. Haley figured he was probably about her age. The picture next to it was the photo of Gail and Ben sledding. Haley looked around at her Christmas Camp group.

"I still can't believe you're all here!" she said. She couldn't stop smiling.

"I heard there was a Christmas party and who can say no to that!" John joked.

"And after you left Ben told us about how you're helping him save his inn and his Christmas Camp by expanding to other resorts," Gail said.

"It's amazing, Haley, that you can help him do that," John said.

"It really is," Ian added.

"But just to be clear, Ben, we're only coming to your Christmas Camp at Holly Peak Inn," Susie said. "Because it's our new Christmas tradition; right, honey?"

Ian put his arm around Susie. "That's right, and we're adding sledding and even turkey to the list of our new traditions."

"Very nice!" Ben said. "And Laura wanted to be here, too, but she's spending time with her family."

"Well, please tell her we all missed her," Haley said. "Especially her cookies."

Gail smiled at her. "Well, if you come help me in the kitchen I might just have some that she sent along with Ben."

"Really?" Haley's eyes grew big and her mouth began to water. "I've been dreaming of those cookies. I'm in. Where's your kitchen?"

Everyone laughed.

"Save some for the rest of us," John called out as Gail and Haley disappeared into the kitchen.

As soon as they walked in, Haley noticed a group of Santa mugs lined up on the counter.

"Hey, those look just like the mugs we had at Christmas Camp!"

Gail nodded and smiled. "They're exactly the same. Ben knew how much I loved them and got them for me for Christmas."

"That's so sweet," Haley said.

"It really is. He's a very sweet man."

"Yes, he is," Haley agreed, and loved that it looked like she'd been right about a potential match between Ben and Gail.

"And I have something for you," Gail said, and went over and picked Jeff's scarf off the kitchen table. "You loaned this to me and I didn't get a chance to give it back to you."

When Haley took the scarf, her heart hurt. "Thank you, but it's not mine. It's Jeff's. You should just give it to Ben to give to him."

Gail had already started pouring some hot chocolate into the Santa mugs when her cell phone rang. "Haley, can you grab that for me. My hands are full."

"Sure." Haley picked up the phone, but when she saw who was calling she quickly ran over to Gail and took the hot chocolate from her. "You need to get this."

"What?" Gail looked confused until she saw it was Ryan calling on FaceTime. Her hand shook as she answered. "Ryan? Is everything okay?"

Ryan grinned back at her. "Everything's great, Mom. I only have a few minutes, but I just wanted to call and say I love you. Merry Christmas."

Gail's eyes filled with grateful tears. "I love you so much. I miss you . . ."

Haley's own eyes were tearing up as she slipped out of the kitchen to give Gail some privacy. As she entered the living room everyone was talking and having a great time. When she looked over at Susie and Ian sitting by the fire holding hands, she saw so much love . . . and it reminded her of what she didn't have. She needed to get some fresh air.

As she slipped out the front door the chilly night air whirled around her. When she realized she was still holding Jeff's scarf, she wrapped it around her neck, savoring how it felt. She walked over to the snowman and noticed Madison's scarf, Blake's gloves, and John's hat. The hat was a little lopsided, so she adjusted it and then looked up at the stars.

"You can see the stars a lot better at Christmas Camp."

Haley spun around, and when she saw Jeff walking toward her, for a moment she wasn't sure if it was real. It had begun to snow and in the darkness everything was starting to blur. But as he got closer she knew it was him. She felt it before she could even see him clearly.

"I didn't think you were coming . . ." she said, still straining to see in the darkness.

"I had to come," he said as he got closer.

"To see everyone?"

"To see *you*." He had now stepped into a stream of light that was coming from the Christmas lights decorating the house.

Haley also stepped into the light, meeting him halfway. She'd thought about it, so many times, what she'd say to him if she saw him again, but now that she had the chance, her mind was blank and her heart was racing. Finally, she just looked up at him and said, "I'm sorry."

As he came closer he looked into her eyes. "I'm the one who's sorry. I know you were only trying to help my dad," he said.

When Haley shivered he immediately took off his coat and wrapped it around her. "I just really believe that I knew what was best for him, and I was wrong."

Haley touched his arm. "You love him. You were just trying to help."

"I was, but my dad and my mom have always followed their hearts, no matter what the risk, and the inn is part of my dad's heart. I'm grateful to you for finding a way he might be able to keep it."

"Really?" Haley asked, her voice full of hope.

Jeff took her hands in his. "And I need to follow my heart, no matter what the risk, and that's why I'm here tonight. I know we've haven't known each other very long, but I know that my life is already better with you in it. I don't know if you can forgive me, but I was hoping maybe we could start over and—"

Before he could finish Haley kissed him with all the love and hope in her heart, and when he kissed her back, she could feel that love returned along with the promise of many more Christmases together.

When she looked into Jeff's eyes she saw her future. "I finally made my Christmas wish," she told him. "I wished for you."

When they kissed again she heard Ben say . . .

"Now that's Christmas spirit!"

When Haley and Jeff turned around they saw the whole gang had gathered by the door and all of them were watching them and celebrating.

She looked embarrassed, hiding her face, but Jeff smiled back at them.

"It looks like we have a fan club," he said as he took her hand and held both their hands up in the air.

Everyone cheered.

"Do you know another reason I had to come back?" Jeff asked, turning back to face her.

"No, what is it?"

Jeff took both ends of her scarf and pulled her closer to him. "To get back the scarf you stole."

Haley laughed and snuggled into the scarf. "I think it looks better on me."

Jeff kissed the tip of her nose. "So do I."

When she turned back to the group, her eyes lit up and she took Jeff's hand. "Look at your dad and Gail," she whispered. Gail had just kissed Ben's cheek and Ben was holding her hand. "I think something special might be happening there."

Jeff smiled when he saw how happy his dad looked. "I hope so."

When Haley kissed his cheek just like Gail had kissed Ben's, everyone watching cheered again.

Haley and Jeff laughed.

"Merry Christmas!" Haley called out to everyone.

They all answered back in unison . . .

"Merry Christmas!"

When Haley looked up at Jeff and saw so much love in his eyes, she felt so thankful that she had been able to open her heart to Christmas, and to love, and she couldn't wait to see what would happen next.

ACKNOWLEDGMENTS

Storytelling. It's what I've always done. Ask my mom. She loves telling people how when I was two, at the grocery store, some woman looked at me and asked her, "Does she ever stop talking?" and my mom smiled and said, "Only when she's sleeping." Thankfully, my mom, Lao Schaler, and my bonus mom, Kathy Bezold, encouraged my storytelling and are still the first to read everything I write. Knowing I always have their unconditional support is everything.

When I wrote my original TV movie *Christmas Camp,* inspired by my Travel Therapy TV series showing how transformative travel and new experiences can be, I fell in love with my *Christmas Camp* characters. I wanted to share more of their story, and knew the best way to do that was in books. This movie-to-book crossover wouldn't have been possible without three people who all took a chance and believed in my vision, starting with my entertainment attorney, Neville Johnson, my champion for helping me transcend the way things are "usually" done.

My next gladiator is Foundry Literary + Media agent Jessica Regel, who fearlessly took on this project, despite the challenging roadblocks we faced with traditional publishing deadlines. Her yes gave me a chance.

My next yes, from executive editor May Chen at HarperCollins, changed everything. With Liate Stehlik and Jennifer Hart, May not only understood my vision but also embraced it, welcoming me into the publishing family. This incredible team, including associate editor Elle Keck, copy editor Martin Karlow and Anne Sharpe, Amelia Wood in marketing, managing editor Karen Davy, publicist Pamela Jaffee, and art director Elsie Lyons, who created our magical book cover, has truly made *Christmas Camp* and *Christmas Camp Wedding* an inspiring and empowering publishing experience. I feel grateful and blessed to be part of this new amazing "family."

It takes a village, and mine also includes my treasured friend Heather Mikesell, who did a fantastic job copyediting my first drafts quickly so I could make my tight deadlines and Denise Seomin at the Phoenician, a Luxury Collection Resort, for believing in and embracing the Christmas Camp concept and helping me bring my Christmas Camp concept to life at the property. I'm also thankful to Greta, Samuel, Denise, Lee, Lorianne, Lisa, Delia, Clint, Amy, Tim, and Jeryl for their loyal friendship and support and to the rest of my family, my dad, Harry; Jon, David, Margaret, Deb, Wynn, John and Nathan who are always cheering me on.

I also want to thank and honor my stepdad, John Bezold, my grandma Irene and grandpa Harry Schaler, my grandpa Walter, and my inspiration for all I do, my grandma, Patricia Crane, who lived a happy, healthy 103 years, and read a book every day. When I look up at the sky at night and see the stars, I always think of all of you.

The journey continues . . .

CHRISTMAS CAMP RECIPES

So you can re-create your own Christmas Camp experience with your family and friends, here are two of our favorite Christmas Camp recipes and our favorite activity, Christmas Camp Charades.

Enjoy and Merry Christmas!

Christmas Camp Hot Chocolate
SERVES 2

Ingredients
2½ cups any combination of milk (cow's, almond, soy, etc.)
4 heaping tablespoons unsweetened cocoa powder
1 teaspoon cinnamon
1 teaspoon nutmeg
1 teaspoon vanilla extract
1–2 tablespoons sugar or honey to desired sweetness
   (optional)

Whipped cream
1 tablespoon dark chocolate shavings
1 tablespoon fresh finely crushed candy cane plus 2 whole
   candy canes to use as stir sticks
1 shot peppermint schnapps (optional)

Instructions

1. Heat the milk in a saucepan over medium-high heat (do not boil). Whisk in the cocoa, cinnamon, nutmeg, and sugar and cook, constantly stirring, about 4 minutes.
2. Remove from heat and add in the vanilla.
3. Divide the hot chocolate into 2 favorite Christmas mugs.
4. Add a shot of peppermint schnapps, if using, and top with whipped cream, dark chocolate shavings, and fresh, finely crushed candy cane.
5. Serve with candy canes as your stir sticks.

Christmas Camp Sugar Cookies Secret Recipe
MAKES 24 COOKIES

Ingredients

2¾ cups flour
1 teaspoon baking soda
½ teaspoon baking powder
½ teaspoon salt
1 cup softened butter
1¼ cups sugar
1 egg
1 teaspoon vanilla extract
½–1 teaspoon peppermint extract
1 16-oz. can cream-cheese frosting at room temperature
½ to 1 cup finely crushed candy canes

Instructions

Note: Hand mix all ingredients. Using a mixer makes the cookies tough.

1. Preheat oven to 375°F.
2. Mix the flour, baking soda, baking powder, and salt in small bowl.

3. In a large bowl, cream together the butter and sugar.
4. Beat in the egg, followed by the vanilla and peppermint extracts.
5. Slowly add in the dry ingredients and mix until combined.
6. Roll the dough into 2-inch balls and put on ungreased cookie sheets.
7. Gently flatten the balls slightly with the palm of your hand.
8. Bake 9 to 11 minutes. Let cool on cookie sheet for 2–3 minutes, then transfer to wire racks or parchment paper.
9. Let cookies cool for ½ hour before generously covering entire cookie with the cream cheese frosting and adding lots of crushed candy canes on top. Enjoy!

Optional: Add some red or green food coloring to the frosting.

CHRISTMAS CAMP CHARADES

Equipment:
1 Christmas stocking to hold song selections
Small blank strips of paper to write song selections on
Notepad and pen for scorekeeping
Christmas Camp sugar cookies and hot chocolate (of
    course)

Directions:
All players should be wearing Christmas sweaters, the
crazier the better!

   Divide players into two teams. Put one person in charge
of selecting Christmas songs (see following suggestions),
write those song titles on the slips of paper, and put them
into the Christmas stocking. This person will also act as
the Christmas Camp referee, making sure all rules are
followed. Decide how many rounds you will play.
   Each team will pick one player to compete against the
other, at the same time, with the first person who guesses
correctly winning, and scoring 1 point for their team.
The next two competitors face off and this continues until you have reached the number of rounds you want to

play. The team with the most victories wins, with team members earning the title of Christmas Camp Charade Champions!

Optional: Little presents or Christmas treats, like candy canes, Christmas cookies, fudge and fruit, can be given out the winners of each round or given to the winning team.

Rules:
- Christmas spirit must be maintained at all times.
- Competitors acting out songs can't talk. Laughter is the exception.
- Competitors can point to their nose if a teammate guesses a word correctly.
- No cheating is allowed or you'll end up on the Naughty List.

Christmas Camp Charades Song Suggestions:
- "Santa Baby"
- "Hark! The Herald Angels Sing"
- "The Little Drummer Boy"
- "I Saw Mommy Kissing Santa Claus"
- "Joy to the World"
- "Jingle Bells"
- "O Christmas Tree"
- "Deck the Halls"
- "Rudolph, the Red-Nosed Reindeer"
- "Winter Wonderland"

Dying to know what happens
next for Haley and Jeff?

Exclusively for this edition, keep reading for
the bonus short story

CHRISTMAS CAMP
WEDDING

CHAPTER 1

Haley Hanson was right in the middle of one of those once-in-a-lifetime moments every girl supposedly dreams of. She was trying on a spectacular wedding dress. But looking at herself in the mirror, instead of feeling overjoyed, she almost felt—guilty, because this had never been her dream.

A successful career woman and the youngest partner at one of Boston's most prestigious advertising agencies, Haley had always been more of a realist than a fairy-tale kind of girl. But somehow, in the most unlikely way, she had found her HEA, her Happily Ever After.

Meeting Jeff had changed everything.

Even as she thought about him now, she had to catch her breath. He had a way of doing that to her, taking her breath away. His love, his kindness, his dedication to family, his passion for life and his work, and most of all, his unconditional love for her had opened a door to a future she had never dared dream of. The fact that he was also incredibly handsome was just a bonus.

From the moment she had met Jeff and his dad, Ben, at

Christmas Camp a year ago, the path she had always been on shifted. With Jeff, her journey to find love had been far from easy. There were bumpy roads, wrong turns, detours, and delays, but in the end, she knew that right now, even if this hadn't been a dream she'd grown up with, she was exactly where she was meant to be, standing on a dressing room platform, inside one of Boston's beautiful boutique bridal stores.

As she did a slow spin in front of the mirror, taking in her stunning silk-sheath wedding dress, she still couldn't believe how trusting her heart had led her here.

It was really happening.

She was marrying Jeff in forty-eight hours, on Christmas Eve!

She still couldn't believe how fast the last year had flown by. The last few months especially were a blur, planning the wedding while helping Jeff's dad franchise his Christmas Camp concept.

When she first pitched Ben the idea, she believed it would be successful, but nothing had prepared them for the overwhelming response of people wanting to do the Christmas Camps, not just in the United States but in Europe, as well.

Working in advertising, she knew one of the keys to being successful was creating something people needed. She had learned firsthand just how powerful and life changing a Christmas Camp experience could be. She knew the day she had given up a prestigious national account to help Ben launch the Christmas Camp franchise idea that she was doing the right thing, just like she knew now, two days before her wedding, that she was marrying the right person for all the right reasons.

The fact that she had no doubts left her with an incredible sense of gratitude and wonder at how this could now be her life. She had gone from being nicknamed the Grinch to having her own Christmas miracle.

As her sparkling oval-cut engagement ring caught the light, she smiled remembering how Jeff had proposed to her at the same place his dad had proposed to his mom, at Star Peak, overlooking a breathtaking snow-covered mountain range.

Jeff had started off by having them both look for a pinecone so they could make a Christmas wish together, a tradition in Jeff's family. After he had helped Haley pick the perfect pinecone, she had found a stunning engagement ring tucked inside. Jeff had told her it was his dad's idea to use diamonds from his mom's wedding ring to have a special ring created just for her, to continue the tradition of true love. He had then gotten down on one knee and proposed, saying how much he loved her and that he wanted to spend every Christmas together for the rest of their lives.

Knowing that Jeff had proposed to her at Star Peak, just like his dad had proposed to his mom, meant everything to her. Now that his mom had passed away, she knew it was even more important to him to honor her memory by keeping special traditions like this alive.

Haley would be the first to admit that when she first met Jeff and his dad, Christmas traditions weren't exactly her thing. That's why her boss, Larry, had sent her to Holly Peak Inn, to Christmas Camp, to find her Christmas spirit, hoping it would help her land a huge new holiday advertising campaign.

For years, Haley's idea of celebrating Christmas meant getting out of town and taking her parents to the Caribbean to avoid all the Christmas craziness and celebrating the holiday. While her parents would vacation on the beach, she would always work, using the time not celebrating Christmas to get ahead, while her competitors took time off.

But as soon as Haley had arrived at Christmas Camp, she quickly found there was no avoiding the Christmas craziness there. She was surrounded by Christmas 24–7, from the decorations, to the activities, to the meals, you name it. If it had anything to do with Christmas, it was happening at Christmas Camp. Haley had desperately wanted to escape, but when her boss insisted she stay the entire week, all she could do was try to find ways to avoid all the holiday hoopla. But every time she tried to take a shortcut, she kept running into one big roadblock.

Jeff.

Jeff's dad, Ben, owned the inn and ran the Christmas Camp, so Jeff had made it his personal mission to keep an eye on Haley. He'd known she didn't want to be there and had told her he wanted to make sure she didn't wreck the other guests' experiences. That's when she had nicknamed him the "Christmas Camp Police."

But what had started out as Christmas Camp chaos had turned into something much more meaningful for Haley. Through Christmas Camp, she was able to learn what mattered most at Christmas—family, friends, community, and love—and was then able to open her heart to finding her Christmas spirit and finding true love.

If someone had told her back then that the following Christmas she'd be marrying the "Christmas Camp Police," she would have laughed them all the way to the North Pole.

But yet, here she was, wearing a wedding dress. It was crazy. Christmas crazy, in a good way.

Haley twirled around one more time in front of the mirror. "So what do you think?" She looked over at her best friend, Kathy, who was enjoying the posh surroundings, lounging on a white velvet settee, sipping champagne.

Kathy lifted her glass in a toast. "I think it's perfect for you. It's simple but chic, classy but not stuffy, expensive but not showy. It's totally you. I love it!"

Haley smiled brightly. "So do I. They did a great job with the alterations."

"It's going to be perfect for the pictures," Kathy said.

"I hope so." Haley reverently touched her silky dress. "You know, at first, I only agreed to do all of this—the designer dress, the fancy cake, and all the flowers—because my mom and dad needed some promotional pictures to get ready to open their B&B. But now, honestly, I'm really getting into it. I guess it's happened. I've officially caught bridal fever."

"And why not?" Kathy said. "You only do this once. You deserve this."

"I'm just glad I was able to get everyone to donate everything in exchange for all the publicity this will hopefully bring them."

Kathy nodded. "Your parents are lucky they have a brand specialist for a daughter who can work her magic and make all these things happen."

"I'm just thankful all the renovations are finally done at the Money Pit, in time for the wedding, and to open after Christmas," Haley said.

Kathy gave her a look. "Hey, remember, you're not supposed to call it the Money Pit anymore? That's bad karma. It's now your parents' beautifully restored Victorian that's going to be one of the hottest B&Bs in Massachusetts."

Haley laughed. "As long as I'm still paying the bills on it, I'm calling it the Money Pit."

"Fair enough," Kathy said and smiled back at her.

A pretty salesclerk walked over to Haley holding a fabulous bejeweled tiara and veil. "Are you ready to try this on?" she asked.

Haley nodded, excited.

As the salesclerk arranged the veil, Haley shut her eyes.

"Okay, you can open your eyes now," she said.

When Haley opened her eyes and looked at her reflection in the mirror, she let out a small gasp. As she fought back tears of happiness, she couldn't believe this was really her life. She was getting married to a man who was better than any dream she'd ever had. "I feel like . . ."

"Cinderella?" Kathy asked.

"No," Haley laughed, breaking the spell. "I could never do those glass slippers." She thought about it for a moment, then smiled. "I feel like Meghan Markel in my own fairy tale."

They all laughed.

When Haley struck the perfect princess pose, Kathy snapped a quick picture with her phone. "Well, no one deserves a fairy tale more than you and Meghan." Kathy lifted her glass of champagne for a toast. "To the fairy tale . . ."

Haley held out her empty hands. "Wait, where's my champagne?"

Kathy was already pouring her a glass. "After you get out of your dress."

"I think that's our cue," the salesclerk said to Haley, as she led her back into the dressing room and carefully helped her out of her dress. Haley, with a grateful smile, handed her the veil and tiara. "Thank you, this is all perfect."

The salesclerk smiled back at her. "We'll have it all ready for you up front. You're going to look beautiful. This dress is perfect on you. We can't wait to see the pictures."

"Thank you, again, for everything." Haley gave her a grateful smile.

A few minutes later, Haley came out of the dressing room wearing chic black pants, strappy high heels, and a sapphire-blue leather coat. She looked every inch the success she was.

When Kathy handed her a glass of champagne, they clinked glasses. "Now we can toast together. To my best friend getting married, chasing her dreams, and creating her own happily ever after. You're my inspiration."

Haley gave Kathy a heartfelt hug. "And thank you for being here and doing all this with me."

Kathy sipped her champagne, smiled. "You're my best friend. Where else would I be? Plus, I love the dress I get to wear." Kathy walked over to a gorgeous burgundy velvet cocktail dress that was hanging up.

"Only the best for my best woman," Haley said. "It really is going to look amazing on you."

"I love that you're not calling me your maid of honor," Kathy said. "The word 'maid' is too close to the word 'old maid,' and I don't need to be reminded . . ."

Haley laughed. "We're only thirty-three. You're not an old maid."

"Yeah, well tell that to my dating app where all the guys only want to date hot twenty-year-olds."

"Then you need to find a better place to meet guys," Haley said.

"Well, one of those places is supposed to be a wedding, but then you decided to have this small, intimate wedding, so you're not helping me out one bit."

Haley laughed. "So, you're saying I should have done a big wedding so you could meet someone?"

Kathy poured herself more champagne. "Exactly. You're supposed to help me get my HEA."

Haley put her arm around her. "I'm sorry I let you down on this one, but I know your happily ever after is just around the corner. Jeff's dad always says at Christmas anything is possible. You just have to believe."

Kathy laughed. "And to think a year ago I was calling you Grinchy."

Haley grinned back at her. "I guess my heart has grown three sizes, just like the Grinch's."

"And then some," Kathy agreed.

Haley put down her champagne glass. "Now that we're done here, I need to head over to the Money Pit to make sure everything's perfect for our shoot. We need some great pictures to launch the B&B's website and social media pages."

Kathy gave her a look. "You mean you need to go to your parents' fabulous B&B?"

Haley laughed.

"You know, it really does look amazing now that the renovations are finally done. Jeff did a great job helping finish everything up."

Haley agreed. "The perks of marrying an architect who specializes in restoration projects. I think he loves our old Victorian as much as my parents do. They all see the potential . . ."

"Where you've only seen the problems," Kathy finished for her.

"Well, there have certainly been enough of them, but thankfully, that's all in the past," Haley said. "So, do you want to come with me? We're shooting the wedding cake and flower pictures today. I could use your creative eye. You are one of my favorite graphic designers at work."

Kathy arched an eyebrow. "One of your favorites?"

Haley laughed. "Sorry, I meant my favorite, first and foremost, and always and forever."

"Okay, now you just sound like you're practicing your wedding vows."

Haley's smile faded. "Thanks for reminding me. I still have to write them."

Kathy looked surprised. "You haven't written them yet? You're getting married in forty-eight hours."

Haley shook her head. "I know. I need to do it. I've just been so busy with everything, I haven't had a chance."

"I'm sure you'll come up with something fabulous. You come up with slogans and advertising copy for a living. Piece of cake."

Haley smiled, nodded. She didn't want to admit to Kathy, or anyone else, that she had tried to write her vows several times, but she could never seem to find the right words. She wanted everything to be perfect, starting with this first photo shoot. "Okay, let's get going." Haley headed for the checkout counter where the salesclerk was waiting with both of their dresses. "Are you with me?"

Kathy caught up with her. "Always."

"And wait until you see the incredible cake." Haley got out her phone and showed Kathy a picture of it. The cake was amazing! It was snow white, with six different tiers all in the shape of different squares. It looked like a bundle of Christmas presents all wrapped up with an elaborate burgundy fondant bow.

"Whoa! That's some cake." Kathy looked impressed. "I've never seen anything like that. It's supposed to be Christmas presents, right?"

"Right." Haley brought up another picture to show her. "I actually saw this picture of it after it won a pastry competition in Paris."

"Nice," Kathy said.

"Right? And you know Jean Michael on Newbury

Street? He was able to re-create it for me. It took forever to make, but it was worth it. Look how beautiful it is."

Kathy gave Haley's hand a little squeeze. "This is going to be the perfect wedding."

Haley nodded. "And I'm getting really excited."

"Just don't turn into a Bridezilla on me," Kathy said.

Haley laughed. "Never." She was about to say something else when her phone rang. She was surprised to see it was Jeff calling on FaceTime. She picked up quickly. "Hey babe, what's up? I thought you were going to be in meetings all day?"

Jeff's handsome face looked troubled. "I was, but . . ."

Haley looked at the phone closer. "Wait, are you at my parents' house?" Her eyes grew huge. "And what's happening behind you? Is that water pouring out of the ceiling?"

Jeff took a deep breath. "Haley, you need to get over here right away. We have to cancel the wedding."

CHAPTER 2

Haley and Kathy stood in her parents' living room and looked around in shock. The scene was horrific. Water was still dripping from the ceiling, and there were buckets of water everywhere. Plastic sheets covered all the furniture and the floors.

"I can't believe this . . ." Haley's voice was overcome with emotion. "Are my parents okay?"

Jeff came over and put his arm around her and cradled her close. "Your parents are fine. They went out to the tree farm to get some fresh garland and holly for the wedding. I've already called them. They're heading back now. So, no one was here to know a pipe had burst until I stopped by to drop off some things for the wedding."

Haley still couldn't believe what she was seeing. As she looked over to the massive dining room table, her shock turned into sadness. "Oh no . . ." She looked up at Jeff.

He looked just as sad. "I know. I'm sorry."

On the table was what used to be her exquisite designer wedding cake. It now didn't look like a cake at all. Instead it was just a lumpy puddle of flour and frosting. The deep crimson stream of melted fondant running across the table made it look like a wedding cake crime scene.

As Haley walked over for a closer look, her heart hurt. The cake had meant something special to her. She always said that Jeff's love was the best Christmas gift she had ever received and having her cake designed to look like Christmas presents symbolized that.

And the cake wasn't the only thing destroyed. All of Haley's flowers for the wedding, dozens and dozens of red and white roses, that she had been getting ready to use for the photo shoot, were now all soggy and drooping, with their petals falling off.

It made her sick to her stomach, realizing that her perfect plan to launch her parents' new B&B and to have a dream wedding had gone the way of the *Titanic*. Everything was underwater.

Haley looked up at the water still dripping from the ceiling. "So, what happened?"

"A pipe burst in the bathroom upstairs," Jeff said. "By the time I got here, most of the damage was done. I already have a plumber upstairs, and we'll be able to put down a new floor tomorrow, and we'll get this place cleaned up really fast."

Haley gave Jeff a hopeful look. "How fast? In time for our wedding on Christmas Eve?"

Jeff shook his head. "No, I'm sorry. Not that fast. We have to check out the electrical and make sure everything is safe. No one can stay here until we get the all clear."

When Haley laughed, it almost sounded like a cry. As she picked up one of the wet rose bouquets, water dripped off the petals. "Everything's ruined." She looked over to

Kathy, who was standing silently in the corner. "You were right. I jinxed this place by still calling it the Money Pit, and I also jinxed my wedding. We're going to have to call the whole thing off."

"There has to be something we can do," Kathy said. Still, she cringed when she looked over at the dining room table.

"Right," Jeff said. He was quick to come to Haley's side and take her hand. "We're not calling off the wedding. We can order another cake and flowers. It'll be fine. The place doesn't matter. As long as we have our friends and each other."

Haley, still reeling from the shock, gave him an incredulous look. "We can't just find another place. It's two days to Christmas. Everything's booked. Nothing's available. That's one of the reasons we decided to have it here in the first place. And your friend Steve, the best man, he's flying in from LA. He was supposed to stay here and so was your dad and everyone else, so we could all spend Christmas together after the wedding." Haley's voice was getting higher and higher. She knew she was starting to spiral out of control, but she couldn't help herself. All she could think about was how disappointed her parents were going to be. She had come up with the perfect plan to have her wedding at the B&B to get the publicity photos for the website and now none of that was going to happen. "This is a nightmare."

Jeff grabbed both of her hands and looked into her eyes. "It's going to be okay."

"How?" Haley asked. She was close to tears. "My parents planned to open right after Christmas. They have worked so hard on this. This is their dream."

"And they'll still be able to open on time. It looks a lot

worse than it is," Jeff said. "I promise you. I already have guys lined up who said they'll work around the clock getting this place fixed up."

"But if we can't have the wedding here, we can't do all the publicity photos for them."

"You have all those other photos that are great," Jeff said. "You have more than enough for the website."

"But they don't show a wedding, and everyone loves a wedding. That's why we were doing this."

"I thought we were doing this because we love each other and wanted to get married," Jeff said in a teasing voice. Haley knew he was just trying to lighten the moment, but right now she felt like the weight of the world was on her shoulders.

Kathy came over. She had a more positive look on her face now. "Jeff's right. The other photos we've already shot are fantastic. Your parents are going to be fine. Right now, we just need to concentrate on where you're going to get married. That's the most important thing."

Haley didn't look like she agreed.

Jeff looked into Haley's eyes. "Kathy's right. I love you. I want to marry you, and I don't care where or how we do it."

"I want to marry you, too, but it's not that easy," Haley said. "It's almost Christmas. Most places are either booked or closed."

Jeff put his arm around her. "I've already made a call, and I've worked everything out."

Haley and Kathy both gave him a skeptical look.

"You found us a place to get married and for everyone to stay?" Haley asked.

Jeff kissed the top of her head. "I did, and it's perfect."

"Where?" Kathy asked. "Because Haley's right. Everything's booked."

When Jeff smiled at them both, he looked quite pleased with himself. "Except us. We never book the inn at Christmas. That time is just for family."

Haley's eyes grew huge. "You want us to get married at Christmas Camp?!"

Jeff nodded as he looked into her eyes. "It's where we met, fell in love, where I proposed—it's perfect."

Haley shook her head, trying to take it all in. Jeff's dad's Holly Peak Inn was in a remote area, up in the woods. It had a special rustic charm, but Haley couldn't even imagine how they could ever pull off a wedding there. "But I thought your dad shuts down now until New Year's," Haley said just as some more water from the ceiling dripped on her head. Jeff quickly pulled her out of the way.

"He is shut down, so he could be here for the wedding, but I've already called him, and he's called Laura, and she's going to help, as well, and they're going to open back up just for us," Jeff said.

"Who's Laura?" Kathy asked.

"She's the chef I told you about that did the Christmas Camp," Haley answered.

Kathy smiled and nodded. "The one who made the Christmas cookies you loved."

"That's the one," Jeff said. "We all love those cookies, and now she can make them for the wedding. I'm sure she can make a wedding cake, as well."

Haley gave Jeff an incredulous look. "It's not that easy to just whip up a wedding cake, especially when she'll have to do all the other meals, as well. We can't ask her to do all that."

"Laura volunteered," Jeff said, "and you know how she's practically part of the family. She was coming to the wedding anyway."

Haley looked stressed. "Coming to the wedding and working the wedding are two different things."

Jeff wasn't fazed by her tone. "The point is, everyone can help. They're all waiting for us to get up there. We can make this work. Think of it as an adventure."

Haley stared at Jeff. She didn't look happy. "So now our wedding's an adventure? We've gone from our goal of having it be picture-perfect to get publicity shots for my parents' B&B to an adventure. Seriously? What else can go wrong?"

"Don't say that!" Kathy grabbed Haley's hand. "You'll jinx us again." Kathy looked so serious it made Haley laugh and for that she was grateful.

She knew she needed to stop having a pity party and put things in perspective. While the burst pipe had caused a huge mess and meant canceling the wedding at her parents', no one was hurt, and that was the most important thing. Everything in the house could be fixed, everything but her beautiful wedding cake. Just as Haley looked over at the cake again, more drops of water from the ceiling dripped into the puddle of what used to be her cake, making the already gooey mess even more pathetic looking.

As she looked over at Jeff, there was only one thing she knew for sure, how much she loved him, and he was right. It didn't matter where or how they got married as long as they got married and started their lives together as a team. That was the important thing.

If she was honest with herself, it was when she had decided to combine her wedding with her personal work project to help get publicity for her parents' B&B that she had gotten swept up into the whole perfect wedding thing. She knew right now she was dangerously close to being one of those Bridezillas you always hear about instead of just being thankful she had a great guy in the first place who loved her and wanted to spend the rest of his life with her.

She mentally pulled herself together and walked over to Jeff and gave him a kiss.

He looked surprised in a good way. "What was that for?"

"For being you. I love you, and you're right, the rest doesn't matter. We can even go down to City Hall and get married. I don't care."

"Actually, you can't," Kathy said. "It's closed for the holidays."

Haley laughed. "Okay, no City Hall."

"We don't need City Hall, we have Christmas Camp," Jeff said. He looked excited. "You'll see—it's going to be great. We already have all the beautiful decorations set up at the inn for Christmas Camp, and the rooms are ready. This can totally work. Dad even has a wedding planner already pulling things together for us."

Haley looked surprised. "How in the world did your dad find a wedding planner at the last minute like this?"

Jeff shrugged. "You know my dad. He said something about knowing someone who knew someone or something, but the point is, we can make this work. Right?"

When Haley looked into his eyes, she remembered all the reasons she loved him so much, including his always-positive can-do attitude. She took a deep breath and smiled. "We can make it work. Let the adventure begin."

Jeff, looking relieved, pulled her into his arms for a heartfelt hug. "That's the spirit."

Haley laughed. "The Christmas spirit? Is this another Christmas Camp lesson?"

"Hey, you said it. Not me," Jeff laughed. "But you know what my dad would say."

Haley looked into Jeff's eyes. "He would love it."

"Just like I love you."

When they kissed, Kathy waited a few seconds then cleared her throat. "Okay, you two lovebirds. Stop it. We have a wedding to plan."

Jeff laughed. "She's right. You just need to go home and pack and get up to the inn as fast as you can. Dad says the wedding planner is waiting to meet you. I'll go to the airport and pick up Steve. We'll share a room to make space for everyone else. It'll be just like at college. It'll all work out. Don't worry. I'll see you at the inn. I already told your parents the plan. They're heading up as soon as they get back and grab some stuff. I'll also let Gail know what's happening."

"Gail's not already up there with your dad?" Haley asked. "I thought she was helping him with the Christmas Camps?"

"She has been, but she came back into Boston yesterday, thinking the wedding was here," Jeff said. "She said something about wanting to get her hair and nails done, all that girl stuff. So, now I told her the change of plans, and she's getting what she needs and heading back tomorrow morning."

Haley turned to Kathy. "Gail was part of my Christmas Camp group, and she and Ben hit it off."

"What about the rest of the Christmas Camp crew that was coming?" Haley asked.

"I already texted John, and he's letting everyone know."

"Are these the guys who did the camp with you last year?" Kathy asked.

Haley nodded. "They're all great. I can't wait for you to meet them. There's John and his two kids, Madison and Blake, and then Ian and Susie, this fun couple in their twenties. Susie is Miss Christmas. You'll love her."

"They all sound great," Kathy said. "I can't wait."

"My boss, Larry, is traveling for the holidays to see his daughters, and so are a lot of other friends. We knew that was going to happen, but it was really important for us to get married during Christmas."

"So, we're just doing a really small wedding now, and then, we'll have a big party in January to celebrate with everyone," Jeff said. "But when the Christmas Camp crew heard about the wedding, they all wanted to come."

Haley looked worried. "That's when it was in the city. You're sure everyone's okay with heading up to the mountains to the inn?"

Jeff laughed. "Are you kidding? John said he's really excited to get out of the city, and the kids have been talking about all the fun things they did at Christmas Camp last year and they want to go sledding again, so they're thrilled."

Kathy looked so excited. "I am loving this Christmas Camp already."

Jeff gave Kathy a high five. "Just wait until you get there. Okay, so the new plan is, everyone's coming up tomorrow morning, the day before the wedding, and we'll have the wedding on Christmas Eve, as planned."

Haley looked impressed. "Wow, okay. So this could really work."

"Of course it will work. It's going to be great," Jeff said. "But you should get going. You know how the roads can be this time of year. You want to get up there tonight before dark. I have to go get Steve, and we'll meet you girls up there." Jeff kissed Haley one more time before heading out. "Love you."

"Love you, too."

As soon as Jeff left, Haley stood there, looking at the dripping ceiling. She looked a little dazed.

"You okay?" Kathy asked.

Haley nodded. "I guess. I just can't believe how quickly all our wedding plans have changed."

Kathy walked over to the dining room table. She picked up a soggy rose. "Is there anything we can salvage here and take up with us?"

When Haley looked at the sad little rose, she shook her head. "No. Let's just get going. I still have to take back my wedding dress. They were only letting me have it as a trade for the publicity they would be getting, but now that there's not going to be any photos or publicity . . ."

"No dress?" Kathy asked. She looked bummed.

"Exactly," Haley said with a sigh.

"What are you going to wear?"

Haley shrugged. "It doesn't really matter. Now it's just going to be a small casual wedding up in the woods. I'm sure I have something that will work."

Kathy came over and linked arms with Haley. "It's gonna be okay. You'll see. You're always saying, anything's possible at Christmas. You just have to believe."

Haley took a deep breath as they headed for the front door. "I believe Jeff is right. This is going to be one big adventure."

CHAPTER 3

Driving the last stretch of winding mountain road to the Holly Peak Inn, Haley was thankful that the roads had recently been plowed and were clear of snow and ice. All around her, it looked like a winter wonderland. A blanket of fresh snow covered the hillside and clung to the tree branches.

She thought about the first time she'd come up to Christmas Camp, when her boss had made her come. At that time, she hadn't even noticed the spectacular scenery. All she had cared about was getting up to the inn and getting the whole Christmas Camp experience done as soon as possible so she could get back to work in Boston. It seemed like a lifetime ago, not just a year ago.

"It really is so beautiful up here," Kathy said. She was taking pictures with her phone.

"And we couldn't have gotten a better day for a drive," Haley said.

The sky was clear and a brilliant sapphire blue, and the sun was just starting to set, making all the snow shimmer and sparkle.

Kathy nodded and kept taking pictures. "This really does look like a Christmas dream. I feel like we're living in one of those Christmas movies."

Haley laughed. "Right? And who doesn't want to do that. I feel like I have to pinch myself every time I come up here to make sure it's real. But Jeff and I have been so busy at work—he has been restoring another wharf on the waterfront, and I've been working nonstop on Ben's Christmas Camp franchise, plus helping my parents get ready to launch their B&B—we haven't been up since Thanksgiving."

"Do you usually come up more?" Kathy asked.

"Jeff likes to come up as much as possible to help his dad with the Christmas Camps, but now that Gail's been helping so much, it's worked out well for all of us."

"So Jeff's okay with that?" Kathy asked. "Gail and his dad?"

"Oh absolutely. We love Gail. She's amazing," Haley said. "I know Jeff's really happy his dad has someone to spend time with so he's not up here all alone. Plus, Gail loves helping out with the Christmas Camps. It's really a perfect fit. They're so cute together. You'll see."

"I can't believe how fast the Christmas Camp franchise has taken off," Kathy said. "You've been working nonstop since you got the idea."

Haley smiled. "I know, but it's worth it. I love thinking about how many people can experience the Christmas Camps now, and the numbers just keep going up. Did I tell you my parents are considering doing a Christmas Camp at the B&B?"

"What? No. That's so cool," Kathy said. "The B&B would be perfect for people who can't get away up here to the mountains but still want the experience."

"That's the idea, but first we have to get the place

open." Haley already had ideas for her parents' B&B having the Christmas Camps. She could even see the pictures on the website. She knew it would just mean more work for her, but she didn't mind. She loved her job and she loved doing everything she could to help Jeff's dad share the Christmas Camp experience. Jeff kept telling her she needed to hire an assistant, but at this point, she felt she needed to be completely hands-on to get the franchise off the ground properly.

She knew Ben had put his life savings into launching the franchise, and she wasn't going to let him or Jeff down. She'd also had a lot invested personally and professionally. This franchise idea was her baby, and she was going to make sure it grew up just the way it should. She didn't want it to grow too fast and lose the authenticity of what made the Christmas Camps so special.

"We're almost here," Haley said as she took the last turn to the Holly Peak Inn. As they drove slowly down the meandering tree-lined road, Kathy took more pictures.

"Wow, it's even more amazing than the website pictures. You need to update their website," Kathy said.

Haley laughed. "Thanks, another job. Just what I need." She smiled at Kathy. "No, seriously, you're right. Get me some good pictures, and I'll put them up."

"Deal," Kathy said.

As they turned the last corner and the Holly Peak Inn came into full view, Kathy was so in awe she forgot to take pictures.

"Wow!" Kathy said, taking it all in. "I can't believe all the Christmas decorations."

Haley laughed. "Oh, you haven't seen anything yet. Just wait. I told you. Jeff's dad, Ben, goes all out for Christmas and his Christmas Camps."

Haley parked the car. "Looks like we beat Jeff here."

When they both got out of the car, Kathy looked around in awe.

"I love it here," Kathy said, linking arms with Haley.

"Me, too," Haley said as they both stood and admired the quaint and charming inn. It was tucked away in the woods and outlined with white twinkling Christmas lights. All the surrounding trees were also glowing. They were covered with red, green, silver, and gold Christmas lights. The inn was a pristine white with black shutters, and on every window there was a beautiful wreath made out of fresh fir tree branches, holly, and pinecones. The largest wreath was on the front door.

The whole setting was dreamlike.

Before Haley could even get their bags out of the trunk, she was greeted with a loud bark, as Max, Ben's adorable golden retriever, came racing toward them.

"Max!" Haley got down onto one knee, so she could give him a hug. He was the first friend she'd made at Christmas Camp, and she loved him dearly.

Max looked just as excited to see her. He was wagging his tail and licking her face.

Kathy laughed. "Does Jeff know about this relationship? Because clearly this is your first love."

"Oh, he knows," Haley said. "Doesn't he, Max. He knows you're my favorite."

"Hey, I heard that!" Ben said. He was laughing and looked excited to see them.

"Ben!" Haley rushed over to him and gave him a heartfelt hug. "I've missed you!"

He smiled, as he hugged her back. "We talk almost every day."

"Email and calls aren't the same, and that's all about work . . ."

Ben nodded and looked into her eyes. "And for the

next few days, no work. You know my rules at Christmas Camp. To be in the moment and enjoy what's around you, and of course, get you married to my son!"

They all shared a laugh.

"Ben, this is my best friend, and coworker, Kathy. She's actually worked on the Christmas Camp franchise. She's the best graphic designer in Boston."

Kathy came over and took Ben's hand. "And now you see why we're friends. It's so wonderful to finally meet you. I've heard so much about you from both Haley and Jeff."

Ben took her hand and pulled Kathy in for a hug. "And I've heard so much about you. Welcome."

Max barked.

Haley laughed. "Max welcomes you, too."

Kathy leaned down to pet him, and Max loved every minute of it.

Haley looked around at all the decorations. "The place looks great. It looks like you put up some new things."

Ben's eyes twinkled. "You have to keep things fresh. Isn't that what you say?"

Haley laughed and put her arm around Ben. "Actually, it is. If I'm not careful you're going to be taking my job." They both laughed, as Haley continued to look around. "And I see you have Jeff's favorite reindeer ready to go." Haley motioned over to a group of life-sized LED wired reindeer set up like they were about to pull Santa's sleigh.

"Of course," Ben said. "It wouldn't be Christmas without the reindeer."

Kathy walked over so she could get a closer look. "These are great. What's the story with the reindeer? You said they're Jeff's favorite?"

Ben and Haley shared a knowing smile.

"Ben's mom got them when he was little," Ben said. "He was so excited when he saw them all set up, waiting for Santa, until he couldn't find one with a red nose."

"And he was convinced Rudolph had gotten lost," Haley said.

"Oh no, poor, Jeff," Kathy said.

"But his mom came to the rescue," Ben said. "That night when Jeff was sleeping, she made a red nose and put it on one of the reindeer. She then moved it so it was a little bit away from the rest of the group, like it maybe had gotten lost, and when she took Jeff out the next morning, and he saw it, he was over the moon happy. He was convinced that Rudolph had used his nose to find his way home."

"Of course," Haley said.

Kathy laughed. "That's too cute."

"The kids still love it, and so do we," Ben said. "We have a lot of wonderful memories here. Every year, we try to make more, and now look at the one we'll be making this year!"

"I can't wait to be part of it," Kathy said.

Haley took Ben's hand and looked into his eyes. "Thank you so much for doing all of this last minute for the wedding. Don't worry—we're not planning anything fancy. We can just do a little ceremony on Christmas Eve. My dad is the officiate. He got his license, figuring it could come in handy at the B&B, so we'll just keep things really simple."

Ben chuckled. "I'm thrilled that you're here and that we can have the wedding here. I know Jeff's mom would be so pleased," Ben said. "We haven't had a wedding here before, and I can't think of a better wedding to start with. And don't worry, we have a wedding planner, so she can help with everything. You can just relax and enjoy this moment. So let's get inside, so you can meet her. We don't have any time to waste."

Kathy turned to Haley and gave her a confident smile. "See, this is all going to work out great."

Haley nodded, as they followed Ben and Max to the inn.

"It is," Ben agreed. He sounded upbeat and chipper. "You don't worry about a thing. You're here now. We've got everything under control. Laura's already putting together some menu options for you, and Gail's coming back up tomorrow, and she can't wait to help out, too. We're all very excited about this."

Haley gave Ben a knowing look. "So, how's everything going with you and Gail? She's been spending a lot of time up here."

Ben smiled like a man in love and blushed a little. It was endearing. "I'm one lucky guy for sure," he said. "Gail's wonderful. She loves helping out with the Christmas Camps, and the guests love her, too. She has some really great ideas that we've added and some new decorating ideas. I can't wait to show you."

"And?" Haley waited. She gave Ben a teasing look. She wasn't about to let him off the hook. She wanted to hear him say it.

Ben laughed. "And she has been great company. Gail is a very special person."

"Yes, she is," Haley agreed. She loved seeing Ben look so happy. "And she says the same about you."

Kathy looked intrigued. "So, wait, Haley, you met Jeff here at Christmas Camp, and Ben, you met Gail. This sounds more like a Matchmaker Christmas Camp to me, and if that's the case, sign me up. I'm still waiting to meet my Prince Charming."

Ben and Haley laughed.

When they got to the front door, Haley smiled at the adorable life-sized elf figurine. "Looking good, little guy," she said as she patted his head.

Kathy cheerfully patted the elf's head, too. "Does this bring you good luck?"

Haley laughed. "I don't know about that."

"Well you met Jeff here so I'm going to do whatever you do," Kathy said. She looked completely serious.

When Ben opened the door for them Haley's face lit up. Laura was waiting with an adorable reindeer tray that was holding colorful Santa mugs that all had huge swirls of whipped cream on top and candy canes for stir sticks.

"Laura! It's so good to see you," Haley said.

"Merry Christmas," Laura said. Her smile was genuine and warm. "I thought you might want some Christmas Camp hot chocolate to help warm you up."

Haley laughed as she took a Santa mug. "Laura, you know me so well. Thank you." Haley handed the mug to Kathy. "You're going to love this."

Kathy gave Laura an excited look. "Oh, I've heard all about this hot chocolate." She took a quick sip and blissfully shut her eyes. "Yup, it's just as good as Haley promised. Amazing. Thank you."

Haley took the other mug and gave Laura a heartfelt smile. "I'm so glad you're here and not just because of this hot chocolate."

"You know I wouldn't have missed this for the world," Laura said.

Haley looked grateful. "And you've probably already guessed but this is my best friend, Kathy."

Laura smiled at Kathy. "It's so good to finally meet you. I've heard so much about you.

"Not as much as I've heard about you." Kathy smiled back at her. "And if I'm not mistaken you're also responsible for the famous cookies Haley hasn't stopped talking about."

Everyone laughed.

"That would be me," Laura said. "And I have a batch in the oven right now."

"Here, let me get that for you," Ben said as he took the tray from Laura and set it on the table.

Haley gave Kathy a look. "Watch out. They're addicting."

Haley took Laura's hand. "Thank you for doing all this for me. Are you sure it's okay? I don't want to take you away from your family at Christmas."

Laura laughed. "Are you kidding? My husband is thrilled to get to watch football all day, and we're seeing our kids next week when we go to my daughter's house in Florida, so this worked out great."

"If you're sure . . ." Haley said.

Laura gave Haley's hand a little squeeze. "I'm sure that nothing would make me happier than being a part of your special day. When are your parents coming up?"

"Tomorrow morning, so they can get everything settled at the B&B."

Ben smiled at Haley. "I talked to them and promised them you were in good hands and that we had everything under control here."

Haley looked touched. "Thank you so much for coming to the rescue. I can't tell you what this all means to me."

Ben put his arm around her. "We're family. This is what family does, and we all love you very much. We can't wait to officially make you part of the family."

When Max barked and wagged his tail, everyone laughed.

"We're all looking forward to it," Ben said. "Especially Max."

As they all followed Ben into the sitting room, Haley smiled when she saw all the stockings hanging from the fireplace. There was one with her name on it that also had a pretty angel on it. It was the same stocking Ben had first given her when she had arrived at Christmas Camp a year ago.

Kathy looked mesmerized by the room full of Christmas decorations. She turned around slowly, taking everything in, from Ben's impressive Santa figurine collection, to a variety of beautiful snow globes, to all the colorful nutcrackers lined up by the fireplace. "This really is like a Christmas dream." Her look of wonder grew when she spotted the giant Christmas tree in the corner. She walked over and looked at all the unique handmade ornaments. "And this tree. I don't think I've ever seen one like it."

Ben joined her at the tree. "No, you haven't. This is our special Christmas Camp tree. Every guest who comes to the camp has to make an ornament to hang on the tree using things that inspire them from nature or things they find around the inn. This was Haley's."

Haley laughed and covered her face, embarrassed, when Ben held up the dog biscuit ornament she had made. "I can't believe you kept it, or that Max didn't eat it."

"Oh, he sure tried," Ben said. "But I wouldn't let him. Your ornament and all the rest here are part of our Christmas Camp tradition. It's one of my favorite things, decorating with these ornaments every year and remembering everyone who made them. We all have to make one this year, too. After the wedding, when we have more time."

"I love that," Kathy said.

Haley smiled at Ben. "Me, too."

Laura walked over and picked up the tray Ben had put down. "Excuse me, everyone, but I need to get back in the kitchen and check on those cookies. Haley, as soon as you finalize the menu with Trisha for the wedding reception and dinner, just let us know and I'll start getting everything ready."

"Trisha?" Haley asked.

Ben's eyes lit up. "Your wedding planner. You're going to love her. She's in her room right now making a few calls, wedding planning stuff I think, but she'll be down soon. And don't worry, we saved the angel room for you."

Haley laughed. "Of course you did."

"And if it's okay, I'd love to go up to my room and get settled," Kathy said.

Ben grabbed Kathy's bags. "I'll be happy to show you your room. I put you in the star room—it's Gail's favorite."

Kathy looked excited. "That sounds great. Thank you."

As Ben led Kathy up the stairs, he turned back around and smiled at Haley. "Welcome home, Haley."

Haley gave him a grateful look. "Thank you. Thank you for everything."

After everyone was gone, Haley walked over to the fireplace where Max was curled up. He was watching her. "So, it looks like it's just you and me, Max."

"And me, if that's okay."

Haley looked up to see a very pretty girl walk into the room. She was in her early thirties, designer chic and perfectly put together from head to toe. She had a confidence about her that was impressive. She looked very much in control and at home at the inn.

"I'm Trisha, your wedding planner." Trisha held out her hand. "And you must be Haley, Jeff's girlfriend . . ."

Haley smiled, as she took her hand. "And now fiancée, bride-to-be. That's me."

Trisha was all business. She was already swiping through some pages on the computer tablet she was holding. "We should really get started. We don't have a lot of time."

Haley looked a little surprised by Trisha's intensity. "I don't know what Ben told you, and I'm so appreciative that you're here, but we're just going to do a really small, simple ceremony. We don't have time to do anything else."

When Trisha looked up from her tablet, she looked determined. "No matter how little time you have, we can still plan a proper wedding," Trisha said. "Don't you worry. This is what I do for a living, and I'm very good at it. That's why Ben asked for my help. I've already put some ideas together for you. Let's get started."

Without waiting for Haley's answer, Trisha headed for the couch. Haley quickly followed and sat down next to her. When Max came running over, Haley waited to pet him, but when he instead sat down at Trisha's feet, Haley looked surprised. "It looks like you've already made a friend with Max."

Trisha laughed as she leaned down to pet Max. "Oh, Max and I go way back. Don't we, boy?" When he happily tried to lick her face, she pulled back and gave him a stern look. "Max, you know the rule. No licking the face."

Haley looked confused. "So, you've been here before?"

Trisha smiled her perfect smile. "Yes, many times."

"But I didn't think they'd ever done a wedding here before?"

Trisha continued to pet Max. "Oh, they haven't. This will be a first. That's for sure."

Haley was feeling more confused by the second.

Trisha held up her tablet. "Here, let me show you my first idea."

Before Haley could ask any more questions, the front

door opened, and Max took off running toward it. When Haley saw Jeff, she jumped up excitedly and went to the door.

"You made it," she said. "I was starting to worry."

Jeff kissed her quickly just as Steve came inside.

"Sorry, that was my fault," Steve said. "My plane was late."

Haley smiled at Steve. She had seen pictures of Jeff's college best friend, but they didn't do him justice. He was handsome, the same age as Jeff, in his midthirties, with a smile that could melt any girl's heart. Haley instantly liked him. "It's so good to finally meet you. I've heard so many stories."

Steve laughed. He pretended to look nervous. He patted Jeff on the back. "Don't believe anything this guy tells you, unless it's all good, then believe it all."

They all three laughed.

Steve stood back and smiled at Haley. "And you must be the beautiful bride, Haley." Steve gave her a hug. "You're obviously too good for this guy," he said, teasing. "Are you sure you don't want to rethink this whole wedding thing . . ."

Jeff playfully pushed Steve away from Haley. "Watch it, Romeo, she's all mine." When Jeff kissed Haley, she was still laughing.

She grabbed Jeff's hand. "Come in. You're just in time to meet our wedding planner."

"Great." As Jeff and Steve entered the sitting room with Haley, Trisha slowly stood up. She was smiling.

Steve looked surprised. "Trisha?"

Trisha came over and gave Steve a kiss on the cheek. "Steve, Merry Christmas."

Haley looked from Trisha to Steve. "You two know each other?"

When Steve whipped around to face Jeff, it was the first time she saw the look on Jeff's face. He looked surprised, and there was something else Haley couldn't quite define.

"What is it?" she asked Jeff.

But before Jeff could answer, Trisha walked up to him and gave him a kiss on the cheek, too, only this kiss lingered a little longer.

Trisha looked into Jeff's eyes. "Merry Christmas, Jeff."

Jeff finally found his voice. "Trisha, what are you doing here?"

Trisha smiled. "I'm your wedding planner."

Steve coughed, but it sounded more like he was choking.

Now Haley was totally confused. She looked at all three of them. "How do you all know each other?"

Jeff opened his mouth to say something, but before he could, Trisha jumped in.

"I met Steve through Jeff."

Haley looked at Trisha. She was still smiling at Jeff. But it wasn't just any ordinary smile, it was a flirty smile. Haley didn't know what was going on, except that she didn't like it. She turned to Jeff. "And how do you know Trisha?"

"I've been coming up here for years," Trisha answered for Jeff, never taking her eyes off him.

"As a guest?" Haley asked.

"No." Trisha laughed, as she continued looking at Jeff. "As his girlfriend."

CHAPTER 4

Haley gave Jeff an incredulous look and waited for him to say something. When she noted how uncomfortable he looked, that made her even more concerned. When she looked over at Trisha, Trisha was smiling like she was as happy as could be. Haley, not liking how this was looking, turned back to Jeff.

"What's going on?" Haley asked.

Kathy interrupted the awkward moment by entering the room. "Hey, no fair having a party without me." She came over and hooked arms with Haley. "Introduce me to everyone."

Trisha held out her hand to Kathy. "Hi, I'm Trisha. I'm . . ."

"Jeff's girlfriend." Haley finished for her.

Kathy looked shocked. "Wait . . . What?"

Jeff jumped in. "My ex-girlfriend. She's my old girlfriend."

"And longtime friend of the family," Trisha said and smiled sweetly, too sweetly for Haley's liking.

Haley put her hands on her hips. She locked eyes with Jeff. "So, which is it? Old girlfriend or old family friend?"

Trisha walked over and stood next to Jeff and looked up at him. "It's both," she said. She was still smiling. Haley was not.

Haley turned to Kathy, who looked equally confused. "And she's my wedding planner."

Kathy's mouth dropped open. She quickly recovered, but you could still see the shock in her eyes.

Steve looked as uncomfortable as everyone else. "So, I was going to head into the kitchen. I think I smell Laura's cookies . . ."

Kathy immediately took the hint. "I'll go with you. I'm dying to try these cookies."

Steve looked over at Trisha. Trisha wasn't taking the hint. "Trisha, why don't you come with us? We can catch up. It's been a while."

As everyone stared at Trisha, it was clear she didn't want to leave.

Steve came over and put his arm around her. "Let's get caught up." As Steve started guiding Trisha away, she looked back at Jeff and smiled.

"But we need to catch up, too, Jeff," Trisha said. She then looked at Haley. "I can't wait to hear all about how you met. It was a big surprise hearing about the wedding."

Steve walked faster. "Okay, let's go. Those cookies are waiting."

As soon as they were alone in the room, Haley turned to Jeff. She just looked at him. She didn't even know where to start. She had never heard about Trisha before.

"I can explain," Jeff said.

"Okay," Haley said. She walked over to the Christmas tree and pretended to study some ornaments when actually her mind was whirling a million miles a minute. She had questions, lots of questions. She turned back around and faced Jeff. "But first, just answer one thing. Is our wedding planner really your ex-girlfriend, because that just seems a little crazy . . ." When Haley saw Jeff take a deep breath, her eyes widened. "Okay. So it's true."

Jeff joined her over at the tree. He took her hand and looked into her eyes. "I swear I didn't know anything about this."

Haley let go of his hand and picked up a snow globe off the mantel and started shaking it, hard. "How long ago did you date? She clearly still has a thing for you."

Jeff, looking apologetic, gently took the snow globe out of her hand. He took a deep breath. "I've known Trisha a long time. I'm sure my dad was just trying to help and find someone fast. He's always treated her like family."

Haley stared at him. Hearing that Ben thought of Trisha as family only made Haley feel worse. "So when did you date? In college? Is that where you met?"

Jeff looked over at Max lying by the fireplace. Max put his head down on his paws. Jeff looked back at Haley. "No, we didn't meet in college."

Haley gave him an impatient look.

"We met here at the inn," Jeff said. He hesitated a moment. "When her family came for Christmas Camp."

Haley's eyes grew huge. She laughed, but it wasn't a happy laugh. "So, you met her at Christmas Camp, just like you met me? Okay, wow." Haley shook her head, trying to take it all in. "How long did you date?"

"Five years."

Haley's jaw dropped open. She didn't even try to pretend she was cool with that. "Five years. That's a long time, and you've never once mentioned her . . ."

"We haven't talked that much about exes."

Haley laughed. "That's because I didn't really have any serious old boyfriends. You know I've been concentrating on my career, but you apparently have had this serious relationship that I've known nothing about . . ."

"I didn't bring it up because Trisha's my past, and I want to concentrate on my future with you," Jeff said.

Haley started pacing around the room. "But yet here she is, your past, and she's about to become part of our future." Haley picked up a Santa figurine, stared at it, but didn't really see it.

"When did you break up?" Haley asked.

"About three years ago," Jeff answered.

Haley shook her head. "What I don't understand is, why would your dad ask your old girlfriend to be our wedding planner?"

"Because he has always liked Trisha," Jeff said. "When we were dating, we'd come up here all the time, and it wasn't a bad breakup. We parted as friends."

This made Haley feel even worse. "Then why did you break up?"

Jeff stared into the fire. "I broke things off after my mom passed away. I wanted to spend more time with my dad. He needed to be my number one focus. I didn't have time for a girlfriend."

Haley's heart was beating so fast, she had to take a breath. She was waiting for him to say they'd broken up because they weren't a good fit, because he didn't love her, not because his mom had passed away and he needed to take care of his dad.

Not wanting Jeff to see how upset and worried she was, she walked over to the window and looked out. As she watched the snow start to fall, she fought to stay calm. She couldn't help wondering now if Jeff had ever really gotten over Trisha. Five years was a long time to be with anyone. She'd only known Jeff a year and still couldn't believe how much she loved him. For the first time, she felt insecure about Jeff's love for her, and it was the worst feeling in the world. She felt sick to her stomach. Her mind was whirling. Doubt clawed at her heart. What if Jeff had only broken up with Trisha because he was heartbroken about his mom, and now, now that he was better, now that he'd had some time to heal, his old feelings for Trisha could resurface. She took several deep breaths and willed herself to try to be rational and not jump to any conclusions, but she was scared, really scared. The thought of losing Jeff was unbearable.

When Jeff joined her at the window and put his arm around her, she didn't resist. Instead, she put her head on his shoulder; seeking the comfort he always gave her. He always made her feel loved. Not just by saying the words—and he did that a lot—but by the actions he did every day, the little things that showed her how much he cared. She had seen the way Trisha looked at him. It was clear she still had feelings for him, and now, Haley worried that Jeff, after seeing Trisha again, would also start to have feelings for her again, now that he had healed emotionally and was able to move on with his life.

"Haley, talk to me. What is it? Ask me anything, and you know I'll answer you."

Haley turned around. "Do you still have feelings for her?"

Jeff looked surprised. "What? For Trisha? No, of course not. You know I love you. We're getting married in two days."

"But you two only broke up because of what happened with your mom."

Jeff took Haley's hand and led her over to the couch

and sat down. "Honestly, I don't even remember every-thing that happened back then except how upset I was about losing my mom."

Haley looked worried. "That's what I mean. If that's the only reason you two broke up . . ."

Jeff looked into her eyes. "Here's what I do know. I love you. She's my past. You're my future. I know what I want, and I want to marry you on Christmas Eve . . ."

"With your old girlfriend being our wedding plan-ner?" Haley said. She couldn't believe the words even as she said them.

When Jeff laughed a little, it only made Haley more upset.

"You better not be laughing at me. This isn't funny," she insisted.

Jeff took both her hands and pulled her toward him. He smiled as he looked into her eyes. "You're cute when you're jealous. I've never seen you jealous before."

Haley looked up at him. She didn't even try to deny it. "Because I've never had a reason to be before."

"And you don't have a reason now. I promise," Jeff said. "I'm not sure how all this went down. I'll talk to my dad, but I'm sure Trisha is just trying to help my dad and us and she's really good at what she does."

This didn't make Haley feel any better. She saw the way Trisha had looked at Jeff and even if Jeff was clue-less, she knew Trisha still had feelings for him. Her spi-raling thoughts were interrupted when Jeff gently lifted her chin so she was looking into his eyes.

"You're the only one I love," Jeff said. "You're stuck with me, this Christmas and every Christmas for the rest of our lives."

When he kissed her, Haley forgot about everything but

the love she felt in that kiss. It was the perfect kiss—until they were interrupted.

"So who's ready to plan a wedding?" Trisha asked. She walked into the room holding up her tablet. "I have some great ideas here I know you'll like, Jeff." Trisha sat down on the couch, looked at Jeff and patted the space next to her, urging him to sit.

When Haley gave Jeff an incredulous look, he kissed her quickly, got up, and headed for the kitchen. "I'll like whatever Haley likes, so you two plan away. I'm going to go find Steve and Kathy and those cookies. Have fun."

The look Haley gave him said she'd rather eat broken glass, but when she turned back to Trisha, she forced herself to smile. No matter how insane she thought this whole situation was, she knew right now she was stuck, and she had to make the best of it. She sat down next to Trish and looked at her tablet. "Okay, let's see what you have."

Trisha stood up. "Maybe we should wait for Jeff."

"No, I'm good," Haley said. "Like you said, we don't have a lot of time, so let's do this."

Trisha reluctantly sat down. "Okay. Here's what I'm thinking." She brought up some pictures on her tablet. "Here are some ideas I have for the cake, for the flowers, for the menu. I know Jeff doesn't like white cake, and he likes prime rib better than turkey, and Laura makes a great prime rib. For flowers, we're a bit limited, but I know Jeff likes red roses—he used to always get them for me. They're his favorite."

Haley gave Trisha a look like she had sprouted two heads, but Trisha didn't see it. She was too busy pulling up more pictures. Speechless, Haley looked over to Max lounging by the fire. He got up and trotted over to them.

At first it looked like he was going to sit by Trisha again, but then he changed his mind and sat down at Haley's feet instead. She instantly felt a rush of victory. She knew it was ridiculous to be jealous of Max also liking Trisha. As she petted him, she decided she could share Max, but there wasn't a snowball's chance in the desert she was going to share Jeff, and the sooner Trisha knew that, the better.

"So what do you think?" Trisha asked, finally looking up from her tablet.

Haley locked eyes with her. "I think you're still in love with my fiancé."

Trisha didn't even pretend to be shocked. She simply smiled and stared back at Haley. "I've always been in love with Jeff, and he was in love with me for many years. Jeff, Ben, Jeff's mom, this place, has been a big part of my life and always will be."

Haley just stared back at her. Trisha wasn't pulling any punches. She almost admired her for not trying to deny how she obviously still felt about Jeff. But this was a problem, a big problem. So Haley chose her words carefully, using the same words Jeff had said to her. "I understand Jeff was your past, but he's my future. We're together now, and we love each other very much." She paused a moment and waited for Trisha to say something, but when Trisha just kept flipping through pictures on her tablet, she continued. "I just want you to understand and respect that we're together now. We're getting married . . ."

Trisha looked up from the tablet. "Obviously, or Ben wouldn't have asked me to help plan your wedding. I don't want to let him down—he's done a lot for me over the years—so let me show you what I'm thinking for a menu, so we can get Laura started."

Haley couldn't tell if Trisha was being genuine or sarcastic. She didn't know what to say, so instead, confused, she looked down at the menu Trisha had pulled up on her tablet. The more Trisha talked about what appetizers they should have, the more surreal the whole thing felt to Haley. She was more than a little relieved when Kathy and Steve walked back in.

"So, how's the wedding planning going?" Kathy asked cheerfully.

"Great." Both Haley and Trisha answered at the same time. But the tones of their voices suggested differently.

Steve held up a platter of Christmas cookies. "Who needs a sugar break?"

Haley grabbed one and took a big bite.

Trisha waved them away. "I don't eat carbs."

Haley took another big bite of her cookie.

Steve put the cookies down. "I was going to head outside. Ben wanted me to check out some new Christmas lights he just put up before it gets dark. Trisha, you always had a great eye for decorations. Why don't you come with me? I could use your help."

Trisha's smile seemed forced. "Sure." She gave Haley her tablet. "Why don't you look over my ideas and let me know what you like, and we'll get this thing done."

As Trisha walked out of the room with Steve, Kathy turned to Haley. "We'll get this thing done? That doesn't sound very romantic or weddinglike to me. I'm sensing a little tension here."

"You think?" Haley shook her head, frustrated.

"If you don't want her here, just tell Jeff we can plan this wedding. It's not brain surgery."

"Oh sure, and then I look like the insecure jealous girlfriend who sent Trisha home after she came all the way up here, at Christmas, to help with the wedding. Ben apparently loves her. That's why he asked her to come. Even Max loves her. As long as Jeff doesn't love her, I can handle it."

Kathy gave her a sharp look. "You sure?"

Haley nodded, forced a smile. "Yes, I can be the bigger person, for Jeff and for Ben. But don't you think it's strange he never told me about her? They dated for five years."

Kathy looked surprised. "I really don't know. I don't know the whole story."

"That's the problem," Haley said. She looked worried. "Neither do I."

"If you have any doubts, just talk to Jeff. I know he's crazy about you."

Haley nodded, but still didn't look convinced.

Kathy sat down next to her. "Okay, then let's see what Trisha's thinking for the wedding. Does she have good ideas?"

Haley sighed. "Yeah, she's put together everything Jeff would want."

"But what do you want?"

Haley shook her head sadly. "I just want to marry Jeff, but honestly, I was really looking forward to wearing the dress, all the flowers, the cake. I know at first that didn't matter to me, but then I got all caught up in doing the pictures for my parents' B&B, and I guess I drank the wedding Kool-Aid. Now that it's gone, I want it back. I sound like Bridezilla, right?"

"No, of course not," Kathy said. "You have every right to be disappointed after everything that's happened. You're worried about your parents and the B&B, and now you come up here and you have to deal with Jeff's old girlfriend and start over planning a wedding when you have less than two days to do it. No, you're entitled to freak out a little. Bridezilla away. You've earned it."

Haley laughed. Kathy always had a way of making her feel better. "You're the best."

Kathy got up and walked over and picked up a Santa figurine. "I know."

They shared a laugh.

"But seriously," Kathy said, "we're up here at Christmas Camp, and this place is so magical. This is where you fell in love. Sure, your wedding is going to be different, but it can still be special."

"I agree," Jeff said as he entered the room.

When Haley stood up, Kathy gave her a quick hug. "I'm going to go catch up with Steve and Trisha and see if there's anything I can help with." Kathy turned to Jeff. "By the way, your friend Steve . . . what's his story? Is he single?"

"Kathy!" Haley playfully swatted her.

"What? He's hot. It's a fair question."

Jeff laughed. "He is single, but he's a tough one to pin down. He's always traveling with work."

"Well, he's here now," Kathy said as she headed out the door. "Let's see if I can catch him."

"Seriously?" Haley threw up her hands.

"I meant, catch up to him outside," Kathy said with a wink, before she left the room.

Jeff took the tablet from Haley. "So, let's plan our wedding."

Haley watched him flip through a couple of pages. "Wow, it looks like she has all my favorite things here."

"Uh-huh," Haley said. She sounded less than thrilled.

Jeff looked up immediately. "You're sure you're going to be okay with this?"

Ben entered the room. "Okay with what? Is there a problem?"

"Trisha," Jeff said. "Haley's a little uncomfortable with her planning our wedding."

Haley gave Jeff a look. She didn't want to look like the bad guy. "I was just thinking, there's not a lot to do since we're just having a simple ceremony. It doesn't make sense to have Trisha here when she should be home with her family at Christmas."

"That's the thing," Ben said. "Trisha doesn't have any family close by and usually spends Christmas up here with us, so she doesn't have to be alone."

Haley gave Jeff a surprised look. "So, even after you broke up, she still came up here for Christmas?"

Ben answered for him. "Yes. It's a tradition for her, except last year when she was traveling—that's why you didn't meet her. I thought this was a good thing. We have a last-minute wedding to plan and she's a wedding planner and was happy to help."

I bet, Haley thought.

Ben saw the look on Haley's face. "Is there a problem?"

Haley wanted to say that there was a huge problem. She wanted to tell Ben that Trisha obviously still had feelings for Jeff and that the way she kept looking at him made Haley very uneasy. She didn't trust her. She had wanted a small wedding with just close family and friends, and while Ben thought Trisha was a family friend, Haley wanted to say she was very nervous about just how friendly Trisha wanted to be with Jeff. But when she opened her mouth to express her concerns, she was stopped by the look on Ben's face. He was eagerly waiting for her response. She knew Ben would never intentionally do anything to hurt her and that he had asked for Trisha's help genuinely thinking he was doing her a favor.

"I wanted you to have a special wedding," Ben said. "I know how disappointed you are that you can't have it at your parents', so I thought Trisha could help make the best of things here since that's what she does for a living, and she's very good at it." Ben was starting to look concerned.

When Haley couldn't find her words, Jeff came to her rescue. "Haley's just a little uncomfortable knowing I dated Trisha . . ."

Ben gave Haley a surprised look. "But that was several years ago. That's water under the bridge, and you and Trisha remained good friends."

"We have," Jeff agreed. "But . . ."

Ben's shoulders slumped. He looked at Haley then back at Jeff. "But, I messed up. I'm really sorry, Haley. Everything happened so fast. I just wanted to help and thought Trisha could do that . . ."

Haley hated seeing Ben look so disappointed. She rushed over and gave him a hug. "It was very thoughtful of you. You're always trying to help and thinking about other people. That's what I love about you."

"But you want her to go?" Ben asked. He looked troubled. "I just don't think she has anywhere else to go now for Christmas . . . But you come first. Just tell me what you want me to do."

Jeff looked at Haley.

Haley forced herself to smile. As much as she wanted Trisha to go, she didn't want to disappoint or upset Jeff and Ben. They meant everything to her. So, if that meant she would have to put up with Trisha, she would do it.

"It wouldn't be right to ask her to leave now, so close to Christmas. She should just stay," Haley said.

"Are you sure?" Ben asked. "I can ask her to leave right now."

"No, I'm sure," Haley said and forced a smile for Ben's sake.

When Jeff gave her a concerned look, Haley nodded to let him know she was okay, but the truth was, she wasn't. She needed a moment to regroup.

"I think I'm going to run upstairs and freshen up," Haley said.

Jeff held up the tablet. "But what about the wedding plans?"

"You go ahead and look at everything. I'm sure whatever you want will be fine, and you know best what we can and can't do up here."

Jeff looked concerned. "Haley . . ."

She smiled back at him. "No, really, it's okay. At the end of the day, all I want to do is marry you. Whatever you want is fine with me." Haley gave him a quick kiss. "As long as you're standing next to me on Christmas Eve and we're getting married, I'll be happy."

"Are you sure?" Jeff asked, looking into her eyes.

She smiled but looked away quickly and started heading out of the room. "I'm sure."

"Okay," Jeff said. "I'll look at everything, and we can decide together later."

"Sounds good," Haley said and picked up her pace. She didn't want anyone to see she was crying.

CHAPTER 5

As Haley entered the all-white angel bedroom, the same room she had when she first came to Christmas Camp, she shut the door behind her and leaned against it. She impatiently brushed away her tears. She was mad at herself for getting so emotional. That wasn't like her. She wasn't usually the type to cry. The tears had just come out of nowhere. *Okay*, she thought, *maybe not nowhere*. In the last few hours, she had gone from planning a beautiful wedding that was also going to help launch her parents' new B&B business to having everything underwater at the B&B, moving the wedding at the last minute to Christmas Camp, and having Jeff's ex be the wedding planner.

She shut her eyes and took a deep breath to steady herself. When she opened them again, the first thing she saw was all the angel figurines staring back at her. The angel room was decorated with dozens of different kinds of angels, from the angel figurines on the dresser and nightstands to the pictures on the wall and the pillows on the bed.

She smiled a little, remembering how they used to freak her out and how she'd hidden them all away the first time she'd stayed. But now as she looked at them, they felt like old friends and brought her comfort.

She had meant what she'd said to Jeff about the most important thing to her was marrying him, not the who, what, why, and where. She loved him. More than she had ever loved anyone before. But loving someone that much scared her. She couldn't imagine the pain of losing him. Hearing about Trisha and how they'd dated for five years had her feeling insecure for the first time about the relationship they'd built.

"This is crazy, right?" Haley said out loud. She was talking to the angels, as she started pacing around the room. "I know how much Jeff loves me. Trisha is his past. I'm just stressed and tired and overreacting." Haley stopped and looked at one of the pictures of an angel. "Good, you're not talking back, because if you were then I'd know I was really losing it."

Haley fell back onto the bed and closed her eyes. She told herself she just needed some rest, and then she'd feel better. But after a few minutes, when her mind refused to turn off, she opened her eyes, frustrated, and stared at the ceiling. She knew there was no way she could rest.

She got up and grabbed her laptop out of her bag and sat back down on her bed. Work was the one thing that always made her feel better. The one place she always felt safe and in control. She opened up a file that had photos of her parents' B&B and started scanning through them. When she looked up and saw the angels were staring at her, she gave them a look.

"What? I know I told Jeff I would take a break and not work while I'm here, but his old girlfriend also wasn't supposed to be my wedding planner, so it is what it is. I get a pass."

An hour later, Haley was still working when she heard a knock on her door.

"Come in," Haley said.

Kathy opened the door. "Ah, now I see why you're hiding out. You're working."

Haley closed her laptop. "I'm not hiding."

"But you are working? I thought you promised Jeff . . ."

Haley held up her hand to stop her. "Don't even say it. There were some things I needed to do."

Kathy sat down on the bed next to her. "Needed to do, or are you just working because that's what you do when you're upset and don't want to deal with something."

"You make it sound like working is a bad thing. It's what has made me so successful."

"And I thought you learned your lesson here last year at Christmas Camp that sometimes you just need to take a break and concentrate on what really matters most, and right now, that would be your wedding, Jeff, your friends, me, and your family. You know, the important stuff. With me being at the top of the list, of course."

Haley couldn't help but laugh. "Of course."

Kathy shut Haley's laptop, stood up, and grabbed Haley's hand and pulled her up, too. "Jeff and Ben sent me to come get you. Ben made a fresh batch of hot chocolate. He said it's your favorite."

Haley couldn't help but smile. "Everything they do up here is my favorite."

Kathy linked arms with her. "I'm beginning to see why."

As they walked out, arm in arm, Haley dropped her head to Kathy's shoulder. "Thanks."

"For what?"

"For being a good friend."

"Always."

When they came down the stairs, Jeff was waiting for them. He looked into Haley's eyes.

"All good?" he asked. He still looked concerned.

She smiled back at him and took his hand. "All good." When she said it, she really wanted to mean it more than anything in the world, but she was still worried, and what she hated most was that she wasn't sure what she could do about it.

As they walked into the kitchen, Jeff smiled at her, but when he looked up, his smile faded.

"What happened in here?" Jeff asked as he looked around. "What are all these new decorations? And why do we have a Christmas tree in the kitchen?"

Ben grinned back at him. "Isn't it great? It was all Gail's idea. She brought some of her decorations from home and gave the kitchen a whole new look."

Jeff gave his dad an incredulous look. "But the kitchen didn't need a whole new look. Mom always had her special way to decorate in here, and where are all of Mom's poinsettias? I didn't see them when I came in. They're usually everywhere, in the living room, dining room, in here. They were her favorite. Where are they?"

Jeff, Haley, and Kathy all looked at Ben.

He smiled as he handed each of them hot chocolate.

When Jeff got his mug, he looked even more upset. "And what are these?" Jeff held up his mug. It was an adorable snowman mug. Jeff shook his head. "Where are the Santa mugs we always use?"

"We got some new mugs," Ben said. "Gail thought they'd go great with our Santa mugs. All the guests love them."

"They're adorable," Kathy said, but when Jeff gave her a look, she quickly stopped talking.

Jeff put down his mug without drinking anything. "I just don't understand why we need all these changes. Christmas Camp has always been about celebrating tradition, and we always do our traditional decorations. That's what the guests love and count on."

"But now we're adding some of Gail's traditions. It means a lot to her, and the guests really do love it, too. It's always nice to start some new traditions, don't you think?"

But the look on Jeff's face said he didn't agree at all.

Haley took his hand. "I think it looks great. Sharing traditions is what Christmas Camp is all about, right?"

Trisha walked into the kitchen and looked around. "But it does look a lot different than what your mom always did."

Jeff let go of Haley's hand and pointed at Trisha. "Exactly."

When Haley saw Ben's disappointed look, she went and stood next to him. "I think there's always room for new traditions."

"I agree," Ben said.

Jeff clearly didn't. "So, where are the poinsettias? That's one of our oldest traditions."

"The thing about the poinsettias is they can be poisonous for cats, so we've been using Christmas lilies this year instead," Ben said. "Gail's going to bring some when she comes up tomorrow. Now that we'll be spending Christmas here."

Jeff gave his dad an incredulous look. "What are you talking about? We don't have a cat, and we always do Mom's poinsettias."

As if on cue, an adorable white fur ball of a cat with

huge emerald-green eyes strutted into the kitchen and straight over to Jeff and rubbed up against Jeff's leg and meowed, Jeff gave his dad a stunned look.

"What is this?"

Ben chuckled as he picked up the pretty kitty and snuggled her. "This is Snowball. She's the newest addition to our family. I got her for Gail last month for her birthday. We found her at the same shelter we found Max." Ben held Snowball up to Jeff. "Do you want to hold her?"

"No." Jeff backed away. He looked overwhelmed. "I need some air." When he turned to leave, Trisha went to follow him.

Haley stopped her. "No, I'll go."

Ben looked worried. "I think he's really upset."

"It'll be okay. I'll give him a second and then go talk to him."

Ben nodded and cuddled Snowball. Haley petted Snowball, too.

Max came over and sat down at Ben's feet.

"So, how is Max with Snowball?" Haley asked.

Ben put Snowball down, and Max nuzzled her. "He loves her. I think he likes having a friend, and Snowball pretty much does her own thing. You know how cats are. So, she's usually hiding somewhere and doesn't take any of the attention away from Max. That's probably why he's okay with it."

Haley smiled and watched Max and Snowball sniff each other. "Well, I think she's a wonderful addition."

"Now I just need my son to think so," Ben said.

Haley nodded. "I'll go talk to him." She gave Ben a hug. "Don't worry—everything will be okay."

By the time Haley caught up with Jeff outside, he had one of the LED reindeer decorations upside down. He was adjusting its leg so it would stand up straighter.

Haley knew when Jeff was upset he always had to fix something. Remembering the story of Jeff and his mom and the reindeer, Haley wasn't surprised to see Jeff working on the reindeer that had the makeshift red nose. She knew why he was so upset, and her heart ached for him.

"You okay?" she asked quietly.

"Yeah, just fixing this reindeer."

When Jeff didn't look up at her, she kneeled down next to him. When he finally looked at her, she could see the pain in his eyes.

"I know how much you miss her," Haley said.

Overwhelmed with emotion, he could only nod.

As they both stood up together, she gave him a hug and held on tight.

"It's going to be okay."

Jeff pulled back slowly. He looked up into the sky. "I know she's gone. It's been three years, and we all have to move on but . . ."

Haley took his hand. "But it's hard."

Jeff nodded. "You know I think Gail's great. I'm so glad my dad has someone to keep him company. It just seems like everything is happening so fast, so many changes. Did you see the cat? We have a cat!"

"It was a cute cat." Haley tried to lighten the mood.

"It was a cat!" Jeff said as he shook his head in disbelief. "I'm not a cat person."

"Maybe she'll grow on you."

"And who names a cat Snowball?" Jeff rolled his eyes.

"Someone who owns a Christmas Camp."

When Jeff couldn't help but laugh, Haley looked relieved. "Just talk to your dad. Tell him how you feel. He'll understand."

"That's hard to do when I don't even know how I feel. Does that make sense?"

Haley nodded. She understood only too well. That's how she felt about the Trisha situation. Christmas Camp had never felt so complicated.

As they walked back to the inn together, Haley kissed Jeff. "I love you."

Jeff gave her a look that was filled with love. "Love you, too." He looked up into the sky. It was just starting to get dark, and the first stars were showing up. "I wish you'd been able to meet my mom . . ."

Haley put her arm around him. "Me, too. But I really love what your dad always says, that the stars in the sky are the people we've loved and lost watching over us. I like to think your mom is doing that . . ."

They both looked up together at the sky.

Jeff nodded. "I'd like to think that, too."

A FEW HOURS LATER, as everyone—Ben, Jeff, Haley, Trisha, Steve, Kathy, and Laura—all gathered around the beautifully set dinner table, the mood was much lighter. There was laughter and joy, and looking around, Haley felt grateful. At that moment, she didn't even mind that Trisha was part of the group or that she had snagged the seat on the other side of Jeff. What was getting all of Haley's attention now was watching Kathy's and Steve's reaction to the remarkable meal Laura had prepared. Beyond her always-popular pot roast, Laura had also served roasted cauliflower with melted white cheddar cheese, Brussels sprouts with bacon, roasted baby potatoes, and tomato salad with feta.

"This meal is amazing," Kathy said. "I can't believe you put this all together so quickly not knowing any of us were going to be here."

Laura smiled as she passed the Brussels sprouts to Ben. "I'd already planned the pot roast for my family. It's always a dish we have this time of year, because it's easy to make and you have lots of leftovers."

"Except for tonight," Jeff said as he took a big slice of roast and put an equally big slice on Haley's plate for her. "You know your pot roast is one of my favorites."

Laura nodded. "And that's why I knew it was perfect for tonight. A pot roast is great comfort food. It's like serving a big, warm hug, and I thought you and Haley might be needing that tonight with everything that's happened today."

Kathy looked at Laura. "That is so sweet. That settles it. I'm never leaving here."

Everyone laughed.

"Thank you, Laura. I know we all appreciate this," Haley said and gave her a grateful look, "but what about your family? If we're eating your pot roast, what are they eating?"

"A pizza," Laura said. "I never let them order pizza. They're loving it."

Everyone laughed again.

When Haley tried to pass the potatoes to Trisha, Trisha shook her head. "No, thank you. I don't do carbs."

Instead, Trisha helped herself to some salad and smiled at Laura. "Thank you for making my favorite salad. I always look forward to it."

Haley fought to keep her smile on her face.

Kathy, seeing Haley struggling, held up her plate. "I'll take some potatoes. They look delicious, just like everything else. It's a good thing I'm only staying a few days here, or I'd be in trouble. I've already packed on a few pounds from overindulging at all the Christmas parties."

Steve gave Kathy an admiring look. "Well, whatever you're doing, it looks great on you."

Kathy, flattered, smiled back at him. "Flattery will get you everywhere."

Steve laughed and held up his wineglass. "That's what I'm hoping."

Haley watched as Kathy laughed and clinked her wineglass to Steve's. She knew that look on her best friend's face. Kathy was falling for Steve. She needed to find out Steve's story. She only knew what Jeff had told her about how he always traveled for work and never stayed in one place long enough to have a long-term relationship. She didn't want Kathy getting hurt, falling for someone who was unattainable.

Ben stood up and held up his wineglass. "Before we enjoy this lovely meal, I want to make a quick toast."

Jeff looked into Haley's eyes, and they shared a special smile, as they picked up their wineglasses together.

"First I want to thank you all for being here and everyone coming together at the last minute to make this wedding special for my son and soon-to-be daughter-in-law," Ben said. When Ben looked over at Jeff and Haley, Jeff gave Haley a quick kiss on the cheek. Haley looked over and saw Trisha was the only one not smiling. Ben continued, "We have a traditional toast we do at our Christmas Camp, and I thought it would be perfect for this occasion, as well. Son, will you help me?"

"Of course," Jeff said. He got up and went to stand over by his dad.

Both Jeff and Ben held up their glasses.

"To our family, friends, and community . . ." Ben looked at Jeff to continue the toast.

"To the people we've lost but will never forget . . ." Jeff looked back at his dad to finish.

"To love everlasting. Merry Christmas!" Ben said.

Everyone joined in the toast. "Merry Christmas."

As everyone toasted, Haley watched as Ben turned to Jeff. "We have so many wonderful traditions that we will always honor, like this one, and the ones we had with your mom. But I believe as we bring new people into our lives"—Ben looked over at Haley—"that we can also bring in new traditions."

Haley smiled back at them both. The two men she had come to love so much.

Jeff nodded and put his arm around his dad. "I think you're right, and I'm sorry for overreacting earlier. It just caught me off guard. You know I love Gail."

"And I do, too," Ben said. "We can talk more later, but I just wanted you to know how much I love you and the life we've built here and all our traditions that we'll always honor."

When Ben and Jeff hugged, Haley felt so relieved. She smiled at Jeff when he looked over and nodded her approval.

Once Jeff and Ben sat back down everyone started enjoying their dinner. After the meal was done, Laura got up and started clearing away the dishes until Ben and Jeff stopped her. Jeff took a plate from her. "You know the rules, Laura. You cook. You don't clean. We got this, don't we, Dad?"

Ben smiled at Laura. "We sure do, and thank you for another wonderful dinner."

"It really was fantastic," Kathy said.

Laura smiled. You could tell the compliments meant a lot to her. "Thank you, and there's dessert in the kitchen when you're ready. Fresh berry pie."

When Jeff quickly headed for the kitchen, Haley grabbed his arm. "You can't seriously have room for that right now?"

"What?" Jeff tried to look innocent. "I'm putting the dishes away."

"Uh-huh." Haley laughed. "I know you, and I know you love berry pie."

"Not as much as I love you." Jeff gave her a quick kiss.

Kathy laughed. "Oh, he's good."

"Right?" Haley shook her head. "His sweet tooth is incredible."

Ben looked around the room. "You know what it's time for?"

Haley shook her head. "What?"

"Christmas Camp Charades!" Ben said, sounding excited. "Let me just finish cleaning up, and we can play."

Jeff laughed. "I think everyone's too tired tonight."

Ben looked disappointed.

"We should wait until everyone gets here," Haley said. "Then we can really have a great game."

"That's true. The more the merrier, and Gail does love the game. Okay, then tomorrow night."

Steve stood up from the table. "I'd love some dessert, but first I think I need to walk off some of this amazing meal." Steve patted his perfectly flat six-pack of a stomach. "Anyone want to join me?" Steve looked right at Kathy.

Kathy grinned back at him and stood up. "That sounds like a great idea."

"Anyone else?" Steve asked.

Haley was about to say something, but when Kathy gave her a look, she shut her mouth.

Kathy turned back to Steve. "Looks like it's just us."

"And I should be getting back to my family before they order a second pizza," Laura said.

Haley gave her a heartfelt hug. "Thank you so much for dinner tonight, and all you're doing for the wedding. I couldn't do this without you."

"Well, you could. You'd just be eating a lot of pizza," Laura said.

Haley laughed.

"And we really do need to decide the menu for the rehearsal dinner and the wedding first thing tomorrow morning, so we have a chance to shop for everything," Trisha said.

Laura smiled back at Trisha. "I'll be back tomorrow morning, and we'll figure it all out. But I agree, the sooner the better. Our little grocery store has a limited selection, and I'm sure right now a lot is probably sold out."

"I can always have my mom pick up whatever we need before they come up from Boston," Haley said.

Laura nodded. "That's an excellent idea. That will really help. Okay, sounds like we're all set. I'll see everyone in the morning."

"How far away do you live, Laura?" Kathy asked.

"I'm just a few miles away, right before the turnoff to the inn," Laura answered. "Very convenient. Just another reason why I love working here."

Trisha stood up. "I think I'm going to turn in," Trisha said. "We have a lot to do tomorrow. Good night, everyone."

Everyone answered, "Good night."

When Haley started helping to pick up dishes, Ben stopped her. "It is going to be a big day tomorrow. Why don't you turn in, too? Jeff and I have this."

"Are you sure?" Haley asked.

Jeff came into the dining room, holding a plate, eating a piece of Laura's pie. "We're sure."

Haley couldn't help but laugh. She went over and kissed Jeff's cheek. "Behave yourself. Save some pie for the rest of us."

"Of course," Jeff said, feigning innocence. When Jeff held out a piece of pie for Haley to eat, she smiled and took the bite, and then laughing, she headed out of the room.

SEVERAL HOURS LATER, Haley was cozy in bed with her laptop, working on her parents' B&B website. Kathy was right. The website was looking really strong and even though the wedding pictures would have been a great addition, they weren't needed. The B&B impressed on its own.

She smiled at the picture of her parents, arm in arm, in front of the B&B. Their smiles were so welcoming and sincere. Haley knew that picture alone would draw people in. She couldn't wait to see them and everyone else tomorrow.

This wedding was really happening, but before it did, she still wanted and needed to talk to Jeff one more time about Trisha and make sure he really had moved on and was really ready to marry her. She knew she was being paranoid. He'd already explained everything to her, but for her own peace of mind, she had a few more questions she wanted to ask him before she could truly stop worrying. She knew it was going to be a big day tomorrow and the thing she needed the most right now was to get some sleep. She was exhausted.

After turning off the light and snuggling deeper under the covers, she smiled at one of the angel figurines that was glowing in the moonlight, before drifting off to sleep.

CHAPTER 6

Haley woke up to a familiar sound, a single, insistent bark from Max. She laughed as she got out of bed and opened her door. Max, wearing a red-and-green-striped Christmas sweater, trotted into the room, carrying his leash in his mouth. He dropped it at Haley's feet.

Haley gave him a look. "Are you up to your old tricks again? Did Jeff already walk you, and you're just trying to con me into another walk, like you always do?"

For an answer Max tilted his head and gave her his best innocent, adorable look. It worked. It always worked. Haley headed for the closet.

"Okay, Max, you win. Give me a second to get dressed. But it has to be a short walk. I have a wedding to plan today!"

WITH MAX HAPPILY walking along beside her, Haley opened the front door of the inn and was startled by the icy blast of cold air.

"Whoa, the temperature sure did drop." She wrapped her scarf tighter around her neck and hurried to keep up with Max, who was pulling at his leash, anxious for his walk. As she stepped outside, she looked up at the sky and saw thick, grey, low-level clouds. She looked at Max. "Let's make this quick. It looks like it's going to snow."

"I thought I might find you two out here."

Haley turned around smiling, as Jeff came out the front door. He walked over and gave her a kiss. "Good morning, beautiful."

Max barked and wagged his tail.

Haley laughed. "I think he was talking to me, Max."

Jeff petted Max. "But you're really cute, too." Jeff looked up at Haley. "Trisha's looking for you."

"Already? When did you see her?"

"She was up, already working, when I took Max for a walk earlier," Jeff said.

Haley looked surprised. She gave Max a look. "So, you already walked Max this morning? I thought he needed to go out."

Jeff laughed. "That's Max's favorite trick and looks like you fell for it."

"Seriously?" When Haley stared down at Max he just wagged his tail.

"She says you wanted to plan a menu and get some things for your mom to pick up before they leave Boston and head up here today."

Haley sighed. "She's right. But before I go in, I wanted to talk to you about Trisha."

"Sure," Jeff said.

Haley took a deep breath, as they continued to walk Max together. "I know you've already explained everything, but we're getting married tomorrow, and I just want to make sure you don't have any doubts about us. I just keep wondering how you know for sure that I'm the one you want to spend the rest of your life with. You were with Trisha for five years, and like you said yourself, you didn't have a big fight or anything like that. You broke up because you were devastated about your mom's death. That's totally understandable, but it looks like she's been holding on to hope this whole time that someday, when the timing was better, you'd be able to get back together." Haley took a deep breath. "Did you ever really deal with the feelings you had for her?" She stopped to look up at him. "I'm sorry—it's just that all of this is what keeps going around in my head. We've always been able to talk about anything, so I want you to know, you can be honest with me now about this. I can handle it. I just need to know." Haley's voice wavered at the end. She was getting emotional again. The thought of losing Jeff terrified her. She believed he would never lie to her, but she worried he didn't really know his own feelings and that maybe deep down he still felt something for Trisha that he hadn't even realized yet.

Jeff stopped walking and without saying anything, put his arms around her, and gave her a hug. It made her feel safe and cared for, and she loved him even more for it.

When she looked up at him, he smiled at her. "Do you know one of the things I love most about you?" he asked.

She shook her head.

"I love that you always talk to me about how you feel. You don't just hold it all inside and expect me to read your mind. You come right out, like this, and ask me. Communication is everything in a relationship, and I think you and I do it really well."

Haley nodded. "I agree. I feel like everything is moving so fast, I just want to make sure you and I are okay. I know seeing Trisha was a surprise for you, too. How can you be sure you don't still have feelings for her?"

"I'll always care about her," Jeff said. "We have a history together, but I never felt about her the way I feel about you. When Trisha and I dated, we had a good relationship, but we never talked about getting married. Looking back, I'm not sure why. Maybe because we both had our careers, and we enjoyed each other's company, but we never had the kind of connection you and I have. Trisha will always matter to me. I truly see her as a friend, but even when we dated I never thought this is someone I can't live without and that's how I feel about you. You're my everything. You're the one I see spending the rest of my life with. I have no doubts. Not one. There's a lot I don't know, but what I do know is that no matter what our future brings, as long as we're together, it will be okay. I love you, Haley. You've changed my life, and I can't wait to start building our life together."

Haley didn't even try to stop herself from crying this time, because these were tears of joy and gratitude. "I love you, too."

A light snow was just starting to fall when Jeff kissed her. It was one of those beautiful romantic moments Haley knew she'd remember for the rest of her life.

After they kissed, Haley gave Jeff another heartfelt hug. "Thanks for always making me feel like I can talk to you about anything. Even if it seems like I'm being crazy or I'm being insecure. Knowing you'll always listen makes me feel like together we can work anything out."

"I couldn't agree more," Jeff said. He gave her another quick kiss. "It's getting cold out here. Go inside. I'll take Max."

Haley smiled a brilliant smile. "This is really happening. We're getting married!" At this moment, she didn't even mind that she had to plan her wedding with Trisha.

Jeff smiled at her. "We sure are. Nothing can stop us."

"That's right!" Haley called over her shoulder as she hurried toward the inn. She was still smiling when she opened the front door and saw Trisha coming down the stairs. She was immaculately dressed, hair and makeup perfect.

"There you are," Trisha said. "When Jeff and I had breakfast together, I told him I was looking for you."

Haley looked surprised. "You two already had breakfast?"

Trisha nodded, smiled. "We were both up early and were starving so Jeff made one of his famous omelets. You know the ones with the mushrooms and sautéed peppers. They're my favorite."

Haley smiled back. "Mine, too." Now that she felt confident about Jeff's feelings for her, she actually felt a little sorry for Trisha. She continued up the stairs. "I'm just going to take a quick shower and see if Kathy's up. I want her input on the menu, and we'll be back down, and we can get everything all set."

"The sooner, the better," Trisha said.

"Agreed." Haley hurried up the stairs and was heading to her room when she ran into a tired-looking Kathy coming out of her room wearing her robe.

"Late night?" Haley asked.

Kathy yawned and then smiled. "Steve and I actually stayed up late watching old Christmas movies. I think I went to bed around three."

"You and Steve, huh?" Haley gave her a look.

Kathy smiled back at her, she looked happy, really happy. "He's a great guy."

"You just met him."

"But when you know, you know, right?" Kathy asked. "Plus, he's Jeff's best friend so he has to be great."

"You've spent more time with him than I have," Haley

said. "But he does seem like a good guy. Still, be careful. I know how fast you can fall."

Kathy put her arm around Haley. "Don't worry. I have a good feeling about this one."

"Okay, but right now I need your help," Haley said. "Our wedding planner is downstairs, and she has us on a very tight schedule. So, take a quick shower and meet me downstairs in twenty minutes."

AN HOUR AND a half later, all three girls were getting up from the kitchen table. Everyone looked pleased.

"I think the menu for tonight's rehearsal dinner and tomorrow for the wedding is going to work out great," Haley said. "Thanks for all the help."

"We just need to make sure to get all the ingredients," Trisha said and handed Haley a sheet of paper. "Here's the list for your mom. There's a lot on it, but Laura's right, the store up here doesn't have much."

Haley took the list. "I'm on it. I'll call her right now. She's standing by."

"When are they heading up here?" Kathy asked.

"They said the plumbers were just finishing cleaning everything up, so they should be able to take off about noon."

"Perfect," Trisha said. "And when is everyone else coming?"

"Jeff said the rest of the gang are also heading up this afternoon," Haley said. "So, by tonight, we should have a full house. It's going to be so great to see everyone."

Trisha looked at her tablet and frowned. "We have a lot to do before everyone gets here."

Laura walked in, overhearing the last of the conversation. "Then I'd say, it's time we divide and conquer." She took the list from Haley. "I can call your mom and give her the list. Because I'm making the meals, I can answer any questions she might have."

Haley gave Laura a grateful look. "That would be great. Thank you."

"Okay, let's go down the rest of our checklist," Trisha said. "Who has the rings?"

"My dad does. They had to be sized. He's picking them up today," Haley said.

"Great." Trisha marked another thing off her list. "And Ben said your dad is also going to officiate the wedding?"

Haley smiled. "He is, and he's very excited about it. He took the online course last year, so they could hold weddings at the B&B and he could officiate if someone wanted him to. But I'll be the first one he has done."

"That's so sweet," Kathy said.

"Well, I hope he's practicing," Trisha said. She looked worried.

Haley laughed. "Don't worry. He is. It'll be fine."

Trisha looked back at her tablet. "Okay, who is bringing the flowers?"

Haley and Kathy looked at each other.

"The flowers died in the flood," Haley said.

"It wasn't pretty," Kathy added.

Jeff walked into the kitchen. "What are you girls up to?" He headed straight for a cupboard, took out a pretty Christmas tin, opened it up, and took out one of the famous Christmas Camp sugar cookies.

"There they are!" Haley hurried over and took one. She smiled up at Jeff as she took a bite.

Kathy laughed. "Does Laura really hide them?"

Jeff and Haley, still chewing their cookies, nodded.

"I guess she would have to," Kathy said. "Hand one over." Kathy took a cookie. "Trisha, do you want one?"

"She doesn't do carbs, right?" Haley said.

"Right," Trisha answered. "Okay, we need to get back to work."

"How's the wedding planning coming along?" Jeff asked. "Did you see Dad's inspirational word for the day?" He pointed over to the chalkboard where Ben always did a Christmas countdown. Right now the chalkboard said *2 Days to Christmas* and the inspirational word for the day was *Devotion*.

"Devotion," Trisha said. "That's perfect because I'm devoted to making this wedding actually happen in the next twenty-four hours." She looked back at her tablet. "So who's bringing the flowers?" Trisha looked at Haley then at Jeff.

"Uh, no one," Haley said. "There wasn't any time to get any flowers."

Trisha looked horrified. "You can't have a wedding without flowers."

"Actually, you can," Haley said. "It's not that big of a deal."

"Well, flowers are kind of a big deal," Kathy said.

Haley gave her a look. "Whose side are you on?"

Kathy laughed. "The flowers' side?"

Trisha looked at Jeff. He looked at Haley.

"Flowers would be nice," he said. "We usually have all the poinsettias my mother loved, but now we don't have anything . . ."

Haley felt bad.

"Hold on. Let me see what I can do." Trisha left the room.

Stress eating, Haley grabbed another cookie from the tin and took a big bite.

"What happened to that sugar detox you were doing?" Kathy asked.

Haley laughed. "Oh, that was so last year."

Jeff laughed. "Thank goodness you gave that up."

When Trisha came back into the kitchen, she had a smug smile on her face. "Haley, we need to go."

"Where?" Haley asked.

"To get you some flowers. I called the flower shop in town. They think they might be able to help us figure something out. But we have to go now."

"Okay, let's go," Kathy said.

"Actually, Kathy, I have you going with Laura to get groceries, and Jeff, you need to work with your dad on those decorations we were talking about, and everyone needs to meet back here in two hours so we can go through the rest of the list."

"Decorations? What decorations?" Haley asked.

Jeff kissed her on the cheek. "It's a surprise. I gotta get going. I'll see you later. Good luck."

"You, too," Haley called out as he left the kitchen. She looked at Kathy. "Are you good with helping Laura?"

"Absolutely. Whatever you need."

"Great, then let's go," Trisha said, looking at Haley. "They're waiting for us."

"Wait, I have a question," Kathy said. "What about a photographer? I think that's even more important than flowers. The pictures you take you have for the rest of your life. The photographer we had in Boston couldn't make the trip up here."

"It's okay," Haley said. "We can just get some pictures with our phones. My mom's bringing up her camera. We'll make it work."

"We will do better than just make it work," Trisha said. "I've already found a photographer for you."

Haley looked amazed. "How did you do that? At the last minute. At Christmas?"

"He's a friend of mine," Trisha said. "Curt's parents

have a place up here, not too far away, and he said he'd stop by on Christmas Eve and take some pictures as a favor to me. He is an excellent photographer."

Haley smiled at Trisha. "Thank you so much. That's so great. I really appreciate it."

Trisha nodded. "I know how much Jeff and Ben love pictures."

"And my family does, too," Haley said. "My mom still has pictures of her great-grandmother's wedding."

"We really do need to go," Trisha said.

"Okay, let's go," Haley said. "See you in a few hours, Kathy, and make sure Laura has enough ingredients to make some more Christmas cookies. In case Jeff has found her other hiding places."

Kathy laughed. "I'm on it."

THE LITTLE FLOWER shop in town, Petal Dreams, was as cute as its name. Out front, there was a stand next to the door with pretty pink, white, and red poinsettias, and gorgeous wreaths made out of fresh tree branches, holly, and pinecones. In the window, there was a cascade of white and silver stars, in different shapes and sizes. They twinkled when they caught the light.

Haley stopped to admire them as Trisha breezed into the shop.

"Haley, come on," Trisha called over her shoulder.

Haley quickly followed Trisha inside.

As soon as they entered, a man in his sixties, with a joyful smile, greeted them. Haley was surprised to see him give Trisha a hug.

"Trisha, it is so good to see you," the man said. He smiled at Haley. "Merry Christmas. You must be the bride."

Haley smiled back at him. "I am. Merry Christmas, and thanks again for helping us."

"Haley, this is Toby. Toby and his wife, Betty, have owned this flower shop for . . . how many years is it now, Toby?"

"Forty-three years." Toby beamed back at them. "Betty's in the back getting what we have left ready for you to see."

Haley looked around in awe at all the beautiful flower arrangements. She started to get really excited. She couldn't believe that such a tiny flower shop, tucked away up in the woods, could have so much. "Your selection here is amazing. I don't know what half these flowers are, but I know I love them all."

Toby looked pleased by the compliment. He happily guided her over to the roses. "Now, I know you know what these are. Our red roses and their connection to love are always a favorite choice at Christmas, and for weddings, our white roses are always popular, as they traditionally signify new beginnings."

Haley nodded, intrigued. "I didn't know that about white roses."

Toby continued walking her around and proudly pointed out different flowers. They all were in a deep rich Christmassy hue. "Also popular at Christmas are our dahlias, our ranunculus, and the amaranthus."

Haley laughed. "I can't even say half of those, but I love them all . . ." Haley's voice trailed off when she saw a stunning display of peonies and walked quickly toward it. "Now, these I know. I love peonies, but I've never seen them in this color."

Toby joined her. "These are called Red Charm Peonies. They're known for their rich burgundy color."

Haley looked over at Trisha, who was eyeing the red

roses. "Trisha, I think these peonies would be perfect for the wedding. They're so beautiful and this color is the same color Kathy and my mom will be wearing."

Trisha held up a red rose. "But red roses are Jeff's favorite."

Haley fought to keep the smile on her face. "I'm sure he'll love these, too." But when Haley turned back to Toby, she saw the regretful look on his face.

"I'm afraid I don't have any peonies left. Or any red roses, or any of the flowers out here," Toby said.

"What do you mean?" Trisha asked. "You have so many."

Toby picked up the red roses Trisha was looking at and moved them over to the counter. "Unfortunately, they're all spoken for. We have a lot of Christmas Eve and Christmas parties and some weddings. Everyone is coming by today to pick up their orders for their big events. So everything you see here has already been sold."

Haley felt a crush of disappointment. "So, you don't have any of the peonies left? What about paperwhites? They're always so pretty at Christmas."

Toby shook his head. "No, I'm sorry. We hardly have any flowers left at all. We had to make an emergency run into Boston to get enough to finish one of our orders when they called last minute and ordered more table settings for a wedding. We got several last-minute rush orders that we weren't prepared for."

"Like us," Trisha said.

"But we only need a few flowers," Haley said. "I'm having a very small ceremony and usually there are poinsettias all around the house, but . . ."

Toby nodded. "I know. Ben usually orders them from me, but not this year."

"It's Snowball's fault," Haley said.

"Snowball?" Toby looked confused.

"The new cat," Trisha said.

Toby laughed. "Well, then that explains it. Gail has come in several times to get some Christmas lilies but she never mentioned Snowball. That's a cute name."

"It's a cute cat," Haley said.

Trisha checked the time on her phone. "We're on a tight schedule. You said you had put some things in the back for us?"

"Yes, come with me," Toby said. "I'll show you what we have."

Haley and Trisha followed Toby to the back room where his pretty and petite wife, Betty, was waiting with some greenery laid out on a table.

"Trisha, you remember, Betty, my wife," Toby said.

"Of course I do," Trisha said. "So good to see you, Betty. This is Jeff's fiancée, Haley."

Betty looked confused. "Your old boyfriend, Jeff? Ben's son?"

Trisha smiled. "Yes."

"And you're planning their wedding?" Betty gave Haley a surprised look.

Haley laughed. "Trust me. This wedding has been full of surprises. I'm thankful for Trisha's help and for yours with the flowers. Your shop is lovely. I'll be back when I have more time to spend."

"Thank you." Betty beamed back at her. "I wish we had more for you to choose from today, but I'm sure Toby told you, we're out of almost everything. But I had an idea for you."

Trisha walked up to see what Betty had laid out. "We're listening."

"I know you're getting married at Ben's place, where he does his Christmas Camps."

"That's right," Haley said.

"I've heard one of the activities they have you do is to go out in nature and create ornaments out of what you find," Betty said.

Haley smiled. "That's right. You are supposed to pick things that inspire you. Everyone loves that activity."

Betty picked up some Douglas fir branches and some holly branches from the table. "So, I thought what you might like to do for your bridal bouquet is use that inspiration and go gather things like this, from around the inn, like you do with the activity." Betty gathered up the branches, the holly with the red berries, and some other evergreens, and held them all together. "You then just need to tie a string at the top and bottom really tight to keep everything together and use some burlap ribbon like this to cover the stems and make a bow if you like." Betty held up her creation. It was beautiful.

Haley held her hand to her heart. "I love it. It's perfect. It will really mean something to everyone, and I know Jeff will love it, too."

"But it's not flowers," Trisha said, frowning.

"But it doesn't have to be flowers. I love that it can be anything that inspires us from nature. This way it will really mean something to us," Haley said and turned back to Betty. "But I know we don't have all of this at the inn—like holly."

Betty smiled. "We have some extra holly that we can spare. See how the holly has all the beautiful bright shiny red berries? They'll be perfect to add that pop of red. Just be careful, it's prickly. You only need a couple of branches to really make an impact. The main filler is Douglas fir branches, and I know you have a lot of those by the inn. You can use some other evergreens as well, like Balsam fir, if you want some variety." Betty picked up some green floral foam and a plastic tray. "Then you can also easily make some centerpieces by covering this foam with the Douglas fir branches and adding in some holly and anything else you like. You can put it in a container or a wicker basket."

Trisha nodded. She was quickly writing down notes in her tablet. "We have the wicker baskets Ben always uses for the Christmas Camp when people gather ingredients for their ornaments, so we can use some of those, and I've made some centerpieces. So I'm sure I can pull something together."

"That would be great," Haley said. "Thank you so much, everyone."

Betty walked over to the flower cooler and opened the door and took out one dozen perfect pristine white roses. "These are the last roses we have. We were going to use them for our own Christmas centerpiece, but we would like to give them to you for your wedding," Betty said.

Haley looked touched. "Oh no, I couldn't take your roses."

"Please, we insist," Toby said. "We know how much joy flowers bring. It's why we do what we do, and we would really like you to have these for your wedding."

Betty came over and took one of the roses and put it in Haley's bouquet. "See, even adding one or two roses can really make a difference, and with the white roses signifying new beginnings, I think they are perfect for your wedding."

Haley nodded and gave Toby and Betty a grateful look. "They are perfect. This is so kind of you. Thank you so much."

Toby smiled back at Haley. "It's our pleasure. Merry Christmas."

Haley smelled her white roses and smiled back. "Merry Christmas."

CHAPTER 7

As Haley and Trisha drove up to the inn, they saw the guys taking some Christmas lights to the backyard.

"Does this have something to do with my surprise?" Haley asked Trisha.

Trisha just shrugged.

Haley shivered as she got out of the car. The temperatures were really dropping, and the light snow that had started earlier was starting to pick up. When they opened the door and stepped inside, Snowball zipped by them. "I still can't get used to seeing a cat here," Haley said.

"Let's go see how Laura and Kathy did," Trisha said. Haley followed her into the kitchen where Laura was just putting out two pizza boxes.

"What is this?" Haley asked, laughing. "Pizza? No? We've never had pizza here."

"And we've also never planned a wedding in forty-eight hours," Laura laughed. "I'm making an exception. I know everyone's hungry, and I need time to start preparing our rehearsal dinner for tonight and making some of the hors d'oeuvres for the wedding tomorrow." Laura opened the pizza boxes. "So we have pepperoni and sausage and Canadian bacon and pineapple."

"That's Jeff's favorite and mine," Haley said.

Laura nodded. "I know, and it's your wedding, so we had to have your favorite."

Haley looked concerned. She came over and took Laura's hand. "This all sounds like way too much. Honestly, we don't need a cake or anything fancy. We could have pizza at my wedding for all I care. As long as we're all together."

Laura smiled and gave her hand a reassuring squeeze. "Now, don't you worry about a thing. You know I'm used to making big meals every night, and this time, I have all this help coming. Your mom said she's ready to pitch in, and so are Gail and Susie."

"And I'll help," Kathy said.

Haley laughed. "You don't cook! I think the best way you can help is stay out of the kitchen."

Kathy laughed. "Look who's talking."

"I agree," Haley said. "That's why you won't see me in here. I'm going to leave this to the pros or we will be ordering pizza."

Laura laughed. "Nobody's going to be ordering any more pizza after today."

Haley gave Laura a heartfelt hug. "You really are the best. I love you."

"I love you, too, sweetie. Now grab a slice of pizza before the guys get in here, and it disappears."

Haley laughed.

Laura went over to the refrigerator and took out a salad and gave it to Trisha. "I whipped up a quick salad for you. I know you don't eat pizza."

Trisha smiled. "Thank you, Laura. That's very sweet."

"Who doesn't eat pizza?" Steve said as he, Jeff, and

Ben walked into the kitchen. "Trisha, you don't know what you're missing."

Trisha held up her salad. "I'm good. I have my salad."

Jeff came over and put his arm around Haley. "How did the flower trip go?"

Haley smiled a brilliant smile. "Amazing."

"What did you get?" Jeff asked. "Let's see."

Haley shook her head. "Nope, it's going to be a surprise. We're going to put everything together when the rest of the gang gets here, but there is something you guys can do for me."

"Whatever you need," Ben said.

"You know the wicker baskets you use for Christmas Camp? If you would fill several of those with some Douglas fir branches that are around twelve to fourteen inches long, that would be perfect."

Jeff looked intrigued.

"Consider it done," Ben said. "We can go get some right after lunch."

Trisha checked the time on her phone again. "Haley, we need to wrap up here to stay on schedule."

Haley took a big bite of her pizza. "What's left? I think we've done everything until the rest of the group gets here."

Trisha shook her head. "I need to see what you're both wearing so I can tell our photographer what to expect."

"I brought the tux I was planning to wear and a suit. I wasn't sure what would be best," Jeff said.

Trisha and Haley spoke at the same time.

"The suit," Haley said.

"The tux," Trisha said.

Haley laughed. "You were only wearing the tux before for the photos for the B&B. I don't even know if you need to wear a suit with a tie and all that for this wedding. This is just going to be a simple ceremony."

Trisha looked appalled. "This is a wedding not a barbecue. This is one of the most important moments in your life, and it's going to be photographed. You're going to have those photographs forever."

"I have to agree with Trisha on this one," Jeff said. "I want to look my best for you. It's our wedding, and you said you had an amazing dress. So, I'm thinking I need to wear the tux."

Haley's shoulders slumped. "Had a dress. I don't have it anymore."

"What do you mean?" Trisha asked. "What happened to your dress?"

"Nothing happened to it. I'm sure it's perfectly fine hanging back up at the boutique in Boston. I was doing a trade with them. They were giving me the dress for all the publicity photos we were doing, and I was going to give them some, as well, for their own advertising. But all that got canceled, so I had to give back the dress."

Trisha looked so upset you'd think she was the one getting married. "So, what did you bring to wear?"

Haley cringed. She had no idea this was going to be such a big deal. Seeing the way everyone was looking at her made her regret her next words. "I brought some black pants and a nice top."

"No, I meant, what did you bring to wear for the wedding?" Trisha asked impatiently.

Haley looked at Jeff before looking back to Trisha. "That's it. That's what I brought for the wedding. I was in a hurry and still upset and not even sure what we would be able to do up here, so I just grabbed something I thought would work."

The room was silent.

By the look on everyone's faces, Haley knew she had really messed up. "Okay, maybe I should have brought a dress. I was just thinking we were going to be up here in the woods. Pants seemed more practical. They're nice pants, designer . . ."

More silence.

Ben walked over and put his arm around Haley. "It's okay. I have an idea."

A FEW MINUTES LATER, Ben, Haley, Trisha, and Kathy were all upstairs in Ben's bedroom. He was holding a white garment bag.

"My wife, Grace, was very sentimental," Ben said. "She never could give away her wedding dress, and while I donated most of her clothes to charity, I just couldn't part with this." Reverently, he handed it to Haley. "I know she would want you to have it."

Haley looked overwhelmed with emotion.

Kathy had tears in her own eyes.

"But, I couldn't . . ." Haley said. She was at a loss for words.

Ben smiled. "You don't have to wear it if you don't want to, but I would like you to have it. Grace would have loved you so much, just like I do." Ben kissed Haley on the cheek and left the room.

Haley turned to Kathy. "I don't know what to say."

Trisha took the dress from her. "Let's see the dress."

Kathy took it back from Trisha and gave it to Haley. "It's Haley's dress. She can decide what to do with it."

"It seems pretty simple to me. You need a dress. Here's a dress. Let's see if it fits. You two are about the same size," Trisha said.

Haley nodded. "I know. Jeff let me wear some of her

clothes the first time I came to Christmas Camp and hadn't packed properly. But a wedding dress is a whole different story, and I don't know if wearing Jeff's mom's dress is the right thing to do . . ."

"I think it's absolutely the right thing to do," Trisha said. "This way you would be honoring his mother's memory, and she would be part of the wedding. I know that would mean a lot to Ben, too."

Kathy nodded. "I think she's right. I think it would be really special. But only you can decide what's right for you."

Trisha eyed the garment bag. "So? Why don't you look at the dress and then you can decide. I need to go check with the guys about the decorations. Let me know what you decide." Trisha left the room.

Once she was gone, Haley turned to Kathy. "I don't know what to do."

Kathy put her arm around her. "Take a deep breath. It's all going to be okay. Let's just look at the dress and see what you think. Okay?"

Haley took a deep breath and nodded slowly. "Okay." Her hands trembled as she slowly unzipped the bag and carefully took out a lovely classic satin sheath wedding dress. It had a simple scoop neck and long sleeves. Haley caught her breath when she saw it and fought back tears. "It's perfect," she whispered, holding the dress up to her. She looked at Kathy.

The tears were back in Kathy's eyes. "It sure is," Kathy said. "Try it on. See how it fits." When Kathy took the dress from her, Haley quickly slipped out of her clothes and carefully, with Kathy's help, put on the dress.

Amazed, Kathy stood back and looked at her. "I can't believe it. It fits like it was made for you."

Haley didn't look surprised at all. She looked grateful. "Or like it was meant to be."

Kathy nodded. "Exactly."

Haley took a deep breath and smiled. "Everything's finally all coming together. I have flowers. I have a photographer, a dress. This wedding is really going to work . . ."

"Wait, don't say that, you might jinx . . ." But the rest of what Kathy was about to say was cut off by Trisha yelling up to them from downstairs.

"Haley!" Trisha hollered. "You need to come down here right away!"

HALEY WAS SMILING and humming the Christmas song *We Wish You a Merry Christmas* with Kathy as they headed down the stairs, but when they got to the bottom and saw everyone gathered in the sitting room looking concerned, Haley stopped singing.

"What's wrong?" she asked.

Jeff came over and took both her hands. "There's really no good way to tell you this, so I'm just going to give it to you straight."

"Okay, now you're starting to really scare me," Haley said. "Is everyone okay?"

Jeff nodded. "Everyone's fine, but a weather system has moved in. We thought it was going to miss us, but it changed course, and we're getting a direct hit now. The snow is coming down hard, and it's supposed to last for several days."

"But it was fine earlier," Haley said. "It wasn't snowing that much." Haley walked over to the window and looked out. She was stunned. The snow was now coming down so hard all she could see was a whiteout.

Jeff joined her. "They've just closed Alpine Road and some other roads as a precaution."

"But Alpine Road is the only way to get here," Haley said. When Jeff nodded, it hit her full force. "So, this means no one can get here for the wedding—my parents, Gail, everyone from Christmas Camp . . ."

"Or Laura," Ben added. "Thankfully, she left earlier right after lunch to get some things from home, but she won't be able to get back here now."

"And our wedding photographer won't be able to get here either," Trisha said. She looked as upset as Haley. "And your parents were bringing most of the food, the wedding rings, and your dad was officiating."

Haley nodded. She was still struggling to comprehend what was happening.

"So, what does this mean?" Kathy asked.

Haley, heartbroken, looked at Jeff. "It means we have to cancel the wedding. Again."

CHAPTER 8

Haley numbly left the group and walked over to the front door. When she opened it, a blast of wind and snow hit her full force, but she didn't flinch. She just kept staring out into the bleakness. She couldn't see more than a few inches in front of her, but that didn't stop her from taking a few more steps outside. "Why is this happening?" she whispered as more blinding snow hit her in the face.

Jeff quickly joined her, grabbed her hand, and pulled her back inside and shut the door. "Haley, come on. You can't go out there."

Haley laughed. It was the kind of laugh you heard right before someone lost it. "I can't go outside. I can't have my wedding. What else can't I do? I can't do anything. We can't do anything. This is . . ."

When Jeff took her into his arms, she finally calmed down, but with the calm came more pain. When she looked up, there were tears in her eyes. "I just wanted to marry you. This shouldn't be that hard . . ."

Jeff nodded. "I know."

"So, what do we do now?" Haley asked. "We were supposed to get married tomorrow, Christmas Eve . . ."

"We find another time," Jeff said. "We reschedule."

Haley looked brokenhearted. "But it meant so much to us, to all of us, to get married at Christmas, when we first met and fell in love . . ."

"Are you saying you want to wait until next Christmas?" Jeff asked.

"No. I mean, I don't know." Haley looked confused. "I don't know about any of this."

"Let's not make any decisions right now," Jeff said. "We should be grateful no one's stuck in this storm. Everyone's home safe. We're all here together. It's almost Christmas. Let's make the best of it."

Haley nodded. It was just another reason she loved Jeff so much. He was always looking at the positive side of things and didn't usually let stress get to him.

When there was a loud knock on the door, they both looked startled. Jeff immediately opened it and found Gail standing there covered in snow.

"Merry Christmas," she said, brushing snow off her.

Jeff pulled her quickly inside. "What are you doing here? How did you get here? Are you okay? Dad, Gail's here."

Ben came rushing over and gave her a hug. "I was so worried about you. I've been calling and calling but no answer. I knew you weren't going to leave Boston until later, and I left you a message about the storm, but when I couldn't reach you I got worried."

Gail kissed his cheek. "I'm sorry I worried you. I wanted to surprise you all, so I left really early this morning and luckily I was almost here when the snow really hit. They closed the road behind me."

Haley gave Gail a hug. "I'm so glad you're okay."

Jeff hugged her, too. "We all are."

Snowball came running over to her. Gail picked her up and cuddled her. "There's my little Snowball." She handed Snowball to Ben. "But right now I'd just really like to get out of these wet clothes." She headed for the stairs. "I'll be back down soon."

"I'll make you some hot chocolate," Ben said.

"That sounds perfect," Gail said, smiling back at him.

A HALF HOUR LATER, they were all gathered in the kitchen. Haley watched as Gail helped Ben make the hot chocolate. They were so cute together. You could see how much they cared for each other. Haley looked over and saw that Jeff was watching them, too, and he was smiling. When Gail went to get out the mugs, she only took out the Santa mugs. Haley watched her exchange a look with Ben and saw that Jeff saw the look, too.

Jeff walked over to Gail and gave her another hug. "I'm so glad you're here." He reached up into the cupboard and took out one of Gail's new snowman mugs. "I'd like to try one of these mugs. Seems perfect on a snowy day like this."

Gail touched Jeff's hand. "Are you sure? The Santa mugs are a tradition."

Jeff nodded. "And I say it's time we start making a new tradition with these snowmen."

Haley walked over and joined them and took out a snowman mug, too. "I agree."

Gail looked touched. "Thank you."

Haley knew Gail was thanking them for much more than just using the mugs.

Jeff smiled back at her. "You're welcome."

Just as they clinked snowman mugs together, the lights went out.

Haley laughed. "Seriously?"

Kathy laughed, too, and looked over at Haley. "What did you say to jinx us this time?"

Haley shook her head. "I swear I didn't say anything."

Ben tried the light switch but got nothing. "The power's out. It must be the storm." He opened a drawer and took out some flashlights and passed them around. "I'm going to go check on the generator. I don't hear it kicking in."

"I'll come with you," Jeff said.

A FEW MINUTES LATER when the guys returned Ben had a smile on his face. "So I have some good news and some bad news. What do you want first?"

"The bad news," Haley said.

"The bad news is the generator isn't working."

"And the good news?" Haley asked.

Ben grinned back at them all. "Now we can play Christmas Camp Charades."

Everyone laughed.

"Nice try, Dad," Jeff said.

Ben smiled back at him. "I'm serious. Who wants to play?"

"I do!" Kathy said. "I love games."

"Me, too," Steve chimed in. "But exactly what is this?"

Haley laughed at their enthusiasm. "It's something Ben does at all the Christmas Camps. It's like charades, only we play using Christmas songs, and you split into two teams. Each team gets a different song, and you compete at the same time. The first team to guess right, wins. It's hilarious."

Gail laughed. "Especially when you're wearing the crazy Christmas sweaters."

"Oh, that's right," Haley said. "How could I forget that part? Luckily, we don't have the sweaters this year."

Ben's smile grew. "Want to bet?"

AND A FEW minutes later everyone was wearing one of Ben's crazy Christmas sweaters, because of course, he had a collection of them, and they were playing Christmas Camp Charades. There was a lot of joking around and laughter, and once again, Haley ruled, winning her round against Jeff. The song she had gotten was Dean Martin's *Let It Snow, Let It Snow, Let It Snow*. For her clue, she had run outside and scooped up a bunch of snow and brought it in and dumped it on Jeff's head. By the time the game was over, Haley had laughed so much her stomach hurt. The crazy Christmas Camp Charades was exactly what she had needed to take her mind off of having to cancel her wedding for the second time.

AFTER CHARADES, BEN had another game for them to play that was all about how to make dinner without the groceries Haley's parents were bringing and without any electricity. It became a scavenger hunt through the kitchen where anyone who found something that could work would put it on the counter. Haley was rummaging through the pantry when Steve joined her.

He picked up a box of crackers. "How about these?" he asked.

"Sure," Haley said. "I saw some different cheeses and things in the refrigerator that Laura was going to use to make appetizers, so we can always do cheese and crackers."

"I'm pretty good at whipping things together," Steve said. "I'll go take a look at what we have."

Steve was about to leave when Haley stopped him. "Hey, I've been meaning to talk to you about something."

"Sure," Steve said. "What about?"

"Kathy."

Steve nodded, laughed a little. "Okay."

Haley chose her words carefully. "I've noticed you two hanging out a lot and you seem to be getting along well."

"We are. She's really great."

"She is," Haley said. "Look, I'm just going to say it. Jeff told me you traveled a lot. You're not one to really stay in one place for very long . . ."

"That's true," Steve said.

"So, how does that work with your relationships?"

"You mean, how would that work with Kathy."

"Yes," Haley said. "That's exactly what I mean. I just don't want to see her get hurt. I'm not saying you would do that intentionally. She just seems to really like you . . ."

"She's great. We're talking about maybe hanging out for Christmas Eve while I'm in town and then I guess we'll see."

Haley nodded. "Sorry if I seem a little overprotective . . ."

"You just care about your friend," Steve said. "I get it. All I can tell you right now is that Kathy is someone I want to get to know better and I'm not leading her on or anything like that. I would never do that."

"And now I see why you're Jeff's best friend," Haley said. She smiled. "Thanks for this little talk."

"Anytime." Steve grinned back at her. "But now I better go see what Laura has in the refrigerator to make us something to eat and I'm going to put as much as I can into the freezer. Even with the power out the freezer will keep things cold for forty-eight hours if you don't open it again."

LATER THAT NIGHT everyone was gathered around the fire, staying warm, with blankets wrapped around them. The electricity was still off, so the room was only lit by the fireplace and candles. It looked beautiful and romantic.

Haley was standing over by the fire. Jeff joined her. "Not exactly the rehearsal dinner we were planning," Jeff said. "But, I have to admit, Steve, you did a great job with what we had. How did you know that about the freezer and when did you learn how to cook? The only thing you used to make in college was mac and cheese from the box."

Steve laughed. "Luckily, I've picked up a thing or two in all my travels."

Kathy was sitting next to Steve on the couch. She looked impressed. "Those goat cheese balls you made with the chopped walnuts and parsley were great."

"And so were those hummus cucumber rolls," Gail said.

Steve held out his hands. "I take tips."

Everyone laughed.

"But I can't really take the credit. The appetizer recipes were Laura's," Steve said. "She calls the goat cheese balls her *Christmas Camp Goat Cheese Delights*, and I agree, they're great and so easy to make, luckily. And I have to give credit to Trisha and Gail for putting together a great spinach apple salad. I think we all pitched in and made a great team."

Gail laughed. "Using flashlights and candles to see with."

"I have to get you some of those electric lanterns for emergencies like this," Jeff said.

"It's a good idea," Ben agreed. "We've just so rarely ever had the power go out up here. We've been spoiled. And speaking of spoiled . . ." Ben picked up a platter of Christmas cookies and started passing them around. "Who wants dessert?"

"Me!" Jeff said as he took a cookie and got one for Haley, too. "Always my favorite part."

"So, what's on the agenda for tomorrow?" Steve asked.

Everyone looked at Trisha. She was sitting in a chair, trying to get her tablet to work but not having any luck. "So far, nothing. It looks like the power on my tablet died, and I can't recharge without any electricity. Not that it matters, because we're not planning a wedding anymore."

Haley gave Jeff a sad look. He kissed her on the cheek. "At least not for Christmas Eve. But we're definitely getting married."

"Someday," Haley said.

Trisha stood up. "I think I'm going to go upstairs and turn in for the night. Ben, is it okay if I take one of these candles with me?"

Ben shook his head. "It's going to get really cold tonight without any heat. We should all stay down here by the fire." He walked over to a stack of rolled-up sleeping bags. "I got these out for everyone. You'll be toasty warm." He tossed one to Trisha. She looked at it like she'd never slept in a sleeping bag before. When Ben tossed one to Kathy, she, on the other hand, looked excited.

"Fun, just like camping!" Kathy said.

"When have you ever gone camping?" Haley asked her.

Kathy smiled. "I've seen it in the movies. I've always wanted to go."

"I've camped all over the world, and I love it," Steve said. "Fire one of those bags over here, Ben."

Ben laughed as he threw one over to Steve.

Jeff went over and helped his dad hand out the rest. When he tossed a bag to Haley, he winked at her. "I told you this would be an adventure."

Haley couldn't help but laugh.

HOURS LATER, HALEY woke not knowing where she was. When she abruptly sat up in her sleeping bag, she realized she was in the sitting room with the rest of the group, sleeping on the floor by the fire. Max was by her side. He was awake, as well. She looked over at Jeff on the other side of her. He was sleeping peacefully. Looking at him, she felt a rush of pure undeniable love. She gently kissed his cheek.

She saw Ben sleeping on one couch, and Gail sleeping on the other. Trisha was sleeping in a chair. Kathy and Steve were also sleeping next to the fire and next to each other. Even Snowball the cat had come out of hiding and was curled up on the couch with Ben.

Haley shivered. It was getting cold. The fire was almost out. Carefully, quietly, she got up and put several more logs on the fire, and it roared back to life. She quickly ran back over to her sleeping bag and snuggled up inside. She looked over at Max, who was watching her. When he put his head down on her chest, she cuddled up with him before closing her eyes and falling back to sleep.

CHAPTER 9

Haley woke up early the next morning to Max licking her face.

"What are you doing?" she whispered as she sat up. Max dropped his leash in front of her and wagged his tail and ran toward the front door. "Are you crazy?" she whispered to him. She looked around, and everyone was still sleeping. "We can't go out there. There's too much snow."

But when Max started circling and looked like he was about to bark, Haley jumped up and put her finger in front of her lips. "Shhhhhh," she whispered. "Everyone's sleeping. Okay, I'll take you out quickly. Just don't bark."

She quickly grabbed Jeff's big snow coat and his boots out of the closet and put on his hat and scarf and put the leash on Max. "I can't believe you're making me go out here in this snowstorm. This was supposed to be my wedding day. You should take pity on me."

Max wagged his tail and waited for her to open the front door. When she did, she was stunned. It wasn't

424   KAREN SCHALER

snowing anymore. The sun was just starting to come up, and there wasn't a cloud in the sky.

"Whoa, what happened to the storm?"

For an answer, Max pulled her forward, and she had to run to keep up with him as he started playing in the fresh snow. Haley laughed. He was hilarious. He would bite the snow and jump and then bite the snow again. She made a snowball and threw it at him. He instantly devoured it. She was laughing again when a snowball hit her on the back.

"Hey!" She whirled around and found Jeff walking toward her. She laughed. "What are you doing?"

"Sticking up for Max. I saw you throw that snowball at him." Jeff joined her and kissed her. "Good morning." He shivered. He wasn't wearing a coat.

"Oh no, I stole your coat," Haley laughed. "I'm sorry." She took off his scarf and wrapped it around his neck.

He laughed and looked up at the sky. "It's warmed up a lot."

"I know," Haley said. "What happened to the storm?"

"It's gone."

"But it's still cold and you don't have a coat," Haley said. "Let's get you inside."

Before they got to the door, it opened and Trisha was standing there. "Haley! Jeff! Get in here."

"What's wrong?" Haley asked as she and Jeff hurried toward the door. As soon as they were inside, they saw everyone was up in the sitting room, rolling up their sleeping bags.

"Nothing's wrong," Trisha said. "Everything's finally right. Ben just got a call. Because the storm has passed and the snowplows are already out, they're going to re-open Alpine Road."

Ben and Gail joined them. "That means . . ."

"We have a wedding plan!" Trisha said.

"What?" Haley looked at Jeff. Her eyes were full of hope. "Really?"

"Really," Gail said. "Ben's been calling everyone, and they're all coming."

Haley gave Jeff an incredulous look. "So we can really get married. Tonight . . ."

"On Christmas Eve, just like we always wanted." When Jeff kissed her, Max barked happily, and even Snowball made an appearance and meowed.

FOR HALEY, THE next few hours flew by like a whirlwind. She still couldn't believe the storm was gone, and it was a perfect sunny winter day. It was her wedding day. It was really happening.

Laura had even surprised them all by showing up with her husband on a snowmobile. He dropped her off and said he'd be back with the car once the road reopened. Laura told them she didn't want to miss anything. And now it was such a beautiful day, it had been perfect for a snowmobile trip.

Haley smiled, thinking about how Laura was already in the kitchen working away with Gail. After she'd heard about Steve's success the night before, she had recruited him to help as well, while they waited for Haley's mom to bring the rest of the ingredients. Since they only had a few hours to get everything ready, the original menu wasn't going to work anymore, but Laura had assured Haley there were still enough things they could make that would be wonderful.

Haley had assured them that whatever they made, she knew it would be special, because it had been made with love.

As soon as they knew the wedding was back on, Trisha

gathered everyone together and started handing out assignments. Haley had to admit it was impressive how quickly Trisha could shift gears and make things happen. There was no doubt she was a great wedding planner and everyone respected that, including Haley.

The guys were assigned to go get the Douglas fir branches they hadn't been able to get the night before because of the storm. As soon as they got back, Trisha started showing Haley and Kathy how to put together a beautiful arrangement using all the things from the flower shop, including the white roses. Haley couldn't believe how incredible they turned out.

As the sun started to go down, Haley kept looking out the window, excited for people to start arriving. But Trisha was firm, insisting that Haley wait until after the ceremony to see everyone, so she had time to get ready and could make a grand entrance.

Haley didn't care at all about making a grand entrance, but when she saw how hard Trisha was working to make the day special, she agreed to do what Trisha asked. Trisha had even had the photographer, Curt, bring along his sister, who specialized in doing hair and makeup. Haley agreed to stay upstairs and wait to see everyone.

Kathy had also pointed out it was bad luck to see the groom before the wedding, and with the way this wedding had gone, they all agreed they didn't want to take that chance and jinx anything.

At least Trisha had let Haley's mom and dad come up to see her, and they were all able to catch up while Haley was getting her hair and makeup done. Curt captured everything, getting some wonderful family candid shots that Haley's mom was already raving about.

Everything, dare she even think it, was going wonderfully.

The last thing for Haley to do was put on Jeff's mom's wedding dress. Her own mom and Kathy helped her, as Curt took more pictures. It was a beautiful moment, and at one point, all three of them were crying. Trisha had instantly appeared with tissues for each of them. Trisha stood back admiring Haley in the dress. "The dress is beautiful on you," she said, smiling a genuine smile. "Grace was a very special person. She was always like another mom to me. She was so kind and loving . . ." When Trisha's voice got choked up with emotion and trailed off, Haley looked over and saw Trisha was holding back tears. She was surprised. It was the first time Haley thought about the fact that Trisha had known Grace and she had lost Grace, too. Her heart went out to her. She took Trisha's hand. "You have done a beautiful job with this wedding, and I'm sure Grace is so thankful that you've done all this for Jeff and for Ben. That you were here when she couldn't be."

When Trisha's eyes filled with tears, Haley handed her a tissue.

They smiled at each other—a real smile, for the first time.

"Thank you for saying that," Trisha said. "I miss her very much, and Jeff and Ben, they've been like my family. I've missed them, too, these last few years." Trisha wiped her tears and pulled herself together. "I'm sorry for the way I acted when we met. I really do love Jeff, but I've realized, watching you two, we never had what you have, and what I really loved was being part of this family. I can see how much Jeff loves you, and Ben, too. You make them happy and that's all I want."

Haley, touched, reached out and took Trisha's hand. "Thank you." She was starting to tear up, too.

As soon as Trisha saw that, she went right back into wedding planner mode.

"Don't you even think about crying," Trisha said. "You'll ruin your makeup."

Haley laughed. Trisha gave her a stern look, then after a moment, laughed with her. "Okay, let's do this wedding," Trisha said. "Before something else goes wrong."

Haley laughed again. "Don't even say that!"

Trisha headed for the bedroom door. "I'm going to go check downstairs to make sure everything is ready. We should be getting started in seven minutes."

After Trisha left the room, Haley looked down and saw both Max and Snowball looking up at her.

"I'm about to officially become part of your family. I hope you guys are okay with that?"

Haley laughed when Max barked and wagged his tail. She decided to take that as a yes. As she slowly walked over and looked at her reflection in the mirror, she smiled and took a deep breath. With her eyes closed, she whispered softly, "I promise I will love and take care of your son, Jeff, and Ben, always." She opened her eyes just as Kathy came into the room.

Kathy looked stunning in her burgundy velvet cocktail dress. She twirled around in front of Haley. "I'm so glad I kept this dress."

Haley smiled at her. "And it looks amazing on you. You're glowing, but I don't think it's just from the dress . . ."

Kathy couldn't stop smiling. Excited, she took Haley's hand. "It's Steve. I know you said not to get carried away, but I honestly think he might be the one to give me a chance at my own HEA, my happily ever after."

"You know there's nothing I want more for you," Haley said. "He seems to really like you, too. This could be the start of something really special."

Kathy shook her head. "I'm sorry. Look at me going on and on when today is about you. I think I just feel so much love all around me here, with you and Jeff and Ben and Gail. It's really beautiful, and speaking of beautiful, I don't know how all this worked out so well but you are truly one of the most beautiful brides I've ever seen. I am so happy for you. I love you, and I love Jeff." Kathy walked over and picked up Haley's bridal bouquet that was on the dresser. It looked magical. "This turned out so well. Wait, you added a pinecone . . ."

Haley smiled. "I did. It's a Christmas tradition in Jeff's family and now mine, too. When Jeff's dad proposed to his mom he put the ring in a pinecone and proposed up at Star Peak. Ever since, it has been a tradition in Jeff's family to go up to Star Peak every Christmas and get a pinecone to make a Christmas wish. Then you bring the pinecone back to the inn and put it in that basket of pinecones by the fire, with all the other Christmas wishes."

Kathy smiled. "I saw that basket! I love this."

Haley nodded. "And Jeff proposed to me the same way, up at Star Peak." Haley smiled, looking at the pinecone in her bouquet. "This pinecone is my Christmas wish. I know Jeff will see it and understand."

"Who knew all you needed was a pinecone to make a Christmas wish," Kathy said. "I'm going to go find one immediately."

They shared a laugh.

"Okay, let's make sure you have everything," Kathy said. "Where are your vows?"

Haley touched her heart. "They're right here."

Kathy looked concerned. "You don't have a copy written down?"

"I never got a chance," Haley said, "but that's okay. It doesn't have to be perfect. I know what I want to say. I don't need to write anything down."

Kathy smiled at her. "I knew you would figure it out. Okay, next. Making sure we have something borrowed—the dress that also counts for something old. You have the pinecone—that's something new—but what about something blue? Wait, we forgot something blue!"

Haley reached out and took Kathy's hand. "It's okay. Don't worry about it. We don't need it."

"What?" Kathy gave her an incredulous look. "Yes, we do. We are not taking any more chances jinxing this wedding."

Trisha walked in smiling. "Don't worry. There will be no more jinxing." She held up a pretty white lace garter with a tiny blue bow.

Haley laughed. "No. That's so old school. I don't need that . . ."

Trisha and Kathy interrupted at the same time. "Yes, you do!"

Trisha gave it to Haley. "Keep it. I have plenty. It's part of the wedding planner emergency kit I always have with me."

"Wow, okay, if you both insist," Haley said.

"We do," Trisha said. "And it's time to get started. Are you ready?"

Haley quickly slipped on the something blue and nodded. She knew, without a doubt, she was 100 percent ready.

CHAPTER 10

Right as Haley was about to leave her room, her dad appeared. He looked so handsome in his black suit and burgundy tie. He smiled when he saw her.

"There's my beautiful girl," he said and took both her hands. "I just wanted to check in on you one more time to make sure you're ready." He kissed her hands.

Haley looked into his eyes. "I am." She smiled. "Do you believe this is really happening, after everything we've been through?"

"I do," he said. "Because when two people love each other as much as you and Jeff do, you're meant to be together. Nothing can stop you. Not a flood, or a snowstorm, nothing."

Haley kissed her dad on the cheek. "Thanks, Dad. You know, I started to get scared, but then I remembered what you'd always say about you and mom when times were tough . . ."

"That true loves only gets stronger during the tough times . . ."

"And better," Haley finished for him. "Because I love him with my whole heart."

"That's my girl. You know your mom and I have been talking, and we talked to Ben, and we've decided that we're going to do a Christmas Camp at the B&B. We saw how much coming here helped you and we want to be able to create that same kind of experience for our guests. This is just the beginning for all of us and I just wanted to tell you how much your mom and I love you and how happy we are for you."

Haley nodded. For a moment she was too emotional to say anything, but as he left she called after him. "I love you both so much."

Haley took a deep breath, as she waited in her room alone. She knew that when the Christmas song *Have Yourself a Merry Little Christmas* started playing that was her cue to start walking down the stairs where everyone would be gathered below waiting for her. The fact that it was Christmas Eve and that she would be walking down the same stairs she had walked down a year ago, when she had reluctantly come to Christmas Camp for the first time, never dreaming how much her life would change, felt like the perfect start to her own happily ever after.

Over the last year, by opening up her heart for the first time, she had experienced so much joy and love and laughter, and she couldn't wait to start her new life with Jeff.

When she heard her cue she took a deep breath and looked around at all the angels in the room, she smiled. She felt so grateful for the journey she'd been on, even with all the ups and downs, because it had brought her here, where she knew she was meant to be. By finally learning how to open her heart and let love in, her entire future had changed. She couldn't wait to marry Jeff and start that future together.

Feeling excited and confident, Haley opened her bedroom door and couldn't help but laugh when she saw Max waiting there for her.

"You are the other love of my life. You know that, right?" Haley said.

Max wagged his tail and walked by her side as she headed for the stairs.

When Haley got to the top of the stairs her smile was radiant. There was a collective "ahhh" when everyone standing below looked up and saw her for the first time.

Haley could feel the love and knew this was the wedding she was meant to have.

As she slowly descended the staircase she looked around and saw all the people from her Christmas Camp—John and his kids, Madison and Blake; and Susie and Ian—she felt so blessed. They had been such a big part of the journey last year when she had rediscovered her Christmas spirit, allowing her to let Jeff into her heart.

Standing next to them was Laura and her husband. Laura wore a pretty black dress with a burgundy shawl. She knew how much Laura loved Jeff and Ben and felt thankful that she now was also included in that love.

The next person she saw was Gail standing next to Ben. She looked beautiful holding little Snowball, who had a burgundy ribbon tied around her neck. Ben looked distinguished and proud in his black suit. He touched his heart and had tears of joy in his eyes when he saw Haley was wearing Jeff's mom's dress.

When Haley looked over to her parents, she also saw

tears of happiness in her mom's eyes. When her mom mouthed the words "I love you," Haley whispered, "I love you."

And then there was Jeff, the love of her life, standing there, wearing his tuxedo, looking more handsome than she had ever seen him look. But what really mattered most to her was how he was looking back at her. In his eyes, she saw so much genuine love that it made her feel safe and cherished. She knew that together they could handle anything, and she couldn't wait for their own adventure to begin.

When she got to the bottom of the stairs and he took her hand, he looked into her eyes and softly said, "I love you."

She smiled back at him. "I love you, too."

As he led her into the sitting room, she stopped and looked around in awe. The entire ceiling was covered with rows and rows of white twinkling lights. The only other light came from candles and the fireplace. It was magical. Now she knew why Trisha had wanted her to stay upstairs, so they could surprise her.

As Jeff guided her over to the fireplace, where her dad was waiting to officiate the wedding, she looked up at him and whispered, "It's beautiful."

THE CEREMONY WAS equally beautiful. Haley and Jeff recited their own vows that had people laughing and crying all at the same time. It was a true celebration of their love. After the ceremony, Trisha orchestrated the picture taking, making sure everyone got a special picture with Haley and Jeff. The whole time, Haley was in a daze of happiness. She kept looking at her wedding ring and at Jeff, making sure it all wasn't just a dream, that this was real. She still couldn't believe she was married to someone who loved her and that she loved with all her heart.

They had just finished taking a picture with John, Madison, and Blake, when Trisha ushered them into the dining room to get a picture with the wedding cake.

Haley looked confused. "But we didn't make a cake. We didn't have time."

Trisha, looking stern, walked up to Haley. "Any wedding I organize has a cake." When Trisha moved out of the way, Haley gasped.

On the dining room table was her dream wedding cake. Just like the one that was destroyed at her parents'. Only instead of six different snow-white tiers, there were three smaller tiers, all in the shape of different squares so it looked like a bundle of Christmas presents all wrapped up with a pretty burgundy fondant bow.

Stunned, she looked at Jeff. "How did you do this?" She wiped tears from her eyes. "You know how much this meant to me."

Jeff kissed her cheek. "I didn't. Trisha did."

Haley spun around to look at Trisha. "What? How?"

"Kathy showed me the picture on your phone and told me what happened . . ."

Haley looked from Trisha to Kathy.

Trisha continued. "I called in a favor with a pastry chef I know, a big favor because they pretty much worked around the clock to make it happen, and I had Gail pick it up and bring it here. I wanted it to be a surprise."

Incredulous, Haley walked over to Trisha and took her hand. "Thank you. This means so much to me."

Trisha smiled a genuine smile. "I'm glad I could do it for you."

When Haley hugged Trisha, Jeff and Ben came over and hugged her, as well.

"Thank you, Trisha," Jeff said. "For everything."

Trisha smiled back at him and at Haley. "You're welcome."

Jeff picked up the cake knife. "Okay, who wants cake?"

Haley, laughing, took the knife from him. "We haven't even had dinner yet . . ."

Jeff smiled and gave her a confused look. "So?"

Haley laughed and kissed him. "I love you so much."

When they kissed, the photographer got the perfect shot. In the picture, you see Haley and Jeff kissing, and in the background, there's Ben and Gail, also looking very much in love, and Kathy and Steve holding hands, and you know another Christmas Camp love story is about to begin . . .

CHRISTMAS CAMP WEDDING ACTIVITY AND RECIPE

In case you'd like to make your own holiday arrangement like Haley made for her wedding, we've included the simple instructions, along with the easy recipe for the always popular Goat Cheese Delights.

Christmas Camp Wedding Greenery Arrangement

Materials Needed:
1 14–16 inch wicker basket (with waterproof liner) or decorative container
1 floral foam (make sure it is for fresh flowers) and a tray for water
Wire wooded pegs to anchor pinecones
Douglas fir branches cut 12–14 inches long
4–6 holly branches with bright red berries
4–6 flowers of choice (Haley used white roses. Red carnations also last a long time.)
Several pinecones for your own Christmas wishes

Please adjust the amount of materials based on the size of the arrangement you would like. These approximate numbers are based on a basket 14–16 inches wide. The amount of branches you will use will depend on the fullness of each branch.

Additional Decorative Ideas:
Additional evergreens, like Balsam fir, if wanted for variety
Small red ornaments to hang on branches
Burlap or red velvet ribbon for a bow

Directions:
1. Cut all stems at an angle and soak in water for a half hour before creating.
2. Soak floral foam all the way through, put on tray and into lined basket.
3. Start by putting the Douglas fir branches into the foam, horizontally, all around the bottom, then adding diagonally and vertically in the middle, doing the top last. The goal is not to see the foam.
4. Next, disperse the holly branches all around the basket.
5. Add flowers (be sure to strip flowers of all thorns and leaves, just leaving the stem).
6. Attach pinecones to wooden pegs and add to the arrangement. Make your wish!

Tips:
1. Make sure tray always has water and store in a cool place away from the sun.
2. Mist lightly every few days with water and trade out flowers if needed.

Here's Laura's recipe for an easy delicious party appetizer you can whip up in no time, even if the power goes out!

Christmas Camp Wedding
Goat Cheese Delights Recipe

Prep time: 10 minutes
Skill Level: Easy
Makes: 20

Ingredients:

1 pound of soft goat cheese
½ cup crushed walnuts
4 tablespoons parsley (flat leaf)
1–2 teaspoons black pepper (optional)
Honey to drizzle on top (optional)

Directions:

1. Combine crushed walnuts and parsley in medium bowl and set aside.
2. Combine soft goat cheese with pepper.
3. Use goat cheese to make 20 small bite-sized balls.
4. Roll balls in the walnut/parsley mix until generously covered.
5. Drizzle with honey (optional).
6. Eat immediately or refrigerate until ready to serve. Serve at room temperature.
7. Serve with crackers and bread or eat alone.

Optional Ingredients:

Cranberries
Pecans
Pistachios
Rosemary
Thyme

*G*ive in to your Impulses!

These unforgettable stories only take a second to buy and give you hours of reading pleasure!

Go to ***www.AvonImpulse.com*** and see what we have to offer.

Available wherever e-books are sold.

AVONIMPULSE

IMP 0811